Chrissy —

SHADES OF YOU

Enjoy the journey!

SHADES
of You

Calypso Key
SERIES

SHADES OF YOU

Calypso Key Series

ERIN BROCKUS

GREEN SAGE
PRESS

Edited by Lawrence Editing Services

Cover design by GetCovers

Ebook ISBN: 978-1-957003-38-2

Paperback ISBN: 978-1-957003-39-9

Hardcover ISBN:

Chapter One

Hunter

I HATED CHEATING SPOUSES. I gently closed the front door after the woman left, trying not to see how her shoulders drooped as I stared through the glass pane. But this was part of what I did—I provided the ugly truths wrapped in sterile manila folders. Truths about husbands who strayed, business partners who embezzled, or people who didn't know when to stop. What the client did with the information I'd provided was now up to her.

After she backed out of the parking stall, I padded to the front picture window of KeyMark Security, my hands finding the back pockets of my black jeans. Outside, Main Street hummed with activity, a postcard of small-town Florida Keys charm come to life. Cheery hanging baskets swayed gently in the breeze, their bursts of color complementing the crisp, colorful paint of the shopfronts. My soon-to-be sister-in-law's bakery, Sweet Dreams, lay across the street and a couple of buildings down. I hadn't chosen this site for any particular reason—the location for my new business had simply been too good to pass up.

Two figures walked past, their laughter reaching me even through the glass. I recognized my former schoolmates, both guys I'd known once. Instinctively, I ducked away from sight, a shadow dressed in all black amidst the brightness of the day. The irony wasn't lost on me. Here I was, trying to carve out a space on the most visible street in town, yet craving the anonymity I'd once taken for granted under the cloak of night and covert ops. Except that obscurity was a luxury I could no longer afford. Not if I was going to make this new venture work. And in order to do that, I needed to unpack.

I took in the large, open expanse of my new enterprise. KeyMark Security, the symbolic title I'd chosen for my business, was a simple mixture of both my last name and where I was setting up shop. And maybe a subtle reminder that I was still a Markham, regardless of all that had happened.

The space, with its cluster of metal desks and office in the corner, wasn't just a workplace. This little slice of Dove Key was a clean slate. Taking a deep breath, I let the silence wrap around me, a comforting reminder that while some chapters closed with pain and desolation, others opened with promise.

The promise of home. And maybe if I was really reaching—of forgiveness.

I moved through the stillness of the open area to my office. Framed black-and-white beach scenes adorned the white walls. The prints were designed to instill a sense of peace, the ocean's timeless rhythm captured in still life—a stark contrast to the turbulent lives that walked through my door. A thick catcher's mitt was visible inside my gym bag, but I ignored it. That was an off-duty item.

I crossed the floor to unpack one of several cardboard boxes neatly lined up against the wall. Peeling back the flaps of a box, I found myself face to face with the clutter of transferring from one life to another—pens that had seen better days and a tangle of office supplies. As I methodically placed each item in its new home, my thoughts drifted to the dual purpose of my return. Though Dove Key held the promise of becoming home, it wasn't quite the real thing. But I wasn't sure I'd ever be a part of Calypso Key again. For now, providing security for my family's Calypso Key Resort would have to be enough. And moving back would certainly bring on the unresolved whisper of another name. Brenna Coleridge. The name that had seen me through so many dark times.

I chose another box at random and opened it. My breath caught, and my body assumed the precise stillness that was second nature. I reached in and pulled out a framed photograph. Then light flickered off something else in the box, and my eye landed on the trophy I'd packed around for years.

The damn trophy.

I wasn't ready to deal with that, though the frame in my hands didn't fill me with euphoria either. I swallowed over a suddenly parched throat as I studied the photo. Two smiling boys stared back at me, young and oblivious to what the future would hold. Evan and me, arms slung over each other's shoulders at a beach outing.

I traced the edge of the frame, the weight of our complicated relationship pressing down. Gently, I placed the picture inside a desk drawer, not ready to hang it on the wall. I'd kept it nearby all these years, but displaying it would be a symbol of our reconciliation. And we were a long way from that.

I dropped into my chair. My brother had every right to hate me, considering what I'd done to him. Evan was trying to reconcile, and so was I. So far, it had been a tentative, awkward reunion. Could he actually forgive me?

Even more importantly, did I deserve forgiveness?

As DUSK FELL, I stood and stretched, the toll of the day seeping into my bones. The office was quiet as I locked up, and outside, the hum of Main Street's night was awakening. I headed for the staircase near the back of the large space.

Upstairs, my apartment welcomed me with the scent of fresh paint and the comfort of simplicity. The light-gray modern couch was sleek and inviting, but first things first. After kicking off my boots by the door, I padded across the new plush carpet. The modern, efficient kitchen lay at the other end of the open space.

I sprawled on the sofa, one arm bent behind my head as I flipped through channels. A day of grieving wives and unpacking had sapped me of the desire to do anything other than seek out the simple pleasure of an evening baseball game.

My phone chimed, an alert tone from my own security system app, and I picked it up. My sister, Stella's, name flashed on the screen, indicating she'd entered her code to access my building. A thumbnail photo showed her ascending the stairs, and her arms were full of... something. That sparked a flicker of curiosity, enough to coax me into sitting up straight. I shut off the television.

Almost on cue, there was a knock at the door, promptly followed by the sound of it swinging open. Stella didn't wait for an invitation or a beckoned entrance. She simply waltzed in like she owned the place. She was the embodiment of Markham traits—dark hair that danced in the ocean breeze, eyes like pools of aged bourbon, and a height that made her stand out in any crowd. Though her genes hadn't gone as overboard in that department as mine had.

"Ever heard of waiting for someone to answer the door?" I mock-frowned at her. "For all you knew, I could've been lying here naked."

She breezed toward me with that familiar athletic grace of hers, hair swinging as she laughed. "Please. With your security fetish, I bet you have a system rigged that warned you the second I made the decision to come over." She shot me a teasing glance. "And don't worry. I'd avert my eyes if you were in your, uh, unmentionables."

"Sure you would." I rolled my eyes, unable to suppress the smirk tugging at my lips. There was no denying the comfort that came with Stella's presence—even if she was invading my personal space with the subtlety of a tropical storm.

The handles of a canvas bag draped over one of her arms, and I couldn't make out what she held in the other. "I'm surprised you didn't have your front door locked."

I scowled at her. "I'm alone inside my own home with both exterior entrances armed. You're the one invading." I didn't mention I was well equipped to handle any situation if that thumbnail had shown someone I *didn't* want ascending my stairs.

Stella's stride didn't falter as she approached, her face alight with a mischievous smile that set off alarm bells in my head. Whatever she was up to, it spelled trouble. She reached me and, without missing a beat, deposited a small, wriggling black bundle right onto my lap.

"It's your lucky day," she chirped, barely containing her

excitement before continuing past me and toward the kitchen. The canvas bag she carried landed with a soft thud on the quartz counter, its contents a mystery.

"Stel, what the—" My words halted at the surprise she'd dropped on me. It was a tiny fluffball, but one equipped with an arsenal. Miniature daggers sank into my thighs through the fabric of my black jeans, eliciting an involuntary hiss from me. The creature looked up, its bright green eyes meeting mine, and let out a plaintive meow that was somehow both demanding and endearing. "What is this thing?"

Stella's laughter floated from the kitchen. "It's a kitten, Einstein."

"Never would've guessed," I shot back, frowning as it began to knead my leg in earnest, those tiny daggers a rhythmic torture. The damn thing had the sort of face that could make a guy forget he was supposed to be tough. "What am I supposed to do with it?"

"It happens to be a him," she replied, a playful lilt in her voice. "I picked the black one because it matches your wardrobe. You two will match for those stealthy midnight snacks, though I drew the line at tattooing him. Meet your new roommate." There was a teasing glint in her eye as she leaned one hip against the counter.

"Stella, you can't be serious!" Ignoring her remark about my tattoos, I peered down at the little animal that had made itself comfortable on my lap. The kitten's short black coat blended in with my black jeans and its four white paws—socks, Stella would call them—moved with its rhythmic motions. Despite myself, I gently lifted the kitten and inspected its front paws. Sure enough, each paw boasted an extra toe. "A Hemingway cat? Really?"

"Really." After padding across the room, she stopped

before me and folded her arms in satisfaction. "You're a Markham, Hunter. And every Markham needs one of our legendary cats—even if they're living off the Key."

I'd completely forgotten that Pilar, the current resident Hemingway cat at the Big House of Calypso Key, had given birth to a litter. Rolling my eyes, I set the kitten down on the couch beside me. He quickly scrambled back onto my lap. "And what makes you think I need this thing?"

"Because it's time you settled into more than just this apartment." Stella's voice softened, her determination to play big sister evident in her stance. "Having something to care for can change a person. It's good for the soul. His name is Pedro."

"Pedro?" I echoed, unable to suppress the twitch of my lips. *The Sun Also Rises*, huh?"

Stella gave me a deliberate nod. "See? It's fate. You're the only person I know who would get that Hemingway reference right away. The book is about starting fresh and finding your place. And now you've got a kitten named after a character. Seems fitting, don't you think?"

"All our cats have the names of Hemingway characters."

Our. Such a small word.

And yet one I wasn't sure I could use yet.

I sighed at the small creature purring contentedly on my thighs. My skeptical gaze met Stella's unwavering one, and I knew resistance was futile. "Fine," I relented, scratching behind the kitten's ears and eliciting a louder purr. "But if he starts using my favorite boots as a scratching post, I'm giving him back."

"He'd never do that." Then her smug smile fell, her face becoming serious. "But he'll always have a home on Calypso Key. Just like you do."

I concentrated on Pedro, breathing through a sudden swell of emotion that had come from nowhere.

Stella seemed to realize I needed a moment and crossed the room back to the open kitchen. She returned carrying the canvas bag, and her smile reappeared as she handed it to me. Shiny food and water bowls, along with a small bag of dry cat food, were nestled inside. "He's going to need to eat, and I figured you wouldn't have anything suitable."

"Gee, you think?" I grumbled, peeking at the feline treasure she had brought. The kitten, meanwhile, seemed quite content making himself at home on me.

"Wait here," Stella said with a grin that meant more surprises were in store. She opened my front door and disappeared briefly, then reemerged with a brand-new litter box and a box of litter. "Can't forget this!"

"Well, aren't you helpful," I deadpanned, but secretly, her thoughtfulness touched me. It was just like Stella to make sure every detail was accounted for.

After patting the litter box, she straightened. "Hey, you ready for our game? The Marathon Marlins aren't pushovers, you know."

"Yeah, I'll be there."

"Good. We need your big muscles for some serious slugging." She flexed an arm in imitation of me at bat. "If only we had a better pitcher than Gabe…"

I snapped my gaze up to meet hers. A silent understanding flickered between us, heavy with unspoken thoughts about Evan still refusing to step into the role he was made for. The role I had ended permanently. We held the look for a heartbeat too long before each of us averted our gazes. "Gabe's a great pitcher, and we've won our first three games."

"I know. He's just been grumbling that he's too old to play anymore."

I snorted. "Give me a break. He's all of thirty-seven." Gabe was the eldest of our siblings, with Stella next. At thirty-two, Evan was less than a year older than me, partly why we'd been inseparable growing up.

She panned her gaze around my mostly unpacked living room, pausing at my fully stocked bookshelf. "It might have taken a few months to iron out the details, but here you are!"

I'd found my building with its second-floor apartment several months ago. Such a perfect location was worth waiting for the tenant's lease to end before opening KeyMark. Now it was mid-January, and we were in full swing.

"Here I am. So how's Aiden?"

Her eyes lit up like bioluminescent waves at night. "Fantastic! When we were at the farmer's market last week-end, he got me another orchid. A gorgeous bicolor Catt-leya." Her tone shifted to the reverence usually reserved for sacred things.

"Sounds like a keeper. Aiden and the flower." I smiled at her laugh. Aiden was good for her, and that meant he was all right by me. He was possibly the only thing Stella was more in love with than orchids or her position as top chef at the aptly named Orchid, our family resort's fine dining restaurant.

There was that *our* again.

As I tried to get used to the new weight on my legs, she wandered over to a security system box I'd casually tossed on a side table. I could practically see her thoughts change as her smirk faded. A series of thefts the previous summer had made our family realize they needed a closer eye on the resort, which had brought me back.

"I saw Myles last night," she said. "He was like a shadow. There but barely noticeable."

"Of course. That's the plan," I replied, pride swelling within me for the team I'd put together at KeyMark. "Garrett and Myles are trading off seven-night shifts while I work days here to get the business off the ground. We'll keep everything locked down tight." Garret Decker, Myles Howard, and I went way back—all the way to the Marines.

"Dad is very happy to have you handling security," she said. "We're all glad you're back."

I tried to take that at face value, and to ignore that Evan most definitely had mixed feelings about my return. Then Pedro shifted, returning my attention to him. My fingers hovered over his back. Pedro's fur was as black as the ocean at midnight, and when I finally let my hand brush against him, the kitten gazed up at me with those bright green eyes. "How old is he?"

"Eight weeks. Pilar had seven kittens and we're keeping two. You should be honored—I think Pedro is the pick of the litter."

"I already said I'd keep him," I griped.

"He'll be good for you. And you for him too. I'll leave you two to get acquainted."

Depositing the kitten on the couch, I pushed to my feet. Stella wrapped her arms around me in a spontaneous hug that squeezed the reluctance right out of me.

"I love you."

"Thanks, Stel. Love you too."

She pulled away, and the corners of my mouth twitched upward despite the weight of her words. After shooting me one last knowing look, she sauntered out and left me alone with Pedro. Once the door clicked shut behind her, I sighed and glanced down at my unexpected charge. He was already curling up, prepared to nap as though he belonged here. Shaking my head, I went about setting up his new world. The food and water bowls clinked together as I placed them on the floor near the fridge and filled them. The kitten was so tiny, I was worried he might hurt himself jumping off the couch, so I picked him up and set him on the floor. Pedro stretched lazily before ambling over to inspect his provisions.

"Welcome to bachelor life," I told him as he sniffed at his meal, then began to eat.

I found a spot for his litter box in the laundry room, tucked neatly out of sight but easily accessible. Left alone with my thoughts, I settled onto the couch, not bothering to turn the TV back on. After a while, Pedro hopped up beside me, dispelling my concern about his physical prowess. His presence was a warm weight as he settled next to my leg. And though part of me was pissed as hell at Stella for doing this, I knew one thing. I might not get overly attached to my new charge, but I was going to take care of him.

I didn't know if I'd ever fully embrace the Markham traditions or if I'd forever be the black sheep. My gaze drifted to the window. In the distance, just beyond the reach of Dove Key's quaint charm, lay Calypso Key. Silhouetted against the twilight sky, it was my true home, and yet somewhere I wasn't comfortable being yet. I didn't belong. This small town, with its salty air and tight-knit community, was supposed to be a fresh start. Yet everywhere I looked lay the ghosts of my past—and not just Evan.

The past also included Brenna Coleridge.

She had known me before I became the guy with a dark,

shadowed reputation. In high school, we'd been friends, bonding over our love of books. I'd been a gangly, shy tower of a teen, too scared to let her know how I felt about her. But she'd never left my thoughts in the decade-plus since. Dark, black years that she had provided light in, whether she knew it or not. And now? I had no idea who she was. And she sure as hell didn't know me.

It was ironic how, after all my narrow escapes as a Marine, the thought of her this close was what unraveled me. I had to smile at the absurdity.

Facing down insurgents? No problem.

Dodging IEDs and hollow-point bullets? Been there.

Yet the thought of talking to Brenna Coleridge made my stomach clench.

I could almost picture her caramel-colored hair reflecting the sun's rays, her laughter mingling with the ocean breeze. But even our friendship had contained dangerous undercurrents—two families with long-held, simmering resentments. I had come back to make amends, but maybe I'd also come back for a second chance at the life I thought I'd lost.

I was an expert at surveilling others, distilling their lives down to evidence and reports. But when it came to facing my own need for redemption, I was as green as a rookie during spring training. The Markhams were a baseball family. Evan and I had grown up playing ball, dreaming of grand slams and perfect games. And it had been more than a dream for Evan.

Until I ruined it.

But Stella and our youngest sibling, Maia, had convinced me to play once again. Strictly recreational league, but I was part of a team again and able to feel the rush of camaraderie. And if I could face down fastballs and curveballs, I could surely navigate the complexities of a conversation with Brenna.

With one last look at the dark outline of Calypso Key, determination filled me. It was time to stop watching shades of a life lived from the shadows. Enough was enough. Maybe Pedro wasn't the only thing I needed in my life.

Chapter Two

Brenna

I DELICATELY POSITIONED the last batch of thrillers on the warm mahogany shelves. Bookstore in Paradise wasn't just a haven for book lovers. It was a reflection of my heart, standing tall and proud on Main Street of Dove Key. The scent of vanilla and sandalwood mingled in the air, dancing with the soft glow of candles that flickered on the counter-top. As I aligned the spines with meticulous care, my fingers brushed over the colorful covers. The chime above the door jingled softly, a gentle reminder of the world outside. I stepped back, admiring the orderly array I had created, a vibrant mosaic of storytelling.

"Looks inviting, Brenna!" Michelle approached with her usual sunny smile, her sandals slapping softly against the floor. "These new releases are pretty tempting."

"Thanks. There's nothing like a good book to kick off the week." I smiled back at her, tucking a stray lock of hair behind my ear. Michelle was a regular, her presence as much a part of the store as the weathered armchairs and stacks of bestsellers.

"Have you heard the latest?" she asked nonchalantly, picking up a novel with a beach on the cover. "Hunter Markham is back in town."

My hand paused mid-air. The atmosphere shifted slightly, as if the mention of Hunter's name had stirred something invisible. "Is he?" I kept my voice even, feigning a casual interest that my racing heart betrayed.

Michelle, oblivious to the history that clung to that name, continued. "Yep. Supposedly, he bought a place on Main Street not far from here, but I'm not sure which. Could be interesting, don't you think?" Her eyes sparkled with the allure of fresh gossip.

A two-story building three down from mine had recently undergone renovations, but I hadn't investigated the new business, except to note it was some sort of security firm. "Interesting for sure," I agreed.

"Didn't you know him way back when?"

"Kind of," I hedged. Hunter and I had been close once upon a time, before life took us down divergent paths. "We hung out back in high school, but I haven't heard from him since."

"Maybe he's planning to open a business or something. I wonder what kind. Another Markham would liven things up around here." Then she sighed. "After his rift with Evan, I wonder if he wasn't welcome on Calypso Key."

"Maybe." My curiosity was piqued despite my reservations. Could Hunter really be back?

"Anyway, I'll let you get back to it." Michelle gave me a friendly wave as she strolled toward the door. "I'm still working through my TBR pile. I swear you've become my dealer!"

"See you later." Laughing, I called after her, my gaze lingering on the doorway.

After Michelle disappeared, I reached for a stack of brightly covered paperbacks, my hands mechanically adjusting their arrangement on the display table. But my thoughts were far from the task at hand.

Hunter Markham.

The name echoed in my mind like a song from another life. We used to share secrets between the stacks of the library, dreams scribbled on the margins of our notebooks. He had been my confidant, my partner in literary crimes. But school had been over a decade ago. Uncounted rumors had swirled around Dove Key about Hunter in the years since. Unsettling stories from far-off lands about a man, not a boy.

With an impatient huff, I straightened a row of contemporary romances. A gossipy rumor was hardly confirmation, and I had plenty else to occupy my thoughts. Like my family. A pang of concern wound its way through me. Siesta Sunset, the resort my family had poured generations of heart and soul into, was hanging on by its metaphorical fingernails. Part of me felt the weight of responsibility, a constant reminder that I needed to do more. Though I had elected a different path as a Coleridge, that didn't mean guilt didn't gnaw at me occasionally. But I also had my own business to run.

There were displays to organize, recommendations to make, and a book club meeting to prepare for. Yet, in this quiet moment of reflection, I couldn't shake the worry for my family's legacy. With a deep breath, I banished thoughts of struggling finances and old flames. I needed to concentrate on the present.

Dove Key was my home, Bookstore in Paradise my sanctuary.

The next time the door opened, I was placing an order. My brother, Ben, pushed through, a gust of tropical air sneaking in behind him. His light-brown hair was mussed from working outside, his skin bronzed and lightly freckled across the bridge of his straight nose—a testament to the long hours he'd been putting in under the sun. The image sharply contrasted the man who had once been more interested in living life by the seat of his pants than shouldering responsibility.

"Hey," he called out, his voice carrying over the quiet hum of the bookstore.

"Ben! What brings you here?" I stepped from behind the counter.

"Needed a break from the resort." He wore an easy smile, though I caught a glimpse of weariness in his eyes he couldn't quite mask.

"You look tired. Let's have a seat." Concern laced my words as I led him over to the cozy reading nook nestled near the front picture window.

"Ah, just the usual grind." He brushed off my concern, sinking into the plush burgundy armchair across from me. "Glad to be done with the job at Calypso Key, though."

"I'm sure you are," I said hesitantly, not wanting to dredge trouble but needing to address the obvious. "It can't have been enjoyable to be called a thief."

Ben's jaw set, a shadow passing over his features. "It wasn't. You know how the Markhams can be."

I shifted to face him more directly. "Didn't you say that Stella apologized to you?"

He looked at me, surprise flickering in his expression before it softened. "She did. Took me aback, honestly."

"Maybe it's a sign," I suggested, warming to one of my other favorite subjects. "A sign to end this feud between our families. It's old news, Ben. We could move past it."

"Yeah, right." He leaned back with a snort.

"The two families have held onto this animosity for too long. It's past time we find some common ground."

The Coleridges and Markhams had been at odds for over a century—ever since a Markham had won Calypso Key from our ancestor in a high-stakes poker game. The Coleridges had once owned most of Dove Key in addition to Calypso Key, but our holdings had whittled away over the decades. Sold off in the name of making ends meet, while the Markhams and their resort had thrived.

Decades of resentment and animosity had been passed down too.

"Stella reaching out... that's not nothing," Ben conceded, his gaze meeting mine. "But it'll take a hell of a lot more than that for me to ever trust one of those vipers."

"Well, with that attitude, no wonder!" The news I'd just heard about Hunter entered my mind, but I stayed silent. Ben would not be pleased to hear the errant Markham had returned. Then again, all I had was a rumor. Michelle hadn't actually laid eyes on Hunter, had she?

Ben's skepticism was as clear as the glass chimes hanging above the bookstore's entrance. His deep sigh held a heaviness that spoke of endless worries. "Look"—he rubbed the back of his neck—"I appreciate Stella's apology. But words won't change what people think of me overnight."

It pained me to see him like this—tired lines etching his face, the harsh judgment of our small community dimming the spark in his blue eyes. Ben was working two jobs. In addition to working full time with a local landscaping company, he worked on his off hours around the resort. Doing whatever needed to be done, and fixing the million things that seemed in need of constant repair.

"Ben, you're turning things around, really putting your heart into Siesta Sunset. People will see that." I smiled, trying to infuse some hope into the conversation.

When our father had deserted our mother—and the whole rest of the family—ten years ago, Ben had reacted by sowing a very large can of wild oats. But as the years wore on and our mother struggled to pick up the pieces, she leaned more and more on her eldest child. Ben. Though he never complained, I knew the mantle of leadership had been a heavy one to bear.

"Maybe," he said with a shrug. "But it feels like for every step forward, there's someone waiting to push me two steps back."

"Give it time," I said gently, reaching across to squeeze his hand. "You're more than your past. Slowly but surely, everyone else will see that too."

Before he could respond, the cheerful ring of the door chime signaled a new customer. A woman with sunburned skin and an adventurous glint in her eye wandered in, her gaze immediately drawn to the travel section. I gave Ben's hand a final reassuring pat before moving toward the newcomer, who had tourist written all over her. In no time, I had the perfect book selected for her, a guide to the Keys full of out-of-the-way haunts just waiting to be discovered that a local author had written. As I rang up her purchase, a pang of longing hit me. Exploring new places, seeking adventure—Hunter and I used to dream about that when we were kids, tucked away in the corners of the local library.

"Enjoy your adventure," I told the woman, handing her

the bagged book. As she walked out, she left a trail of excitement behind her.

My brother smiled faintly at our exchange as he rose from his chair. "You've got a gift, Bren. Always have."

"Thanks." The boards squeaked reassuringly as I crossed the worn wooden floor. "Just doing what I love."

He nodded, and though his shoulders still bore that heavy weight, there was a slight lift in his posture. "I better get back to the resort. I need to repair a railing on the dock."

"Get some rest, okay? And remember, you're not alone in this."

"Thanks. I know," he said, though we both knew it was a promise stretched thin by circumstance.

Alone again among the bookshelves, I roamed between the stacks. My fingertips grazed the spines of countless stories until my eyes landed on a contemporary romance and I pulled it out for a closer look.

"That's the one." The glossy cover flaunted two celebrities locked in a clinch that promised both passion and secrets. Perfect for next month's book club selection. I returned to my computer and ordered twenty copies.

Bookstore in Paradise had always been a place where different worlds collided and harmonized with the scent of aged paper and scented candles. Yet, even in this tranquil setting, thoughts of Hunter stirred my calm waters. His possible return to Dove Key was like a rogue wave, unexpected and potentially tumultuous. As kids, a friendship between a Coleridge and a Markham had raised eyebrows. But as adults? It would be even more complicated.

If the rumors about him are true, I doubt he's picked up a book in years. I'm probably the last person he's interested in seeing.

I shook my head, dispelling any thoughts that threatened to dampen my spirits. Our monthly Sips and Pages book club was a testament to how family divides could be bridged. April Markham, with her infectious laughter, and Liv Jacobson, who was Evan Markham's fiancée, had become unlikely allies over the past couple of years. Then more, friends. They were proof that the past didn't have to dictate the future.

They had been there to console me after a recent breakup. Worse—it had been a second breakup. I'd given Knox Crandall another chance, but our relationship hadn't been any more fulfilling the second time, at least for me. He tried so hard to do the right thing, but trouble seemed to follow him everywhere. And when I'd been despondent, my two friends had come over, bearing Liv's exceptional coffee and donuts—sugary circles of comfort that made the heartache more bearable. Their kindness meant everything. It was high time the rest of our two rival keys caught up with us, recognizing that feuds belonged in history books, not in the heart of our community.

My phone buzzed from within the pocket of my apron. I hesitated, my hand hovering over the fabric. When I finally pulled it out, Knox's name flashed on the screen, another message to add to last night's that I hadn't answered.

Knox: Can we talk? Please?

Memories ebbed and flowed. Knox, with his easy grin and artfully disheveled brown hair, always looking like he'd stepped off a postcard for Dove Key. But I was done with him and his late nights at the bar. Too bad he wasn't. A soft sigh escaped my lips as I locked my phone and straightened the throw pillows on the chairs Ben and I had used, though

21

it wasn't my ex-boyfriend who drifted into my thoughts. It was Hunter. The sweet bookworm whose shy smiles could light up the darkest corners.

"Who are you now, Hunter Markham?"

The question lingered in the air, unanswered. My curiosity was piqued, yet it was tempered with caution. Everyone knew Hunter had joined the Marines after Evan's accident, but no one knew exactly what he'd done. Rumors swirled about his appearance, his actions, and none of them were good. People change, after all, and I couldn't help but wonder if time and trials had rewritten the boy who once spoke in quotes and dreams.

Dove Key was a small town. The chances were good that if Hunter had moved back, our paths would cross at some point.

Chapter Three

Brenna

THE FOLLOWING AFTERNOON, sunlight filtered through the blind covering the big picture window, throwing slanted beams of light across the floor of my little bookstore. I stood behind the checkout counter, thumbing through the delicate pages of a first edition of *Catcher in the Rye* that smelled faintly of adventure and time. The store was quiet, winding down from another day. After carefully replacing the Steinbeck in my display of treasured books, I reached for a Hemingway. I was admiring its rugged cover— a mirror to the author himself—when the chime above the door jangled.

Glancing up, I froze.

The man who entered was dressed in all black and seemed too large for the cozy confines. Easily six and a half feet tall, he was stunningly handsome, his face a chiseled formation of angles that a trimmed, dark beard perfected. Said face was paired with an alarming amount of muscles on his arms and chest, with tattoos marking his skin. The sight made my heart race as I considered the cash in my drawer. Was I about to be robbed? Then, with a sharp intake of breath, recognition dawned on me like a switch being flipped. There was no mistaking it.

Hunter Markham stood at the threshold of my store.

As I took him in from the crown of his almost-black hair to the pair of giant feet inside work boots, the differences between the boy who'd left and the man who stood before me were legion. The rumors had done nothing to prepare me for this Hunter. Gone was the near-skeletal, wiry frame that couldn't take in enough calories. In its place stood a man with shoulders broad enough to carry the weight of any world. His upper arms, visible beneath the rolled-up sleeves of his shirt, were canvases of ink. Elaborate tribal tattoos reached toward his elbows, leaving his forearms unmarked. More ink covered the upper part of his chest, visible where his shirt collar was open.

His frame was bulging with muscle, the result of what had to be countless hours of disciplined physical exertion. Yet, it wasn't just his physique that was intimidating. It was the aura around him, an almost visible force that spoke of strength and power. My heart continued its wild gallop as shock and fear turned to recognition. Not to mention the barest glimmers of raw attraction.

Good God. He's the most gorgeous man I've ever seen!

Hunter's jaw was set, his cheekbones high. His hair, once a rebellious mop, was now cropped short, giving him an older, more martial appearance. His eyes were the same shade of stormy dark brown I remembered, but where they had once looked at me with youthful hope and mischief, now they held secrets, guarded and unreadable.

"Hello, Brenna." His voice was deeper than I remembered, resonating through the quiet space between us.

I cleared my throat, trying to remember how to speak. "Hunter." At least my voice came out steadier than I felt.

"Been a while," he added, his eyes cautiously surveying the shop.

"Years." My hands involuntarily smoothed the front of my apron. "I... You look different."

He gave a noncommittal grunt, his posture stiff as he shrugged.

My curiosity got the better of me as I decided to test how much of the bookworm remained. "I'd heard a rumor that you returned. Did moving away give you what you needed?"

A spark of recognition ignited in his eyes, softening them. "You can't get away from yourself by moving from one place to another. There's nothing to that."

That was all it took. I recognized in his voice the boy I had once sat in the library with for hours. My heart leaped, and I couldn't suppress the smile breaking across my face. Understanding my question, he'd answered with a line from *The Sun Also Rises* by Ernest Hemingway, a book we had both loved.

Without hesitation, I responded with the next one. "Hell. We could have a good life anywhere."

Hunter's warm expression slowly morphed into a full smile. The transformation was startling, like watching someone step out of a shadow. The sight of it brought an unexpected warmth to my chest, a soft glow that pushed back against the years apart. It also brought a different kind of flutter in my stomach.

"Still remember your Hemingway, huh?" I observed, my voice lighter now.

"I was told recently it's part of my DNA." His smile changed his whole demeanor. For a moment, the imposing

25

figure before me was just Hunter—the same person who debated literature with me, whose laughter used to fill my ears. Only now he was drop-dead attractive in that imposing, towering body.

"Time does have a way of changing things, though." My surprise mingled with a sense of relief. My sweet friend hadn't been completely lost to time and distance after all. Once again, I couldn't contain my curiosity about him. "So what have you been up to all these years?" I stepped around the counter and leaned back against it, trying to sound casual. But inside, my mind was racing with the rumors that had occasionally trickled back to me.

Hunter's expression closed off again, the shields coming back up as if by reflex. "I was in the Marines," he said, voice even but guarded. "After I got out a few years ago, I lived in South Beach. I just moved back here and started my own security agency down the street."

"Security, huh?"

"Yeah." He nodded, his gaze briefly flicking away before locking back onto mine. There was a coiled readiness in his posture that spoke of experiences being left unsaid. More lurked behind his eyes, utterly unreadable, except for the brief time we'd spoken about books. Books...

"Did you come in for something to read?" The change in topic seemed to catch him off guard, and a hint of shyness crept into his posture, a stark contrast to the confident, intimidating man who had walked in moments ago.

"Uh, yeah. Yes, I did." He cleared his throat, looking slightly embarrassed.

Is he here to see me?

"Action and adventure are over there." I pointed back toward the section that housed tales of daring exploits and heart-pounding suspense. "You always did like books full of thrills."

"I still do. Thanks." Hunter's voice softened at my gesture. He gave me a nod and went toward the back of the store. Walking quietly and softly over the wooden floor despite his bulk, his movements betrayed nothing of the internal currents I sensed swirling within him. He disappeared between the aisles, the set of his shoulders a shadow against the spines of countless adventures.

To distract my nervous hands, I moved to an antique oak table and rearranged the display of candles I'd set up. These were lavender and vanilla and gave off a pleasant, bookish scent I loved. The chime of the door pulled me from my thoughts. And once again, I got a shock when I glanced up.

Knox stepped in, stumbling slightly over the entry. His light hair was mussed and stuck up on one side. He reeked of alcohol and desperation, and my heart plummeted.

"Knox." My voice held an uneven mix of surprise and discomfort. "What are you—"

"Brenna." My name on his tongue was clumsy and thick. His hazel eyes locked onto mine with unsettling intensity. Knox had always been unpredictable when he drank.

"You need to leave," I insisted, trying to muster authority into my voice. "Now."

"Come on." He moved closer, reaching out as if he could bridge the chasm between us with his unsteady fingers. "You don't mean that. We were good together. We can be again."

"Absolutely not," I countered sharply, my stomach clenching. This was not the reunion any girl dreamed of. "We're through. You need to go."

But he was undeterred, stepping forward to grab my arm, making me wince at his touch. What I had once craved now felt like an invasion. "We're worth another shot, Brenna. We can work out our problems."

"Get out of here," I hissed, shaking off his grasp as my heart galloped in my chest.

That's when Knox vanished from my sight in an abrupt blur of motion. He was in front of me and then *gone*. My breath caught in my throat as I turned my head. Hunter had him hoisted in the air, pressing him against the end of a bookcase with an ease that defied belief. One of Hunter's hands was bunched in the fabric of Knox's shirt collar, and the other held him by the waistband of his jeans like he weighed nothing.

"The lady told you to leave." Hunter's voice was low and menacing, a stark contrast to the gentle cadence he'd used just minutes earlier. "What part of that don't you get? Maybe I can clear it up for you." He twisted the hand holding Knox's pants slightly, and my ex's face went pale.

"Okay! I'm leaving. I'm leaving!" Knox's voice broke into a higher pitch at Hunter's motion, sounding almost comical if the situation weren't so frightening.

Hunter released him abruptly, both hands letting go. Knox crumpled down to the floor, then regained his footing with a stumble. His eyes were wide, darting between Hunter and me, but it was clear where the power lay.

"Out. Now." Hunter's tone left no room for argument.

Knox jerked a nod as he scrambled backward, staring at Hunter with wide eyes the entire time. The shop was completely silent as he slunk out of the store without another word. The bell above the door chimed mockingly as he exited, and I jumped at the jarring noise. I took a steadying breath, suddenly aware of the sweat covering my back. I turned to look at Hunter, who remained still, his gaze following Knox until he was certain my ex was gone.

Then, without moving, he slid his eyes to me. "Are you all right?" His voice returned to something softer, though the underlying strength was unmistakable. He didn't look remotely upset, like throwing unruly drunks out of stores was something he did every day.

"Yes," I managed to say, my voice somewhat creaky. I cleared my throat. "Thank you." I couldn't control the tremor in my hands—a reaction to the fear, the shock, and the confusing sense of safety Hunter's actions had provided.

"I take it that guy isn't a friend?"

I shook my head, taking a few steps closer to Hunter. "No, definitely not a friend. Just an ex who doesn't understand boundaries." The familiar pang of regret washed over me as I spoke those words. At how Knox had been charming at first, hiding the person he became when drinking.

Hunter's gaze lingered on me. "You deserve better than that. Has he been a problem before?"

I shrugged, feeling a weird mix of vulnerability and relief at Hunter's presence. "He's texted a couple of times, but nothing like this. I thought we were done for good, but he seems to be having a hard time letting go."

Hunter nodded, his expression serious. "Do you want my number?" My shock must have shown on my face because his posture relaxed. "I'm in private security, Brenna. Dealing with shit like him is what I do for a living."

Something in his tone sent a shiver down my spine. And I was sure Knox had gotten his message loud and clear. "No —I'm fine. I'm sure we just saw the last of him. Thank you for your help."

"Are you sure you're all right?" he asked again, stepping

closer to me. His gaze traced over my face as if searching for any signs of distress I might be hiding.

"Yes." I clasped my trembling hands together to steady them, and tried not to notice how his huge presence that should have filled me with alarm—especially given what I'd just witnessed—was doing quite the opposite. "I'm fine now."

Hunter's eyes lingered on me before he finally nodded once, as if confirming something to himself. "Good," he said simply and headed back toward the stacks of books as if nothing had happened.

As if he hadn't just manhandled my drunken ex with the same ease as flipping through the pages of one of my cherished books. What had life done to him? I returned to the glass check-out counter, mindlessly straightening a stand of watercolor bookmarks.

Moments later, Hunter returned, a Clive Cussler novel in hand, its spine cracked with use. "I'll take this one," he said with a faint smile. His voice was back to what it had been before Knox's rude entrance. "How much?"

"Oh, no charge," I insisted, pushing his extended cash back toward him. "After what you did, it's yours."

The shadow that passed over his features was like a storm cloud over the sun. "I can't ignore someone in trouble. Especially... someone who means something to me. It's what I do."

"Protect people?"

"Something like that," he replied, pocketing his money.

I managed a shaky smile, feeling the weight of his gaze as I motioned to the book in his hand. "Enjoy your adventure."

"Thanks." That nearly imperceptible softening around his eyes made an encore. "It was good to see you."

"Likewise, Hunter." His name still felt strange on my tongue, like a word from a forgotten language I was learning all over again.

He paused at the door, a hint of a smile playing at his lips. "I'll be back. Clive Cussler did write quite a few books, after all." He held up the battered paperback in a salute, his smile widening before he stepped out into the waning day.

The door closed softly behind him, and I was alone in the quiet shop once more. My legs gave out, and I slumped against the counter, my hands trembling. Who was this man who had just walked out of my store? The boy who'd left town years ago, the one who whispered Hemingway and Shakespeare as he smiled shyly had been transformed. He was as daunting as he was mesmerizing, a living paradox wrapped in tattoos and mystery.

My heart raced, not just with fear but with a curiosity that bordered on yearning. Because of that small sentence he'd uttered. *"Especially... someone who means something to me."*

I knew who Hunter Markham used to be, but the question was, who was he now? And more importantly, was it safe to find out?

Chapter Four

Hunter

THE UNMISTAKABLE CRACK of bat against ball snapped me back to the present as I crouched behind home plate. I vaulted to my feet with a curse as the batter hit a clean double through the gap between first and second. He didn't need to sprint to reach first base.

Shit! Gotta get my head in the game here.

The Calypso Key Stingrays were up against the Marathon Marlins today, and the heat wasn't just coming from the blazing afternoon sun. Gabe wound up another pitch, and my muscles tensed in anticipation.

We were in the ninth inning, but I'd had trouble concentrating all game. My mind wouldn't stop drifting back to Brenna's bookstore. When I'd first walked through the door, it was like stepping into a different world. A quiet, familiar world I hadn't realized how much I'd missed. I'd spent so many years imagining what she might look like now. And when I'd finally seen her yesterday, it had hit me like a punch to the gut.

My fantasies couldn't hold a candle to the real thing.

Her light-brown hair had cascaded like a waterfall touched by the sun's golden fingers. Her eyes, an easy soft green, seemed to reach right into me. She still moved with the effortless grace I remembered, but the rest of her was nothing like my old friend.

I'd frozen on the doorstep, completely flummoxed by how gorgeous she was. Tall, willowy, her skin held the faintest blush from the sun. Sharp cheekbones framed a full mouth. When she first saw me, her eyes had been full of surprise and maybe even a hint of fear. I was used to my appearance causing that reaction in people. But fear was the last thing I wanted Brenna feeling in my presence. Fortunately, after she recognized me, I'd actually been able to string a few sentences together.

The way the store had been decorated—the beachy pictures along with paintings of Main Street, the perfect mixture of new books and well-thumbed paperbacks with ratty covers. All of that made it clear that Bookshop in Paradise was more of an extension of herself than a business she ran. The awkwardness between us had eased and we'd been on the way to an honest-to-God real reunion.

Until her ex showed up and ruined everything. When I heard the petulant whine in his voice and Brenna's tight refusal, I'd acted automatically. I hadn't even thought twice before manhandling the guy. And like most bullies, he'd backed down quickly upon facing someone who could fight back. But that look on Brenna's face afterward... like she didn't know whether to be grateful to me or fear me—

"Hey, daydreamer, wake up! We're trying to win a game here!" Maia's voice cut through my memories like the crack of a whip. I blinked and refocused on the diamond before me.

I waved an apology, then adjusted my catcher's mitt as my gaze flitted over to first base, where Maia stood with her hands on her hips. Her straight brown hair was tied back in a no-nonsense ponytail that matched her personality—tough and businesslike on the field but with a laugh that could light up even my moods. A smattering of freckles danced across her nose when she grinned, but right now my little sister and team manager was scowling at me and no doubt wondering where my head was at.

From the mound, Gabe lifted an arm out and glared at me. "You still with us?"

"Absolutely," I replied with a nod and waited for the next batter to approach.

Though a few inches shorter, Gabe was a big brother personified and not someone I wanted pissed at me. I'd seen him plenty angry at me not too long ago, and I didn't want a repeat performance. As I crouched back down, I steeled myself, pushing all thoughts of Brenna aside. The dull thud of the ball hitting my mitt helped settle me. My reflexes snapped into place, sharp and ready, and I hurled the ball back to Gabe with precision. He caught it neatly, rotating his shoulder with a slight grimace. He'd asked about ice earlier, but you wouldn't know he was feeling any discomfort from the quality of his pitching.

The batter in front of me hit a hard line drive. Stella's boyfriend, Aiden, was at third. He leaped with impressive agility, snagging the ball from its flight before landing and tagging the current runner on the base in one fluid motion.

The sparse crowd erupted in cheers as the umpire's hand sliced through the air. "Out!"

"Nice play, Aiden!" I shouted, clapping my glove as we jogged off the field. Aiden had been a great addition to the team. He played with a casual grace that made impossible plays look easy. As we settled into the dugout and the sound of bats clinking and teammates chattering filled the air, I kept my head down, trying not to think beyond the game.

Stella and Liv sat to my right, their heads together. "Hey, don't worry about it," Stella said to Liv, who had a frown tugging at her lips. "You're doing great out there in right field."

Liv shifted on the metal bench, smoothing her team jersey over her curves. "Easy for you to say," she mumbled. "You look like you were born on a diamond. I swear I'm the most unathletic person on earth."

Stella laughed, her athletic form relaxed as she draped an arm over Liv's shoulder. Like Gabe and me, she was a regular runner. "Trust me, I've had my share of outfield blunders. It's all about having fun, remember?"

I nodded in agreement, trying to focus on their conversation. Stella met my eyes before leaning forward to speak quietly to Liv. "Do you think I should talk to Evan again about joining the team? It could be good for him, right?"

Images flooded my mind at the mention of Evan—his total concentration while on the mound, and the way he could pitch with pinpoint accuracy. I remembered the awe I felt playing catch with him, how the baseball seemed to obey his command. He'd been a rookie phenom, headed toward the Major Leagues when I'd changed the entire course of his life in one day. In one dive. And changed my future too.

"It would be great to see him out here," I managed to say, though memories made my voice feel distant, like I was talking from the end of a long tunnel.

Liv chewed her lip, concern creasing her brow. "It would. But I don't know if he's ready for that. Baseball used to be his world, and how could this not bring all that back?"

She trailed off, her lowered brows and tight mouth an expression of protective love. Her man had been through the wringer, and here we were, talking about tossing him into a game that might rake up more than just dirt.

"Maybe he doesn't have to start on the mound," I suggested, trying to navigate our shared history with as much tact as I could muster. "He could just come in to hit and play first base or something. No pressure. Besides, Evan was an amazing hitter, remember?"

Stella nodded, her big brown eyes shining with a mix of hope and nostalgia. "So are you."

I shrugged off her compliment, not wanting to think about my own skills—they paled in comparison to Evan's. More than anything in the world, I wanted to see my brother at ease with me. The two of us had spent hours on baseball fields once.

Liv panned her gaze around the field, then gave Stella a firm nod. "Go ahead and talk to him. If he's not ready yet, he'll say so."

The dugout chatter faded as I approached the batter's box, gripping the bat like it was an old friend. The Stingrays needed this win, and I needed... well, I needed to focus on something other than the long, creamy curve of Brenna's neck and the way her green eyes seemed brighter than the outfield grass I was staring at.

We played on one of several baseball fields adjacent to a school in Big Pine Key. The four diamonds were shaped like a four-leaf clover, with the backstops at the center. Taking a deep breath, I stepped into position and my stance felt as natural as breathing. The Marlins' pitcher wound up, releasing the ball in a blur toward home plate. Time slowed down as my eyes locked onto the incoming pitch, my body coiling like a spring.

Crack!

The sound was sweet, the vibration through the aluminum bat just right. The ball sliced into the gap past the second baseman, and by the time the fielders scrambled, the ball was kissing the grass in the outfield. I rounded first, the cheers from the bleachers spurring me on as I pushed for second base.

"Go, go, go!" Maia's voice cut through the roar of the crowd.

Sliding into third, I kicked up a cloud of dust, the umpire's hand slicing through the air. "Safe!" I whipped my head up as Anselm, a chef at Dorado, ran across home plate just behind Gabe.

"Two runs score! The Stingrays win!"

Adrenaline surged through me as my teammates stood and cheered. I pushed to my feet, brushing dirt from my pants, and a smile fought its way across my face despite my best efforts to stay level-headed. Maybe it was more than just a game, after all. Maybe it was a momentary escape from the complexities of life in paradise, from the tension of reunions both romantic and sibling, from the thoughts about Brenna that had been gnawing at my insides like a persistent hunger.

"Nice hit, little brother!" Stella beamed at me, pride radiating from her.

"Thanks, Stel." I returned her smile. For now, this small victory would have to be enough. I was still catching my breath when they started making plans to hit the Conch Republic Brewpub, Dove Key's most popular watering hole.

"Come on, Hunter! First round's on me," Gabe called out, his arm slung over April's shoulder as they made their way toward the dugout exit. Her stomach was getting round with pregnancy, and she'd made the decision to cheer us from the stands rather than play herself.

"Nah, you go ahead," I said, swiping the back of my hand across my forehead. "Stayed up late on a security detail last night. I'm beat."

"Your loss, man," Maia chimed in with a playful punch to my arm. "But we'll toast to your triple."

"Appreciate it." I forced a smile. It wasn't the late night that had me wanting solitude. It was the need for quiet that sometimes overtook me when faced with loud crowds. For this foray into a fun sports league was about me trying to move on too.

After parking and entering my building, I took the stairs two at a time, ignoring the familiar ache in my muscles from the game and the day's tensions. Pushing open the door to my apartment, the silence welcomed me like an old friend. The Clive Cussler book still lay unopened on the table next to the door. Pedro, my little black six-toed sidekick, lay curled up on the couch, a tiny reminder that not everything in life was as complicated as human emotions.

At the sound of my entrance, he lifted his head. His green eyes fixed on me before he stretched and hopped down, his extra toes making his paws look somehow more endearing. Padding over, he weaved between my legs and demanded attention in his feline way.

"What, you missed me? Don't expect me to get attached, little dude."

With a frown, I reluctantly scooped him up into my arms. His purr vibrated against my chest, a rumble that seemed to say all was right in his world. I set him down long enough to refill his water dish and check his food—still plenty. As he took a few laps of water, a part of me envied his simple needs, his uncomplicated life.

But in the short time I'd been living here, I'd found my sanctuary. After grabbing a protein shake from the fridge, I crossed to my bookcase. The Cussler could wait—I wanted something more literary tonight. After picking up my favorite translation of Homer's *The Odyssey*, I climbed the narrow staircase tucked away behind what looked like an ordinary closet door. I emerged onto the rooftop of my modest apartment. The sky above was a canvas of deep indigo, dotted with stars that shimmered like diamonds scattered across velvet.

The rooftop had become a place where the chaos of the day dissolved into the tranquil whispers of night. I'd set up a little oasis, with a patio cover shielding a cozy rug and an inviting outdoor seating area with couches and throw pillows. Crisscrossing strings of outdoor lights hung over the area, dark now. Tonight, it was the lounger that called to me. I pulled it out and settled down before taking a long drink of my shake and opening my book. Soon, I was lost in the exploits of Odysseus and his crew fighting to find their way home.

A soft, muffled mewing caught my attention, followed by scratching. Frowning, I turned my head toward the door. I didn't want that damn cat to distract me. It was moments like these when I could almost fool myself into believing life was simple. And pets were obligations. Complications.

I snorted. I had plenty of complications and could hardly remember a time when my life had been without them. Evan and I had had some tentative interactions. As much as I missed the brother I'd idolized, I couldn't blame him for hating me and finding it hard to trust me.

I felt the same damn way.

After another plaintive cry, I set *The Odyssey* aside and pushed to my feet. I crossed the cement ground and opened the door, staring down. Pedro called out to me, his four white socks almost glowing in the dark space. My gaze widened to take in the dark stairwell behind him. It couldn't have been easy for him to jump up all those stairs. The kitten squeaked another meow at me, a tiny sound in a cavernous space.

A small creature who had also been displaced. Removed from everything he'd known.

"Dammit, Stella."

I lifted him into my arms and returned to the lounger. Now purring happily, he curled up on my abdomen, digging his daggers in nicely in the process. My fingers moved rhythmically through Pedro's fur, the soft vibrations of his purr comforting against me. And inevitably, my mind turned to Brenna and her mane of hair that made me want to bury my face in it and just inhale.

The wildcard was her ex, Knox. Was he a disgruntled afterthought who'd had too much to drink? Or was he serious about making sure he and Brenna got back together? I'd worked some domestic abuse situations and a few stalker cases. Enough not to take Knox lightly, though Brenna hadn't seemed overly scared.

And then there was me. The guy who'd been too late more than once, and I still remembered the weight of failure. The first was with Brenna, and she didn't even know about it.

And the other time...

No, I refused to let my mind go back there. Pedro shifted position, as if sensing my mental walls flying up. With a long, cleansing exhale, I gazed up at the stars, the pinpricks of light offering silent reassurance. They'd witnessed eons of human struggle and triumph, and yet they endured, burning steadily in the vast darkness.

That first meeting with Brenna hadn't gone how either of us had expected. She certainly hadn't anticipated Knox's visit. But something had been forged by me in those minutes.

Concern. A need to protect.

Maybe Knox would never show his face again, and we could go back to our tentative connections over much-loved books. But if Brenna needed help, I would be the sentinel between her and whatever threats might come creeping from the shadows. Because some things, some people, were worth fighting for. Even when the battle was waged silently under a blanket of stars.

Chapter Five

Brenna

AS I MEANDERED through the stalls of the weekly Dove Key farmer's market, the air buzzed with haggling and laughter. The scent of fresh produce mingled with the sea's saltiness that always seemed to linger in town. I basked in the vibrant tableau spread before me—crates brimming with plump tomatoes, hand-stitched quilts waving in the gentle breeze, jars of artisan honey glistening like captured sunlight.

I hadn't heard anything further from the two men who had wandered into my shop earlier in the week. And that time had given me some perspective, putting my mind at ease. Knox's silence indicated he had gotten the message we were through. And though he had irritated and embarrassed me, I'd never felt threatened by him. Hunter was the huge unknown—shockingly attractive but possibly dangerous.

"Nice morning, isn't it?" someone said from behind me.

At the sound of Knox's voice, I fought off the urge to groan.

So much for getting the message.

I turned to find him standing there, looking out of place among the laid-back hustle of the market. His hair was neater than a few days ago and his clothes were pressed and clean. He stood erect, a certain confidence in the set of his shoulders, but his eyes betrayed him. They fixed on me with a glimmer of despair, like a man clinging to the edge of a cliff and trying to appear casual about it.

"Knox. This is a surprise. What are you doing here?"

He cleared his throat as he shifted his weight. "I'm sorry about the other day. Can we talk?"

Well, at least he's apologizing.

I narrowed my eyes at the idea of him showing up at the farmer's market, of all places. "Did you follow me here?"

His jaw tightened, but he held my gaze. "No. I was driving by and saw your parked car. We need to talk, babe. Let's find someplace a little more private, okay?"

I noted the curious glances from a nearby vendor. My heart beat a staccato rhythm against my ribcage. Knox had never been one for public scenes, and he'd never been violent. And if he was making the effort to clean up, maybe I ought to encourage that by listening.

"Sure," I replied, curiosity piqued despite my misgivings.

We wove through the crowd, the smell of fresh bread and ripe pineapple fading as we headed down a cozy alley that ran between a whitewashed taffy store and boutique. The noise from the market dulled to a murmur.

"Look, Brenna." Knox's voice was low and intimate in the seclusion of the alley. "I know things haven't been... great between us."

I crossed my arms, tension coiling in my stomach. "That's one way to put it."

His pleading eyes searched mine. "I'll change, okay? I'll knock off the booze and quit calling out at the boatyard. I guess I just want you to know I'm trying."

I didn't really know how to reply to that, so I remained quiet.

He stuffed his hands in his pockets. "Who was that goon who threw me out of your store?"

At hearing Hunter described that way, red-hot anger lanced through me. Why was I talking to Knox? I didn't owe him anything. "Just someone who realized you were way out of line and stepped in to help me."

"It won't happen again. That's what I'm trying to tell you."

The sincerity in his tone was disarming, but it was too late now. "Knox, I can't do this again." My voice wavered despite my resolve. "We tried, and it just... it didn't work."

"Because I was a mess." He pulled his hands from his pockets and emphasized his words as he stepped closer. The space between us became charged with the ghosts of our history. "But I'm cleaning up my act. I can be the man you need."

"Stop it." I took a step back, my heart thudding against my ribs like a trapped bird. "Please, just stop. We're through! This was a mistake. I'm leaving."

As I turned away, he reached out and curled his fingers around my forearm with more force than I expected. His grip tightened, and I gasped as a jolt of pain shot through me.

"Listen to me, Brenna." Desperation tinged his features now as he hissed through gritted teeth. "Don't just walk away from me!"

The pain in my forearm intensified as the despondency in his eyes morphed into anger. He squeezed harder, his grip like a vise. Fear coursed through my veins, and I struggled to free myself from his grasp. With a surge of adrenaline, I mustered all my strength and twisted my arm forcefully, breaking free from his hold. Pain shot up my arm, but I didn't have time to register it. I stumbled back and toward the crowd.

"Get out of here," I called out, fear lacing my voice. "Leave me alone!"

His eyes widened, and for a moment, I saw the flicker of the man I'd been attracted to once—a man who would never want to cause me pain. But then it was gone, the hardness that had become so much more common masking it. He glanced around, as if suddenly aware that our semi-secluded alley was mere feet away from the bustling market.

"Fine," he spat out. "You don't deserve me, you dumb bitch." Before I could react to that, he turned on his heel and strode away.

The adrenaline raging through me waned, leaving my legs shaky. My hand went to my forearm. It was already red with a blossoming bruise and tender to the touch, and my elbow throbbed. As I hurried from the alley, the lively chatter of the farmer's market felt surreal, like a distant melody unable to reach me through the fog of my thoughts.

How did it come to this?

Sweet-turned-bitter memories with Knox swirled in my mind, the sting of his grip tainting them. I deserved better. Better than heated arguments, and better than love that hurt. I had to distance myself from him, from us, once and for all. I fumbled for my phone, needing a voice of reason, a touchstone to reality.

"Hey, Harper," I said when my sister answered, relief flooding through me. "Don't suppose you're free right now, are you?"

"Actually, I was just going to grab something to eat. What's the matter? Your voice doesn't sound right."

"I could use my big sister. Could you meet me at Island Breeze in fifteen minutes?"

"Of course, Bren. Are you okay?"

"Yeah. I just need to bounce some things off you."

The walk to Island Breeze Bistro was a blur, and my determination to find solace carried me as much as my steps did. The diner's exterior was painted a bright yellow with a red-and-white striped awning stretched over the entrance. Inside, the walls were lined with photographs of the town's history and locals enjoying meals and events.

Harper was already there when I arrived, her soothing presence drawing me like a beacon as I approached our usual table by the window. We shared a similar shade of light-brown hair, but hers had a gorgeous wave I envied. Though she was only a few years older than me, her young son Finn gave her the maternal warmth I sometimes craved more than our own mother. And Mom was visiting her sister in Georgia for several months anyway. The booth I slipped into was upholstered in soft red vinyl and the seats were slightly worn from constant use.

Harper's brow wrinkled as she noticed me rubbing my forearm, her hazel eyes zeroing in on me. "What's going on?"

I hesitated before answering, not wanting to alarm her. After my walk, the entire scene had become removed, like a bad dream I couldn't quite remember. "I ran into Knox at the farmer's market."

"Did he hurt you?" Harper's voice was steady, but her face was rigid.

"No, no, it's not like that. He hasn't taken our breakup

well and wanted to talk to me. When I turned to leave, he grabbed me."

Her gaze shifted to my arm, and she gasped as she gently touched the darkening mark on my skin. "But he did hurt you."

"I don't think he meant to hurt me," I explained, wincing as I rotated my arm to show her the full extent of the bruise. "He looked shocked about it afterward."

Harper's hand covered mine on the table and gave it a reassuring squeeze. "If he's dangerous—"

"He's not," I cut in, almost too quickly. "Just frustrated. And we're over now, truly."

"Are you sure about that?"

I gave Harper a laugh, swallowing quickly at how shaky it sounded. "I'm sure. He told me I was a dumb bitch and then stormed away. We're through for good."

"Good riddance to the asshole," she said firmly. "You know you can always count on me, right?"

After the server brought our iced teas, I smiled at Harper, grateful to have her. "Of course—that's why I called you. I needed someone to vent to. I was definitely shaken up. But looking back, I'm pretty sure that little episode just put an exclamation point on our entire relationship."

But when Harper gave me a relieved smile, a different image seared its way to the forefront of my thoughts— Hunter stepping in, his presence like a shield. In stark contrast to Knox, there had been a confident fluidity to Hunter's movements, an ease with which he'd defused the tension. A protector in the guise of the town's bad boy. A shiver ran through me at the memory, a war waging inside. I was drawn to him, undoubtedly. But there was caution there too.

If Hunter handles conflict like it's second nature, does that make him more or less dangerous?

My thoughts circled the question, but I clamped down on them. This wasn't the time or place, not with my sister across from me. She would balk at the idea of me getting entangled with a Markham. And after my traumatic breakup with Knox, a dangerously attractive man was the last thing I should be thinking about.

"Brenna?" Harper's voice brought me back to the present.

"Sorry." I shook off the thoughts of Hunter with a twitch of my lips. "Just... processing. Let's eat."

After we placed our lunch orders, I toyed with the edge of my napkin, lost in thought. The urge to reach out to April and Liv gnawed at me—they'd seen me through the worst after Knox and I split. Yet they were firmly on the Markham side, a line drawn so deep in the sand it might as well have been carved into stone. A sigh escaped me, the weight of old grudges heavy on my shoulders. "This war between us and the Markhams is so stupid."

Harper's eyes went wide as she held her glass of iced tea. "Where did that come from?"

I half-smiled, feeling a little foolish. "Oh. My mind wandered to my friends who helped after I broke up with Knox. April and Liv, who are both involved with Markhams. They understood, you know? But I still hesitate a little to reach out. This family feud is so... exhausting."

Harper gave me a sympathetic look. "It's hard to change generations of animosity. But you're allowed to have friends wherever you please, you know."

"Try telling that to the rest of our family," I murmured. She was open-minded, and I didn't doubt she was fine with me having friends on the other side of the divide. But dating a Markham? Sleeping with one? Just the thought of seeing all those muscles I couldn't *not* notice under Hunter's shirt was enough to banish Knox from my mind forever.

We settled into our meals, and with each bite, the memory of Knox's grip on my arm grew fainter. Too bad the bruise and soreness were growing stronger. But I pressed the encounter firmly away. The room around us buzzed with the easygoing rhythm of a small-town café, and I found myself relaxing despite the morning's events.

Lunch passed in a blend of sisterly conversation and laughter, a soothing balm that enveloped me. But eventually, Harper glanced at her watch and sighed. "I need to pick Finn up from school, so I should get going. Then it's back to the resort. We've had two housekeepers quit this week, and I've been filling in where I can." As general manager of the resort and a single mother, Harper had her hands full.

"Yeah, I talked to Ben the other day. Sounds like he's been helping a lot too." I frowned, hating to see them all stretched so thin.

"Ah, we'll manage." Harper waved off my concern. "You stick to your books. I'm proud of how successful you've made that shop. Beaches are my battlefield, not yours."

"I promise I'll come by soon." My smile returned, wholeheartedly this time. "Maybe Eli can take us diving."

"Good luck finding a free slot." Harper laughed as she stood up. "Our big brother is becoming quite the celebrity dive instructor in these parts."

We hugged, a tight embrace that said everything words couldn't. Then we parted ways in the parking lot, and I slowly strolled back to where my car was parked by the farmer's market. The sky stretched out above me, a canopy of endless possibilities, but its brilliant azure mocked the turmoil within me. Mindlessly, I tapped a rhythm on the steering wheel as I drove home. A rhythm that soon morphed into the memory of Hunter's steady presence when he'd stood so close. I shook my head, trying to dislodge the thought of him.

The animosity between our families had gone on too long. And here I was, caught in the middle and yearning for peace. Or perhaps something even more foolish. After parking behind my building, I entered the quiet space where solitude wrapped around me like a comforting shawl. My eyes were drawn to the spot where Hunter had stood, larger than life. Protective. Mysterious. Unpredictable.

What would happen next? I didn't have the answer, but I was ready to find out.

Chapter Six

Hunter

THE SOUND of kibble hitting the metal bowl echoed in my sparsely furnished apartment. Pedro looked up at me with those bright, inscrutable eyes before he padded over and nudged my leg with his head.

"What? You're more interested in me than your food? Don't get any ideas, furball," I muttered even as I reached down to scratch behind his ears. Pedro responded with a rumbling vibration that seemed impossibly loud for such a small creature. With a sigh, I plopped onto the couch and let him climb into my lap. He curled up on my abdomen as I gave in and scratched under his chin.

My gaze landed on the untouched Clive Cussler novel sitting near the door. A prop. That's all it had been—a good excuse to see Brenna, to step into that cozy little world she'd built. I couldn't shake her from my thoughts, the image of her when she'd finally smiled flickering through my mind like sunlight on water.

"Guess if it worked once, might as well try it again."

I gently dislodged the cat from my stomach and pushed to my feet. "Sorry, buddy. Gotta go out for a while." After emitting a squeak at being disturbed, Pedro tilted his head, regarding me steadily. I rolled my eyes, slipping into my shoes. "Why am I talking to a cat?" Getting no answer, I closed the door behind me with a click.

As I PUSHED into Bookstore in Paradise, a wave of coffee and musty paper washed over me. My stomach did that stupid jump like the last time I entered, and I fought to keep my cool. Brenna stood behind the counter, leafing through a book in front of her. When she lifted her head, her expression shifted from concentration to surprise.

"Hey, Brenna," I managed, though it sounded more like a croak than the smooth greeting I had planned in my head. Her eyes crinkled at the corners, and damn if my heart didn't skip a beat or two. I quickly scanned the large space, my alert senses telling me no one else was present.

"Hunter!" Her voice was as warm as the sunbeam bathing her. "Back so soon?"

I shrugged and crossed the wooden floor to stop in front of her. "It's been almost a week. Plus, Clive Cussler writes page-turners, you know?" I refused to feel guilty for my ruse —I would read the book eventually. But right now, a plausible excuse to see her was more important.

"Wrote," she said with a sad smile. "Though others are carrying on his legacy."

"You've got a great bookstore here. I couldn't stay away." I hoped my joke would mask the truth of my words. Then I saw the title of the book before her, written at the top of the worn pages. "*Robinson Crusoe*," I said with enthusiasm now that I was on firmer ground. "Always one of my favorites. I see you still have good taste in books."

"Well, it is my job, after all. And I remember that you loved this book."

When she smiled at me, the air in the room became still. My lungs suddenly forgot how to work as our eyes held. To cover my discomfort, I glanced down at the book, taking in the worn appearance. Other aged books stood in the glass case underneath. "You've got a lot of old books down there. Are you still fascinated by first editions?"

"Oh, yes. There's nothing like leafing through a treasure that's been around for years. I love to take them out and read them—gently. You can feel the love between the pages. I even have a first edition of *Great Expectations*." She laughed softly. "Maybe that's why I quoted Hemingway when you first walked into my shop. An antique store down the street has a first edition of *The Sun Also Rises* I've been dying to get my hands on."

"Too spendy?"

Her smile remained as she shook her head. "The owner won't sell—the book has sentimental value to him. Maybe I'll wear him down eventually."

But her smile faded as she slowly moved her arm to *Robinson Crusoe's* cover, softly closing the book. The motion was stiff, and she flinched ever so slightly, favoring her left arm.

I stiffened and zeroed in on her pained expression. My gaze dropped to the arm she cradled against her body. The world around me faded at the sight of the angry fingermarks marring the porcelain skin of her forearm. A dark, swollen bruise accompanied them. A rush of protective fury so potent it was like a physical blow quickly enveloped me.

"Whoa, Brenna. What happened there?" I kept my

voice soft and even despite the blood roaring through my body. I reached out slowly, as if approaching a wounded animal that might spook. I took her bruised arm in my hands, touching her softly, mindful not to cause her more pain.

She glanced down at where my fingers held her delicate forearm. Then her eyes darted up to meet mine before looking away. Walls went up behind her gaze, her instinct to guard whatever had caused this. I recognized the reaction, and it made my blood boil.

"Nothing. It was just a silly accident," she muttered, trying to pull her arm back.

I let go instantly, but I wasn't buying it. I knew the signs of harm inflicted by another person all too well. Hell, I was an expert at it. As much as I wished I could leave my past behind, this knowledge came with the territory. And right now, my protective instincts were screaming.

"That doesn't look like nothing, Bren. Talk to me."

Her eyes flickered with something unreadable for a moment, a silent battle raging within her. I waited, giving her the space to find the words. My jaw clenched in anticipation, ready to defend her, and to do it right this time around.

Brenna's silence was a thick veil, her eyes darting away as if the answer might be scrawled in invisible ink among the spines of the books that surrounded us. When she finally met my gaze again, her voice was soft and halting. "It was Knox. He just... he wanted to talk. And when I tried to leave, he got upset."

"That's twice now he's laid a hand on you," I said through gritted teeth. "Where does he live?" The question came out more forceful than I intended, and a flicker of alarm crossed her face.

"Please don't do anything stupid, Hunter," she pleaded, worry etching deeper lines into her already troubled expression.

I took a slow breath, fighting to keep the edge from my voice as I straightened and forced my shoulders to relax. "I'm not going to hurt him. I just want to find him and make sure he understands the score."

"And what is the score?"

"That if he thinks he can hurt you, he's going to have to come through me."

Something flickered in her eyes. I'm pretty sure it was relief, and that only made me more determined. "Hey." My voice softened, reaching for the warmth that had been between us mere moments ago. "We were good friends once. And I can't—won't—stand by and watch you get hurt like this. You might not want to hear this, but Knox could be dangerous."

"I really don't think he is."

"Let me be the judge of that, okay? I do this kind of thing for a living."

And I used to do a whole lot more than this.

She hesitated, her gaze dropping before meeting mine again with a glint of resolve. "He lives at 436 Driftwood Lane. And works at the Dove Key boatyard."

"Thank you. I'll let you know what I find out." I gave her a reassuring nod before turning on my heel and leaving her shop. I hurried down Main Street and trotted to the alley behind the KeyMark building, then slid into my Range Rover and pulled out. Driftwood Avenue was in the residential district of Dove Key, and it wouldn't take long to get there.

After leaving my SUV parked on the street, I could feel the weight of each step as I headed toward Knox's apartment. My hands balled into fists at my sides. When I arrived, I took a moment to collect myself before knocking, trying to stifle the drumming of my heart against my ribcage. I loosened my hands, pushing down the urge to throttle him as soon as I saw him.

The door swung open, but the face that greeted me wasn't Knox's. The guy wore a dirty T-shirt and shorts, his hair all messed up. Behind him, the apartment was in disarray—clothes strewn about, dishes piled high. "I need to talk to Knox."

"Haven't seen him in days," he said, a wary look creeping onto his face as he stared up at me—at my clenched jaw and tense posture.

Without another word, I turned around and left, the mess of Knox's life imprinted in my mind. Refusing to let frustration seep in, I checked the Dove Key boatyard next. After parking in a utilitarian dirt lot, my pace picked up as I edged around a long one-story building, thoughts racing faster than my feet. What would I say? What would I do when I found Knox?

But the answers never came. The bastard wasn't at the boatyard either.

"Called in sick the last two days," his boss informed me with a frown.

That didn't sit right with me. Neither his job nor his roommate had seen him. The fact that he was hiding out raised every red flag in my gut. "Thanks," I said tersely, returning to my SUV as my frustration mounted.

Knox was in hiding, and that meant Brenna wasn't safe. My jaw set in a hard line, and determination replaced any uncertainty I had felt before. Memories came crashing down and I inhaled a deep breath through my nose before letting it out through my mouth in a rush. "No, dammit. I won't let it happen again."

This time, I wouldn't be too late. Not for Brenna. Not ever again.

When I entered the bookstore, she was unpacking a box of the latest bestseller near the front window. The sight of her stirred a whirlwind of worry within me. Her green eyes, wide and questioning, locked onto mine as if searching for answers. Then her gaze skipped over my face and down my body. Probably looking for signs of a fight.

I scanned the shop, confirming it was empty, then approached her with a grim set to my mouth. "I couldn't find Knox. He's gone underground or something. His room-mate hasn't seen him in several days, and he's not at work."

Brenna's frown deepened, that little crease between her brows telling me more than words could. She shook her head slightly, disbelief etched into every feature. "Knox can be an asshole. But dangerous?"

I leaned in closer, dropping my voice to a hushed tone. My protective instincts clawed their way to the surface. "Look. We can't afford to take chances."

She processed my words, and hesitation flickered across her face. In the silence that stretched between us, she peaked a delicate brow. "What are you suggesting? If he left, maybe that's for the best."

"Except I'm not sure he's gone. I've seen this before."

A case in South Beach flitted through my mind—a woman who couldn't believe her estranged husband was capable of harm. Until I caught him trying to sneak through a locked window. I straightened to my full height and folded my arms over my chest. "You're staying with me until I find him. It's not safe for you to be alone right now."

Brenna's eyes widened, shock painting her features as she took a big step back. The gears in her mind churned visibly as she absorbed my statement. *"What?* Stay at your place?"

Chapter Seven

Brenna

"I CAN'T MOVE in with you, Hunter! I haven't seen you in over ten years." The words tumbled out of my mouth like a cascade of marbles, each one clattering against the next. I straightened, trying to keep my jaw off the floor. The rush of emotion I'd felt when he walked in the door turned to numbness as shock rolled through me. Over the past few days, I'd half convinced myself he wouldn't be as gorgeous, or as alluring, certainly not as magnetic.

He was all of that and more.

And as shocking as his proposal was, the idea of it didn't frighten me. Stun me a little? Yes. Intrigue me a bit? Maybe. Because this new Hunter who had strolled back into my life was very intriguing.

Except that the whole idea was ludicrous.

Hunter's jaw clenched before he exhaled slowly, his chest deflating beneath the fabric of his fitted black shirt. "Brenna, I'm not trying to be some kind of predator here." A twinge of exasperation sliced through his otherwise calm demeanor. He raked a hand through his dark hair, which only seemed to enhance the bad-boy aura that clung to him like a shadow. "I have two bedrooms, so you'd have your own space and privacy. It's a simple offer."

"Simple?" I asked, incredulous. The idea was anything but simple. My heart hammered against my ribcage, and I couldn't shake the worry knotted tight in my stomach. I still wasn't sure if Knox was dangerous, but he could be lurking anywhere.

Hunter took a step closer, his gaze holding fast to mine. "Brenna, I just want you to be safe. I won't let anything happen to you."

His words struck a chord deep within me, stirring up a whirlwind of conflicting emotions. He was right—I needed to prioritize my safety above everything else. And if staying with Hunter was the best option, then maybe I should consider it.

But it wasn't just about safety anymore. There was something else, an attraction that had been simmering beneath the surface since he walked into my shop the first time.

Taking a deep breath, I tried to steady myself. "I appreciate the offer, really. But you have to understand—this is a lot to process."

My arm brushed against the table, sending a painful jolt through it. As if I needed any reminders of what Knox had become. I cradled my sore arm, staring at the bruised and swollen flesh.

Hunter leaned back against the display table. His intense eyes never left mine, and they held a fervent blaze of protectiveness that felt both foreign and familiar. "Your arm proves you're not safe right now. And I won't stand by when you might be at risk. Not when I can do something about it."

The tension between us cracked with electricity, igniting the air with a silent current that held whispers of the past and possibilities of right now. I wanted to dismiss his offer, to laugh it off as absurd. But the truth was, I did feel safer when Hunter was around. His presence was like an unspoken but deeply felt promise. "Being around you again is... complicated."

"I know," he said quietly, and for a heartbeat, we were just two people bound by a history that refused to let us go. "But I can't sit back and do nothing."

Complicated was an understatement. Hunter was a complete mystery, and I was just a simple bookstore owner. But now he stood before me, a pillar of strength offering sanctuary. It was tempting, oh so tempting, to lean into that power. I took a deep breath, the weight of my decision almost a tangible thing. Moving in with Hunter—even temporarily, just for safety—meant entangling our lives again and the complications of who we were. My family would hardly be thrilled, even if I explained there was nothing romantic between us. I swallowed to wet my parched throat.

Nothing romantic?

I wasn't sure about that. In school, I'd never looked at Hunter as anything but a friend. But I'd been a girl then. Now I was a woman who fully recognized the pull of the man in front of me. This new Hunter also meant safety, and a part of me longed for the protective embrace of someone who cared.

"Okay, let's say I consider this..." I paced over the creaky floor, my mind racing with the pros and cons. "It doesn't mean anything's changed between us. It's just... temporary. A safe haven."

A flicker of humor entered his eyes. "Of course. I'm not kidnapping you, Brenna. Or holding you hostage."

"Why? Why go through all this trouble?" My voice betrayed the mix of curiosity and suspicion plaguing me, but I needed to know. I needed to understand what drove this man who seemed nothing like the shy boy I'd known.

He blinked, taken aback, as though the idea of not helping me had never crossed his mind. "Things happened while I was a Marine," he said after a moment. "There were times when I wanted to do something—anything—but couldn't. It changes you."

"Changes how?" I pressed, while emotions played across his face, a myriad of shadows and light.

"Let's just say it made me never want to stand by when I could act. To never put those I care about at risk if I can help it. I've got more than my fair share of experience with that." He met my gaze squarely, and in his guarded eyes, a glimpse of the burden he carried revealed itself.

Silence enveloped the room as Hunter wrestled with something deep inside him. He seemed to be standing at a crossroads only he could see, choosing his words with care. "Look, it started when Evan had his accident, but there have been more times than I can count where I was power-less. I swore I'd never let that happen again."

He paused, and I could almost hear the echo of distant battles in his voice. His jaw tensed, a muscle working as his gaze locked onto mine. "I've failed people too many times. And it eats at me every day. I'm not letting it happen this time. Not with you."

I swallowed, the words of his confession settling around us like a cloak. "All right. I'll stay in your spare bedroom for a couple of days. If you can't find Knox in that amount of time, he's probably taken off. Then I'll move back to my place." It was a compromise, a middle ground on a battlefield where neither of us knew the rules.

"Thank you." Relief shined through in his tone, the kind that came from sharing a heavy load. Hunter wasn't just offering me shelter—he was offering protection. Safety. And perhaps, just maybe, I was offering him a chance at redemption.

Hunter's eyes held mine for a moment longer before those broad shoulders relaxed. "It might take more than just a couple of days if I need to hunt Knox down. But we can cross that bridge if we get there."

I drew in a deep breath, trying to quell the storm in my stomach. "Hunter, this situation has... consequences. What am I supposed to tell my family? Or you yours?"

He shrugged, unrepentant. "I don't care what they think." Then his gaze softened as though he could sense every doubt that flickered through my mind. "I know this is a lot to process. We'll take things one step at a time. If you feel you need to leave, we'll talk about it. We were always able to talk to each other. Okay?"

"All right." I tried to put some determination in my reply, but the waver betrayed me. "When... when do you want me to move in?"

"Now. Tonight," he replied without hesitation, and those two words made my head spin like I'd been caught in a whirlpool.

"Tonight?"

The reality of the situation hit me hard at the thought of leaving behind the tiny semblance of stability I had in my apartment. I grabbed my long hair and twisted it over my shoulder, coiling it over and over.

Hunter's nod was resolute, reassuring in a way. "I'll

keep an eye out down here and let you get packed in privacy."

With a shaky exhale, I took a tentative step toward the stairs that led to my apartment. As I entered my home, dragging my leaden feet, my heart was a flurry of wings—a chaotic mix of anxiety and something else, something dangerously close to excitement.

My apartment, usually a haven of soft blues and greens that mimicked the nearby ocean, now felt too vast, too empty. I moved as if I were underwater, each decision to fold a shirt or select a pair of jeans seeming monumental and surreal. The zipper on my suitcase sounded louder than it should have as I closed it, the finality of the act sending another shiver through me. I glanced at my somewhat dazed face in the mirror. My reflection offered no reassurance, just the image of a woman caught between the mistake of one relationship in the past and the uncertainty of something new.

With the suitcase in hand, I descended the stairs. I stared at the cozy shop with its stacks of books and nooks for reading. "What about work? I can't just hide out in your apartment twenty-four seven. I have a business to run!"

Hunter loomed near the counter, his presence grounding and intimidating at the same time. "The bookshop should be safe enough. I—or one of the two guys who work for me—will stake it out. No one will get in who's not supposed to."

I opened and closed my mouth a few times but was unable to refute his logic. "All right then."

It was near enough to closing time, and the setting sun beyond the windows cast a golden sheen over the shelves of books. I flipped the sign to *Closed*, turned off the lights, and finally locked the door, each action like sealing away a part of myself.

Hunter waited patiently. Once we stepped outside the back door, he stooped to carry my suitcase and together we walked down the alley toward his building. I took in his towering form beside me, the way his muscles shifted beneath his shirt with every step, the tattoos on his arms dancing with his movement.

I couldn't say whether placing my safety—and maybe my heart—in the hands of this man was the smartest or dumbest decision of my life. But with each step I took, anticipation grew inside me like a diver teetering on the edge of a cliff, ready to plunge into the unknown depths below.

Chapter Eight

Hunter

BRENNA'S PRESENCE was just a breath away from my back as I typed in my security code at the back door. "I'll write down the code for you. There's no key." I tried to impart some confidence in my voice.

She nodded, and I adjusted my sweaty grip on her suitcase. After climbing the stairs and swinging the door open, the spartan landscape of my living room was revealed. I couldn't help but see it through her eyes—the stark walls unadorned with pictures, the practical furniture set that echoed my own utilitarian approach to life.

But there was one exception to the otherwise sterile environment. A mahogany bookcase Gabe had crafted for me was the focal point of one wall. It held a collection that mirrored my mindset—every title by Hemingway, a ton of modern adventure novels, Hawthorne, Shakespeare, Salinger.

"Very practical and no-nonsense," Brenna stated, her voice pulling me back from my introspection. I caught the flicker of surprise in her green eyes as they snagged on the bookcase, and nerves clawed in my stomach. My space felt exposed, too much like the inner workings of my mind laid bare. I set down the suitcase and shoved my hands into my pockets, wondering what the hell we were going to do now.

Then her attention shifted, and her face softened as she spotted Pedro curled up on the couch. In an instant, she was across the room, lifting the fluffball with a smile that made my heart clench tighter. As she nuzzled him, her laughter was like music in the starkness of my home. "I can't believe you have a kitten! What's his name?"

"Uh, Pedro."

"He's so cute!" She held him up before her face and he squeaked at her. "How old is he?"

"Nine, ten weeks, I think. Or something like that." I mumbled the words, and they tumbled out awkwardly. All of a sudden, my body felt too big for the room. Brenna had glided in like she belonged there, and obviously Pedro was a fan as she gathered him in her arms. I frowned at the cat. "Getting a kitten wasn't my idea. Stella made me take him." As Brenna glanced at me, her smile reached her eyes, and I knew my attempt to appear nonchalant had failed spectacularly.

"Looks like he's found himself a good home," she said, still cradling Pedro, who purred contentedly in her arms.

My chest tightened, a strange sensation spreading through me as I tried to deny feeling jealous of a damned *kitten*. I forced a shrug, trying to shake off the warmth Brenna radiated. "Well, the jury's still out on that."

Then she glanced more closely at his paws. "Oh, look at that! Six toes. Figures your sister would bring you a Hemingway cat."

I shrugged yet again, unable to get my mouth to work

properly. The floral-patterned dress she wore accented her tall, willowy frame. Her long hair hung loose, and I had to press my hand against my hip to fight off the urge to run my fingers through it.

Then her eyes became unfocused, staring through the window that showed the scrubby shoreline. "Pedro... don't you guys give your cats literary names? From Hemingway stories? It's been so long I can't remember."

The Sun Also Rises.

She whipped her head back to me, her eyes widening. "That's it!" Then, laughing, she held the tiny cat up, so his white paws hung in the air as he faced her. "Pleased to meet you, Pedro."

Walking back to her suitcase, I quickly changed the subject, eager to regain some semblance of control over the situation. "I'll show you to your room."

"Oh. Right," Brenna said, setting Pedro down. He immediately padded behind us as we walked toward the hallway.

Thank God she was behind me, so I didn't have to stare at the way her ass moved under that dress. The way she laughed, full-body and unreserved, stirred something deep within me. For a moment, I imagined what it would be like to pull her into my arms and taste that laughter right from her lips. My hand clenched the suitcase, damn near cracking the handle. The need to touch her was nearly overwhelming.

We passed my room and the guest bath, arriving at the end of the hall. "Here's your room," I said abruptly and more gruffly than I intended before pushing open the guest bedroom door. Anything to distract myself from the dangerous thoughts swirling in my head.

Brenna stepped inside, taking in the sparse surroundings. The room was clean, almost sterile with its queen-sized bed, solid wood dresser, and bare walls.

"Well, it's... minimalist." A playful smirk tugged at the corner of her mouth.

"Decorating hasn't been a priority lately," I lied as I leaned against the doorframe. Decorating had never been a thing for me. I lived in a world devoid of color, where shades of black and gray were my constant companions.

"Could use a personal touch, though," Brenna added, glancing around once more before turning to face me. Her eyes held mine, and for a second, something like understanding flickered across her features.

"I haven't lived here long enough to get around to it," I said, my voice flat. I didn't mention how this place wasn't really a home to me, just a space to exist in between the hours of work and restless sleep.

"Sure."

"Anyway, make yourself at home. I'll be out here if you need anything." I retreated hastily, practically bolting back down the hallway as Pedro followed behind me.

The smooth chill from the quartz countertop seeped through my skin as I pressed my hands to it, taking slow, measured breaths. Pedro hopped onto the couch and washed his ears. "Get it together, man," I muttered under my breath, raking a hand through my hair.

The possibility that I was overreacting to Knox's threat lingered at the back of my mind. But a primal and fierce protective instinct drowned it out—I had to keep her safe. It didn't matter what it cost me personally. The silence of the apartment was a stark contrast to the chaos unfolding inside my head—vivid images of a woman and two children flashing behind my eyes like some cruel slideshow. There were others, but those three were the ghosts that haunted me most often.

Well, them and Evan. He was always there too.

I'd failed all of them, and no matter what actions I'd taken toward redemption, nothing changed that. It tore at me, that old guilt. But I shoved it down, locking it away in a place I hoped Brenna would never see. She didn't need a man like me, with a past so tarnished it could black out the sun. My heart raced at the mere idea of being more to her than just a guardian or a friend, and I knew that path led nowhere good. Not for her.

Inhaling a deep breath, I tried to quash the surge of desire that had blindsided me. If I could protect her, maybe I could atone for the past, even if she never knew about it. I exhaled slowly as Brenna's gentle footsteps approached from down the hall.

"All unpacked. I didn't bring a lot." Her tone was soft, but her smile was quick to follow. I stared at her but couldn't speak, caught in the storm inside my mind. The silence drew out until her gaze drifted to the kitten, who had made himself king of my couch. "Where does Pedro sleep?" she asked, settling him in her arms. He stretched out and purred, content in the cradle of her warmth. I could relate.

"Uh, he's got a bed." My words felt clumsy and ragged. My cheeks flushed with heat. "In my room. I bought it after he cried at the door the first night. Now I leave it open. He goes in and out."

Brenna glanced at me, her eyes dancing with unspoken laughter. "But not on your bed, am I right?"

"Definitely not," I replied, trying to sound stern. I had a feeling I was failing miserably.

"Pedro's lucky—" But before another word could be

exchanged, her stomach growled, loud enough for both of us to hear. "Oh. Sorry."

"Nothing to apologize for," I said quickly, welcoming the distraction. Glancing at my refrigerator, I ran through a mental inventory of what was inside. Or wasn't. Dammit, Stella was the chef, not me. "But I don't really have much here. Premade meals mostly. Will frozen pizza do?" I moved to the freezer and pulled out the box, feeling inexplicably tense as if the act of cooking for her, even just heating up a pizza, was somehow intimate.

"Perfect," she said, her smile returning.

As the oven preheated, I found myself losing words again, unsure how to bridge the gap between us. I was acutely aware of her presence in my space. Even the air smelled different now. Lighter, better. It was unsettling how powerful the pull was, how much I wanted to reach out to her. But I couldn't—wouldn't—let myself go there.

I slid the pizza into the oven and set the timer with a click that echoed in the quiet tension of the kitchen. Brenna leaned against the counter, her arms folded. I could sense her gaze on me, heavy and curious, like she was trying to read the chapters of my life I kept firmly shut. I searched for a topic of conversation but came up empty. Again.

She took a deep breath, then let it rush out. "So what do you do for fun?"

Her question caught me off guard. The concept felt foreign, like a language I'd once been fluent in but had long since forgotten. Baseball was serious business, not fun—it was as much about reconnecting with my family as recreation. My mind was blank, just like my apartment's walls. "Fun?"

She tilted her head, a strand of light brown hair falling over her face. God, I wanted to brush it back, feel how warm her skin would be. What her hair would smell like. Whirling to the fridge, I pulled out a bagged salad.

"Well, how about diving?" She took the bag and emptied it into the bowl I'd set out. "Have you gone since you moved back? We used to love diving in high school."

"For me, diving was work. It stopped being fun a long time ago."

A frown creased her brow and her eyes clouded with confusion. "But you were a Marine, not a SEAL, right?"

"Yes." I nodded, pressing my lips together as memories of dark waters and covert operations flashed like snapshots in my mind. Bright, colorful ones, and others that were dark and forbidding. All had one thing in common—a brotherhood I'd found when I desperately needed it. "But my unit did dive ops, too."

"Sounds intense," she murmured, picking up on my reluctance to elaborate.

The word SEAL brought back the last time I'd had a conversation with one of the Navy's elites, and I made an expression somewhere between a smirk and a scowl.

Brenna saw it. "What's that expression about?"

"I was just remembering the last conversation I had with a SEAL It was at Gabe's wedding and the guy kept me from punching Evan. I never got the chance to thank him."

Her eyes filled with sympathy. "I heard some rumors about that. What happened?"

Gabe had personally asked me to attend, so I came, balancing on a razor's edge. Both hoping and dreading seeing Evan again as adrenaline surged through me. To keep myself busy, I pulled two beers out of the fridge and opened them, then handed one to her. "I'd kept to the shadows during the ceremony behind the Big House and finally worked up the courage to make an official appearance at the reception. Evan saw me and went apeshit. He rushed me and pushed us both into the pool. When we got out, we started sniping at each other. I was this ball of emotion, and I didn't know how to handle myself. I was this close"—I held my thumb and index finger a centimeter apart—"to punching his lights out when the SEAL got between us and ordered me to stand down. I was so out of it I didn't even correct him for calling me soldier instead of Marine, something I normally do without thinking. It took a while for him to get through the red haze in front of my eyes, but obeying direct orders is too ingrained in me. And this guy was obviously an officer used to giving commands. I stepped back and he got me out of there. Things would have gotten really ugly between Evan and me if he hadn't stepped in."

"I'm so sorry for what you've been through. You and Evan were so close."

I took a long pull of beer. "At least some good came from it. Evan realized that his hatred of me wasn't helping, and I realized I needed to be part of my family. We're trying to... reconnect."

A sympathetic smile stretched her full lips. "I'm glad to hear that. I hope it works out between you two."

"We'll see. There's a lot of shit to process. For both of us." My mood started to darken as memories rushed through my mind. Rolling my head around on my neck, I tried to keep my shoulders from stiffening.

Brenna must have seen. She changed tack, reaching out to poke my bicep, and her touch sent an unexpected jolt through me. "What about this? Obviously, you work out a lot."

I willed my fiery blood to cool, fighting off my reaction. It took me a second to remember we had been talking about what we enjoyed doing. "That is definitely not fun," I said, a smile finally tugging at the corner of my mouth. She had a way of lightening the mood, even when the shadows loomed close. "Just part of the routine. I joined a gym in Dove Key and work out there."

"Ah, the glamorous life of a security expert," she teased gently.

"Something like that." The timer dinged, and I pulled out the pizza, then served it onto two plates.

"Thanks," she said. As I handed her the plate, our fingers brushed briefly.

"Of course," I replied. "I'll try to get to the market tomorrow and get some more... real food."

We settled at the kitchen table, an island in the stormy sea that had become my thoughts. As she took a bite, her eyes closed in appreciation. Something twisted deep inside me.

This was a terrible idea.

Protecting her should've been straightforward—keep her safe, end of story. But with every familiar smile and gentle tease, the line between duty and desire blurred. If one of my guys were this entangled, I'd have reassigned him faster than you could say *conflict of interest*. And yet here I was, unable to take my own advice. And I sure as hell wasn't about to say anything to Miles or Garrett about what Brenna meant to me. The pull toward her was gravitational, undeniable. How the hell was I supposed to keep my hands to myself when every cell in my body screamed to close the distance between us?

Pedro hopped off the couch and sauntered over to the table. He sat and curled his tail around his legs, staring between us. I grabbed at the subject change. "Never thought I'd be a pet person."

"Life's funny like that," she said softly. "You think you know exactly what you want, who you are... Then someone or something comes along, and suddenly you're not so sure."

Her words were too close to the bone, echoing the chaos churning inside me. "True. But some things are nonnegotiable." Like keeping her safe. Like resisting the urge to cross lines that shouldn't even be in view.

"Like what?" Brenna prodded gently, her gaze searching mine.

"Like... professionalism," I managed, seizing on the word like a lifeline.

"Of course," she replied, and a shadow flitted over her face, like she was disappointed at my answer.

I dropped my eyes to my plate again. I'd always had a thing for her. It had kept me going during dark times, been a lifeline of happy memories in a churning, dark ocean. And now, at last, she was more than a memory. And I couldn't act on my desires. We ate in silence for a few moments, the weight of my unspoken words pressing down on me like the humid air outside. I was supposed to protect her, but who would protect her from me? From the intensity of what I felt?

Chapter Nine

Brenna

THE UNFAMILIAR ROOM around me was quiet, and I was blissfully comfortable. I stretched luxuriously, surprisingly refreshed despite the turmoil that had sent me seeking refuge in Hunter's apartment. After crossing the plush, carpeted floor, I found the robe I'd draped over the chair during my unpacking session yesterday. Wrapping it around myself, I experienced a momentary sense of intimacy as if he were somehow holding me with the fabric. I padded out of the room and down the hall, anticipation building steadily.

But Hunter wasn't there, and an unexpected twinge of disappointment caught me off guard. "Guess it's just you and me, Pedro," I murmured to the kitten, who blinked at me lazily before resuming his nap on the sunny windowsill. A smile rose on my lips as I remembered Hunter's embarrassed mumbling about buying the kitten a bed and placing it in his bedroom when the fluff bundle had been scared. All while denying he was becoming attached.

"You don't fool me, you big lug."

The bookshop would remain closed today, which was probably for the best. I needed time to think, to process all that had happened in the past twenty-four hours. After a hot shower that did little to calm the flutter in my stomach, I slipped into shorts and a faded T-shirt. Descending the stairs, I braced myself for whatever remnants of last night's chaos awaited.

But it wasn't chaos that greeted me—it was the sight of Hunter. He was sitting at a cluster of desks within the big open area of KeyMark Security. Two unfamiliar faces sat with him, all deep in conversation. During dinner, he had told me that his two employees were friends and fellow Marines who had worked with him in South Beach, then followed him on his new venture. They certainly looked the part. My heart did an odd skip at the sight of Hunter, clad in black and looking every bit the part of the brooding protector. His button-down shirt was rolled up at the sleeves, revealing strong forearms, and the jet-black jeans clung to him.

"Morning," I called out, more cheerfully than I felt.

Hunter looked up, a flicker of something unidentifiable crossing his features. "Hey, Brenna. Sleep well?"

"Like a rock, surprisingly." I couldn't help but add a light-hearted tone to mask my inner disarray.

"Good to hear," Hunter replied, his voice low and even.

I glanced at the two strangers, who gave me polite nods as I leaned against the wall. Seeing Hunter among allies, a cascade of relief washed over me. There was safety in numbers, or so I wanted to believe. Despite the security of Hunter's apartment, it was his physical presence that truly made me feel safe. As if the danger that lurked beyond these walls couldn't possibly touch us while he was here. It was a ridiculous notion, but in that moment, I clung to it.

"Guys, this is Brenna Coleridge," Hunter introduced with a casual wave in my direction. Then, turning to me, "Brenna, Myles Decker and Garrett Howard."

Myles, with sandy hair cut high and tight, offered me a warm smile. His tan spoke of hours in the sun, and his stretched-out legs crossed at the ankles suggested an easy-going nature. But my impression changed when he rose from his chair, the movement effortless in a way that suggested coiled strength ready to be loosed. He extended a hand, which I shook, finding his grip firm yet unassuming.

"Nice to meet you, Brenna. Heard a lot about Bookshop in Paradise," Myles said, his voice tinged with a coastal drawl.

"Only good things, I hope," I replied with a smile, immediately at ease with him.

"Of course, though Hunter's the real bookworm."

Garrett was a different story. His posture was rigid, like a soldier standing at attention, and his gaze held a focus that seemed to weigh and measure me in a glance. Dark stubble lined his jaw, and his piercing blue eyes flickered to Hunter before resting back on me. As if he was looking for something unsaid, an undercurrent beneath the surface. I expected a crushing grip when we shook but found my hand unsmashed.

"Myles is just coming off shift at Calypso Key, so he's heading home to sleep," Hunter explained. "I asked him to stop by so I could fill him in on the developments. Garrett will be keeping an eye out for you while I look for Knox."

"What?" The word slipped out before I could censor it, my hesitancy clear.

Garrett smiled, and his face transformed. The stern,

intimidating Marine vanished, and I relaxed a little. "Trust me, you won't even notice I'm there."

"Uh, thank you," I managed, mustering a polite smile. "I appreciate it, though I'm still not sure all this is necessary."

Hunter eyed me, not giving an inch. "If it becomes necessary, you'll be very glad to have Garrett there."

I couldn't argue with that. I turned to give Garrett a smile but found him contemplating Hunter—a long, evaluating look like he was trying to put pieces of a puzzle together. As the men continued their discussion, I drifted toward the window. Outside, small-town beach life stirred awake, the sky a canvas of pastel hues, all of it a stark contrast to the turmoil brewing within me.

When I climbed back upstairs, Hunter's bookshelf caught my eye, a solid mahogany case that stretched seven feet high, filled with an array of titles. My fingers trailed over the spines, pausing on a worn, well-used collection of Hemingway titles. I couldn't help but smile—at least some things never changed. In these small details, I glimpsed the boy I once knew, before he became this enigma shrouded in danger and allure.

He had all of Hemingway's works, from *The Old Man and the Sea* to *The Sun Always Rises*, my favorite. Each book seemed to echo a part of Hunter's soul, the adventure, the stoicism, the unspoken wounds. In my mind's eye, I could see him sprawled on the couch and lost in those pages. He was the storm itself, and yet here I was, standing in the eye of it and finding peace.

After selecting a James Patterson thriller, I spent several hours lost in thrills, yet finding comfort in the soft bundle of fur on my lap. After a quick lunch, I was filled with restless energy. And with my store closed, I sought the familiar confines of home. My car was still parked behind the bookstore, and after letting Garrett know I was leaving, I trotted down to it and got in. Reaching Main Street, I turned west and made my way toward Siesta Sunset Resort. The Florida sun was generous today, giving the town a golden hue as I crossed the short distance to the family business. The resort was like a snapshot from a bygone era—cozy and homey, with two blocks of rooms painted in soft seafoam green with crisp white trim. Each room had its own little porch or deck, complete with a sitting area. I parked behind a rectangular structure made from cinderblocks painted a gentle blue.

The familiar sights filled me with a mix of nostalgia and sadness. It was a place that held so many memories of my childhood, of running around with my brothers and helping my parents with odd jobs. But now, it stood as a reminder of the struggles my family faced and the remnants of my parents' shattered marriage.

As I approached the reception area, I could see Harper inside, her brow furrowed as she stared at the computer screen. Her bouncy brown curls looked like she'd run a hand through them. She'd taken over manager duties from Dad when he left and had shouldered the burden without complaint.

But the lobby wasn't my destination today, and with a guilty pang, I bypassed the building. I let my feet guide me through the resort. Siesta Sunset exuded a casual coastal vibe, with its two-story room blocks arranged around the central amenities and pool. At the heart of the resort stood the main restaurant, Driftwood Grill, and the resort pool with palm trees whispering in the breeze. Near the beach, I passed Tidal Hops, the brewpub that was my brother Braden's pride and joy. The pub's white picket fence and turquoise signboard welcomed guests to dine in the shade or inside in the cool air.

I strolled farther, drawn by the rhythmic lapping of waves against the shore. A crescent of beach unfolded before me. Powdery salt-and-pepper sand gave way to gentle azure waters. A weathered yet solid wooden pier stood on this little haven, anchored by a simple structure made of sun-bleached wood at the far end. Adorned with nets and buoys that spoke of the deep blue beyond, a red-and-white dive flag flapped from the top of the roof.

The house I'd grown up in, and that Ben was staying at while our mother was away, was barely visible in the distance, tucked away among sea grape bushes and the whispering fronds of palm trees. As I walked down the pier, the planks creaked under my weight with a comforting sound. I pushed open the glass door to find my brother Eli behind the counter, arranging dive gear with practiced ease.

"Bren! Long time no see." Grinning, he swept a lock of slightly too long light-brown hair out of his eyes. We Coleridges had been graced with a variety of eye colors, but I loved Eli's bright blue shade.

"Hey, you," I replied, leaning against the counter. "Busy today?"

"Two-tank trip is out right now, and I've got a student in another hour. You know, the boat's going out tomorrow, and I just happen to have a spot with your name on it. Or if you're up for some shore diving, just say the word."

I laughed. Four years older than me, Eli and I had gotten certified together. Where I found a hobby I enjoyed, he'd fallen utterly in love and discovered his calling. He never missed a chance to get me in the water.

"Thanks, but I'm back to work tomorrow. Maybe another time. I was just talking about diving last night with a friend."

A friend. One I was afraid to even discuss with my

protective big brother, so I kept quiet. The subject would only stir up trouble, and God knows I had enough of that. It weighed on me, though. Hunter hadn't said anything about payment for his services—he just wanted to be sure I was safe. And yet I couldn't discuss his generosity with my own brother.

Because he was a Markham. And I was a Coleridge.

So stupid.

When we'd discussed diving last night, the glimmers of an idea had formed in my head. How I could spend time with him and pay him back for his help at the same time—by submerging in a shared passion. But diving with Hunter was a complicated subject. Even though it was an activity we had loved doing back in the day, Hunter had terrible memories involved with diving. Evan's accident had precipitated him leaving Calypso Key in the first place. And I didn't want to know what his dives in the Marines had involved. But I couldn't shake the idea that going diving with him could be the perfect way to ease some of those shadows from his eyes and help him remember how magical the watery world could be. After ensuring I could borrow dive equipment sometime to use with a friend I was careful not to name, Eli and I chitchatted until the dive boat's motor indicated its return and he had to go help.

Leaving the dive shack, I allowed myself a moment on the pier. The sea stretching out before me was a reminder of the vast reaches beneath the surface, waiting to be rediscovered. Maybe diving was exactly what I needed to clear my own head. But for now, the intricacies of life above water called me back.

As I weaved through the resort to my car, I was reminded that although Siesta Sunset was home, it wasn't my home. My home was a two-story structure on Main

Street. Except now I was denied even that. With a sigh, I headed back to Main Street. And Hunter.

The distant glint of a vehicle trailed behind me as I left the resort, and I glanced in the rearview mirror. The SUV was nondescript and blended in with the other tourist-packed vehicles—a testament to Garrett's subtlety. Hunter's friend had promised to be a shadow, and he'd lived up to that. If he'd been around while I was at the resort, I never saw him.

After parking next to Hunter's sleek black SUV, I tapped on my phone screen, pulling up the security code he'd sent. The keypad beeped in compliance, then I entered to find the open office area empty and closed up for the evening. I ascended the stairs to his apartment with a flutter in my chest, but I couldn't tell if it was anticipation or anxiety.

Hunter stood in the kitchen, the setting sun streaming through the window outlining his silhouette. He updated me on Knox, keeping his voice even, though I caught a hint of frustration as he discussed his search. Finally, he threw a hand up in apology. "I spent the whole day chasing down leads. Nothing yet."

"Maybe he's checked out and left the area." My gaze fell upon the sizzling pan on the stove. The sight of Hunter cooking chicken breasts—just for me—coaxed a smile onto my lips, along with a warmth that had nothing to do with the heat from the burners.

"Figured I'd try to do better than pizza tonight." He flashed a half-smile, his eyes softening before he turned back to the stove. "I went shopping this afternoon and stocked up. Hungry?"

"Starving, actually." I accepted the glass of white wine he offered. The cool glass was a contrast to the heat that seemed to simmer every time I came near him. I perched on a stool, swinging one leg languidly.

"Do anything interesting today?" Hunter asked, his back to me as he tended to our meal.

"Just went home." I hesitated. Home used to mean something simple and comforting. Now it was woven with complications. I took a sip of wine to help gather my thoughts. "The resort's struggling a bit. Harper is doing her best, but... Everything is so complicated."

"You didn't tell your family you're here with me?"

"No." I traced the rim of the glass with my finger. "They wouldn't understand. Not with everything that's happened between our families."

He snorted as he poured a bag of salad into a bowl. "More than that. They'd probably expect the worst from me."

I didn't bother to deny that. Many of the unsettling rumors about Hunter I'd heard over the years had been from the mouths of my brothers, especially Ben. Weren't rumors supposed to be grounded in truth? I studied Hunter as he stepped around his small kitchen. He moved with incredible grace for a man his size, his actions economical and precise. He paused, utensils in hand, and turned to face me. Our gazes locked, and the air between us thickened, becoming charged.

"I'm not sure I could convince them that nothing's going on between us." My voice was firm, but the lie was brittle, crumbling under the intensity of his gaze.

"Nothing at all." The corner of his mouth twitched as if he wanted to smirk or scowl—I couldn't tell which.

The room seemed to shrink, bringing us closer even though we hadn't moved an inch. My heart thrummed and a strong roll of desire unfurled within me, making it difficult to focus on anything other than the man standing across from me. Under the counter, I clenched my hand, trying to fight off the image of what his dark beard might feel like under my fingertips. And those muscles... tattoos...

"Let's eat," he said finally, breaking the spell as he plated our food.

After we sat at the table, I forked a bite of grilled chicken, the perfect sear flaking away under the tines. "You know, I've been thinking about this ridiculous feud between our families."

Hunter's dark eyes met mine from across the kitchen table, his hands still as he listened. They were large, capable hands that had probably seen more than their fair share of hard work. What other things had they done? What things could they do to me?

That hot roll came back, and I swallowed over a thick throat, getting back to the subject at hand. "It's a century-old grudge holding us all back. I want it to end."

He leaned back in his chair, a muscle ticking in his jaw. "I agree. It's stupid, but not easily forgotten."

"Maybe not." I moved some pieces of lettuce around on my plate, then sighed. "I couldn't even discuss what's going on right now with my brother today. And that makes me sad."

"I'm sorry. Hopefully, I'll find Knox tomorrow. When I do, I'll make sure he doesn't bother you anymore."

I snapped my head up at that. Hunter answered with a smile, but it didn't reach his eyes. "Don't worry. I won't do anything illegal. But that asshole needs to understand that he's not going to lay a finger on you ever again."

The air hung heavy with implications and unasked questions. His presence was like a magnet, pulling me in despite every logical reason I should resist. It wasn't just his looks—though those could stop traffic—it was the aura that clung to him like a second skin.

With effort, I focused back on my plate. We ate in silence for a few minutes before I dared to sneak another glance at him. The way his black shirt stretched over his broad shoulders, how he'd roll his lips inward thoughtfully. The sheer maleness of him captivated me. What would it feel like to have those strong hands cup my face, to taste those full lips in a stolen kiss? The air around me warmed.

As the meal wound down, our connection seemed to solidify with each shared smile and lingering look. Yet the unresolved tension of our family legacies draped over us like a net.

"Thank you for dinner," I said softly, my gratitude genuine but also tinged with something deeper, something akin to yearning.

"You're welcome. It's nice having company."

There it was again—that electric charge, the pull that neither of us seemed willing to acknowledge fully. Then Pedro meowed loudly, breaking the spell as only a pet can.

"Looks like someone's jealous." I laughed and reached down to scratch behind his ears, grateful for the distraction.

"Can't blame him," Hunter quipped, a smile playing on his lips as he collected the dishes. "I make a pretty good chicken."

"Undoubtedly," I agreed, standing up to help with the cleanup. But as I brushed past him, our arms touched, and the simple contact sent an electric jolt through me.

This was dangerous territory, a path leading to forbidden pleasures and inevitable complications. And yet, as I stared at that broad back as he cleared the table, I wondered if it was already too late to turn back.

Chapter Ten

Hunter

THE NEXT MORNING, I sat downstairs at our group of desks with the scent of fresh coffee in the air. I used my office when I needed solitude, but I liked being in the middle of the space. In the thick of things. Across from me, Brenna leaned against a metal bookshelf with arms folded, her eyes clouded with concern that mirrored the morning fog drifting in from the shore.

"Garrett will stake out your shop today," I said, and my friend nodded.

"How am I supposed to operate my business with a bodyguard around?"

"I'll stay in my car," Garrett replied, leaning back in his chair with an easy confidence that came from years of military discipline. "I've already found a spot that will give me a view of both the front and the back. No one will get in who shouldn't."

She pressed her lips together, then nodded slowly. "That works, I guess. Thanks." The tension about Knox's

87

whereabouts was a shadow clinging to the corners of the room.

"I'm hoping to hear back from some of my sources today or tomorrow," I said. "Then I'll have some more places I can check out."

She shook her head, a loose curl falling across her forehead. I wanted to get up and brush it back. "And what if you can't find him?"

"Hey," I said softly, finally reaching out to gently nudge her forearm and doing my best to ignore the ball of unease in my gut. That craving need to protect her. "People don't usually disappear into thin air. Give me a couple of days."

Brenna offered me a brief nod, then turned toward the stairs. "I'll get my things and be down in a few minutes."

Her frame was stiff and halting as she left—worried. I hated seeing her move like that, and it only made me more determined to find the son of a bitch.

"What's going on between you two?"

Garrett's voice snapped my head around. "Nothing."

He lifted a brow, a smirk rising. "Your eyes follow her everywhere. That's not nothing."

I scowled, pissed I wasn't doing a better job of hiding my feelings. "She's an old friend, okay? I'm worried about her. And shouldn't you be getting ready too?"

Rolling his eyes, Garrett pushed to his feet. "Fine. Keep your secrets."

I didn't reply as he moved to the back of the room, where we each had generous-sized lockers to hold our belongings and supplies. After stuffing what he needed into a bag, he shut his locker. "Enjoy your morning out at Calypso Key."

"I will."

I hoped. But his comment brought back the earlier

conversation we'd had with Myles before our day shifts started and Myles went home for rack time. We all agreed on what needed to be done at the resort, security-wise. Now I had to convince my family.

Brenna stepped softly down the stairs, a backpack slung over one shoulder. "Let's go, Garrett." She caught my glance, and a silent exchange passed between us, a flicker of something deeper than concern for Knox or the day's tasks. Or was that just wishful thinking on my part?

"See you tonight," I told her.

The door clicked shut behind Brenna and Garrett, leaving an empty silence. The air was laced with a subtle, floral scent I tried not to notice. I paced back to the staircase, each step heavy with thoughts I shouldn't be entertaining. Upstairs, my apartment was quiet too.

As my eyes landed on the guest bedroom, I padded down the hall without thinking about it. I peered through the open door at a sliver of Brenna's world—neat and clean, just like her. And not unlike me, either. I took several steps inside, and as I breathed in her scent that lingered in the room, guilt gnawed at my insides. It wasn't right to be here without her okay, but something pulled me—the same gravity that had been pulling me since the day I moved back. Spinning around, I reached the doorway in two large strides, then halted.

"Shit." Before I knew what I was doing, I whirled around and stalked to her bed. Her pillow sat neatly atop the bedspread. My hand reached out, fingers grazing the fabric before gripping it and lifting it to my face.

As I inhaled deeply, she filled my senses—a crisp scent like the ocean breeze mingling with the soft floral hint of her shampoo. It was clean, invigorating, and utterly Brenna. I smashed my face into the softness as a surge of desire rocketed through me, so potent it could've lit up the island. I sucked in another breath, and her fragrance wrapped around me like a siren's call. My mind painted her image—her world-class breasts, her slim waist, the curves I'd only allowed myself to skim in my dreams. Goddamn, how I wanted to trace those lines in reality, to taste her lips and claim them as mine.

With a groan that came from deep within, I released the pillow and smoothed it back in place. Like I might restore order to the chaos inside me. Then I stomped out of her room, my body tense, and my footsteps leaden with the weight of longing I couldn't—shouldn't—indulge.

Stepping out into the late-morning heat, I shook off the remnants of Brenna's scent clinging to my thoughts as I got into my SUV. The drive to Calypso Key was brief, but it gave me enough time to switch gears from overprotective would-be lover to professional security consultant. And brother.

Always brother.

I crossed the causeway between the two islands, and a reluctant smile graced my face at the huge billboard advertising Stella and Orchid. I hardly gave the Big House a glance as I drove by. Continuing down the hill, I passed the Barn, where Gabe, April, and Gabe's daughter, Hailey, lived. It was a busy hive of activity, construction workers buzzing all over it as an addition took shape that would give them more room with the extra family member on the way. The sight made even my cold heart warm. Gabe had been a real lifeline for me after I got out of the Corps and moved to South Beach. He'd lived in Miami at the time. When he and Hailey returned home, I'd felt his absence acutely, but I couldn't resent his obvious happiness at the life he'd created here. And the new addition was proof of it. I smiled at the double meaning.

After parking in the sand employee lot, I strode toward the resort lobby, squinting against the glare of the sun reflecting off the pristine white façade. The large, airy room I entered still held the sharp scent of its recent remodel, and I quickly scanned the room—an automatic assessment of potential threats and multiple exits. My motions were so ingrained, I was hardly even conscious of them. But this was just my family's lobby building. No terrorists or insurgents in sight. Or displaced civilians just trying to survive. Frowning, I pushed the thoughts away as I crossed the tile floor.

Evan's office at the end of the hall was a cool sanctuary with air conditioning humming softly in the background. I forced my slowly coiling body to relax as I tried to convince myself this was just another business meeting.

But it wasn't.

"Morning, Hunter," Evan greeted from behind his desk, his tone cordial yet distant. He stared at me with inscrutable blue eyes, and his clean-cut appearance was a familiar one. I hadn't seen him in all the years he'd worn a beard. The fact that he'd recently shaved and looked remarkably different to everyone else was yet another reminder that I was an outsider.

"Evan." I kept my voice even as I took a seat in an armchair in front of his desk. Gabe was already seated next to me and offered a subtle nod that eased the tightness in my gut. He had a way of bringing calm to any storm. After a few pleasantries, it was time to get down to business.

"Let's talk security," I said as my gaze flicked to the window, and I took in the view of families enjoying the resort grounds. "I think it's time to scale back."

"Scale back?" Evan's brow furrowed slightly. "You were the one who wanted an on-site presence."

"I did. Because I wasn't sure the thefts wouldn't continue."

When small items had started turning up missing, Stella had immediately suspected Ben Coleridge. I'd kept an open mind and set up a sting to catch whoever the thief was. And it had been a member of Stella's own staff, not Ben. But I needed time to ensure he hadn't had a partner. I leaned forward, hands clasped. "Matt's been behind bars for months now, and there hasn't been a single incident since. I think we've got our man. Security seven days and nights per week is overkill."

Gabe's dark eyes were thoughtful as he watched me. "You sure about this? Security at the resort was the whole reason you set up shop down here. Can you afford to lose the contract?"

"Doesn't matter," I said firmly. "I won't charge a client for services they don't need. It'd be a waste of your money. And I'm picking up plenty of jobs. I've got one right now that's keeping both me and Garrett busy." I didn't add that it was a non-paying job. I had plenty of savings if it came to that.

"Money aside," Evan interjected, "we can't risk our guests' safety."

"Absolutely not," I replied. "But with the camera system I've installed, if anything suspicious happens, we'll see it. Plus, Myles, Garrett, and I can swing by for random, on-site visits to maintain a presence."

Evan studied me. Maybe I imagined it, but I thought I saw a flash of respect—or perhaps understanding—in his eyes.

"Sounds like you've got it worked out," Gabe said. It still

felt strange not to have Dad at this meeting. But Gabe was the majority shareholder of the resort and island now. He was the one in charge, while Dad enjoyed leading fishing charters.

Evan still had his poker face on. "You're sure about this?"

"It's not like I want to cancel everything. The resort needed a camera system and we've got that in place. And on-site security will still happen too. This is what I'd recommend to any client in the same situation. I'd never put the resort at risk if I wasn't confident."

A long look passed between Evan and me, but I didn't look away. Finally, Evan gave me a nod. "If you're okay with it, then so am I."

"Okay. Go ahead and pull them," Gabe said before turning to face me fully. "You'll be at the game tomorrow, right?"

"Oh yeah," I replied with a nod, feeling a twitch of excitement for the normalcy of a local game. My gaze slid over to Evan, catching the slight clench of his jaw, the tension that never quite seemed to leave his frame when I was around.

"There's always a spot for you too, Evan," Gabe added gently.

I tried not to stiffen as Evan's eyes flickered to me. "I've got a lot on my plate, but thanks for the offer." His nod was stiff but accepting. And just like that, the topic was closed, the meeting over.

THE EVENING FOUND Brenna and me in my apartment, an easy, domestic scene straight out of some idyllic fantasy.

We sat side by side on the couch, lost in our books after sharing a meal we'd cooked together. The aroma of garlic and basil still lingered in the air, mingling with the salt breeze that drifted in from the open window. I had to admit the Clive Cussler book had reeled me in from the first page when I'd started it last night. Brenna was nose-deep in my copy of *The Sun Also Rises*, perhaps an homage to the kitten who purred on my lap. I stroked his head absently.

But as I turned the page, my mind wasn't really on the book in front of me. Instead, all I noticed was the warmth of Brenna's presence. I enjoyed the comfortable silence we existed in together, and how her brow furrowed in concentration. I wondered what it would feel like to trace those lines with my fingers, my lips. It made me yearn for so much more.

My phone buzzed with a security notification, disrupting the peaceful tableau. A sinking feeling hit the pit of my stomach when I saw who had used her personal code to enter and was on her way up. "Oh, shit. Stella's here."

"Your sister's here?" Brenna looked up with a mix of curiosity and alarm.

"I don't keep the apartment door alarmed when I'm in here awake, and she loves to waltz in whenever she feels like it."

The door swung open, and my sister breezed in. "I can't believe I missed you at the resort today!" Her casual clothing meant it was Stella's night off from Orchid. Her glossy dark hair swung around her shoulders as her gaze swept the room. And landed on Brenna. She stopped dead in the middle of the living room, her eyes growing huge.

"Hey, Stella," Brenna greeted, her voice steady, but her stiff body language betrayed her discomfort.

"Brenna? What are you doing here?" Stella's voice was tight as she turned her wide eyes to me.

"Stella, this isn't—" I started, stumbling over my words, trying to figure out how to explain why Brenna was here.

"Isn't what?" Stella arched an eyebrow as she took in the cozy scene. Her shock was visible, disbelief written all over her face as her gaze alternated between us.

"Brenna's staying with me for security reasons," I said, scratching the back of my neck awkwardly. And while there was nothing to hide, per se, I couldn't help but feel exposed under my sister's scrutinizing gaze.

"Riiight." Stella's tone was laced with skepticism, and she turned back to Brenna. "And what security concerns would cause you to move in with my brother?"

"Knock it off, Stel," I warned.

Brenna bolted to her feet. "I'll just give you two some privacy." Holding her book in a death grip, she scurried down the hall and shut her bedroom door behind her.

"That was out of line. She's my guest." The air was thick with tension as I rose and padded over to the kitchen counter, needing to be in motion.

My sister snorted and crossed the floor to me. "Guest? I remember you two were close in school. And family war or no, I'm sure she wouldn't mind getting her hooks into you. In case you haven't looked in a mirror lately, you're quite a specimen, you know."

"Stella, seriously. It's not like that," I tried again, but even I heard the falter in my voice. I was usually better at this—keeping my cool, deflecting concern. But with Brenna here, everything felt different.

"What am I supposed to think?" Stella demanded, her eyes flashing.

"Look, I'm just keeping an eye on her." I raked a hand

95

through my hair. "Her ex has been causing trouble. It's precautionary."

"Precautionary," she repeated flatly. "And that's the only reason she's here?"

"Yes. There's nothing romantic going on," I lied, the image of Brenna's soft neck flickering behind my eyes, the curve of her hip.

The doubt in Stella's expression didn't waver. She took a step closer, and I braced myself for the onslaught. "Are you sure you can keep things friendly? Because a relationship between a Coleridge and a Markham would set off shockwaves in both families."

"Nothing's going on!" I hissed in an attempt to keep my voice down. "And if it were, it would be none of your goddamn business. Besides, you're not exactly the best judge of Coleridge character, are you? You zeroed in on Ben as the thief from day one. And guess what, Stella? It. Wasn't. Him. So back off."

She held my gaze a moment longer, then held a palm out toward me. "You're right. I was wrong about Ben, but there's a lot more history here than just him. There are a lot of Coleridges, you know." Stella was almost a foot shorter than me but had never had any trouble asserting herself. Finally, she took a step back and nodded. "Fine. I made a mistake accusing Ben—I admit that. But you and Brenna together is a very different situation, okay? If you want to play knight in shining armor, I can't stop you. But I won't stop worrying about you, either. I can't help it, Hunter. I just hope this doesn't blow up in your face."

Then she turned and left, leaving me in my living room with my head spinning.

I stood motionless. With each thumping heartbeat, I became acutely aware of Brenna's presence down the hall.

The last thing I wanted was to talk about this right now. I got flustered and tongue-tied around her at the best of times. I stomped to my room and shut the door loudly enough to ensure she'd hear it. Pedro sat up in his bed and eyed me curiously.

Ignoring him, I started pacing. How could I deny what was happening inside me—the visceral, magnetic pull toward her? I'd thought about her for years, and now only the walls of my apartment separated us. Every moment in Brenna's company was becoming a test of self-control. How perfect her bookshop was, the warmth of her smile, the way her collarbone arched delicately—it was all etched into my heart with precision.

As I flopped onto my bed, I rubbed my temples and tried to soothe the brewing confusion. This was all supposed to be about protection, keeping her safe. That was the job, and I'd never had trouble keeping business and pleasure separate before. But those situations had never involved Brenna. She had slipped past my defenses and denying it felt like trying to hold back the tide with my bare hands.

Chapter Eleven

Brenna

TENSE, muffled voices seeped through the walls of my temporary bedroom, a low rumble followed by a sharp retort. Stella's tone was unmistakable even though her words were lost to me, laced with that commanding tone she wielded as easily as a kitchen knife. I lay on my bed, a squall of guilt churning in my stomach. I wasn't completely sure if my presence was causing their conflict or if it was just another storm in the Markham family saga. Oh, who was I kidding? They were fighting about me.

I rolled onto my back and stared at the ceiling fan as it cut lazy circles above me. Hunter's deep, tight reply sent a guilty pang ringing through me. What was I doing here, adding tension to already strained ties? After a few more minutes, the sharp thump of his bedroom door closing echoed through the apartment in a definitive end to the sibling tête-à-tête. In the thick silence that followed, I couldn't stop my mind from wandering to the room where Hunter had retreated. The mental image of him pacing back and forth made me close my eyes—those powerful legs that ate up the ground in long, confident strides, the broad chest that could shield against anything.

I bit my lip, warmth blooming deep in my belly and spreading like wildfire. His tattoos, which I had only seen in tantalizing glimpses, added layers to the enigma that was Hunter Markham. Desire curled its fingers around my thoughts, fueling my hunger for him. It wasn't just the idea of his body or the raw power that seemed to pulse just beneath his skin that sent shivers dancing through me. It was also the quiet moments we had shared—reading a book or enjoying a kitten's company. The sense of safety that wrapped around me whenever I was in his presence.

But oh, those tattoos!

And the more I envisioned that unseen ink trailing beneath his shirt, the more I wanted to trace each one. To learn their origins and lose myself in the story of Hunter's past, a tale mapped out on his very skin.

With a firm shake of my head, I forced myself to remember the mundane events of my day as a distraction. During my completely normal shift at the store, I'd seen no hints of Garrett's presence, though I had no doubt he was nearby. Knox hadn't come by either. I had spent hours lost among the shelves and helping customers. Yet as the day wore on, I found my thoughts drifting back to Hunter and looking forward to seeing him tonight.

When I had, he'd promptly informed me of coming up empty in his search for Knox, but that he wasn't giving up yet. His persistence in keeping me safe felt personal, and I began to wonder if there was something more behind his protective instincts. Initially, I thought his resolve was tied to his guilt over Evan's accident. But now, suspicion gnawed at me that perhaps it stemmed from a deeper wound, a scar left by his military service. He was a man whose very essence was as dangerous as it was comforting.

But with Knox having made no appearances, I had no logical reason to stay here any longer. Other than wanting to stay close to that mountain of hard flesh. I'd told Hunter I'd stay a couple of days, and I had. With a sigh, I got off the bed and packed my suitcase. Afterward, I peeked my head out the door. Hunter's bedroom door was firmly shut, and the idea of going home and spending the night alone—and unguarded—made me swallow hard. Plus, I was sure I'd never get out of the building without Hunter's alarms going off. And he deserved a goodbye. The word sent a pang slicing through me. Tiptoeing to the guest bath, I then brushed my teeth and prepared for another night in safety. And temptation.

IN THE MORNING, I clutched the handle of my packed suitcase and awkwardly entered Hunter's living room. The sunlight streaming through the windows seemed to mock the turmoil inside me.

"Going somewhere?" Hunter's voice from the kitchen was low and gravelly, the sound of it sending an unbidden but very pleasant shiver down my spine. As usual, he wore all black, but today had on a form-fitting shirt that showed the line of every muscle, even shades of his six-pack.

"I think it's time for me to go home," I said, though my heart hammered its protest. It wasn't just the threat of Knox that tethered me here—it was Hunter himself.

He poured a second cup of coffee and pushed it across the quartz island, placing a bottle of creamer next to it. He'd quickly learned how I liked my coffee. "Don't worry about last night. Stella is nosy, but she won't be an issue."

"Hunter, Knox hasn't bothered me. He might not even be around anymore."

"I'm going to check his job site again today. And I had a report come in overnight that gave me some of his old addresses. Give it one more day."

"I don't know. I don't want to cause any more complications. With Stella or anyone else." I hesitated, torn between my logical reasoning to leave and my desire to stay right where I was. This man had the gravitational pull of a black hole. His eyes bore into mine, an unspoken plea swirling in their depths. Was it just about protecting me from Knox, or was there something more?

"Our families have nothing to do with this. You might be right and Knox has bugged out. Let me be sure of that. Stay." He said the last word simply, and it wasn't a command—it was vulnerability cloaked in a single word.

This wasn't about Stella or Knox. It was about what lay between us—an invisible force building like a tidal wave. What had started out as a simple reconnection between old friends had blown into something altogether different. For better or worse, I couldn't walk away. Not yet. And just like that, my decision was made.

I set my suitcase on the carpet. "Okay, one more day."

"Thank you."

Hunter crossed the room to pick up my suitcase and carried it down the hall once again. I followed. I stood rooted outside the open bedroom door as he set it gently on the carpet inside my room. After turning around, he walked slowly toward me, moving with the grace of a tiger surveying its realm. Our eyes met and held like a tractor beam. With my heart taking off at a dead run, I backed up until I was near the hallway wall. He continued to stalk toward me. We no longer stood in a narrow corridor of plaster and paint. It was now a conduit of pulsing energy, crackling with a tension that made my skin tingle and my breath hitch.

"Tell me," I said, my voice coming out deeper, huskier. The air between us vibrated, heavy with building desire. "This isn't all about protecting me, is it?"

Hunter stopped in front of me, his shadowed figure a towering presence in the dim light. "It doesn't matter what I feel."

I took in the sight of him—broad-shouldered, muscles outlined beneath his shirt, the raw power in his stance—and something inside me unraveled. He was the storm on the horizon, thrilling and dangerous. And I wanted to run straight into the eye of it.

"Doesn't it?" I asked, my gaze never wavering from his darkened eyes.

The words hung between us. Desire surged through me, as undeniable as the pull of the tide, and drawing me ever closer to the edge of reason. He stalked silently forward. I moved backward until I touched the cool and unyielding wall behind me, a stark contrast to the furnace emanating from Hunter. He reached out, his hands forming brackets as they framed my head. Not touching me but close enough that I could imagine the roughness of his palms against my skin.

"I know what you want." My words came out in a whisper, floating on the air. My eyes met his intense gaze, and my heart raced like a wild beast trying to break free. Every fiber of my being was calling out to him, yearning for him. "You want to kiss me."

Hunter's reaction was visceral. He jerked as if I'd

touched a live wire deep inside him. He hesitated, his breath catching in the tight space between us. "I can't kiss you."

His words were strained, and the air appeared to tremble with the effort it took for him to restrain himself. Yet he leaned closer, his fingers now close enough to trace my hair.

My lips parted of their own accord, an invitation I couldn't disguise. We were so close our breath mingled, a warm dance in the charged space.

With deliberate boldness, I asked the question burning on my tongue. "Why can't you kiss me?"

A muscle worked in his jaw, and his chest heaved as if he'd run miles instead of just standing there, inches from me. "Because I'm afraid that if I start, I won't be able to stop."

His confession loosed something deep within me, a dam giving way to the torrential craving I'd tried so hard to contain. It wasn't just lust—it was the terrifying thrill of falling into someone who could break you apart and put you back together all at once. And God, did I want to fall. "Hunter, what if I don't want you to stop?"

His response was a raw, unguarded look that tore straight through me. In an instant, his lips crashed against mine with an intensity that bordered on ferocity. Then he blew that border to smithereens. His hard body slammed me into the wall as if he could shield me from the world with his own flesh. He gripped my face with his hands, both so large they encompassed me from my jaw to the top of my head.

His kiss scorched through me, igniting fires in places I never knew could burn so fiercely. I gasped at the overwhelming sensation, but Hunter swallowed my sounds, deepening the kiss until I was lost in the storm of passion he unleashed. As his tongue explored my mouth, the taste of him was intoxicating, a mix of coffee and something uniquely his own.

My mind reeled with the ferocity of it, fear mingling with a thrill that raced through my veins. But the fear was fleeting, chased away by the awakening hunger that demanded more—more of his taste, more of the heat from his body.

A wrenching moan tore from my throat, and my hands found their way to his shoulders, at last feeling the taut muscles that moved under my touch. Each brush of my fingers seemed to spur him on, our breaths mingling in ragged synchrony. He kissed me hard enough to leave a mark, and I slanted my head, wanting more. As I clung to him, every hard plane and contour of Hunter's body became a map I was desperate to explore. He was all-consuming, a tempest that swept me up and promised no safe harbor.

Then he wrenched his mouth from mine and took a solid, deliberate step back. His absence was a brutal return to reality from the consuming inferno we had been lost in. His dark and stormy eyes met mine.

"Getting close to me... it never ends well," he rasped. And then, without another word, he was gone. The front door shut behind him with a finality that echoed through the suddenly silent apartment.

My knees betrayed me as they buckled, sending me sliding down the cool wall until I was crumpled on the carpet. My body was still humming with the remnants of our kiss, every nerve ending alight with the fire he'd ignited. The air around me was heavy with the scent of him, a mixture of salt and spice that I could taste on my tongue. It made my head swim and my heart ache with a longing that was both sweet and terrifying.

I drew a shaky breath, trying to steady myself, but the emotions swirling inside me were too potent. We'd danced on the edge of a cliff, and now I was left teetering, unsure whether to step back or let myself fall into the abyss of what lay between us.

Questions ricocheted through my mind. What did this mean for us? Could there even be an *us*? Our families, our history, the very fabric of these islands seemed designed to keep us apart. Yet in his arms, none of that had mattered. Despite the chaos of my thoughts, one thing was undeniably clear.

That kiss had changed everything.

Hunter, the man with secrets etched into his very skin, had unraveled me with a single kiss. And as I sat there, my back against the wall and my blood still roaring, the thoughts swirling in my head coalesced into one.

How could a man whose very touch promised danger, make me feel so inexplicably secure?

Chapter Twelve

Hunter

RUSHING DOWN THE STAIRS, my heart thundered against my ribs in a relentless echo of Brenna's name. I lifted a hand to my lips, tracing the sting of a cut—a badge from our kiss that had been too passionate to be considered anything less than dangerous. The memory of her mouth sent a shockwave through my body, leaving me with a deep-rooted sense of forbidden desire.

I craved her.

I wanted her.

I wanted to climb back up those steps, shove open the door, and lose myself in her warmth. The image of Brenna beneath me, with her hair tousled across my pillow, was almost impossible to resist. I pictured mapping every curve of her body, the soft dips and valleys that promised endless pleasure. Her taste lingered in my mouth, a torment that only fueled my hunger for more.

But more wasn't an option.

More was a line I couldn't afford to cross.

Garrett was already at work, his focus on the computer screen on his desk. He glanced up and immediately saw something was off. Damn him for always noticing.

"Morning," he said, the word tinged with suspicion. "You look like you're ready to either run ten miles or pull on some boxing gloves."

"Well, neither is in the cards." I dropped into the chair opposite him. There was comfort in the familiar order of his desk—papers stacked neatly, a half-empty coffee cup on a coaster.

"Spill it. Is this about our new charge?" Garrett stared right into me. "*Your* new charge?"

I hesitated, feeling the internal tug-of-war between wanting to confide in my friend and the instinct to keep everything locked down tight. But secrets had a way of coming out, and Garrett had always been stubborn as a pit bull when he smelled trouble.

"Brenna and I just kissed." My voice was rough, as if dragged over gravel. It was a confession and a condemnation all in one.

"Kissed or *kissed* kissed?" he asked, air quotes heavy with implication.

"Isn't it obvious?" I shot back, rubbing one shoulder where tension knotted. "I never should have let it happen, but I couldn't stop myself. I'm supposed to be protecting her, not exploring her tonsils."

"Getting involved with someone you're guarding is always dicey. Which begs the question. Does she really need to be guarded? Is Knox a threat, or are you looking for excuses to play white knight?"

"Does it matter?" I replied, avoiding the question I

wasn't ready to answer. Protecting Brenna felt as natural as breathing, but whether it was from Knox or from me remained to be seen.

Garrett eyed me, assessing and silent, always the strategist planning his next move. I could practically hear the cogs turning in his head.

"Look, I'm not in the mood for twenty questions," I said, standing abruptly. "I've got things to do. Like trying to find the asshole. Keep watching Brenna today, okay?"

"Sure thing, boss," he replied blandly but let me escape without further interrogation.

I slid into the driver's seat of my SUV. The cool leather against my skin was a stark contrast to the heat Brenna's proximity ignited within me. "Dammit."

I knew what I needed to do—check on Knox. Locate the son of a bitch or confirm that he was out of the picture. And find an excuse to pull back from Brenna before I entangled us in something neither of us could escape. If Knox was truly gone, then so was my reason for staying close to her. And maybe that would be better for both of us.

Except that every cell in my body screamed in protest, wanting to claim what my heart had always thought of as mine. Yet the echo of my past reverberated loudly in my head, reminding me I wasn't the man for her. I pressed the ignition button and the engine roared to life.

AFTER SEVERAL MORE HOURS OF useless searching, a thirty-minute drive brought me to isolated Middle Torch Key, where I staked out an old address I'd found for Knox. I settled into my seat, and my frustration only mounted that I'd still found no sign of him. Earlier, I'd returned to the boatyard, and his boss said he'd just filled out Knox's termination paperwork. Knox's roommate was clueless, offering nothing but shrugged shoulders and empty beer cans as answers. Knox's meager, tattered belongings were still there, untouched and gathering dust—an abandoned life with no forwarding address. The roommate had been more pissed off about needing to find someone else to split the rent.

"Chasing ghosts," I said aloud, my voice echoing off the metal confines of the air-conditioned SUV. The sun outside was relentless, its glare like an accusation. This stakeout at Knox's old place was a last-ditch effort, and I knew it. The ramshackle building stood desolate, a front yard full of nothing but weeds and rusting car parts. All of it a monument to futility.

My phone buzzed, Gabe's text lighting up the screen.

Gabe: You up for a beer?

A beer this early? I drew my brows down, but they flew up after I checked the time. It was mid-afternoon. I'd been sitting here, staring at this empty piece-of-shit house for hours. I quickly texted back.

Hunter: Sure. Conch Republic? I can be there in thirty minutes.

Gabe: See you there.

I could use a drink, but even more, I needed some semblance of normalcy. With a sigh, I pulled out onto the road and away from the ghost house. But as much as I tried to leave my feelings behind, they clung to me, stubborn as the salt air on the breeze. My tongue found the cut where my mouth had torn on my teeth from that amazing kiss. A wave of desire rolled through me. I couldn't abandon Brenna so easily, but now I had no reason to keep her close.

Knox was gone.

The Conch Republic Brewpub was housed in what used to be a cannery. I pushed open the heavy wooden door, and the familiar scent of fried conch and beer welcomed me. The place had a rustic charm, with exposed ductwork overhead and worn wooden tables that held the stories of countless patrons. The brewpub was already humming with a mixture of locals unwinding and tourists seeking authenticity.

"Over here," Gabe called out from a booth by the window where the light caught the lingering dust in the air, turning it into gold. He'd already ordered a pitcher of the house IPA, and frosty condensation beaded down the sides.

"Thanks," I muttered, sliding in opposite him. I poured myself a glass, the frothy head spilling slightly over the rim.

"I ran into Myles this morning as he was coming off his final overnight shift," Gabe said. "You hired two pretty good guys."

I barely heard him as I stared at the bubbles rising through the golden fluid in front of me.

"Hello? What's up with you?"

I snapped my head up at that. Then I rubbed my face with both hands, expelling a sigh that was almost a growl. "I've been working on a new case. And it's eating me alive."

Reluctantly, I told him the whole story. Almost the whole story. I couldn't bring myself to admit I'd been in love with Brenna for years. "I can't let it go any further, but it's looking like her ex is out of the picture. So I guess the whole thing is just going to end." My gut clenched at that.

Gabe cocked his head. "You just said you couldn't see

her due to a conflict of interest. Sounds like that won't be an issue anymore. So what's the problem?"

I took a long pull from my glass, hoping the cool liquid would soothe the heat pulsing through me at the thought of that kiss. "It's complicated."

Gabe leaned back and studied my expression. "Because she's a Coleridge?"

"Please." I scoffed, pushing away thoughts of old arguments and historic bitterness. "That's got nothing to do with it."

"The enmity between our families isn't nothing, Hunter. It's a pretty major complication."

I raised my eyes to meet his. "If one of her brothers wants to pick a fight with me, I'm all for it."

Gabe grinned. "It didn't work out so well for me. Then again, I'm not you, am I? They'd have to be idiots to want to mess with you. Which brings us back to the fact that they *are* Coleridges. Are you hoping to be some modern-day version of Romeo and Juliet or something?"

I gave a reluctant bark of laughter. "Hardly. That didn't end too well for them, did it?"

"Well, if it's not the old family feud, then what is it?"

"It's just..." My words trailed off as I considered how much to reveal. How much of my turmoil could I lay bare before it became too real?

"Come on, man. You can talk to me."

"Let's just say... I'm attracted to her. A lot. But acting on it isn't smart." I leaned forward, resting my elbows on the table and letting my fingers trace along the grooves in the wood.

"Because...?"

"Because I'm not the right guy for her, Gabe." The

admission came out gruff, almost a growl. "And I need to keep my distance before we both get hurt."

Gabe didn't say anything for a moment, just watched me with that all-seeing gaze of his. "Hunter, what happened with Evan was an accident. Even he is starting to acknowledge that. Stop blaming yourself for that and the other things. Stop blaming yourself for people you couldn't save."

I slumped back in my seat. "It's not that easy."

Gabe's expression softened. "I know it's not, but moving back here was a big step. Keep chipping away, Hunter. You've been shouldering the weight of the world for too long."

"Look..." My throat tightened as the words clawed their way out. "I'm just... I'm too screwed up. Brenna, she's—"

"Too good for you? Is that what you're trying to say?" Gabe's tone was gentle, but it prodded the raw edges of my conscience.

"Something like that," I murmured. Memories coursed through me... the last time I'd promised to protect someone and failed. And Evan. I had shattered us both in one single blow of fate. How could I even consider holding Brenna close?

"Remember that summer you and Evan built that treehouse in the yard?" Gabe asked, seemingly out of nowhere. "You two always thought you were invincible."

I smiled despite myself. "Yeah, until I fell out and broke my arm."

"Exactly," he said pointedly. "You fell, you got hurt, and you healed. You're not broken beyond repair, Hunter. Plenty of people care about you."

My chest constricted with a mix of gratitude and pain. Gabe always knew how to cut through the bullshit. He saw the mess inside me and still had this irritating belief I could be more. I stared into the amber depths of my beer, grappling with the conflicting emotions swirling inside me. Would I ever be able to look back without regret and self-hatred? I didn't know, but I was trying.

Taking a deep breath, I met Gabe's gaze. "Thanks, man. I appreciate you looking out for me."

"That's what big brothers are for, remember?" He smiled, but it was tight. Probably because he was thinking the same thing I was.

Evan was also my big brother.

I topped off our glasses with more beer. "Can we talk about something else now? How's the construction at the Barn coming along?"

Gabe hesitated for a moment, then gave in to my subject change. "It's going well. The crew is making good progress."

"I like how you're mixing the old with the new. That place has always been more than just walls and beams."

"The extra two bedrooms are shaping up nicely." Then he dropped his gaze to the tabletop, a shy smile rising. His hand absentmindedly rubbed the back of his neck before he raised his eyes to mine again. "We found out it's a boy."

"Really?" I smiled at the news. "How 'bout that. It looks like the Markham name is secured for another generation, huh?"

He leaned back, uncertainty flickering through his expression. "It is, though I've got mixed feelings about that. Hailey's every bit as much of a Markham as the baby April's carrying." Gabe's daughter was a bright, vivacious child with cascades of brown hair. Gabe shrugged, a gesture of surrender to the weight of tradition. "Maybe she'll hyphenate her name if she gets married, like Maia did. Can't really change over a century of family history, can we?"

"Probably not."

"April's already picking out stuff for the nursery."

"You building a crib for him?" I asked. Gabe was an expert wood artisan and had made cribs for both Hailey and Maia's daughter, Skye.

His eyes lit up. "I'm already working on it. It's going to be the best crib I've ever made."

"To fatherhood." I raised my beer to the center of the table, and we toasted.

Then Gabe's proud smile faded, and I recognized another subject change coming. "Evan's going to join us at Stingrays practice," he dropped mildly, almost too casual.

I blinked, my heart stuttering as my glass slammed down on the table. "He's what?"

Gabe nodded. "You heard me. He changed his mind and agreed to join us—hitting and playing first base so he doesn't have to use his leg too much. No pitching. I think it's good for him. You know, part of the new leaf he's turning over."

"Right." My response was automatic, my mind still grappling with the image of Evan stepping onto the field. Where he'd been poised to start his career. Before I ended it for him.

"Are you okay with that?" Gabe prodded, studying me closely.

"Of course," I lied smoothly, now understanding why Gabe had suggested this meeting. Evan finding his way back to something he loved shouldn't be complicated, except that when it came to my relationship with my brother, nothing was simple. But hell would freeze over before I stood in his way.

"Good." Gabe nodded, satisfied, before taking a swig of his beer. "It'll be good for the team, too. Holy shit. The other teams are going to *die* when they hear Evan's playing again. Even if he's not pitching." He burst into laughter.

"Definitely." The weight of Gabe's news anchored me in a moment of unexpected clarity. Evan joining us wasn't just another event on the calendar. It was a sliver of hope cutting through years of animosity and silence between us.

"Thanks, man," I said, my voice rough. "For telling me about Evan. That's... It means more than you know."

Gabe nodded, his eyes showing he understood the storms that churned beneath my surface. After splitting the bill, we rose and headed out. The thought of Evan at practice, of mending fences long left in disrepair, sparked something akin to hope in the hollows of my chest.

I slid behind the wheel of my Range Rover. Now that I was headed home, my mind drifted back to Brenna. Her lips—soft, insistent—had branded themselves onto mine, leaving a mark that smoldered even now.

A good man would let her go, not keep her tangled in a web weaved from my own darkness. The truth clawed at me —Brenna was my north star, but my life was a battleground of scars and shadows. How could I drag her into that?

If Brenna chose to return to her house, I wouldn't stop her. Knox was a ghost, and without evidence of his threat, what claim did I have? My role was to protect her, even if that meant from myself.

When I arrived at my building, my hand hesitated above the alarm keypad. I clenched it closed as visons of this morning ran through my mind for the millionth time. Tapping in the code would be like a signal flare to my senses, a prelude to the reckoning that awaited me on the other side of the door.

I was in trouble.

I wanted her. God, how I wanted her. To take her to

bed, to explore every willowy curve. But this wasn't about what I wanted. This was about what was right for Brenna, and I was acutely aware that I didn't make the cut. It was time to man up and be strong. I was more than my raging libido and somehow, someway, I needed to find the strength to get hold of myself and pull back from the edge of this cliff. Before it was too late.

I typed in the code and entered.

Chapter Thirteen

Brenna

MY KNIFE SLICED through the bell pepper with a satisfying crunch, and I forced myself to focus on the rhythm of chopping vegetables—anything to keep my mind from spiraling back to that kiss. My hands moved mechanically, dicing carrots next while the baked ziti bubbled in the oven and filled Hunter's kitchen with a rich, comforting aroma.

I hadn't heard from him all day. Since this morning, when everything between us had shifted in one electrifying, shattering moment that had left me breathless and vulnerable.

And confused.

After pulling myself off the floor, I'd managed to dress for work—a miracle considering my knees could well have been replaced with jelly. A glance in the mirror confirmed that my lips were swollen and sore. It was the best kiss I'd ever had. Garrett was downstairs as usual, and he spent the day watching from afar.

The sign above the shop read Bookstore in Paradise, and never had the name felt more ironic. Paradise was far from where my head spun. Customers came and went, their voices muffled as if underwater, while I moved between shelves and counters. I restocked books I didn't see, spoke words I hardly heard, all while my skin thrummed with the memory of how Hunter's granite shoulders had felt under my touch.

The only thing that pierced the fog of my desire was a phone call to Eli, asking to borrow some dive gear. All while trying to sound casual, to deny that I was grasping at a way to keep Hunter in my life. And the idea of diving, of submerging in the clear depths of the ocean with him, seemed appealing—therapeutic, even. And of course, Eli was happy to loan me the equipment. Now all I had to do was put my plan together.

The oven timer's shrill ring yanked me back into the moment. I blinked a few times, grounding myself in Hunter's kitchen with its warm, herb-scented air. My fingers absentmindedly traced the tender spot on my bottom lip where it had bruised against my teeth, the evidence left from a kiss I still couldn't believe the intensity of.

Making dinner helped distract me from wondering which Hunter would walk through the front door. Would it be the bookish friend, the man who had sent my world reeling with one kiss, or the unreadable, walled creature who warned me not to get involved with him?

Pulling oven mitts over my hands, I shook off the thoughts and removed the pasta. The baked ziti sat bubbling on the stovetop when I heard the front door open. Tensing, I turned toward the sound as my heart took off at a dead run.

Hunter stood there, still as a statue framed by the doorway. His eyes found mine immediately, holding my gaze with an intensity that felt like a physical touch. "Hey." His voice was tight, betraying the casualness of the greeting.

"Hi." The room became charged, every nerve ending in my body attuned to his presence. He looked different—a rigidity that seemed to keep him rooted to the spot replacing his usually casual, graceful demeanor.

We stood there for a moment that stretched too long. Awkwardness hung in the air like humidity before a storm. His gaze never wavered from mine, and the memory of our kiss lingered between us, unspoken but omnipresent.

"Smells good," he finally managed, a forced attempt to bridge the distance. But even as he spoke, his guarded posture screamed of mile-high walls firmly in place. And I knew the answer to my unasked question. This was the third, guarded Hunter and part of my heart cried out.

I placed the steaming dish of pasta on the table, and its comforting aroma wrapped around us like a warm embrace I hoped could thaw the chilly tension in the air. "I made dinner," I said, attempting to slice through the tension with a cheerfulness I didn't quite feel. "Baked ziti and a salad."

"Thanks." After closing the door, he moved stiffly, almost robotically, to join me at the table. We sat across from each other, initiating a silent ritual of passing plates and utensils. The clinking sounds seemed disproportionately loud in the silence that hung over us.

"Did you hear anything about Knox?" My voice sounded too eager in my ears, but I needed something, anything, to break the ice.

Hunter exhaled a long breath of frustration as he stared at his plate. "No sign of him. Looks like he's skipped town."

"Ah." I nodded, pushing food around my plate, not

really tasting anything. If Knox had left Dove Key, I had no reason to stay here. More pressingly, why wouldn't Hunter look at me?

"How was your day?" he asked, his tone polite but distant.

"Fine," I replied tersely, the word feeling like a pebble in my mouth. It was clear he wasn't going to mention the kiss that had branded itself onto every corner of my mind.

After a few more moments of chewing in silence, I let out a frustrated breath. "Are we going to talk about what happened this morning?"

Hunter dropped his fork, and the metal clattered against the plate. He met my gaze, his eyes clouded with an emotion I couldn't quite decipher. "I shouldn't have kissed you." His voice was rough and ragged. "I crossed a line I shouldn't have."

His admission stung, leaving a bitter taste that the savory layers of pasta couldn't mask. I'd replayed that moment all day. The heat, the urgency. To hear him speak of it with such remorse—had the passion all been on my side?

"Oh. Okay." My heart sank like a stone in still water.

"I'm sorry," he added, his eyes dancing over my face as if he wanted to say more but couldn't find the words.

"Maybe we're better off being only friends," I lied. A part of me wanted to reach across the table and bridge the gap his apology had widened. And I knew Hunter couldn't be pushed. So friends it was.

"I think that would be best."

After a few more bites, I pushed my half-eaten plate of ziti away. If this was how he wanted it, fine. I'd adjust, but no way would I do it on his turf. "I should go home. I appreciate what you've done for me, but with Knox out of the picture, there's no need to stay here."

Without looking at me, Hunter nodded. His jaw tightened. "You can spend one last night in the guest room, then I'll set up a security system at your place tomorrow morning. That will alert you in case he decides to come back."

"Thanks. How much will the system cost?" I wasn't about to let him think I needed charity, not after everything else that had happened.

He waved a hand dismissively. "Don't worry about it."

"Hunter, I want to pay for the security system. In fact, I insist on it. You haven't said a word about billing me for any of this, and I'm not a freeloader."

He paused, then at last allowed a smile to crack through his stoic façade—a smile that sent a familiar warmth flooding through me. "Brenna, you're the last person I'd ever think of as a freeloader."

"Still, I want to pay."

"All right." He relented with a slight shake of his head. "Three hundred for a basic system. I've got one downstairs. I'll bill you."

"That's more like it." I matched his smile, relieved as some small measure of normalcy returned to our dynamic. If we weren't going to be more than friends, we needed to figure out our new dynamic. The tension eased, leaving a fragile peace in its wake. We finished dinner with light conversation that skirted around anything too deep or dangerous. Like the tide retreating from the shore, leaving behind only shades of what could have been.

After dinner, I stood at the sink, rinsing plates as Hunter placed plastic wrap over the casserole dish. "Need a hand?" he asked, his voice casual as if we were just two friends sharing domestic chores instead of two people who had shared a kiss that had shaken me to my core. And then went back to being friends. Or whatever we were.

"Thanks, but I've got it." I forced a nonchalant smile. "Why don't you relax? You look like you could use it."

He leaned back against the counter, arms folded, and watched me for a moment. I tried not to linger on how the pose made his biceps bulge. His gaze was no longer clouded with the tension that had filled the space between us earlier. Instead, it was softer, as if he was allowing himself to remember that we were once the best of friends—before everything got complicated.

"I talked to Eli today about borrowing some dive gear," I said, changing the subject. I felt miles away from the emotions that swirled inside me when I'd talked with my brother just hours earlier. But I wanted to reach out across this abyss between us.

"Yeah?" Hunter tilted his head slightly, interest piqued.

"I thought it might be fun to get back in the water again. You and me, for old times' sake."

He paused, considering it before letting out a slow breath. "I've been meaning to dive since I got back. Just haven't found the time yet."

"Maybe you need to make the time." My heart sank a bit at his noncommittal response, but I masked it with a teasing lilt.

"I'll check my schedule tomorrow." His small smile didn't quite reach his eyes.

With a fleeting twitch of my lips in reply, my belly gave a wrenching twist. Maybe it was better this way. I wanted him in my life, even as a friend, so we'd need to figure out what that looked like. I dried my hands on a dish towel and turned off the kitchen light, leaving us in the soft glow of the living room lamps. The urge to reach out, to bridge the gap with more than words or shared laughter, tugged at me. But I held back, afraid to shatter the fragile truce we'd built.

Once again, we settled in his living room. The pages of my book were mere blurs as I flipped through them, not really taking in the words. Pedro hopped onto the couch and curled up in the space between us, his black fur a stark contrast against the light gray fabric. The kitten turned his head from Hunter to me and narrowed his eyes, as if trying to decipher the shift in our dynamic.

That makes two of us, little guy.

I cast a glance at Hunter, whose attention seemed genuine on his book. But I knew him well enough by now—or at least, I thought I did—to see the tension in his jaw that belied a focused calm. The clock ticked away in the background, and each second felt like a missed opportunity to speak, to touch. But we both remained silent.

When the hour grew late, we closed our books almost simultaneously, as though some unseen director choreographed our movements even in this . "I should get some sleep," I said, more to fill the silence than out of any real need for rest.

In Hunter's guest room, I stood at the edge of the bed and ran a hand over the smooth comforter. This bed, with its neatly tucked corners and unfamiliar pillows, wasn't where I yearned to be. My eyes wandered to the shut door. This was my last night in Hunter's apartment, but I wasn't about to knock on his door. When I climbed into my bed, the mattress was cool beneath me, unlike the warmth and strength I had clung to in those moments pressed against Hunter.

His sudden shift from barely restrained lust to a careful, deliberate distance left me more confused than ever. What had changed in the hours between? Lying there in the dark,

I tried to reconcile the man who had kissed me senseless with the one who now guarded his heart as fiercely as he did mine. My thoughts spun.

I needed to know which Hunter was real. The one whose touch set me aflame, or the stoic, unknowable guardian angel who watched over me. And I had a suspicion that spending several hours diving together would tell me.

Chapter Fourteen

Hunter

THE DRILL HUMMED STEADILY in my hands as I secured the last camera above the front door of Bookshop in Paradise. The morning breeze blew softly through the open door, making the hanging baskets outside rock slightly. I leaned back slightly on the ladder and surveyed my work with a critical eye. Everything had to be perfect for Brenna.

"Do you want to put cameras inside my apartment too?" Her voice cut through my focus, laced with a hint of concern.

I glanced down at her, offering a reassuring smile. "No, only a camera and alarm outside the door at the top of the stairs."

My fingers deftly twisted wires together, wrapping them with electrical tape before tucking them neatly out of sight. After that awful awkwardness last night, we'd settled back into an easier camaraderie. Not quite what we were before that kiss, but better than I had any right to expect. Spoken words had never been my strength, and last night they'd completely failed me. But I'd rather remain silent than say something I couldn't take back. I'd already done enough of that, and our ease with each other this morning indicated I'd repaired some of the damage I'd done. But now I felt her mood changing.

"Good... What about your apartment? Do you have cameras there?"

I caught her hesitation and gave her my full attention. Her green eyes searched mine, and I knew she was worried whether she'd been filmed while staying with me.

"None inside. I value privacy, Brenna. Yours, mine, everyone's." I made a mental note to double-check the angles of the cameras I'd just installed, ensuring not even a sliver of her personal space would be caught on camera. After descending from my stepladder, I folded it together and moved to the control panel at the back of her shop.

Brenna followed, leaning against a bookshelf as she watched me program the system from her phone, all part of the service at KeyMark Security. I showed her how to access the images and the panic button I'd installed near the cash register, which would make a 911 call. She asked interested, intelligent questions and we slipped closer to our earlier familiarity.

"I wanted to ask..." she trailed off as she tucked a loose strand of hair behind her ear. Then she turned a full smile toward me. "Would you like to go diving tomorrow? We didn't really settle it last night. It will be like old times!"

My heart skipped a beat, torn between the pull of her beautiful, soft body and the caution lights flashing in my mind. Diving with Brenna meant being close to her, too close, in ways that could stir up more than just the ocean currents.

"I'm not sure. I didn't have a chance to check my

calendar this morning." I was half-hoping she'd let me off the hook.

"When was the last day you had off?" she asked, her lips curving into a playful smile. "And Garrett told me he and Myles aren't covering Calypso Key anymore. Sounds like your schedule just cleared up, buddy. And my shop just happens to be closed tomorrow..."

She was right. Myles would be pretty recovered from his night shifts now. I had some leads to follow through on, but I could clear a morning off no problem. And dammit, I wanted to be around her, even as just a friend. I was like a moon orbiting around her, helpless to escape her pull. To cover my awkwardness, I raised both hands into the air. "Okay. I surrender! Let's go diving."

"Great!" Her enthusiasm was infectious as she told me about the gear she had arranged for us. But as I went over the last of my demonstration of her new security features, I couldn't help feeling like I was stepping into uncharted waters.

I glanced at my watch. "You're all set. I'd better get going. I need to catch up on some things and make sure I'm clear tomorrow since the boss gave me orders."

Her answering smile went straight to my heart. This might be a terrible idea, but I wasn't about to change my mind and see her beautiful expression fall.

"See you tomorrow." Her gaze lingered on mine a moment longer than necessary. The words hung between us like a promise or maybe a warning.

Back at KeyMark, I settled into the familiar groove of work. The screen's glow bathed the room as I flicked through leads—emails from potential clients in need of security assessments, and a few inquiries about personal protection. I made a series of phone calls, reaching out to current and prospective clients.

"I just got off the phone with a Mrs. Renaldi, who wants surveillance on her beach house while she's away," I said to Garrett, tapping keys to pull up her file. "High-profile, lots of valuables. I want you on it."

"Got it." His reply was crisp, no-nonsense. "I'll call her and set up the walkthrough."

"Make sure to use the new cams for this one and keep it tight. She's nervous, first time leaving the place since her husband passed."

"No worries."

I trusted Garrett implicitly. He handled each job with a finesse that came from experience. We'd been through enough together to have an unspoken language of glances and gestures, which translated into our professional life. And the same went with Myles, my other brother-in-arms turned employee.

"Myles will be recovered from vampire duty by tomorrow," I said, referring to our phrase for overnight work. I'd already talked to him. "He'll be here first thing tomorrow morning."

Garrett filed away a folder and shut his desk drawer. "Sounds like we've enough business to keep us out of trouble, even without covering nights."

I nodded. "KeyMark's doing fine. There's plenty of work to go around, even without my family drama."

"Always knew you'd kill it when you went solo." Garrett's voice held a note of pride.

"Thanks." I paused, trying to think of a good way to tell him I'd be off tomorrow. And why. "Myles is covering for me tomorrow. I'm going diving."

"Really? About time you did something enjoyable. Are you going with your sister, the divemaster?"

"Uh, no. Brenna."

Garrett just stared at me. Then he gave me a slow nod. "Say no more. Nice work."

I scowled at him. "It's not a date. We decided to be just friends."

Laughing, Garrett pushed to his feet. "Keep telling yourself that, man. I'd better get to work. See you later."

After the front door closed, I leaned back in my chair and stared out the front window. Main Street glinted under the sun, a world away from spreadsheets and strategy. Try as I might to deny it, Garrett might be right about the futility of me keeping things casual with Brenna. I was still terribly conflicted about seeing her tomorrow, and what it might lead to. A mix of anticipation and anxiety fluttered in my stomach, though I had a feeling eagerness to see her again would win out.

But as long as Brenna wasn't involved, I was a man of discipline, and break time was over. When I returned to my office, my eye caught on my catcher's mitt sitting on a chair in the corner and my stomach did a weird floppy thing. I had a couple of hours yet before practice. A momentous practice, but I couldn't afford to be distracted now. Opening my email program, I got back to work.

THE FRESHLY CUT grass smelled sharp and vibrant as I strapped on my shin guards, and a refreshing breeze stirred the palm fronds edging the outfield. "Hey, Hunter, heads up!" Stella called out, tossing me my catcher's mitt.

"Thanks," I said, flexing the leather in my grip.

The Stingrays were a motley crew of family and resort employees. And me. But we'd gelled into a good team, and our practices and games were filled with good-natured ribbing and insults.

But today was different. The atmosphere this afternoon had been charged from the start, and now it reached a new peak as Evan stepped to the plate—a subtle current of hope that was nearly tangible.

"Take it easy on him, Gabe," Maia joked from first base.

"Oh, Evan knows me better than that," Gabe replied, a hint of a smile tugging at the corner of his mouth.

Evan held the bat, his stance tense. His nervousness was obvious even from behind my mask. As he fidgeted with the grip, his eyes flicked around the field.

"Ready?" Gabe asked. When Evan gave a jerk of a nod, he wound up for the pitch.

The ball came in easy, and Evan's swing was tentative, sending a slow grounder toward Maia, who scooped it up effortlessly. A murmur of encouragement rippled through the team as two more pitches had similar results.

"Okay, okay, warm-up's over," Gabe called out, throwing a little more heat with the next pitch.

Evan adjusted, the half-hearted swings morphing into something sharper, more focused. It was like watching an old engine rumbling back to life, each swing bringing him closer to the player we knew he could be.

"Is that all you've got?" Gabe asked and I grinned, knowing Evan couldn't see it. Gabe managed Evan beautifully, slowly building his confidence and now baiting him. From the mound, he shook his head. "I thought you could play."

"Just pitch the ball, asshole," came Evan's growl of a reply.

Gabe pitched to him at full speed and Evan swung hard. The crack of the bat resonated like a shot, the ball rocketing straight back at Gabe and missing him by inches. He jumped out of the way, and we all erupted into laughter as Gabe theatrically checked himself for injuries.

"Damn, Evan! You trying to take me out?" Gabe exclaimed, still smiling wickedly as he caught the ball Aiden tossed him.

"Nope," Evan shot back with a matching grin. "If I wanted you out, you'd be out."

The tension broke, and the practice rolled on with newfound ease. As I crouched behind home plate, pride swelled in my chest. Evan was stepping back into the game, into life itself, and I was here to witness it.

He sent the next pitch streaking along the baseline. Then one into the gap between first and second. He hit the next sharply, lacing it between second and chef Martin at shortstop. The next two were long fly balls that dropped where the outfielders couldn't catch them, including Liv in right field. Aiden, stationed at third, could only gape as another line drive whizzed past him, his glove swinging up a moment too late.

"Nice, Evan!" Stella's voice rang out from second base, her athletic form poised and ready. He hit the next ball directly to her, letting her field it cleanly. Her cheer felt like a bright flag waving amidst our collective awe.

I squatted behind home plate, my heart thrumming in rhythm with each precise hit Evan executed. What had started as a tentative experiment became a spectacle, a masterclass in control and power. Each swing sliced away more of the years he'd been absent from the game.

Memories flooded back to me. The countless afternoons we'd spent on fields just like this one, where I was the only challenger willing to step up to the plate because Evan was so damn good. I remembered the ice packs, the bruises on my palms from catching his fireballs, the pride I felt being his brother.

Now, the longing for that connection—a bond frayed by time and circumstance—pulled taut within me. I wanted to reach across the years and mend the threads I'd let unravel, to be the boys who understood each other without words. Evan's last drive arced high, then plummeted down just inside the third-base line, a perfect hit. As the team clapped and hollered, I rose to my feet and flipped my mask back to rest against the crown of my head.

"Well, you've still got it," I said, my voice tinged with admiration.

Hesitating, his eyes scanned mine, searching for a catch that wasn't there. Then, slowly, the edges of his mouth lifted in a smile. It was a fragile, yet pivotal moment in the slow dance of our reconciliation. "Thanks, Hunter. That felt good. Really good."

"Because it was."

"Hey, Evan! Think you could teach me that swing?" called out Aiden, his lanky frame standing with one foot on third base.

"Sure," Evan replied, the ghost of a smile remaining on his lips. "It's easy. Just don't play for a decade."

Laughter rippled through the team, and Stella, still at second, threw in her two cents. "Don't tease him, Evan. Or you'll end up being our manager instead of Maia."

"Hey!" Maia called. "I like being the manager. Evan, you just back off."

This time, Evan's smile could have cracked his face. He was back where he belonged. Part of a team, where the camaraderie was thick in the air. It was clear we all felt it—

Evan's return wasn't just his victory. It was a win for all of us.

When practice ended, Gabe trotted up to the plate, rolling his shoulder with a wince. As I rose from my crouch, he faced Evan. "You know, if you ever want to try pitching again, I'd gladly hand over the mound."

Evan widened his eyes at the suggestion, his hand rising as if to ward off the very thought. "Pitch? Nah, I couldn't hit the broadside of a barn. Hitting's one thing—pitching is completely different."

I knew full well that Evan could probably out-pitch anyone in the league, decade off or not. But I kept my mouth shut. Pitching for him would be more than just throwing a ball—it was bearing the weight of every eye on you, every expectation resting on your shoulders. For Evan, that would be like stepping right into a hurricane.

April rose from her camp chair behind the backstop and approached us. "Come on, Gabe. Let's get you home and get some ice on that shoulder." She linked her arm through Gabe's and shot us a knowing look, her other hand resting on the swell of her belly.

"As long as the ice is on my shoulder and not in my whisky," Gabe replied, his smile softening as he glanced down at her.

They walked off together in a picture of contentment, leaving the rest of us to bask in the glow of a practice that felt like more than just practice—it felt like the turning of a page.

I clapped the dust off my glove, watching how much more relaxed Evan was, how his shoulders had eased down from where they'd hitched up around his ears. I spoke before I could change my mind, even though I knew my words were risky. "Hey, Evan. If you ever want to throw the ball around, really pitch, I'm game." I tossed my mitt from one hand to another, a casual offer lobbed into the charged air between us.

He met my gaze, his eyes steady and unreadable for a moment that seemed to stretch longer than the shadows creeping across the outfield. Then, with a slow nod that felt like a victory in itself, he said, "Maybe. I'll let you know."

That was enough for me—it was an open door, no matter how slight the crack. As he walked off the field with Liv, the others patted him on the back. I felt like we were all part of something fragile yet fierce.

With the day fading into a painted sky, I returned to my Range Rover and headed back to Dove Key. Brenna would be closing up the shop right about now, her hands brushing against the spines of beloved novels, hair falling across her face in that way that always made me want to reach out and tuck it behind her ear. I missed her already, the way you miss the sun when it dips below the horizon, leaving you longing for its warmth.

The road hummed beneath my tires as I navigated the familiar turns back to my place. A thrill rolled through me. Not just for the dive tomorrow, but for whatever lay ahead with Brenna. Could I really keep up a casual friendship with her? Tomorrow would be a minefield of possibilities and danger. I wasn't the man she deserved. Hell, I was probably the *last* man she needed in her life. Yet at the same time, I couldn't stay away from her. And I had yet to figure out how I was going to reconcile that.

Chapter Fifteen

Brenna

THE MORNING WAS TROPICALLY GLORIOUS, with the sun's rays prying into every crevice of Big Pine Key as Hunter and I laid out our scuba gear on a worn, wooden picnic table. As expected, the strip of sand was deserted. This dive spot was a well-kept local secret, one that Eli had shown me a few years ago. And now I was here with Hunter.

"Don't forget to check your inflator hose," Hunter said, his voice steady and calm.

I glanced at him as he meticulously reviewed each piece of equipment. His motions were practiced and deliberate, those of a man who had performed this action hundreds—thousands?—of times. The fact that Siesta Sunset's dive equipment was unfamiliar didn't faze him in the slightest. His long-sleeved rash guard clung to him like a second skin, emphasizing every ripple and ridge of his upper body. Black, of course, and it suited him, the color of mystery and things hidden. Black-and-gray board shorts highlighted muscular thighs, gray being the only nod to color he seemed willing to make.

But his attire brought one rather important fact to light as I tugged my wetsuit on. "I'm sorry. I grabbed the biggest wetsuit we had in our rental pool. You're a big guy, Hunter Markham."

He tossed me a smile that sent a flutter through me. "Don't worry about it. I'll be fine without one. I've dived in much colder water than this." And there it was again. The gulf of experience that separated the Hunter I'd once been friends with from this... mountain of a man.

Without being obvious, I drank in the sight of him. Friend zone or not, desire unfurled in my belly in a long, hot wave. My body remembered the heat of his kiss, the way he'd pressed against me, unmistakably aroused. The size of him! The memory sent a shiver dancing down my spine, which I tried to deny. We'd settled into an amicable rapport, the last vestiges of that awkward tension in the past now. And I had to be okay with that.

"Here, let me help you." His voice snapped me back to reality. Fully geared up himself, Hunter lifted my tank and held out the shoulder straps of the buoyancy compensation device for me to shrug into. His fingers brushed mine, a fleeting touch that set off a cascade of sparks I pretended I didn't notice.

"Thanks." I clipped shut the buckles of my BCD with an ease born of practice. My injured arm was more of a memory than a hindrance at this point. Hunter's hand found the tank valve behind me, steadying me as we waded into the warm embrace of the ocean together. The water lapped at us, whispering promises of the world beneath the waves.

After donning our fins and masks, we placed our regulators in and started our descent. The weight of the world slipped away, the serene bliss of the underwater realm replacing it. Our exhales came in rhythmic bubbles, a soft accompaniment to the pops and crackles emanating from the living ocean. As we moved deeper, following the sand's gentle trajectory, I couldn't shake the awareness of Hunter's presence beside me. How it was a mixture of the old and familiar with the new and the thrilling.

As we began our exploration, the wondrous delight of diving rekindled within me. There was something about being surrounded by the blue infinity, with only Hunter by my side, that made me feel both inconsequential and incredibly alive.

Our fins propelled us over the reef, an unspoken communication guiding our movements. I caught Hunter's eye and smiled behind my regulator. For a moment, it was as if nothing had changed since those carefree high school dives. But so much had—especially him, his life skewered and seared by circumstance.

He let me lead, staying next to me but a few inches behind in an acknowledgment of my familiarity of the site. The thought made me smile. Hunter might be a giant of a man, but he didn't mind letting a woman be in charge.

Another thought that sent my core clenching.

We were drifting past a high coral ridge, its carpet of multicolored sea fans waving gently in the surge, when a green sea turtle emerged from an elkhorn coral cluster. Its flippers moved with a gentle, unhurried grace that belied the strength within them. The creature stared as if acknowledging us as part of its world, then proceeded to swim alongside us in quiet companionship.

Its serene, almost lazy movements mesmerized me, the way it looked at us with ancient, knowing eyes. A school of yellowtail snappers darted past, their silver bodies glinting like coins tossed into a wishing well. They parted gently around the turtle and us, reforming behind our little trio. And when we encountered the regal glide of a queen angelfish, its vibrant blues and yellows stark against the colors of the reef, Hunter and I stopped to watch its graceful movements.

Memories flooded back—of us as teenagers, wide-eyed and awestruck, exploring every reef we could reach. Back then, he was just Hunter, my dive buddy and bookish friend, the one who could make me laugh even underwater.

I glanced at him, wondering if he too remembered those carefree days, or if the weight of his struggles had sunk those memories deep. His gaze met mine through the clear lenses of our masks, and a flicker of something unspoken passed between us. Even amidst the soft ballet of sea creatures, Hunter's presence was a pull more compelling than the strongest current.

I considered myself a pretty good diver, years of experience making my movements fluid and effortless. Hunter had always been naturally talented at it, but the difference between then and now was obvious. The boy swimming in joyous discovery held little resemblance to the man who had completed deadly missions underwater. He was fluid and utterly graceful, with no unnecessary movement. And he used only slightly more air than I did, which was astonishing given the differences in our sizes.

But too soon, our tanks were light and nearly empty, and it was time to complete our safety stop. As we ascended, I felt the loss acutely. Above us, reality waited— territory far more uncharted than any dive. But down here, with the echoes of a simpler past and the beauty of the present surrounding us, life was so much simpler. In this otherworldly realm, I allowed myself to believe in the possibility of redemption. For the bad boy who'd captured my heart without even trying. And maybe even for us, for whatever we might be together.

The salt on my lips tasted like victory as we emerged onto the warm sand. We both used the freshwater shower near the parking lot to rinse off the saltwater, then toweled off. After wringing out my hair, I pulled on my shirt and board shorts over my bikini. When I looked over at Hunter, he had already exchanged his wet rash guard for a dry black shirt. I couldn't deny the pang of disappointment that I'd missed my chance to see those muscles and what his tattoos looked like in glorious daylight.

"Almost like old times, huh?" His smile was easy and carefree, and I wanted to see more of it.

"It did!" I laughed, tilting my head to take in his silhouette against the bright sky. "Except you didn't look like that in high school." My eyes took in his bulging shoulders, the drape of fabric hinting at the tightly coiled strength beneath.

"Neither did you," he remarked with a casual air.

I straightened, surprised at his comment. "How am I different now?"

"It's been over ten years, Brenna." Then he added, softer, "You're even prettier now." The red rising on his cheeks was a revelation as he quickly unscrewed his regulator from the tank.

I tucked away that blush like a secret treasure, letting it warm me from the inside out. A flying fish skimmed across the waves, and when I turned to point it out to Hunter, I found his eyes trailing slowly down my body. Desire flared through me again, my skin tightening. My urge to grab the front of his shirt and pull him down for a hot, wet kiss could barely be contained. He wanted me. I was sure of it. But I was afraid of driving him away again.

When he bent to pack up his gear, his shirt collar shifted to reveal a sliver of inked skin. Curiosity flared within me. Why was he so casual about that spectacular body? "I don't remember you being so bashful. How come you've kept your shirt on the whole time? Most guys with muscles like that would be strutting all over the beach."

He shifted, and the ghost of a tattoo disappeared, to my disappointment. "Just protecting myself from the sun," he answered flatly, but his nonchalance didn't mask his tight voice. Yet another mystery to this man—there was more to this story too. Which only served to remind me that I didn't want this day to end. Not yet. And spending the morning with him made me realize something else. I didn't want to be his friend.

I wanted to be so much more.

So I searched about for a topic of conversation. "Speaking of protection, my security system's been acting up, or my shop is haunted. One of the cameras keeps sending me ghost alerts."

"The camera angle and width of field probably need adjustment. I can take a look at it for you."

"That would be great. And how about lunch? I've got sandwiches in my apartment." It was an excuse to keep us together, and I was sure we both knew it.

"Lead the way," he said, and there was no mistaking the current running between us. As we drove back to my place, anticipation built within me like a storm. I wanted Hunter Markham. All of him. And to hell with the fallout.

BACK IN MY SHOP, Hunter's fingers danced across the screen of my phone. "There," he said as he handed it back to me. "I adjusted the camera and the settings, so you shouldn't get any more false alerts."

"Thanks. I'm sure that will take care of it." I gave him a smile that hopefully masked the butterflies dancing in my stomach. "Diving always makes me starved. Let's eat."

I led the way up the staircase to the cozy living space above my bookshop. We settled in at my small dining table where I laid out the deli sandwiches I'd picked up yesterday. Turkey and Swiss on rye for him, ham and sprouts on whole wheat for me, nestled next to a bowl of fresh fruit salad.

My nerves didn't dissipate as we ate, and I searched for something to discuss. There was so much I didn't know about him. "So tell me about life in the Marines."

He took a bite of his sandwich, chewing thoughtfully before answering. "It was intense," he said, his voice taking on a distant quality. "I was a Marine Raider, and it wasn't exactly a walk in the park. Lots of training, lots of missions that weren't... your average active duty." His shoulders tensed, the lines around his eyes deepening at distant memories. Or maybe not so distant.

"Sounds tough," I said gently, not wanting to press too hard.

"Yeah. A lot of it was routine training, but other parts were dicey." He cleared his throat. "What about you and Knox? Were you two serious?"

A laugh escaped me at the absurdity of that thought. "No. We dated for five months, but we didn't have much in common. Though it took me long enough to realize that. He's probably the only person on this island who doesn't like the ocean. And my other relationships in the past all kind of fizzled out."

He regarded me with hooded eyes. "You're better off without him, you know."

"No argument there." I scooped up a forkful of salad.

As we ate, silence settled around us. The room seemed to shrink, the heat not entirely due to the afternoon sun. I couldn't help but watch Hunter, the way his throat moved when he swallowed, the neat trim of his dark beard. My heart thrummed as I remembered the feel of that hair brushing against my jaw.

I wiped the corner of my mouth with my napkin. "How's your sandwich?"

He nodded, swallowing. "Good—thanks for thinking of this."

As we finished lunch, we discussed my shop, and I couldn't help feeling that my past sounded boring and uneventful compared to his. When I said so out loud, Hunter just stared at me, wide-eyed.

"Brenna, you're a huge success and your bookshop is absolutely perfect. You've accomplished a lot more than I have in the past decade."

My chest warmed at his praise, but I shook my head. "Hardly. But I'm glad you're back."

My breath stilled as his dark eyes stared straight into me. "So am I."

As we finished, I tried not to be acutely conscious of every move he made. Then I brought over a slice of cheese-cake for us to share for dessert. Leaning over, I forked a bite, enjoying the creamy, sweet texture. It was a sharp contrast to the heat from his gaze that felt like the sun itself.

"You know more about me than I do about you," I said.

"Have you ever been married? You know, during all that time away?"

His face took on that guarded look as he shook his head. "Not even close." There was an undercurrent to him now that wasn't his usual reticence.

"No serious relationships? Have you ever been in love?" I held my breath. It was a bold question, but curiosity was burning through me.

Hunter set down his can of soda, his eyes locking onto mine for a split second before darting away. His jaw clenched, and he ran a hand through his damp hair—a move I'd come to recognize as him grappling with inner turmoil.

"Once," he admitted, his voice rough like gravel. "But it... didn't work out."

My heart skipped, then pounded furiously, unsure whether to rejoice or mourn. A flame of regret shot through me at the thought of some other woman letting go of him. Not returning what he'd offered her.

I cleared my throat, trying to mask the sudden surge of emotions burning through me. "I'm sorry to hear that," I said softly, willing myself to maintain composure. "Love can be... difficult."

His glance flickered back to me, full of something unreadable, before he quickly looked away again. "Yeah, it can."

Seeking normalcy, I stood and stacked our plates, my hands moving robotically, while my mind replayed his words. The thought that another woman had touched his heart made something twist inside me—envy, perhaps. Or was it longing?

"Any woman would be lucky to have you, Hunter," I said as casually as I could manage.

He turned sharply, his piercing gaze searching mine for

any hint of sarcasm. His startled look cracked something open within me. How could this glorious man feel so unworthy?

"Thanks," he muttered, but his voice was low, barely audible.

The emotion inside me solidified. I was jealous of that mysterious woman who had left such an impression on him. I wanted to put my own mark over every inch of him. Claim him as mine. And to hell with patience—I couldn't bear the distance his quiet words put between us.

So, with a few steps, I bridged it before I could second-guess myself. I leaned down to where he sat, letting my fingers trail over his beard and feeling the heat of his skin beneath. "You're special to me, Hunter Markham. Don't forget that."

He closed his eyes and trapped my wrist with his hand. He held it gently, no aggressiveness in the motion. "Brenna. Stop. You don't want to do this."

I moved my arm deliberately, and Hunter immediately loosened his hold. It was the arm Knox had wounded, but I felt none of that as I stood on the precipice. Opening his eyes, Hunter stared up at me. I met his gaze squarely, with intent, and neither of us could look away.

He scooted his chair back and slowly rose to his feet, unfurling himself to his full height. He'd rinsed off at the beach, but a hint of saltwater and pure male wafted from him that made my abdomen clench tight. I reached out and fanned both hands over his chest, stroking the hard, curved muscle underneath.

I said with no hesitation, "Yes, I very much want to do this."

A low groan vibrated from his throat. Then, with a sudden movement that stole the air from my lungs, he swept me up by the hips. In two large strides, he sat me firmly on the kitchen counter as if I weighed nothing. His gaze burned into me as he stood between my knees. The strength in his arms sent a molten roll through me, sparking an inferno that blazed through every nerve. I wrapped my legs around his waist, pulling him closer, needing the heat of his body against me. And then his lips were on mine, slanting across mine with an intensity that stole my breath. This kiss was different from our last—less brutal, yet still wild and untamed.

Perfectly right.

My hands moved of their own accord, exploring the landscape of muscle beneath his shirt, tracing the ridges and planes I was dying to explore.

"I want you, Hunter." I pressed the words against his mouth, my voice thick with desire.

He angled his kiss, teasing his tongue over the roof of my mouth. His chest rose and fell rapidly, matching the rhythm of my own lungs.

"God, Brenna," he breathed out, his voice strained with the same burning need that coursed through me. He pushed against my open legs, the hard length of him rubbing against me. A groan wrenched from my throat.

Hunter's eyes were a storm cloud of doubt as his hands braced on the counter on either side of me. "This is a bad idea." His voice was a gravelly warning that rumbled through my throbbing core. "Every time I get close to someone, it never ends well."

I reached up, fingers slipping through the dark waves of his hair, anchoring him to me. "I refuse to believe that. The past ends right here. Right now." Closing my hand, I gripped his short hair. His eyes were wild with desire, glinting dangerously as he pinned me with them.

My heart pounded with abandon. "You're the match, Hunter. I'm the paper. Burn me. I want you to burn me to cinders."

For a heartbeat, there was stillness, a held breath in time. Then our mouths met in a clash of lips and teeth, a fervent dance of tongues that spoke of withheld yearnings now set free.

I was completely on fire for him. Every touch, every kiss fanned the flames, and I wanted—no, needed—to be utterly consumed. I could feel him, hard and insistent as he ground against me. I arched into the sensation, desperate for the full length of him. Craving every inch.

"Which way is your bedroom?" Hunter broke our kiss to gasp the question.

Hardly capable of speech, I managed to nod toward the hall. He lifted me effortlessly, carrying me in front of him across the living room as my legs tightened around him. Then we were inside my room, where the half open blinds threw shadows across the soft sheets. Setting me down, our gazes locked. And as Hunter drew his finger slowly down the length of my neck, I'd never been so willingly caught in the flames.

Chapter Sixteen

Hunter

BRENNA'S ROOM was awash in soft light that filtered through white gauzy curtains. As I tried to focus on this gorgeous woman before me, my heart thumped like a wild drum. God, I wanted her so bad.

My dream of so many years.

But the brightness was too much. I'd thought about this moment for so long, but I'd only imagined it at night. Not in broad daylight. She stared at me as if I were someone worth wanting, her eyes radiating desire as she skimmed her hands over my pectorals. "I've been thinking about this, Hunter. What you look like under that shirt. I can't wait to find out."

"Your r-room..." I stuttered, but the words got lost somewhere between my racing thoughts and the tightness in my throat. My eyes darted to the framed beach landscapes on the wall, then to the bed with its gray-and-aqua bedding ensemble. The illumination would strip away the shadows to leave me exposed. Not just to the light, but to the woman who had no idea what I'd been through. And now there was no way to hide it.

"What about it?" Brenna asked, her voice a melodic tease that pulled deep within me.

"It's so bright." Again, I scanned the unfamiliar space. It felt charged with a heavy expectation that made my palms sweat.

She nuzzled against my neck. "Good. I want to see you. All of you."

But did she?

Then she pulled back to study me. Our gazes held, and the longing was clear in her eyes. Her raw and unguarded face gave me courage, or maybe it was just the pure need coursing through my veins that compelled me to give in to the light and let go.

I leaned down and claimed her lips with mine, plunging both hands into her silky hair at last. Our kiss was deep, passionate, an unleashing of every suppressed desire.

But in the midst of our tangled embrace, reality jabbed at me. Damn it, I hadn't anticipated that we'd cross this line today, if at all. I groaned. "Wait." I stepped back just enough to look into her eyes. "I don't have a condom. I didn't plan on this happening—"

Brenna cut me off with a small smile, her fingers trailing along my jawline in a way that set me ablaze. "I've got some," she whispered, her breath warm against my mouth.

Relief heightened my arousal even more, and desire throbbed in a hot roll through my core. "Good thing one of us is prepared."

Relaxing slightly that at least one problem was solved, my hands roamed over Brenna's body. I had to see her. Touch her. Skimming her sides, I found the hem of her shirt and pulled it upward. The fabric fluttered to the floor, revealing her soft, bare skin bathed in the filtered daylight streaming through her window.

"Beautiful," I murmured as I stared at her in the bikini top that had tormented me all morning. She'd caught me looking at least once, but the beach was a distant memory now. And it couldn't compare to the very real vision before me.

Unable to wait another second, I unbuckled the clasp and lifted the top away. Her breasts rose and fell with each breath, and I cupped them, aching at the softness. She leaned into my touch, her eyes closing. I couldn't resist drawing her closer, raking my mouth over hers once more as our tongues danced. She moaned against my mouth, a sound so sweet it sent a red-hot jolt straight to my groin.

"More," she breathed. Brenna's fingers trembled as they traced the contours of my abdomen, working their way down to the hem of my shirt. She pulled it up with a kind of urgency that matched the pounding rhythm of my heart, and I steeled myself.

The moment was here.

Taking the black fabric in my hands, I ripped it over my head and let it drop to the floor. My heart stuttered as I froze, unable to move. Unable to breathe, I stood before her.

The reminders of my past life lay exposed under her gaze—scars and bullet holes marring my skin amidst the elaborate American Samoan tribal tattoo covering my chest, shoulders, and upper arms.

I stilled completely, hyper-aware of every one of her featherlight touches. It was vulnerability unlike anything else, having her see the marks of my history—the physical evidence of my failures.

"God, Hunter," she whispered, her green eyes wide

with a mixture of shock and something I dared hope was desire. "You're... you've been through so much."

"Part of the job," I said gruffly.

But Brenna didn't flinch or turn away. Instead, she gazed at me as if I were some kind of warrior, not the broken man I saw in the mirror. Her acceptance was more intimate than any physical touch could be, and it sparked fierce possessiveness within me.

"Only part of who you are," she countered softly, tracing the edges of the ink that obscured some of my scars. Others lay bare and exposed on my abdomen, on my sides.

Brenna's gaze lingered on the jagged lines and puckered skin that marred my body. Her fingers danced across my scars with a reverence that left me breathless. My instinct was to cover up, to shield her from the ugliness of my past deeds. I opened and closed my mouth, trying to find words to explain, but she silenced me with her gentle touch.

"Shh," she breathed, placing a slender finger over my lips. Then she slowly slid it down my chin and across my shoulder to rest on the inked skin covering my wildly beating heart. Her kiss landed softly on the bullet hole near my rib, an act so tender it felt like absolution. "Don't," she murmured against my skin, her breath warm and comforting. "Don't be scared. Or worried."

When she glanced up, her eyes held an understanding and acceptance that words could never capture. An understanding of why I'd changed shirts so fast after our dive and why I never removed my shirt in public. As if she didn't see a man marked by violence. Her touch had the power to rewrite my history, and for a moment, I allowed myself to believe in the new story she offered.

"God, you're so beautiful," she whispered hoarsely, her desire fueling my own. "I need to touch you, Hunter."

Taking my hand, she tugged me toward the bed. The rest of our clothes fell away in a hasty trail, the urgency between us growing with each second. Standing naked before me, Brenna was a vision of perfection. Every curve, every dip of her body was a siren call, and I was utterly entranced. Hot blood roared through my body, screaming through my veins.

"I want you so bad, Hunter." Her voice was thick with need, and my body answered with an almost unbearable throbbing. She reached into the nightstand drawer to pull out a strip of condoms and laid them atop the nightstand.

"I want you more. So much more." My deep voice was barely more than a growl, but at least I could speak again. I covered her mouth with mine, the weight of my desire tightening my arms around her. She was so much smaller than me, delicate even. And for a moment, fear laced through the haze of my lust—fear of hurting her. But Brenna met my gaze squarely, her eyes blazing.

"Then show me," she challenged, reaching down to rub the hard length of me. A soft gasp escaped her as she did.

And in that breath, all my hesitation was obliterated. I walked her backward until the backs of her knees hit the edge of the bed, then raked the covers back. I pushed her onto her back. Crawling on top of her, I pinned her in place with my knees on either side of her legs.

I stared at her. She was ethereal, yet all mine. My hands began their worship of her body, tracing the swell of her breasts, drawing from her sharp intakes of breath and quiet moans that stoked the fire within me. I lowered to her breasts and ran my mouth over one in a long, leisurely swipe.

"Yes," Brenna gasped, her fingers tangling in my hair as I took one hard peak into my mouth, teasing it with my tongue before moving to lavish the same attention on its twin. Her back arched off the bed, pushing herself deeper against my mouth, seeking more contact, more of the pleasure I was determined to give her.

Her skin tasted like salt and sunshine. And dreams realized. Her hands never left me, roaming over the ridges of my shoulders and down the muscles of my back. Each touch ignited another spark within me, and I gave myself over to the fire. I slowly moved down her body, making each kiss a promise. She trembled beneath me.

At last, I lowered my head between her legs, and with the pent-up desire from over a decade of dreams, I tasted her.

Brenna's response was immediate, and a strangled cry escaped her lips as she clutched my head, guiding me with urgent hands. Her body writhed, and the room filled with the sound of her pleasure. I settled in, gripping the milky skin of her hips as she writhed. This was everything I'd ever dreamed of and more. She went wild with abandon, giving herself over to what I was doing to her. When her climax tore through her, she screamed my name. I drowned in every second of her sweet surrender.

As I climbed back up her body, her hands pushed against my chest, trying to roll me over. "Your turn," she panted.

But I shook my head, locking eyes with her as I refused to let her move me. "Later."

I grabbed the foil packet and ripped it open, then slowly rolled it on as she stared at me. My skin was hot, on fire as I positioned myself at her entrance.

I entered her slowly, hyperaware of her every reaction—every hitched breath, every flutter of her lashes. Slow. So agonizingly slow. Despite my size, she urged me deeper, wrapping her legs around my hips and pulling me into her warmth. The sensation was overwhelming, an exquisite pressure that had me gritting my teeth to keep control.

"More, Hunter. I need more," Brenna begged, her nails digging into my back as if she could pull me even closer.

Her words were my undoing, and at last I gave in completely, driving into her with a wild rhythm. Every fear I had about hurting her melted away with her encouragement, with the sheer pleasure that painted her face. Our bodies moved together, passion building until it bordered on pain—the kind of pain you'd beg for, just to feel alive.

Sweat glistened on Brenna's skin, and the air in the room felt alive. Every breath I took was laced with the salt of her sea-kissed flesh. She was wild and untamed beneath me, her passion matching my own fierce hunger.

And then her hands shoved against my shoulders— suddenly, forcefully—and I rolled off to lie flat on my back. Brenna went with me, then loomed over me like some gorgeous goddess claiming victory. She pinned my arms to the bed, her small hands surprisingly strong, her eyes blazing with a fire that could melt steel.

"My turn," she said in a deep, husky voice I couldn't get enough of.

It was a command, one I gladly obeyed. Her hips moved with a rhythm that was primal, harder and faster, as if she were racing against time itself. Her hands fanned out over my pecs, tracing the whorls of my tattoo, then the edges of my scars. I was completely spellbound.

"Oh my God, Brenna," I groaned.

The sight of her, taking everything I had to give and demanding more than I ever thought possible, sent a shudder through me that was so intense it almost hurt. Everything else fell away. There were no feuding families, no past mistakes, just Brenna and me and this all-consuming blaze between us.

I slid my hand between her legs, my fingers finding her tender flesh. I circled once, twice, building her pleasure until she was teetering on the edge. Then, with a few well-timed strokes, I sent her tumbling over. Her body clenched around me, and the world fractured into a thousand stars as we both shattered, our climaxes ripping through us in a maelstrom of sensation that left us gasping, clinging to each other as if we could somehow anchor ourselves in the eye of the storm we'd created.

Slowly, the world came back into focus, our breathing slowing as we returned from wherever we'd been flung. I pulled Brenna into my arms, her body still trembling slightly against mine. Her head rested on my chest, and the rapid beat of her heart slowly synchronized with my own. Our limbs entwined in a tangled mess of satisfaction and contentment.

"Are you okay?" I asked, my voice hoarse with lingering desire and a trace of concern. I brushed a damp strand of hair from her forehead, needing to see her face, to reassure myself I hadn't been too much for her. "Did I hurt you?"

"Maybe a little, but I loved every minute of it," she murmured against my skin, her lips tracing a path along my collarbone. "How about you?"

"I'm not sure I've ever felt better than I do right now."

I marveled at how something that had always seemed forbidden could feel so undeniably right. With Brenna in my arms, every doubtful thought was drowned out by the undeniable truth of what had just happened. We were two pieces of a puzzle that the universe had stubbornly kept apart, now finally interlocking in a way that felt like... destiny.

Chapter Seventeen

Brenna

AS I NESTLED in the sheets with Hunter's arms around me, the wonderful soreness between my legs made everything even more real. The ceiling fan above us stirred the air, carrying a soft breeze to dry the sweat on our skin. He had just unraveled me in ways I didn't know were possible. My head spun at just the sight of him, not only his raw physical beauty, but the map of scars on his skin. I understood that few people knew they existed, yet he'd trusted me enough to bare himself. And I realized that act was every bit as intimate as what we had just shared.

"Did you get all those at once?" My voice was soft as I traced a finger over a particularly wicked scar that snaked its way across his abdomen.

"No, it was over many missions." His words were heavy, like they carried the gravity of each memory. He gently folded his hand over mine and laid it on his chest. His gaze drifted to a bullet hole near his rib, and tightness crept into his jaw. "But this one... and some others were from one mission that went south fast." Shadows passed over his face as if he'd left a part of himself on those foreign battlefields.

"Something went wrong?" My heart clenched for the pain he'd endured, for the stories etched into his flesh that he hadn't shared with me. Yet.

"Yeah."

"I understand if you can't talk about it, but I'd like to hear," I said softly. Not pushing too hard but offering him the space to unfold before me if he chose to.

He stared out the window toward the mangroves that fringed Dove Key. "Her name was Ayesha. She was a young widow with two kids—a boy and a girl. Both smart as whips. She taught English secretly because, well, you know how it is over there. The Taliban... they would have killed her for it."

A knot tightened in my stomach. The idea of children being dragged into such horror felt like a punch to the gut. I couldn't imagine the strength it took to defy such odds, to cling to the belief that education could be a candle in the darkness.

"I gave Ayesha some books to use in her classroom, and we became friends. I told her... I'd protect her and her kids." He stopped to clear his throat, his hand unconsciously stroking my back as if to soothe us both. "We were working to get them out. My unit. We thought the Taliban were still days away. Myles, Garrett, and I went into town for something to eat, thinking we'd be back long before anything happened."

He hadn't spoken much about the two men who worked with him, but his words confirmed my intuition that they had all served together. The hard knot in my gut twisted further. "And something did happen?"

"Yes. All hell broke loose." He swallowed hard, the

Adam's apple in his throat bobbing with the effort. "The sound of gunfire rattled through the streets—it's not something you ever forget. We dropped everything and ran back. The Taliban had already overrun the town, and we engaged every step of the way. Thank God we never went anywhere unarmed. Some shrapnel hit me on the way. On my upper back."

I rubbed my fingers, remembering the ridges of his skin as I'd stroked across that broad back.

He sighed, a sound that weighed a thousand pounds. Then his body tensed as if the memory was a physical blow. "When we got there... It was too late."

"Oh no." A numb wave rolled over me, leaving goose bumps in its wake.

He nodded, a pained expression crossing his features. "Ayesha and her kids... They lay there in their own home, lifeless, and I just..." He moved his hand, his fingers tracing the bullet hole near his rib—the scar I'd traced with my lips not so long before, learning the history etched into his skin. "I completely lost it. Went after the Taliban still around with everything I had. It wasn't about orders or duty anymore. I didn't really care what happened to me. It was personal."

"Revenge?" I asked softly.

"Justice," he corrected, a hollow breath escaping him. "But in the end, what does it matter? They were still gone. And I took another bullet, this time for nothing."

"Nothing?" I echoed, frowning deeply. "You were trying to protect them."

"Key word—trying." Hunter's eyes met mine, filled with a sorrow that twisted everything inside me in knots. "I failed them, just like I failed Evan."

"Your brother's accident wasn't your fault," I said firmly.

Everyone knew the story. It had been an accident, sure. But Hunter had instigated the whole thing and obviously never forgiven himself.

He shook his head, his expression unreadable. "Doesn't change how I feel. I couldn't save them, and Evan was paralyzed for a while because of me. It's why I pushed you away, Brenna. Why I'm still not sure that us"—he gestured vaguely between our entwined bodies—"that this is such a good idea."

"Because you think you're what. Cursed?" I challenged, refusing to accept his self-condemnation. "That you bring disaster wherever you go?"

"It's crossed my mind," he admitted, staring with ancient eyes at the ceiling.

"Then stop." The words came out more forcefully than I intended. "Those things happened *to* you, not because of you. You're just as deserving of love and forgiveness as anyone else, Hunter."

"Sure," he mumbled.

"It's true," I insisted, turning his chin to make him look at me. Even though I felt like my heart was cracking in half. "You've been carrying these burdens alone for far too long. Let me help."

He looked at me then, really looked at me, his deep, dark eyes searching mine for something he couldn't seem to find within himself. "Why do you care so much?"

"Because," I whispered back, pressing my forehead to his. "It kills me to see you like this."

He closed his eyes and pressed a gentle kiss to my temple. I traced a stylized inked turtle on his shoulder, knowing that in his heart, he was still miles away on a battlefield that he couldn't escape. I reached out, my fingers tracing the line of the elaborate tattoo, a gesture meant to tether him back to the present, away from the haunting memories.

"Look at us," I said, allowing a small smile to dance on my lips, hoping it might coax one onto his. "A Coleridge and a Markham, and we're a whole lot more than friends at this point. That means anything's possible."

Hunter let out a groan that seemed to come from deep within. And finally—finally—a wry smile raised his lips. "Not when our families find out."

"Your family..." I hesitated for a moment before plunging ahead. "Do you think they'll hate me? And me being with you?"

He lifted a hand, tenderly brushing a strand of hair away from my face. "No. My family thinks the feud is pretty stupid. And they've learned firsthand that Coleridges have a good side—after that fiasco with Ben and the fact that he was innocent."

I bit my lip, thinking of my own family. "Speaking of Ben. My brothers..." My stomach tightened at the thought. "Hunter, there's a good chance they'll want to kill you."

That slow smile I loved so much stretched Hunter's full mouth, and a devilish glint shone in his eyes. "Is that right? I'd like to see them try."

And at the thought of any of my brothers, all tall, solidly built men who never shied away from conflict, taking on this gigantic Special Forces Marine, my own smile rose. Laughing, I shook my head.

In the dim light that filtered through the curtains, I saw not the fearsome former Marine or the tormented man scarred by war and loss, but Hunter—the man whose resilience was woven tightly with vulnerability, whose strength was matched by curiosity. The man who could quote Hemingway, Shakespeare, and Sun Zhu with ease.

"Maybe I'd better try to talk them out of picking any fights with you." I nudged him playfully with my foot.

We settled into a comfortable silence. As I snuggled closer to Hunter's warmth, my mind wandered back to his harrowing tale, to the woman who had been more than just another soul caught in the crossfire. The schoolteacher... a widow with two children. My heart ached at the memory of the sorrow that had laced his voice. "Ayesha. Was she the one? The woman you said you were once in love with?"

He exhaled a long breath, and for a moment, I thought he might refuse to answer. But then he met my gaze, his eyes back to being a guarded fortress. "No," he said simply, and there was a depth to his denial that begged for no further questions.

I nodded, letting the subject drop, though part of me wanted to delve deeper into the mystery. If the woman from his story wasn't his lost love, then it made me wonder even more who had captured his heart.

And why she wasn't by his side now.

Chapter Eighteen

Hunter

I LAY STILL, not yet willing to open my eyes and let go of the dreamy haze between sleep and wakefulness. That's when I noticed the difference—the gentle weight of an arm draped over my waist, the soft press of her body against mine. After a week of being together, I still wasn't used to it. My senses sharpened as the sweet scent of citrus and vanilla filled my nostrils. Brenna's hair was like a cloud of tropical paradise fanned out across my pillow.

A smile tugged at my lips, involuntary and utterly genuine. It was a smile born of a gratification so deep that it settled into my bones. A contentment borne from baring my soul to her and finding acceptance. Understanding and compassion. I wasn't convinced her faith was justified or wise, but I felt too damn good to worry about it. The warmth from her skin seeped into me, an itch I still couldn't believe had been scratched—though not enough.

I wasn't sure it would ever be enough.

The thought sparked heat in me, eagerness to reignite

the passion we'd discovered within the tangled sheets. But then again, if memory served, yesterday—and last night— had left us both more than a little spent. I couldn't help but laugh silently. We'd settled into a new routine, getting used to each other. Knox hadn't made any appearances, increasing my gut feeling he was out of the picture and out of the area. Good riddance to the bastard. Our separate workdays transitioned to evening hours in each other's arms and long nights full of whispered words and fevered touches. Incredible didn't even begin to cover it.

Now, with morning light filtering through the blinds, her chest rose and fell, her hair a wild tangle of chestnut waves across my pillow. I shifted slightly, pulling her closer, feeling the need to keep her near.

"Morning," Brenna murmured, her eyelids fluttering open. She stretched like a cat before cozying up to me again.

"Hey." My voice was hoarse with sleep and something deeper. I looked into her eyes, filled with a mixture of affection and a hint of playfulness. "How are you feeling this morning?"

She smiled as she shifted slightly, the warmth of her body against mine making me never want to get up. "Absolutely wonderful."

Her response was like music to my ears, and a surge of warmth spread through me. I reached out to tuck a strand of her hair behind her ear, my touch lingering as I murmured, "I'm glad. I want you to feel good, always."

"Well, you've certainly shown you know how to do that."

We had been existing in a sort of secret limbo for the last week, not proclaiming our new passion or status to anyone. She'd even managed to duck out of my place before Myles or Garrett showed up. But it couldn't last forever.

"We have to figure out how this is going to work with our families."

Brenna shrugged and nestled back into my embrace. "Yeah, I know. It's just been so nice having our own forbidden secret. Let's worry about everyone else some other time."

"Have you forgotten we live in a small town?" I poked her side lightly.

Giggling, she nodded, her eyes alight with mischief. "I know, but let them mind their own business for a little longer." Finally exiting the bed, Brenna slipped into her clothes from yesterday—her movements deliberate and unapologetically sensual. She shot me a long side-eye to let me know she could feel my gaze on her.

I gave her a deep, approving rumble in return, then reluctantly rose to pull on clothes for my own day ahead. I looked across the room at the empty pet bed, then at the door I'd left slightly open. "I wonder if Pedro slept in the living room last night."

"Maybe we made too much noise, and it bugged him." She laughed, the sound like music, and teased me about not being as tough as I looked. "Let's go check on your baby."

I refused to rise to the bait and padded out of my room. We entered the living room and found Pedro sprawled on the sunny windowsill, his green eyes fixed on some distant point only he could see. But his relief was immediate when he bounded over, his purrs filling the room as he greeted us both with headbutts and figure-eights around our legs. Refusing to admit to the warmth filling me as I greeted him, I merely grumbled that at least he hadn't shredded anything out here.

Brenna bent down and picked him up, then pressed her cheek to his side. Pedro purred, stretching out to maximize the pleasure of her touch. "You keep an eye on this guy for me, okay?"

"Are you talking to me or the cat?" I asked with a smirk.

Setting him back down, she stuck her tongue out at me. "Either or, smart-ass." Then she gathered her purse from the chair where she'd tossed it last night. "I'd better get back to my place and get ready for work."

"Nearly eight a.m., huh?" I noted, surprised by how late we'd slept. We'd been lost in our own world, but reality was quick to stake its claim.

"Time flies when you're... well, you know." Brenna winked at me.

"Breaking new ground," I supplied, grinning despite the bittersweet edge to the morning's farewell. "I've got a baseball game tonight, by the way."

"With you there, how could your team lose? I know several of the guys from Dove Key talked about joining the league, but they couldn't get the details ironed out in time."

We reached the bottom of the stairs just as Myles strolled into view. His timing was impeccable—or terrible, depending on how you looked at it.

"Well, good morning, Brenna," Myles drawled, mischief dancing in his eyes as he caught sight of her. Though he had been covering Calypso Key when Garrett and I shadowed her, he was well versed in the particulars. And he also knew damn well that the case was over.

"Morning," she replied, nonchalant as ever, and gave him a breezy wave as she headed for the back door.

I pinned Myles with a hard look that hopefully said *later* and followed her outside. After I pulled the door shut, I gathered her close. My hands found the familiar curve of her waist, and I lowered my mouth to hers. And not a sweet little peck either. My tongue parted her lips and skated over the top of her mouth. I didn't want it to end.

"See you later," she murmured against my lips before pulling away with a soft smile.

"Later." I rubbed a finger back and forth across my forehead as she disappeared down the alley back toward her shop. A strange mix of emotions filled me. The deep contentment was still there, but worry and guilt rose to compete like they always did when I had a moment to myself to think about what the hell I was doing.

As I stepped back into the building, my eyes immediately caught sight of Myles, his tall frame draped lazily against his desk. A sly grin played on his lips as he motioned toward a chair next to him. I couldn't fault his work ethic— either his or Garrett's. Dammit.

"Coffee?" he offered, pouring me a cup from the steaming pot on his desk.

"Thanks," I muttered, taking the cup from Myles as I settled into the chair next to him. The rich aroma of freshly brewed coffee filled the space between us, but my mind was still lingering on that final kiss with Brenna.

"Didn't you two look cozy, tiptoeing down the stairs in the morning. I thought the Brenna thing was over."

"Things change." I shrugged, trying to keep my voice casual.

The Brenna thing will never be over.

"Obviously." Myles raised his eyebrows, a teasing lilt to his words.

"What happened between us is new," I stated firmly as I locked eyes with him. "And we're not ready for it to be public knowledge. So keep your mouth shut."

"Gotcha, boss." Myles held up his hands in mock surrender. "Mums the word."

I nodded, satisfied, but as I made my way upstairs to my apartment, the weight of our secret hung heavy in the air. There was no telling how long we could keep this quiet in a town where whispers traveled faster than the wind. But for now, Brenna and I were a silent vow, a promise written in the sand.

I needed to get ready for work, to shift my focus from the softness of Brenna's skin to the real world. After showering, I stood with a towel wrapped around my waist and trimmed my beard. My eyes caught on my tattoo. It was such a part of me that I hardly noticed it anymore. As the black designs radiated outward across my pectorals, they morphed into stylized waves and sea patterns with distinctive arches and hook shapes reminiscent of ocean swells and curling waves. On my shoulders, two detailed sea turtles had been meticulously tattooed, their inky shells comprised of an infinite maze of spines and natural textures that continued in sweeps to my elbows.

I thought of the new life I was trying to start here, the bonds I was attempting to reforge. And my deep desire to protect Brenna, even if Knox's threat had diminished. A bittersweet smile rose to my face as I absently ran my fingers over one pectoral, a memorial inked on me permanently. My gaze drifted toward the ceiling. My friend might have been gone for a long time, but I had to think he'd approve.

Chapter Nineteen

Hunter

I STEPPED up to the plate, gripping the bat with hands calloused from more labor than this leisurely evening game. The Sugarloaf Key Barracudas were on our turf, and despite the mostly friendly rivalry, I was determined to crack the cool façade of their pitcher, Tom. So far, I was oh-for-two. The Barracudas were first in the league, largely thanks to the arm of this pitcher and their power hitter, Brent. The Stingrays were only one game back in the standings, making tonight all the more important.

"Come on, Hunter!" Stella's voice punctuated the hum of the crowd.

I tuned everything out and focused only on the approaching ball. It hurtled toward me, and I tensed. It looked high and I took the pitch.

"Strike!" The umpire's call sliced through my concentration like a knife through water.

My jaw tightened. No way I was letting the next one pass. As the pitcher wound up again, I coiled like a spring.

The pitch came—low and fast, a blur against the backdrop of the fading day. My swing met it with a satisfying crack, sending a sharp line drive whizzing toward left field. For a moment, hope soared. But then the Barracudas' shortstop snagged the ball with a dive, popping up to throw me out at first. Frustration filled me as I trotted off the field.

"Nice hit. Just bad luck," Evan called from where he stood in the dugout, arms folded across his chest.

"Thanks," I grumbled as I put on my catcher's gear, offering him a nod. I'd been on pins and needles all game, trying not to make a big deal of him being there.

Despite everyone on our team knowing it was a huge, monumental deal.

We transitioned to defense, and I crouched behind home plate. Evan stood tall at first base, his figure casting a long shadow in the infield as he scooped up a grounder.

Gabe was on the mound, and the Barracudas were ahead three to one. With each pitch, Gabe strained, his arm losing the fight against fatigue. When a towering pop fly headed Evan's way, he instantly moved into position, then caught it without a hint of strain. Facing the other way, Gabe winced, rubbing his shoulder.

"Nice catch," I said over the cheers, clapping my mitt in quiet support.

"Thanks," Evan replied. His eyes scanned the field, taking in every detail.

The next inning rolled around quickly, and it was Evan's turn to bat. He walked up to the plate with a nonchalance that belied the tension of the moment. He wasn't even limping, though I suspected that easy stroll cost him some effort. Tom wound up and threw a ball that came in high—close to Evan's head. He didn't even flinch. Just stepped out of the batter's box as the umpire yelled, "Ball!"

Maia laughed next to me, not a little pride in it. The next throw had the pitcher releasing a fastball that seemed to scream through the air with the fury of a hundred storms.

Evan swung.

The crack of the bat meeting the ball echoed like a shot across the field. Time slowed as everyone's heads craned to follow the trajectory of the baseball as it soared high and far over the outfield fence. A solo home run.

"Yeah!" I shouted, joining in the eruption of cheers from the Stingrays' bench. We were only one run behind now, with the ninth inning looming ahead.

We held the Barracudas at bay in the top of the ninth, our defense as tight as the knots that tangled my insides. And despite Gabe being a little wilder on the mound, he held them. Pride in my family surged through me. Excitement buzzed through the team as we took our last chance at bat. I toed the chalked box for the fourth time. The last time. The first pitch hurtled toward me, and it looked outside. I held my swing.

"Strike!" The umpire's call pierced the tense silence that had settled over the crowd, and I shot him a dirty look. Probably in his mid-twenties, the kid pursed his lips together but held firm.

"Shake it off, Hunter!" Maia yelled from the dugout. The weight of every gaze was fixed upon me.

Determined, I steadied myself for the next pitch. My hands gripped the bat, the tape pressing into my skin. When the ball came, I swung with all I had but only met air. A swing and a miss.

"Strike two!"

"Goddamn it," I muttered under my breath, stepping out of the batter's box for a moment. My heart hammered against my ribs as I tried to focus, to find that sliver of calm.

I stepped back in, Tom already winding up for what could be the final blow. And then it came—a blur of white heading straight at me.

Another swing. Another miss.

"Strike three! You're out! Game over."

The word *over* knifed through the evening, severing the thread of hope we'd clung to. We lost by one.

"Good game," Wyatt, who was Maia's husband and our center fielder, said quietly as he passed me, his hand briefly touching my shoulder.

"Thanks."

"Next time, Hunter," Stella said, patting me on the back before she joined the others collecting their gear. Her smile was encouraging, but the disappointment in her eyes mirrored my own. Resting the bat on my shoulder, I made my way over to the dugout.

"Hey, Evan," Maia called out, her voice slicing through the murmur of disappointed chatter and the clanking of metal cleats against concrete. "Maybe you should be the one coaching the team, not me."

Evan laughed, the sound somehow both lighthearted and tinged with melancholy. "You're doing a great job, Maia. No need for a last-minute substitution." His eyes didn't quite meet hers as he shoved his glove into his duffel bag.

I turned away from them, my gaze settling on Manuel. As the driver of the resort dive boat, *Shark Bait*, the guy could read the ocean like nobody's business, but now his gaze was fixed on Gabe, who was nursing his pitching arm with a wince.

"Think you might need a break next game?" Manuel's concern was evident even in his casual tone. And he'd pitched in the rec league before.

"Maybe," Gabe grunted, rotating his shoulder with a grimace. "If this doesn't shape up, the mound is yours."

The idea of Manuel stepping onto the pitcher's mound brought a round of good-natured encouragement, but wary glances kept darting toward Evan. He was the elephant in the room—or rather, the hurricane whose presence had changed the dynamics of our team massively.

Then Liv appeared, having made her way in from the outfield. Her approach shifted the atmosphere, drawing Evan's attention. As she reached him, her arm looped around his waist. Evan's shoulders dropped, and the stiffness in his frame melted away under her touch.

"Ready to go?" she asked, her voice low and soothing.

"I am."

And there it was—a smile. It was small, almost hesitant, but genuine. The kind of smile that showed up when guards were let down and comfort seeped in. They walked off toward Liv's Tahoe. I watched them go, feeling a curious mixture of relief and envy. In her company, Evan was different, lighter. He'd found his safe harbor in Liv, someone who helped him navigate his stormy past and anchored him in the present.

I hung back a bit, scanning the now quiet field. After tossing my mitt into my old green duffel bag, I called out my goodbyes. "Take care of that arm, Gabe," I added, clapping him on the back before heading to my SUV. The night air was cooler now and a breeze drifted off the ocean. It held the promise of rain, or maybe that was just the cloud of disappointment following me.

As I drove home, my mind turned to Brenna. I wanted to see her again. Hell, right now. But she'd just broken up with a guy who was more or less stalking her. Nope—I wasn't going to push her.

I tried to wash away the defeat in the shower and ate a quick meal. Settling onto the couch, Pedro hopped into my lap. As I absently stroked his soft fur, I pulled out my phone, hesitating for a moment. My fingers hovered over the keyboard as I weighed calling or texting. Playing it cool seemed like the better strategy, so I sent a text.

> Hunter: Lost the game tonight.

She replied almost immediately, her words lighting up my screen. And, damn it, my mood too.

> Brenna: Sorry to hear that! How are you feeling?

> Hunter: I hate losing, even rec games. How was your day?

> Brenna: You're always a winner in my book. My day was good. Busy. Sold a big boxed set today. Limited edition.

Her response was prompt, warm. Not someone who didn't want to hear from me.

> Hunter: Sounds like your day was more successful than mine.

> Brenna: Success is relative. I can sell a boxed set anytime. But the baseball season isn't much longer, so losses hurt. It's my job to cheer you up!

Her words made me smile, and I could picture the playful glint in her eyes as she typed them out. It was easy banter, a comfortable rhythm we seemed to fall into effortlessly.

> Hunter: Who knew you were such a baseball fan?

> Brenna: Nah. I'm not particularly into sports. Just trying to boost the morale of a certain tall, dark, and handsome slugger I know.

I grinned at her response. The evening stretched out, only the occasional purr of Pedro breaking the quiet of my living room. As our conversation flowed back and forth, I found myself relaxing, the tension from the game slowly dissipating.

> Hunter: Thanks for being my cheerleader tonight.

> Brenna: Always. Someone's got to keep you from getting too down on yourself.

> Hunter: I never feel down when I'm with you. I'd better let you go.

> Brenna: Aw! Sweet talker. Night.

There was something both comforting and exhilarating about this easy exchange of texts. In a way, it felt like we were building something, brick by digital brick. Small experiences shared, little connections made. Even if our families' histories tried to dictate otherwise, here we were, two people tentatively stepping over a century-old line drawn in the sand.

Setting my phone on the couch, I picked up the Clive

Cussler book from the coffee table and thumbed to where I'd left off. Adventure waited between the pages, a welcome distraction from the ache of losing the game, and thoughts of how much I wanted to go over to Brenna's. Thirty minutes slipped by, Cussler's words painting vivid scenes of underwater exploits and treacherous escapades. Pedro had fallen asleep on my thighs.

The sound of my text tone jolted the stillness, startling both me and Pedro. He gave a disgruntled meow as I reached for my phone, eager to read another message from Brenna.

Instead, the screen lit up with an unknown number. As I read the mysterious message, the air in my lungs froze. My entire focus lasered down to the words on the screen.

> (305) 222-6395: You need to tighten up your stance and not take so many pitches. You're so tall, your strike zone is as big as the Grand Canyon. You're never going to draw a walk, especially in a rec league.

Numbness washed over me as I read the text. Then read it again. And again. Only one person could dismantle my batting technique with such precision. Only one person could have sent that text.

Evan.

What the hell should I say?

How should one respond when someone reached for the first time in fourteen years? While at boot camp as a miserable, guilt-ridden eighteen-year-old, I'd deleted Evan's information from my contacts. But who else could it be? Finally, I sent back a response, my thumbs numb and clumsy.

> Hunter: Thanks for the advice. Maia might be a good sister, but she's not the best hitting coach.

My text floated away into the digital ether, carrying with it another huge step in mending the chasm between brothers. Pedro sat up on my lap, sensing my change in mood.

"Come on, come on, Evan." After a pause, another text came through.

> (305) 222-6395: No, but she's good at building a team. So is Stella.

I snorted, an unexpected laugh escaping me despite the tension coiling in my gut. That was typical Evan, always giving credit where it was due. And he wasn't wrong—Stella could rally a group of cats into a swimming race if she put her mind to it. This time I answered more quickly, more confidently. A challenge wrapped in a veiled request.

> Hunter: Maybe the Stingrays need a new hitting coach.

I stared at the small ellipsis that indicated he was typing a response, my heartbeat pounding in my ears. The brief lull felt like being underwater, suspended between two worlds—the surface where everything was light and clear, and the depths where things got murky and unpredictable. My fingers tightened around the phone, its edges digging into my palms. The text bubble popped up again, and I braced myself, ready for whatever Evan threw my way.

> (305) 222-6395: If you need some pointers, I might be able to help you out.

Breath exploded from my lungs as I bolted upright. Screeching, Pedro leaped from my lap. I ignored him, hope flaring in my chest like a beacon.

> Hunter: When and where?

> (305) 222-6395: Let's have a casual batting practice in the garden next to the Big House. Can you come Saturday morning? Dad kept my old batting cage, believe it or not.

> Hunter: I believe it. I'll be there.

Nothing happened for a solid minute, a minute heavy with portent. Pedro cautiously jumped back on the couch and sat with his tail curled around his white paws. I tapped out a final text, adding one confirmatory word at the end.

> Hunter: Thanks, Evan.

The answer came immediately.

> (305) 222-6395: You're welcome.

The phone slipped from my hands, landing on the coffee table with a clatter that spooked Pedro. Once again, he leaped off the couch. This time, he shot me a disgruntled, narrow look before stalking off toward my bedroom. I barely noticed, my head falling back against the wall, and both hands running through my hair.

Evan's words, so simple and casual, were anything but. They rattled around in my head, a chaotic blend of past and future colliding. Baseball had always been our common ground, and now it might just be the thing to bring us back to each other. Picking up my phone again, I opened our conversation and tapped the icon at the top. In place of the bare digits of his phone number, I entered a first name. Nothing else was needed.

Evan.

I could already feel the trimmed grass of the lawn Evan and I had once practiced on as kids, smell the leather of my glove, hear the crack of the bat—a sound that spelled out hope in the only common language Evan and I truly spoke anymore.

For now, that was enough.

Chapter Twenty

Brenna

MY SHOP WAS its usual refuge of much-loved books and fresh coffee, but I barely registered the scents drifting around me. My actions were mechanical as I shelved a group of new non-fiction titles. Hunter Markham had infiltrated my thoughts with the stealth of a shadow.

I could almost feel the press of his lips, the rugged terrain of his scars beneath my fingertips. And the way he'd groan my name in a private confession between entwined bodies. The overwhelming feeling of him inside my body, inside my mouth. Our moments weren't solely forged in passion. I also loved our quiet interludes—two silent figures pressed together on the couch, each lost in a separate world of printed words yet somehow together at the same time.

I forcibly shook my head, hoping to tether my wandering mind. I began gathering the books for this afternoon's book club meeting, arranging them in a neat stack beside the cash register.

The bell above the door chimed its familiar tune. Ben

strode into the bookstore with purpose. His expression tightened and his brows lowered as he scanned the room, like he was searching for someone other than me.

"Everything okay?" I asked, watching him closely. His light-brown hair was ruffled as if he'd run his hands through it.

Ben's gaze landed on me briefly before he continued his search. "Just wanted to stop by."

A frown drew my lips down. He was too busy to stop by without reason. "Need help finding a book?" I asked with an arched brow.

He didn't smile at my pointed joke. "Hardly. Brenna, I've heard a rumor. I came by to see if it was true."

"And what would that be?" I had a suspicion of what he was about to say, and my heart began a steady drumbeat of nerves.

"That you're involved with Hunter Markham. They even said you've moved in with him." His big-brother concern etched lines into his forehead. Ben had always been protective, and it looked like he was preparing himself to step into that role again.

I stalled as I gathered my thoughts. Now that the inevitable moment was here, I found myself wanting to deflect the confrontation. "The thing with Knox got a bit messy, and Hunter offered his place as a safe haven. Only for a few days. It's all settled now, and I'm back home."

Ben narrowed his eyes. "Just like that?"

I sighed, bracing for impact. "We aren't living together, Ben. But we are... romantically involved."

"Dammit," he said heavily, lacing his fingers on top of his head. "That's what I was afraid of."

Anger lanced through me. "Why, exactly? Because he's a Markham?"

Dropping his arms, he crossed the floor toward me and leaned against a bookcase. "That's part of it, sure. I remember that you two were friends a long time ago. But, Brenna, a lot of stories are floating around about that guy. I've heard people say he used to be a hired mercenary, even worked as a contract man in Miami."

I scoffed and rolled my eyes. "That's ridiculous."

"Is it?" He arched an eyebrow, his eyes not leaving mine. "How much do you know about him? Hunter's got a lot of history that no one knows the details of. History that might come back to haunt him. I'm more concerned about it affecting anyone close to him."

"I know plenty, Ben," I said quietly. "And I'm old enough to choose who I'm involved with." Images flashed through my mind of that tortured confession of Ayesha and her two children. Were those the actions of some soulless killer? Next, my brain tried to remind me about how Hunter had all but admitted he'd gone berserk in the aftermath. I tried to push that line of thought aside, but my inner voice got in one final shot.

Are you pushing it away because you're afraid of what he's capable of? Or that he'd had such a deep connection to that Afghani woman?

I firmly took hold of my thoughts and told them to shut the hell up. Then I spread my arms wide. "Look, we just got together, okay? Please don't spread this around the family. If Hunter and I work out, they'll find out soon enough."

"I'm sure they will," he said. "I'm not the only one with friends, you know. But I'll keep your little affair to myself for now."

"Thank you."

I tried to put some steel in my spine and was determined

to deny the fluttering in my stomach. I was the one hell-bent on ending the century-plus feud. Except that now the reality of my family's reaction to Hunter was more unsettling than when it had been a purely theoretical concept. I'd just gotten out of a lousy relationship, but was I only making the same mistake again? Hunter was certainly a complicated man, but I knew the heart that beat inside him.

Didn't I?

Ben stepped closer to hug me. "I need to get going. Call me if that guy needs an ass kicking. I'd have been happy to step in and pummel your last boyfriend, you know. Speak up if you need help, Brenna."

A smile broke across my face as I enjoyed being in the familiar and slightly sweaty embrace of my big brother. And at how Ben was always willing to stand up for me. "I know. And I know I have a tendency to be a little too independent."

After he stepped out into the warm afternoon, I shook off my unease and turned back to prepping for the book club meeting. I needed to leave soon, and the distraction would be welcome.

THE MONTHLY MEETINGS of our Sips and Pages club were held in the residential district of Dove Key. A quaint bungalow with a white picket fence was the venue of our undeclared leader and usual host, though I toyed with the idea of starting my own club at the shop. Liv and April, with their infectious smiles, greeted me warmly as I joined them and set my box of next month's novels next to the couch. The air was filled with anticipation as Liv and I poured ourselves a glass of crisp white wine and April grabbed a bottle of water.

April's radiant smile reached her eyes, making them twinkle as she settled comfortably on the couch between Liv and me. A broad smile rose on my face at the shirt stretching across her broad abdomen. "You look beautiful, April. Seems like the pregnancy is progressing well."

A rosy hue spread across her cheeks. "Thank you. I'm hanging in there, and I'm actually looking forward to the birth just so I won't be pregnant anymore! We're so excited for this little one to arrive."

Liv's eyes danced as she leaned forward from April's other side and studied her friend. "You're positively glowing! Motherhood suits you."

And in that moment, all thoughts of Hunter and his possible past life faded away. We were just three friends, sharing in each other's joys.

"Have you and Evan set a date yet?" I asked Liv, glancing at the diamond ring on her finger.

Liv laughed and shook her head. "Not yet. I'm getting Sweet Dreams Mini off the ground at the resort, so it's been a challenge finding a date. And Evan is really serious about playing for the Stingrays—I don't want to distract him. Him playing baseball again is a huge step." She shrugged both shoulders. "We're not in any rush."

As Liv talked about her and Evan's plans, I contemplated telling them about Hunter and me. It was tempting to share the secret.

I was saved from having to make a decision when the meeting got underway about this month's book, a best friend's brother romance. As we discussed the novel, a spirited debate on the protagonist's choices animated the room. I tried to immerse myself in their dialogue, offering insights while sipping my wine. But beneath the surface, I felt like a swimmer caught in a rip current.

Liv flipped her long, curly hair over one shoulder and pointed to a highlighted section of text. "This part, where she realizes it's always been him. Didn't that just melt your heart?"

A collective sigh floated around the circle, but inside, my stomach knotted. It hit too close to home. Hunter and I had been such good friends once, and now we were so much more. But did I really know the man I was involved with?

"Uh, yeah," I muttered, fumbling with the edge of my bookmark. "It was really something."

"Come on, Brenna, you're usually gushing over these scenes," April teased.

"Guess this one wasn't quite swoony enough for me." I deflected with humor, hoping they'd miss the tightness in my voice.

As conversation swirled, I sank deeper into the couch, and the weight of my secret, forbidden love felt like a stone in my pocket. With each passing comment about fictional romances, my thoughts focused on Hunter. How he growled my name, like it was torn from something deep inside him, and the dangerous past Ben had hinted at.

"Can you imagine keeping a love like that hidden?" April pondered aloud, unknowingly skewering me with her words.

"Impossible," Pam, the leader of our little group, agreed emphatically. "Love like that can't be contained. That's one of the things I didn't like about the book." Then she held up her glass and laughed. "Then again, that was the whole point, wasn't it? That she tried to deny that this A-list movie star could actually love her. But he did."

As the meeting wrapped up, I handed out next month's

book. The club members dispersed, and I said goodbye to my two friends as I headed toward my car. The drive back to my building was short, and Dove Key's residential streets were bathed in a soft late-afternoon light that cast shadows across my windshield. I always closed up the shop early on book club afternoons, so my shop was dark as I parked in the alley.

As I stepped inside, I gasped, my hand flying up to clutch my neck.

Hunter leaned against the wall with his arms casually folded, completely motionless. His tall, broad silhouette was outlined by the light shining through the picture window like a scene straight out of one of our steamy novels.

"God, Hunter! You scared me."

"Sorry, didn't mean to," he said, though the half-grin tugging at his lips told a different story.

I couldn't help but roll my eyes, feeling silly for letting him catch me off guard. As my heart got over the shock, my body came alive with a different emotion. "I guess I should've changed that entry code you gave me."

"Guess you should have," he agreed, pushing himself away from the wall and closing the distance between us with slow, deliberate steps. "But maybe I'd just figure out the new one." His voice was like crushed velvet, and I was helpless to resist it. Him.

Heat radiated off him in his all-black ensemble. He looked like pure temptation crafted from shadows, and I found myself helplessly drifting toward him as if some magnetic force beyond my control pulled me.

"Miss me?" His voice reverberated through the empty space between us.

"Maybe I never thought about you," I murmured, but my tone betrayed my breathlessness.

Our lips met, and the world melted away into a deep kiss that swept me away. A kiss that was reckless, consuming, and everything I shouldn't want—but did. With Hunter, every touch was an adventure, each caress a discovery I never knew I needed.

Was this man my savior or my inevitable downfall? The thought teased at the edge of my consciousness as we broke apart, gasping for air. I remembered daring him to burn me to cinders, and the truth was, I still wanted that. I wanted the all-consuming blaze, the intensity, the passion that threatened to ruin me.

"Come upstairs," I murmured, my hand finding his as I led him toward the staircase.

Halfway up, our restraint crumbled again, and our bodies collided in another desperate kiss. His hands were in my hair, on my waist, everywhere at once, sending waves of desire through me as he pinned me against the wall.

"God, Brenna," he breathed against my lips, the urgency in his voice matching the pounding of my heart. "I couldn't stay away. I had to come over and wait for you."

And then I was being lifted, Hunter's arms strong and unyielding as he carried me effortlessly the rest of the way. We reached my apartment, and he swung open the door. As it clicked shut behind us, I was acutely aware of the precipice we stood upon—of how easily this man could shatter me. Yet, with every breath-stealing kiss, every searing touch, I was more than ready to dance among the shards if it meant feeling alive like this.

Chapter Twenty-One

Hunter

I'M A BASTARD.

The morning sun was still gentle as I pounded the pavement, but the relatively cool breeze couldn't blow away the thought repeating through my head. Or its truth. The rhythmic thud of my running shoes against the concrete sidewalk was a steady drumbeat in the quiet residential district of Dove Key. I'd already put in two hours at the gym —lifting until my muscles screamed—but this run weighed me down more than any dumbbell ever could. No matter how hard I pushed my pace, I couldn't outrun the fact that Brenna deserved so much more than I could give her.

Guilt gnawed at me with hungry, sharp teeth. Even while I was entering Brenna's building, I knew it was wrong. And when I saw her startled face, it hit home even more. Until the thrill of what I'd done eclipsed any rational thought. My pulse had raced, a mix of danger and desire coursing through my veins. And when she'd jumped—hell, it scared me too. But damn if it didn't make me feel alive.

Watching her expression morph from startlement to desire had obliterated any regret I'd had.

Until that regret had come back and taken up permanent residence.

Again.

As I rounded the corner onto Pelican Drive, I shook my head. Because that was the thing—I wasn't the man for her, but I couldn't stay away. I craved her like she was the oasis at the end of the desert, and I hardly dared to believe her reactions to me were real. I'd spent most of the nights since doing my best to make it up to her, and not just physically. Last night, I even read to her in bed from the tattered paperback on her nightstand, which happened to be *Little Women*. Not my type of book but lying there reading out loud with her snuggled up against my chest had been one of the most amazing—most *right*—things I'd ever experienced.

But we were playing with fire by keeping our relationship cloaked in shadows. Every stolen moment was intoxicating. We were supposed to be figuring out how to break the news to our families, except the secrecy added an edge that was too enticing to give up.

The town was stirring now, shutters opening and dogs barking in the distance. With one last look at the horizon where the sky kissed the sea, I turned and headed back. At least in the soft embrace of morning, I could pretend everything was simple. Just me, the open road, and the ghost of Brenna's kiss lingering on my lips.

And that other thing I had to do today.

I was just a normal guy who had fallen in love with his girl over a decade ago but couldn't admit that to her. A guy who happened to have scars crisscrossing his body and his soul.

Sweat clung to my skin as I pushed through the glass

door of KeyMark Security. I entered the large open office space to find my two friends, now employees, already at work.

"Morning," Garrett grunted, not looking up from his computer screen. Myles was at the desk beside him, leaning back in his chair and feet propped on the worktop as he scrolled on his phone.

Myles looked up and grinned. "Yeah, this is about right. The boss takes the day off to relax and we do all the hard work."

I grabbed a cold bottle of water from the small fridge we kept in the room and drank it all in one shot. "It's all part of my grand plan to make you feel useful, Decker."

"Don't taunt him, Myles." Garrett shot him a dirty look. "Otherwise, he'll never leave."

"Yeah, yeah," I said. My eyes darted to my open office door where the picture of Evan and me as kids still sat in the desk drawer. And the trophy lay in a box in the closet. I'd carried that trophy around for so many years, an albatross around my neck. Would today change any of that? Just the thought sent a mixture of uneasiness and dread slithering through me. I needed the distraction of work and pointed to Garrett. "Sorting out the new case?"

Garrett finally glanced up, then updated me on our new case with an ex-wife stalking her husband.

Myles set both feet on the ground. "The guy seemed pretty embarrassed about it at the intake interview, but I think we put him at ease."

I nodded, having been there with Myles. And that was why I'd brought him. Light-haired and with a surfer-dude persona even as a Marine, easygoing Myles Decker had a way of making people feel comfortable. Unlike me. That particular skill of his had been invaluable when we were

Marine Raiders and needed information. Myles could have someone talking before they even knew what had happened. And despite his casual nature, he was utterly ruthless in a fight.

Garrett straightened in his chair. "The guy is convinced she's been following him for weeks. We need to set up surveillance and get eyes on her before things escalate."

It wasn't so different than the situation with Brenna and Knox. Hopefully, it would end as anticlimactically. "Have you set up a schedule for monitoring her movements?" I asked.

"Myles is about to head out for day shift, and I'm covering tonight," Garrett replied, his fingers already dancing over the keyboard, probably updating the schedule.

"Count me in for tomorrow." I had a full day planned today but didn't want the guys thinking I was slacking off too much.

"Noting it now," Garrett responded as he typed.

"All right, I need a shower."

"Pretty much the understatement of the century, dude," Myles said with a laugh.

I grinned and flipped him off, then tossed the empty bottle in the recycling bin and headed for the stairs and my apartment. The pleasant ache of my morning workout pulled at my muscles. But there was also weightlessness, a sense of purpose that came with the job, with being part of something bigger than myself—a brotherhood forged under fire and solidified further in the quiet streets of our small town.

I let the hot water cascade over me, and steam filled the bathroom, enveloping me in a cocoon of warmth and tranquility. My fingers rubbed the shampoo into my hair as my thoughts scattered to the next task on my day's agenda. The big one. A blend of excitement and nervousness built in my chest.

After stepping out of the shower and drying off, I dressed in black athletic shorts and a matching shirt. The fabric clung lightly to my damp skin as I downed a quick breakfast and tried to prepare mentally. When I descended the stairs, Myles called out to me.

"Hey, Hunter."

I turned around and both men were looking at me. Myles was dead serious, not a trace of humor on his face. He nodded gravely. "Good luck today."

I dragged a hand through my hair as Garrett added a solemn nod of his own. These two had known me for over a decade. They knew what today meant. "Thanks, guys."

Then I stepped out the back door and entered my SUV to head toward Calypso Key.

Home. Yet not home.

The Big House loomed as I pulled into the drive, its stone and timber façade contrasting against the backdrop of clear blue sky. After I cut the engine, my hands rested on the steering wheel while I took a deep breath and tried to steady the churn of emotions in my gut.

I just sat there, staring at the grand entrance. The thought of opening and walking through that front door tightened something inside me. Years away from the family legacy, of making choices that set me apart, clung to me like a second skin.

As I stepped out, my heart hammered with each step toward the house. The home I'd grown up in, dammit. The idea of knocking felt absurd—like I was a stranger about to peddle vacuum cleaners. And yet, barging in unannounced seemed... presumptuous coming from the black sheep of the family. I paused twenty feet away, my feet stopping on their own. Maybe the kitchen door would be better. Less formal, more—

The front door swung open before I could decide, revealing my grandmother, Nona, whose long white hair caught the sunlight like a halo. Her eyes, the same shade of blue as the Gulf on a calm day, twinkled with unspoken understanding. Her gentle smile softened the apprehension coiled inside me, and as I met her warm eyes, the tension eased. A flash of warmth drifted through me at her familiar western wear, a soft plaid shirt paired with well-worn jeans.

"Good morning, Hunter." Her voice carried the soft lilt of years gone by. She slowly ambled down the cement pathway to me, her firm step belying her eighty-five years. "I saw you standing there from inside. You look like you're fighting a battle with yourself."

"Maybe."

"Let me tell you something," Nona said, turning around at my side to stare at the imposing manse before us. "When I first married your grandfather and became a Markham, I was petrified. I came from a simple family, and here was this... empire."

She laughed softly, a sound that held both fondness and a touch of melancholy. "I remember standing right where you are, not knowing if I should knock or just walk in. It was silly, but I felt like everything hung on that decision."

I listened, leaning into her story and waiting for the wisdom I knew she'd impart. Her struggles weren't mine, but maybe they shared the same root.

"Then I realized," she continued, her voice steady and sure, "that this wasn't just the Markham estate. It was *my home*. My family. And I belonged there as much as anyone else." She paused, offering me a knowing glance that reached into the depths of me. "Just as it will always be *your* home. And you don't ever need to feel you aren't good enough to walk in the front door. You're a Markham through and through, Hunter."

Her words were simple, yet they cut through the tangled mess whirling inside me. I embraced this tiny yet fierce woman, whose head hardly reached my chest. My throat was tight, and I cleared it roughly. "Thank you."

Eventually, I relaxed my hold so she could let go, and we faced the grand manor—our family legacy. We walked toward that mammoth wooden door. I reached for the doorknob, turned it with resolve, and pushed the door open.

"Always," she said quietly, her eyes crinkling at the corners with a smile.

I ushered her in first, the matriarch deserving of every courtesy. And stepping across the threshold, something shifted inside me—a piece clicking into place. The Big House embraced us with its history, and the walls almost whispered with tales of Markhams past.

"I love you, Nona," I said, wrapping her in another hug.

"And I love you, Grandson." She patted my back gently before pulling away and giving me a soft push. "Go on, now. Evan's in the kitchen." After a nod, she ascended the staircase.

Turning toward the kitchen, the scent of coffee and the subtle tang of cinnamon greeted me as my feet treaded forward inevitably. Evan was there, his broad shoulders relaxed as he filled a reusable water bottle at the sink. He was dressed in a T-shirt and shorts that showed off strong, muscular legs. I breathed a silent sigh at his obvious good health. But it was the cleats he wore, grass-stained and worn, that caught my attention. Memories of us as kids, playing impromptu games on the beach, sent a wave of nostalgia crashing over me.

"Hey." I wiped a sweaty palm on the back of my thigh surreptitiously.

"Morning," Evan replied, glancing up. His eyes flicked to my face, then away as if he too was navigating uncertain waters. The two of us hadn't been in a room without others present since that awful fight fourteen years ago. A lifetime ago.

I leaned against the doorframe, watching him cap the bottle and slide it into his bag. The air between us was thick with words unsaid, but for now, the silence was enough. It had to be.

Chapter Twenty-Two

Hunter

FOLLOWING EVAN, I detoured back to my Range Rover to grab my equipment duffel. When we reached the garden, nostalgia hit me hard. The lawn next to the Big House was a sight to behold, a huge expanse of trimmed grass carpeting the ground like a lush green blanket. A tall hibiscus hedge in full bloom bordered the area, its vibrant red and yellow flowers creating a natural barrier that encased the garden in a riot of color and fragrance. The sweet scent wafted through the air, mingling with a salty breeze from the nearby ocean. This was where I had stood unnoticed while Gabe and April said their vows.

But my memories went further back.

This was our old stomping ground. Mine and Evan's. Where we'd spent countless hours under the sun, the crack of the bat an echo of simpler times. And like those long-ago days, the batting cage stood at the far end of the garden, a large structure made of sturdy metal and thick netting. The sun shined through the netting, creating intricate patterns of light and shadow on the vibrant green grass.

I couldn't help but marvel at how unchanged it all seemed. From the middle of the lawn, a pitching machine pointed at the batting cage. The piece of machinery had seen countless practices and stood as a silent testament to our shared history.

"It looks exactly the same," I remarked, my voice hushed.

Evan shrugged nonchalantly as his gaze followed mine. "Didn't see the point in messing with a good setup."

"Good point."

"You want to take some swings first?" he asked. And maybe his simple offer could end up being a bridge back to the camaraderie we once had before life tore us apart.

I nodded, a smile tugging at the corners of my lips. "Sure. You can help me shrink my Grand Canyon-sized strike zone, maybe."

Evan flashed a grin. "I'll set up the pitching machine. Get yourself warmed up."

I dumped my full, heavy bag on the ground next to the cage. Both aluminum and wood bats were lined up like soldiers against the netting, and I made my choice quickly. We used aluminum in the rec league, so that was all I'd worked with since joining the Stingrays. Wooden bats were for more exalted arms. Taking my stance, I gripped the bat. The familiar weight settled the nerves flying around my stomach as Evan approached at an angle.

He stopped six feet away and folded his arms as the first ball whizzed toward me. "Elbow up a bit," Evan called out with no trace of judgment in his voice. I adjusted my stance and swung, connecting with the next pitch solidly.

"Better," he acknowledged, and something like pride swelled in my chest. God, I had missed this—his guidance, the unspoken bond of brotherhood. With each pitch and hit, the tension unwound from my muscles, leaving room for something akin to peace.

As the pitching machine hummed, sending another ball spinning toward me, I focused on Evan's advice. Elbow up, eyes on the ball, pivot on my foot. The next pitch flew at me, and this time, as I adjusted my stance and crouched slightly, I swung with newfound intention. The bat connected with the ball crisply, sending it soaring through the air in a satisfying arc.

Evan's smile widened, a silent approval that spoke volumes. "Nice hit. Keep that tighter form. You should work on making contact with any pitch you're not positive is a strike—foul it off and stay in the game. Plus, you'll rattle the pitcher."

It was like finding a piece of myself I had long forgotten, rediscovering the joy of simply playing the game. Pitch after pitch, I improved under Evan's watchful eye. Each swing grew sharper, more precise, his subtle pointers and my own determination to do better fueling me.

Finally, I straightened and stepped out. "Thanks. Your turn."

Evan's limp was slight as he moved toward the pitching machine, but it grabbed my attention and held it tight. The shadows of that day on the *Benson* flickered across my mind, and heat rose on my face. I fought not to let the demons rise—to stay in this cocoon of warm happiness. Evan cranked the speed up, then hurried back to casually pick up a wooden bat. When he stepped into the batter's box, his form was impressive. Natural. He swung effortlessly, and the ball soared in a perfect arc against the clear sky.

I tracked its graceful movement. There were no tips I could give him—his swing didn't need them. Instead, I let myself bask in the sight of my brother, the natural-born athlete, the man who had been on the cusp of Major League greatness when I snatched it away. A man who was now slowly, steadily finding his way forward.

I remained silent as he sprayed the ball over the field as he had at practice, words inadequate for the surge of emotion I was holding back. After several minutes of this, Evan opened up and really hit the ball. And I remembered why we'd always put the batting cage at the edge of the garden. Hit after hit soared to the very far end, yet none went over the hibiscus hedge. His control was incredible.

I whistled, shaking my head in disbelief. "Damn, Evan. You've still got it."

He just twitched that half-smile of his and shrugged off the compliment as if it were nothing. But it wasn't nothing—it was everything.

"I've been sneaking in some practice sessions," he admitted with the sun glinting off his hair and turning it to molten bronze.

Too soon, Evan called time on the batting and shut down the machine, its hum dying into the coastal silence. After staring at the ground for a long moment, he raised his head to look me straight in the eye. "What do you say, Hunter? Ready to catch a few?"

A numb wave traveled from my head to my feet, and goose bumps pebbled my arms. I fought to keep my face expressionless, not to show how utterly momentous this was. So I simply nodded. "Sure. I've got everything I need.

My catcher's gear was already in my SUV." That was a white lie. I'd packed my gear bag last night.

Just in case.

Strapping on my shin guards and the heavy breastplate, the rhythm of Calypso Key's heart synced with mine—a slow, steady beat promising new beginnings. I crouched inside the cage and punched my glove as I smiled at the familiar pitcher's mound, now tattered but still hanging in there. Evan walked to a place marked with an X that I knew without asking was sixty feet, six inches away.

Evan started easy, lobbing the ball in a gentle arc that I caught without strain. But soon his pitches came faster, harder, demanding more from both of us. We fell into our old routine with ease, a dance we hadn't performed together in years. Yet I remembered flawlessly—the twist of his arm, the arch of my back, the satisfying smack of the ball against leather. My hand stung inside the thick mitt, but I couldn't suppress the grin splitting my face.

"Nice one!" I called out as another pitch hit my glove dead-on.

Evan flashed me a thumbs-up, sweat beading on his brow. His pitches came at me like a whirlwind, each one the result of his talent and determination. Fastballs screamed with a fierce intensity, curveballs dipped and spun in ways that challenged my reflexes, change-ups deceived me with their subtle shifts in speed, and sliders darted away at the last moment as if mocking my attempts to catch them.

Despite the thick padding of my catcher's gear, the impact of each pitch reverberated through my hand, sending a jolt of pain up my arm. But I gritted my teeth and refused to let it show. This moment was too precious, too rare to let something as trivial as physical discomfort mar it.

Besides, I'd known pain much more profound than catching a baseball.

As Evan continued to unleash his arsenal of pitches, I crouched in awe at his form. His focus was unwavering as he delivered each one with precision and power. The deep *thwack* of the ball meeting my glove echoed in the still afternoon air, a symbol of mending brothers and shared passion for the game.

After half an hour of perfection, Evan's arm whipped forward. But the ball spun out of control and veered off to the side. He bent over, hands on his knees, and let out a hearty laugh. "Man, I think we better call it," he panted, straightening up. His cheeks were flushed, and his eyes gleamed with amusement. "I've got the pitching endurance of an eight-year-old girl."

"Hey, don't sell yourself short." I stood, chucking the ball back to him. My own muscles were singing with the effort and my hand ached like a son of a bitch, but it was a good kind of ache in my bones—the kind you get from doing something you love. "You've still got one hell of an arm."

He shrugged modestly, but I caught the twinge of pride flickering across his face before it disappeared. So different than the old days, when he walked with a natural, unconscious swagger I always admired. Yet I'd just seen that it was still there. I wondered if he realized just how much he'd given me today.

I hesitated, rolling a baseball between my hands as I searched for how to ask the giant question. "So does this mean you're going to take over pitching for Gabe?"

Evan's eyes became guarded. A hint of red crept up his neck, and he scuffed the dirt with his cleat, suddenly shy. "I might give it a shot, but only for an inning or two. Though I'll probably make a fool of myself."

"Come on. Don't be so hard on yourself." A low laugh escaped me as I held up my hand, now tinged a vibrant shade of red with some purple developing. "Look at this. I don't think those poor rec league players will know what the hell to do. You might want to take mercy on them and ease up a bit."

His grin was back, sheepish yet hopeful. It was clear that beneath the layers of self-doubt, a spark had been reignited. Playing catch wasn't just about nostalgia. It was about reawakening dreams we thought were buried forever.

We gathered the balls scattered across the grass, the machine silent now except for ticking as it cooled. Evan tossed one up and caught it, his eyes meeting mine. "Kind of like old times, huh?" The corner of his mouth lifted in a half-smile.

"Yeah, it is." I blinked back a sudden fullness in my eyes.

"Two old men playing catch," Evan quipped, but his tone was warm, appreciative. We both knew it was more than that.

As we packed away the gear, silence developed between us, but it wasn't strained like before. I watched Evan's profile against the sun, the way the light played on his features and highlighted lines time had etched into his face. We walked back to the house, and the red hue of my hand faded to a dull ache.

I couldn't quite wrap my head around the idea that Evan might be inching toward forgiving me. Forgiveness was a luxury I hadn't earned. Probably would never earn. But as I stood beside him in the camaraderie of our old routine—it sparked hope inside me that maybe, *maybe*, I could work toward something that resembled atonement.

"Thanks, Hunter," Evan said, breaking into my thoughts as we reached the porch.

"Anytime, Ev. I mean it. And thanks for helping me with my swing."

His gratitude was a balm, a sign that the chasm between us was narrowing. And as he walked away, a sense of purpose settled within me. I might not be worthy of forgiveness, but I'd take whatever he could give me, one pitch at a time.

Chapter Twenty-Three

Brenna

AS I TURNED the key in the ignition, the familiar rattle of my old sedan filled the air. I glanced at Hunter, his tall frame folded into the passenger seat, and couldn't help the bubbly excitement that surged through me. "Ready for an adventure?"

"Never knew deer were an adventure," Hunter replied, his voice as easy as his smile, the smile I'd seen more of this morning. He'd worked on a new case all day yesterday, so this was the first chance we'd had to be together since his get-together with Evan. Other than a quick text exchange telling me his catch session with his brother had gone really well, I'd let my curiosity simmer. But now I could detect a clear change in him, how his broad shoulders were more relaxed, his posture in the seat more at ease.

Soon, we left behind the familiarity of Dove Key as we headed toward Big Pine Key and our eventual destination—No Name Key. There was always something thrilling about searching for the elusive Key deer. No matter how many times I glimpsed the tiny creatures, I always loved it.

As we crossed onto No Name Key, Hunter let out a low whistle as he peered out the window at the expanding rows of houses and canals, the freshly paved roads. "Looks like progress is trying to swallow up this place too. I can't believe how much this has changed."

I nodded but couldn't suppress my sly grin. "A lot of the Keys are getting developed, but I know some secret places that are still wild."

He turned and laughed at me—actually laughed!—and winked at my innuendo. Steering the car off the main road and onto a sandy trail, I wound through dense, scrubby foliage. The car jostled over the uneven terrain, the under-carriage scraping ominously against a hidden rock.

"We should've brought my four-wheel-drive," Hunter said, gripping the upper door grab as if bracing for impact. "Your little ride might not forgive you for this."

"Ah, she's tougher than she looks," I shot back.

We bounced along the path, stirring up clouds of dust that clung to the rear window. Moments later, I eased the car to a stop, nestling it between two stunted trees whose branches were twisted together in solidarity against the encroaching development.

"We're here," I declared, killing the engine, which gave one last protesting shudder before falling silent.

Hunter's gaze met mine, a spark of that bad-boy charm still flickering there. It was a look that said he was ready for whatever challenge lay ahead. A look that made my adventurous heart beat a little faster.

"Lead the way," he said, popping open the door and unfolding himself from the car with the grace of a man who had spent years learning how to move efficiently.

We ventured into the thick of No Name Key, the calls of distant birds echoing over the soft rustling of leaves. Above us, sea grape trees with their broad, rounded leaves sheltered us from the glaring sun.

"Look at this," I murmured, guiding Hunter's gaze to the vibrant yellow petals of a beach sunflower thriving in the sandy soil. A green anole lizard flicked its red dewlap at us from a nearby rock.

"I forgot about this," Hunter mused, his voice low as he panned his eyes around us. "How tenacious life is here in the Keys."

As we walked farther into the wilderness, the sounds of civilization faded into the background, replaced by the gentle rustling of leaves and the occasional splash of water as we passed by a hidden creek. Hunter stooped to examine a delicate wild orchid tucked away in the shade, his expression one of quiet fascination.

We followed a narrow trail that wound its way through the thick foliage, where the air was heavy with the scent of saltwater and earth. As we rounded a bend in the path, a flash of movement caught my eye. I held out a hand to stop Hunter, my heart racing with anticipation. Ahead, a small group of Key deer grazed peacefully in a sun-dappled clearing. Their tiny, delicate frames moved gracefully as they nibbled on the sparse vegetation. My breath caught in my throat at the sight, a surge of joy and wonder filling me as I observed the rare and beautiful creatures.

Hunter stood beside me, his gaze fixed on the deer with a softness that mirrored my own awe. For a moment, we simply stood there, sharing this magical moment.

"Move quietly," I said, tiptoeing in front of him and heading toward them. "If we're quiet enough, we can get close." I placed my steps with care, barely daring to breathe. But hearing nothing behind me, I scowled.

He's not coming with me?

I'd thought he was as entranced as me, but maybe I was wrong. Unable to help the irritation flickering through me, I spun around with a huff.

And smashed right into a solid wall of hard, male flesh. I squeaked, a high-pitched sound that sent the deer bounding away.

"Dammit, Hunter!" I tried to scold him, but my annoyance melted as soon as I saw the surprise on his face.

"Sorry," he said with a sheepish grin. "I wasn't expecting you to stop like that. You need to hold your fist up and give me a little warning, okay?"

Several military and action movies flitted through my mind. Scenes where the characters had done exactly that to warn each other. "Oh," I said, regaining my composure. "I didn't realize you were such a ghost." Which brought another realization. He'd been behind me, completely silent, the whole time. The man was contradiction after contradiction, all wrapped up in an intoxicating, utterly handsome bundle.

Hunter's smile turned sly, and his dark eyes glinted with mischief. "It was part of my job to move quietly. Being light on my feet has its advantages, you know? Such as crashing into beautiful women."

The humor in his tone was infectious, and I laughed. It was a reminder of how much we had both changed, yet the connection between us felt as warm as ever. "Guess you still have some bad-boy tricks up your sleeve," I teased, and my heartbeat quickened at his proximity. His black shirt was sleeveless and showcased his huge, tattooed arms.

"Only the useful ones," he said softly, and the way his

gaze lingered on mine sent a clear message—that he'd picked up on my inventory of his assets.

We resumed our walk along the sandy path that wound through the scrubby habitat. Hunter joined me to walk alongside as the track widened, and above us, the cry of a lone osprey pierced the serene sky. The sound of waves grew louder as we headed toward the shore. Now that we'd scared off the deer, I searched for another topic and settled on the obvious. "How did it go with Evan? The catch session?"

A wide, unguarded smile broke across Hunter's face, lighting up his eyes. "It was good. Better than good." He kicked at a small shell on the path, sending it skittering into the brush. "I mean, there were a few moments when it felt like the old days."

"Really?"

"Yeah. There was this one pitch..." His expression turned wistful for a second as he recounted a fastball Evan had thrown.

My heart unfurled at his obvious relief. As if with every word he spoke, Hunter was rebuilding the bridge between his present and the past he'd tried so hard to outrun. Which brought me to the other subject I'd wanted to broach since the day he'd walked back into my life. Now was the perfect time, though this topic was sure to eliminate the happy smile on his face.

As we passed through two stunted pine trees, we emerged onto a shelly, coarse beach. "Can I ask"—I paused to swallow before pressing on—"about that day with Evan. The diving accident. I'd like to hear your side if you're okay talking about it."

Sure enough, the smile plummeted off his chiseled face, and for a moment, I regretted asking. But that day was also an ordeal he needed to work through if he was ever to move past it. He nodded. "Yeah. Let's sit down."

We found a driftwood log that time and tides had smoothed, nestled on the fringe where beach met thicket. As we settled onto the sun-bleached wood, the rhythmic lapping of the gentle waves played a soothing, contrasting backdrop to the silence stretching between us. I held my breath, waiting for him to fill it with his truth.

"The whole thing was supposed to be a surprise for Evan. He was expecting to make his Major League debut that season." Not looking at me, his fingers toyed with a splinter on the log. "I wanted to give him something special, you know? Something to show how damn proud I was."

I studied his profile, the way his jaw tightened. There was so much love there, mixed with an ache that seemed to stretch across the years. "So I had this MVP trophy made at a local shop. Shiny and grand, just like Evan's future was supposed to be." A bitter laugh escaped him, and he finally met my eyes. They were filled with so many shades of regret. "I gave it to this guy I knew, Bruce, who did commercial diving, and we set up a plan. He was to place it in the deep room of the *Benson* wreck for me. Evan and I loved diving that thing, and I'd always wanted to enter the deep room at the stern. Bruce and I figured out the day he'd place the trophy, and I scheduled the trip on our backup boat, *Indigo Heaven*, for the following day with Evan. During the dive, I was going to present it to him. Like a secret celebration beneath the sea, just between us."

The image painted itself in my mind—the two brothers, suspended in the silence of a wreck I'd dived many times myself, sharing a moment of triumph. It should have been perfect.

"But that's not what happened," Hunter said, his voice hushed and tight now.

The weight of those words hung heavy in the air between us. I felt it in my chest, a pressure that made it hard to breathe. The pain in Hunter's expression was raw, and it cracked something open inside me—something warm and fierce. I reached for his hand, threading my fingers through his. Rough and calloused, they closed around mine with gentle strength.

"Hey," I said softly, giving his hand a reassuring squeeze. "I'm here for you."

He turned his hand to clasp mine fully, his thumb brushing against my skin. His defenses eased to reveal the boy I once knew—the one who had both a shy, caring nature and a devil-may-care attitude. But I also saw the man he had become, the one multiple tragic experiences had shaped.

And with stunning clarity, I realized I was falling in love. Not with the boy from my memories or the idea of a second chance. I was falling for the real, flawed, incredible man in front of me.

"We reached the deep room... but the trophy wasn't there." Hunter's voice held a note of bewilderment, even now. He lost himself in the memory, his free hand idly working a stick around his fingers as he stared at the horizon. "I looked everywhere, Brenna. It was supposed to be right there and easily visible. That deep room is over one hundred fifty feet down, so Bruce made a point to tell me our air would go quickly and we needed to grab the trophy and get back out. But all I found was empty space and the eerie, dark quiet of the wreck."

"Then what?" I urged gently, my heart beating a steady, fast rhythm.

Hunter eased out a long sigh, still weaving the stick

around his fingers. "I went deeper into the ship, thinking maybe Bruce had put it somewhere else. Hell, I don't know what I thought. Evan followed. But the farther we went, the more twisted the corridors became. Before I knew it, we were lost."

His eyes reflected the shadowed ocean depths where fear had once ruled. "Evan panicked, darting into another room to look for a way out. I might have been only eighteen years old, but I was the better diver. My brother's life was in my hands, so I had to keep it together and get us out."

Instinctively, I moved closer to him on our driftwood perch and pressed the length of my arm against his. I wanted to absorb some of his pain, to offer solace in the silent language of touch.

Hunter's voice trembled slightly as he spoke, like he was diving back into that day with each word. "Finally, I saw a blue glow and we made it out of the ship. Except we were almost out of air and one hundred fifty feet below the surface. Evan... he just lost it. He took off for the surface."

My stomach clenched at the thought of their desperation in the dark water. Evan was less than a year older than Hunter, part of the reason why they'd been so close. Both had been so young to have to face something so terrible.

"Of course, panicking at that depth can be deadly. I tried to catch him, to slow him down." His hand clenched into a fist on his thigh, knuckles white. The stick broke and he tossed it onto the sand.

"Everything I knew about diving safety, all the rules, were screaming at me from inside my head. But none of that mattered. All I could think about was saving my brother. So I went up after him, as fast as I could. And then..."

Hunter paused to ease out a long sigh, almost a hiss. "I ran out of air. Nothing but locked pressure of an empty regulator in my mouth when I tried to breathe. I kept my cool, though. I had to. Evan was all that mattered."

My breath caught as I envisioned him racing for the surface, lungs burning and heart pounding in the shadowy depths of the ocean. Silence enveloped us, the only sound the gentle waves against the shore. My heart no longer beat —it thundered and sweat broke out on my brow. "Oh my God. What happened next?"

Chapter Twenty-Four

Hunter

THE MEMORY HAD CARVED a permanent scar into the fabric of my being. Fourteen years might as well have been fourteen seconds. And the weight of that day clung to my soul like an unwelcome shadow, dimming every moment of joy that dared to surface in my life since. Brenna's quiet presence next to me was comforting, urging me to continue.

"By the time we reached the surface..." I paused, the image of my brother's enraged face flashing before me. "Evan was wild with rage. Like a storm personified. He hit me in the face."

I could feel the punch again, a jarring blow that damn near knocked the breath from my lungs. My head snapped back in the water, the salt stinging my eyes.

"He punched me again and again, and I just took them. God knows I deserved every one. Finally, he got his rage out, and we moved toward the boat and clambered aboard. We got our gear off. Then, without warning, Evan doubled over and puked into the ocean. A wave of freezing dread rolled through me when he flexed his fingers and said they were tingling."

Taking a deep breath, I met Brenna's gaze once more. "Since you're a diver, I don't need to explain the symptoms of decompression sickness. The bends."

Brenna's expression shifted from horror to realization. Her eyes widened, a silent acknowledgment of the danger we had faced, and she nodded slightly.

"As fast as I could, I got the engine going and headed toward home. I radioed ahead and told them Evan had signs of DCS. By the time we reached the island, he couldn't feel his legs."

My hands clenched involuntarily, reliving the helplessness of that moment as Calypso Key grew closer. Each second stretched out like an eternity, filled with the writhing of my brother's agony.

And beneath it all, the horrible, gnawing guilt of knowing I had walked away unscathed.

Brenna was the lighthouse guiding me through a storm of memories, and her gentle eyes were the beacon of understanding I'd been searching for without even realizing it.

After rolling my rock-hard shoulders, I continued. "Once we docked, the ambulance rushed Evan to the recompression chamber in Tavernier. He spent days locked inside that steel cocoon. While he was trapped in there, I haunted our beach like a ghost. I wouldn't talk to anyone—anger and guilt were my only company.

"When the rage finally won out, I found myself standing outside Bruce's run-down shack without even realizing how I got there. I pushed open the door without knocking."

Brenna ran her thumb over the back of my hand. "Was he there?"

Nodding, I exhaled a long breath of that long-ago fury. "Bruce was slouched in a chair with his feet up on some rickety table, clutching a half-empty bottle of rum like it was his lifeline. I stormed across the floor and knocked the bottle out of his hand, demanding to know where the trophy was." I barked a humorless laugh. "He got up and lurched to a table across the room, then lifted a dirty shirt to reveal my trophy. He admitted he'd been on a bender and forgot all about our plan. I snatched the trophy from him, boiling with rage as he dropped onto the stained, dusty recliner, dismissing me. He had no idea what had happened. Of course not. He'd been buried in a bottle, not a recompression chamber. I turned and left without another word."

I'd given Brenna a very shortened version of the events, minimizing the red haze that had descended over me at Bruce's shack. That had been the first time I'd experienced that blind rage. I didn't give in to it, but in later years I would. I found myself absently stroking the bullet hole near my ribs and moved my hand away.

My other hand was still entwined with Brenna's, and I squeezed gently. "I still remember the hospital's cold, sterile smell as I walked to Evan's room. You know how hospitals are, right? That eerie silence that seems to swallow your words before they even leave your mouth. It was like that."

I took a moment to collect my thoughts before continuing. Much of that time was hazy in my mind, but not what happened next. That was etched in crystal-clear high definition. "Evan lay in his bed, looking so small and so... *still* beneath those white sheets. The guy who used to throw pitches that left batters swearing was just lying there."

Brenna tightened her hold on my hand and pressed against my side.

"Evan didn't want me there. He was so furious. And the

more I apologized and tried to make things right, the angrier he got. The louder he got. Finally, he screamed at me to get out. He told me if I really wanted to help him, then I should disappear from his life."

The pain of that moment still cut like a blade. I had backed away from his bed, my heart shattering with each step. There was no redemption there, no forgiveness. Only the truth of what I had wrought. The older brother I'd idolized my entire life was broken because of me.

"I turned and walked away. It was the longest walk of my life. I drove straight to Key Largo, where the military recruiter's office was located. I told the guy to sign me up with the Marines. He wanted to know if I was in trouble with the law. I assured him that wasn't the problem, though I refused to tell him what the problem was. He asked if I was sure about this decision. All I could say was that it was the only certain thing about me."

I stared at the distant horizon where sea met sky but only felt the gaping wound of the empty, tortured boy I'd been. "I'd heard that the Marines break you down and then build you back up. I thought maybe they could make me into someone worthy of forgiveness. That night, I called Dad and told him I wasn't coming back. I left Calypso Key and the person I used to be behind." I let out a long breath, a weight lifting off my chest as I finally reached the end. "And I didn't look back. I never spoke to Evan until Gabe's wedding brought us together again."

Brenna's soft hitch pulled me back to the beach where we sat, her warm, giving presence a stark contrast to the chaotic whirlwind I'd just recounted. A single tear rolled down her cheek, and I resisted the urge to reach out and catch it.

"I've heard about the accident, of course," Brenna said,

her wavering voice betraying her own turmoil. "But I thought you were diving for... lost gold?"

"Gold?" The word felt foreign, almost laughable now. "No, it was never about that stupid imaginary gold. It was a trophy—a goddamn baseball trophy."

She nodded, absorbing the gravity of what a simple object had cost. And her eyes brimmed not with judgment but with a deep well of understanding. It was hard to look at her, to see the sympathy written all over her face. Harder still to admit how a gesture meant to celebrate my brother's achievement had spiraled into the worst event of my life.

"Nobody knows about the trophy," I murmured, my voice hoarse with emotion. "You're the first person I've ever told that part to."

"God, Hunter," Brenna murmured, raising our clasped hands to kiss the back of mine. "I'm so sorry."

I gave her a half-smile, the effort it took making my face feel like it was cracking. "It's not your fault, Brenna. It's no one's fault but mine."

"Stop," she said firmly, fiercely. Her willowy figure turned toward me like a reed in the wind, strong despite its slenderness. "You always do this—take the world's weight on your shoulders. But some things are just... out of our hands."

God, I wanted to believe her. And as I searched her imploring eyes, a sense of relief washed over me. Brenna's presence was as calming as the gentle sea breeze, and for the first time since that fateful day, the crushing weight inside me lifted ever so slightly.

"It feels strange," I said, my voice stronger now. "Like I've been carrying around this lead anchor, and it's just gotten lighter."

"Letting go doesn't mean forgetting, Hunter," Brenna

said softly. "It means you're choosing not to let it pull you down anymore."

Her words struck a chord within me. This woman, whose family had been pitted against mine for over a century, was offering me solace and understanding without a second thought. I lifted her hand to brush my lips over it.

The brush rustled softly, a whisper of life that drew our attention away from the dark memories swirling between me. A doe, the size of a large dog, nudged her way into the clearing, followed by two tiny, spotted fawns that stepped with spindly legs. They were a picture of innocence and resilience, completely oblivious to the weight of human sorrow.

I couldn't help it—the corner of my mouth twitched upward, a reluctant smile breaking through the storm clouds in my soul. The animals before us knew nothing of treachery or the bitterness of regret.

"Well, would you look at that," I whispered.

"Hard to believe how these deer thrive in such a changing world. But they're survivors." She reached up to brush her fingers against my beard. "Just like you are. And your brother."

A tremor ran through me, a seismic shift threatening to shatter the fragile composure I'd cobbled together. My heart clenched, the pain sharp and sudden, but I swallowed it back, refusing to unravel before her.

Instead, I bridged the distance between us, a force stronger than gravity pulling me. Our lips met in a kiss that was both a balm for old wounds and the spark of something new, something bright and terrifying in its intensity. Her lips were soft, yielding, and every bit as healing as the words she had offered me. Pulling back just enough to see her face,

I rested my forehead against hers, the warmth of her skin seeping into mine.

"I feel better," I admitted, the truth of it surprising me. "Thank you for listening."

"Of course." Her gaze locked onto mine with an unwavering certainty that made my chest ache. "I'll always be here for you, Hunter."

The doe glanced over at us, then turned and led her small family back into the bush. And without either of us needing to say anything, the moment was gone. Pushing to my feet, I pulled Brenna up, and we padded through the soft sand. I couldn't quite shake the image of those deer from my mind—the stubborn persistence they represented, the unspoken promise that life endures against odds.

Hope in its most natural form.

As we approached Brenna's car with its faded blue paint reflecting the bright sun, I fought an internal battle. I had laid bare the darkest parts of my past, exposed the festering wounds I fought so hard to conceal from everyone. Brenna's presence, her quiet strength and patient ear, had become an integral part of my healing, as vital as air.

I loved her.

It was as simple and as complicated as that. I loved her now more than ever. More than the desperate wishes I'd clung to in my dark moods over the years.

Yet, how could I ask her to love a man who had caused so much pain?

My heart raced with the words I yearned to say. Her hand felt warm and sure in mine. She didn't recoil from my touch, even knowing the ugliness I hid inside. That alone should've given me courage, but it only intensified my trepidation.

Her obvious feelings for me, the way she looked at me

like I was more hero than villain, only convinced me further that she deserved better than a broken man with a fractured past. But as she unlocked her car and we got in, I knew I wasn't noble enough to end things between us. I might have had the courage to face down the Taliban, but I didn't know how to face a future without her in it.

Chapter Twenty-Five

Brenna

DOVE Key's warm evening breeze ruffled through my hair, carrying the muffled voices spilling from the open doors of bars and shops lining Main Street. Hunter and I strolled hand in hand, and our steps were unhurried as we enjoyed the evening after dinner at a local hideout.

"Did you see Mrs. Henderson's face when you kissed me?" Hunter's voice was a low rumble next to me, his thumb caressing the back of my hand.

"Let her look," I said, arching a brow. "I don't care tonight."

Hunter smiled and pulled me in for a quick peck on the lips—while strolling down Main Street! That kiss at Rousseau's wasn't just a kiss. It was a declaration, one I'd made beneath the soft glow of candlelight and curious onlookers. I was still surprised that I'd stood and leaned across the table to plant a long, fat smooch on his lips, but I'd been unable to resist the urge. Though a corner of my mind was still worried about my family's reaction to the two of us, Hunter's catharsis on No Name Key had solidified that he was working through his trauma. And I couldn't have been happier or prouder.

"Ah, Brenna, what am I going to do with you?" he teased, but his gaze held something warmer. Something very, very sexy.

"Mmm. I can think of a few things."

He slung his arm over my shoulders, and I reached up to lace our hands once more. As we ambled, I caught sight of the antique store nestled between a boutique dress shop and an ice cream parlor. My steps slowed, drawn to the window display like a moth to a flame. The books behind the glass beckoned, their spines rich with history and secrets. Rare tomes, luxurious leather-bound editions, and hand-tooled covers taunted me. And as we stood before these precious, important books, solemnity replaced my mirth. From the corner of my eye, I studied the man beside me.

Again and again this past week, I'd mulled over the story Hunter had told. His confession had shaken me—not because of what he'd said but because of how much it had hurt him to say it. He'd bared his soul, shared a wound so deep I could almost feel its sting myself. But even through all his guilt and pain, there was something beautiful about Hunter's vulnerability. It was raw and real and undeniably human.

A pang hit me hard as I glanced at him from the corner of my eye—his profile etched against the windowpane, eyes focused on the display. His strength and need to protect deeply impressed me. Not just physical strength but emotional resilience too—the kind you only gain from surviving life's harshest battles. I wished I could take away his pain, which had been clear on his face several times in the week since, even when he looked at me. But all I could do was be there for him—a steady presence in his tumultuous world.

And I was coming to realize something else. If I'd learned one thing from our day searching for Key deer, it was that Hunter Markham wasn't just another chapter in my life.

He was turning out to be the whole damn book.

And I knew something else too—love wasn't about perfection. It was about accepting someone with all their flaws and scars. And I was ready to love Hunter, for everything he was and everything he believed he wasn't. Yet, how could I make him see his own worth when he was so hell-bent on believing otherwise?

For now, all I could do was offer him my support and hope it would be enough to help mend his fractured soul. And surely he had to be on the way to healing, for why else would he share such vulnerability with me?

And for us, it always returned to books. No matter how massive and menacing Hunter had become, he was still the boy who loved to read. And that brought the smile back to my face as I studied the window display. A soft sigh escaped my lips when I visualized a particular treasure hidden within the store. It was tucked away from prying eyes and safely ensconced in a locked cabinet.

I turned to Hunter with a wistful smile. "There's a rare first edition of *The Sun Also Rises* inside." I pointed vaguely into the depths of the shop. "I've been trying to persuade the shop owner to part with it for years, but he holds onto it like it's his own personal treasure. He simply won't let it go." I shrugged, a laugh escaping me as I brushed off the minor disappointment.

He bumped my shoulder with his. "I remember you

talking about that book. I imagine there are plenty of other priceless tomes you can covet."

"More than I could count in a lifetime. Which makes me very lucky."

Hunter gave me a wink. "Just as well. Hemingway is my turf. So back off, missy."

"Touché." I let my eyes roam back to the window, where they were drawn to a stunning leather-bound version of *Romeo and Juliet*. Gold lettering shined in the soft light from the streetlamp, making it hard to look away. I couldn't help but wonder about Hunter's past love, if that romance he'd mentioned had been as tragic and all-consuming as Shakespeare's star-crossed lovers. Since he wasn't with her, I doubted their story had a happy ending. The woman in Afghanistan would certainly fit the situation.

Curiosity clawed at my insides, but I clamped down on the questions wanting to spill from my lips. This night was ours, and I wanted nothing more than to revel in the beauty of the present and the chemistry that sizzled between us.

"Am I going to have to toss you over my shoulder to haul you away from this window?" Hunter's voice was soft, his thumb tracing circles over the back of my neck.

That brought me back with a laugh. "You'd probably do it."

He grinned at me and pointed with his head. "Let's keep going. I feel like taking my girl back to my place."

"Oh? That sounds promising. Lead on, good sir."

Our fingers intertwined once again as we continued down Main Street, wrapped up in our own world. One where the ending was yet to be written and every chapter held the promise of passion and redemption. As we approached the stoic façade of KeyMark Security, Hunter's stride slowed, and he turned to me with a glint in his eyes. "How about we head up to my rooftop?"

I tipped my head back, intrigued by his spontaneity. "Sure, but why?"

"You'll see." He flashed me a grin that set off a fluttering sensation deep in my belly. "We haven't gone up there yet, and it's a nice night."

"Very nice night. Now I'm intrigued."

We navigated through the dimly lit open room of his business, then up the stairs. Upon entering his apartment, Pedro sauntered over with that air of regality only cats possessed. And I had to think that was amplified when the cat was six-toed royalty.

"Hey there, buddy," I cooed, bending down to scratch behind his ear. The kitten purred, leaning into my touch as if he approved of this late visit. "You're getting so big!"

"Pedro's been hitting the gym," Hunter joked.

"Clearly." I laughed, giving the cat one last pat before straightening up. Hunter crossed the room and opened what I'd thought was a closet door to reveal a staircase. Together, we made our way up to the rooftop.

As we emerged into the open air, the warm night wrapped around us. Hunter walked over to the corner where a switch was mounted on the wall. With a flick of his wrist, he illuminated the space with an enchanting array of string lights that crisscrossed above our heads. The soft golden glow cast a romantic hue over the rooftop, turning it into a private refuge high above the world below.

Two plush couches, adorned with colorful throw pillows, beckoned from one side of the rooftop. A soft, fluffy rug sprawled beneath the seating area, its intricate patterns resembling ripples in a tranquil pond and promising a comforting touch to bare feet. A solid wooden cover stood over the seating area, protecting it from inclement weather but leaving plenty of the glorious sky visible to enjoy. The string lights above us danced lazily in the night air, creating a magical ambiance.

"Oh," I breathed out, captivated by the transformation as I twirled in a circle. "Hunter, this is beautiful!"

"Thought you might like it." Hunter reached for his phone, and soon the gentle strumming of an acoustic guitar ensemble filled the night air. He extended his hand to me, and I took it without hesitation, feeling like I was stepping into a dream as he pulled me into his arms. We swayed to the music and quickly found a rhythm that felt as natural as the tide coming in.

His arms wrapped around me, drawing me closer until our bodies moved in perfect harmony under the moonlight. The rest of the world fell away, leaving nothing but the entrancing music that played just for us.

"Look at us, dancing on a rooftop like we're the only two people left on earth," I murmured, resting my head against his chest.

"Maybe we are." Hunter's voice was a soothing baritone that vibrated through me. "Everyone else just fades away when I'm with you."

"I had no idea you had such a romantic streak," I said, taking in the chiseled angles and planes of his face.

He flashed me a sexy smile, raising an eyebrow playfully. "Did you forget? I was the one who was the sucker for love stories in high school."

His words made my heart flutter as I recalled those days. When he'd sneak off to read Nicholas Sparks novels behind the bleachers, away from the prying eyes of others. Except for me. It seemed like a lifetime ago, but here we were now, dancing under the stars on his rooftop refuge.

And I knew firsthand that sweet soul was still inside this man. I was one of the few who did.

I laughed softly, a surge of affection rising. "I guess some things never change."

Hunter's gaze held mine, his eyes staring at me with an intensity that raised the temperature inside me. Leaning in closer, he pressed his lips to my temple. "Some things do, though. We're not schoolkids anymore. We're adults now, and I know what I want."

Chapter Twenty-Six

Brenna

HUNTER'S WORDS lingered in the air, heavy with unspoken promises that left me breathless. I locked my wobbly knees as he lowered his head, his lips brushing against mine in a featherlight touch that sent shockwaves spearing through me. I responded eagerly, my fingers tightening around his waist as I pulled him closer. The kiss deepened, and the feel of his hard back muscles under my hands left me dizzy.

I broke our kiss to stare at him, and my skin felt hot everywhere he touched it. His dark and stormy eyes were filled with hunger, which only made me more eager to lose myself to the storm. Hunter took charge, pulling me tight against him as he clenched one hand in my hair and pulled my head back. His lips were warm and full. The taste of him was intoxicating, a heady blend of desire and longing that left me craving more.

So much more.

Hunter walked me backward toward the plush seating

area, never once breaking our kiss. The soft cushions welcomed us as he pressed me down onto the couch, his body fitting perfectly over mine. The music continued to play in the background, adding a melodic backdrop to our dance of lips and tongues. Clothes became unnecessary barriers, and we discarded them with hurried hands and whispered approvals.

Hunter's mouth traced a wet path down my body, his lips exploring every dip and swell with a ravenous need that lit my skin aflame. When he arrived between my thighs, his tongue was my undoing, drawing guttural moans from the depths of my being. My universe contracted to the singular sensation of his mouth against my most intimate flesh. His tongue performed an intricate motion that stoked a mounting tension within me—a crescendo promising sweet release.

I arched into him, and my fingers tangled in his hair, guiding him as I lost myself to the rhythm he set. Then, with a skill that showed exactly how attuned he was to me, Hunter brought me to the edge and over it. My body clenched, seeking and striving until, with a cry that pierced the quiet night, I shattered into a million stars, the explosion echoing through my veins.

Panting, I opened my eyes to find Hunter watching me, a triumphant smile playing on his lips. Leaning off the couch, he reached for his wallet and withdrew the foil packet within. My heart galloped as he pulled out a condom and opened his pants. But before he could do anything else, I stopped him. My hand closed around his wrist like a vice grip, holding him still.

"Let me," I demanded, my voice heavy with the remnants of my climax.

I pushed his hand away and replaced it with my mouth

as he stood in front of me, savoring the taste of him on my lips. I teased and flicked my tongue against him, feeling his body tense and shudder beneath me. His groan reverberated through my body, sparking a new ember within me. The sound he made was raw and desperate, a primal craving that had been seething just beneath the surface.

"Stop, Brenna," he rasped, his hands threading through my hair and holding my head still. "Or this will be over before it even begins."

Letting go, my movements were deliberate and unhurried as I took the foil packet. The crinkle of the wrapper disturbed the still night as I tore it open, locking eyes with him the whole time. His chest rose and fell with ragged breaths, a look of pure greed painted on his handsome face. With care, I rolled the condom down over him, and every touch was a promise.

"Come here," I said, my voice still throaty. "Sit down."

He obeyed, sitting on the couch with his thick shaft very ready. I straddled him, slid down, and took him in slowly, inch by torturous inch. In this position, I could dictate the pace in order to savor the fullness, the stretch, the exquisite friction.

He lounged before me with his eyes half-closed. His mouth was slightly ajar, and I could hear the uneven rhythm of his breaths. A sense of raw power surged within me that he trusted me enough to let me be in control, to surrender willingly. This feeling of confidence coursing through my veins was intoxicating as I held him captive with nothing more than the promise of my touch.

His strong hands gripped my hips, but he continued to let me. A silent conversation of need and desire passed between us. I moved atop him, rising and falling with deliberate slowness as I drew out the pleasure, creating a rhythm that was ours alone. His eyes were the storm personified, and his jaw clenched as he fought to maintain control.

"Hunter," I breathed his name into the night.

"God, Brenna," he groaned in response. "You... you're going to be the end of me."

I smiled at him, my eyes drinking him in as I leaned closer. My hair fell forward over my shoulders, and he plunged both hands into it. Our bodies moved in sync, and our ragged breathing was the only sound.

"I need you," I whispered against his ear, and he shuddered at my words.

"Then take me," he growled.

With that, he reached for my hips, thrusting upward to the point of pain. Our bodies collided, skin sliding against skin, every muscle tensing to meet the other's need. Pain mixed with exquisite, shattering pleasure. Our movements grew more frenzied, each gasp and groan sharing the space between us. His eyes met mine again and something flashed within them.

Anticipation. Need. Surrender.

His hands roamed over my skin with a possessive urgency that only inflamed my desire further. "Oh God." I gasped, clinging to his shoulders as the pressure built again.

"Tell me, Brenna," he murmured against my neck, his breath hot on my sweat-slicked skin. "Tell me you're mine."

"Only yours." The words dissolved into a moan as he surged within me.

"Goddamn right," Hunter growled and locked onto my neck with his teeth. A deep, shuddering moan rippled through me, and his movements grew more insistent, driving us both toward a precipice we were desperate to tumble over.

"Look at me," I demanded. Hunter's eyes met mine,

filled with a wildness that matched my own. "Make me forget everything but this moment,"

I rolled my hips against him, drawing out a low, primal sound from deep within him. "You drive me crazy. I can't get enough."

With a sudden, powerful thrust, Hunter groaned my name as he shuddered beneath me, his release overtaking him. He buried his face in the crook of my neck, his body tensing, then trembling as if he were unleashing every ounce of passion and emotion he possessed. And that was enough to send another climax rushing through me.

As our heartbeats slowed, neither of us moved. I placed my hand over his heart, the thump of it strong under my touch. It gradually slowed to its usual reassuring rhythm. Lifting my head, I brushed a gentle kiss over his lips. I rose off him, but I wasn't ready for clothes yet.

After disposing of the condom, Hunter tossed a fuzzy throw over us. He left his spectacular chest bare and I snuggled up tight, fitting myself against his side as he slid an arm over my shoulders. My fingertips gently skimmed the surface of his skin, following the elaborate tapestry of ink that sprawled across his pecs. The designs were an intricate maze of swirls and patterns, each one meticulously placed to form a stunning visual display. Every curve and line had been thoughtfully considered, weaving a narrative across the broad expanse of his chest and shoulders, extending up to embrace his upper arms.

"This tattoo is incredible. What does it mean?"

Hunter's gaze shifted, and a shadow flickered across the depths of his eyes. "It's a tribute. An American Samoan, Tavita, was in the same unit as me. He was my best friend."

Was.

Emotion swelled within me. Another sad story buried

in his past, but one he wanted to honor. He certainly didn't want pity from me. "Your tattoo is more than ink. It's a story, a legacy."

"We were friends a long time ago, before I met Garret and Myles. Tavita and I went through our Raider training together, and he helped me get through some dark times as I tried to move on from Evan's accident. He was killed during an op... I guess it's been eight years ago. He had a tattoo similar to this, so I got one to help me remember him."

Hunter's eyes held mine. The ghost of his pain flickered there before he masked it with a smile. I wanted to wrap him in words of love, to tell him how deeply he had rooted himself in my heart, but the vulnerability in his gaze held me back. He needed understanding, not declarations that might overwhelm him.

"I'm sure he'd be proud," I said quietly.

"I think so too." Gently cupping the back of my head, he pressed our foreheads together. "But sometimes I feel so broken."

"No, Hunter. *The world breaks everyone and afterward many are strong at the broken places.*'"

He huffed out a quiet laugh. "More Hemingway, huh?"

I stroked my fingers through his dark locks. "You know what it means. Just because you've broken doesn't mean you can't come back even stronger. And you're the strongest person I've ever met."

He sighed another long breath, but this time it sounded more at ease. "You're so perfect. You're the light to my darkness, Brenna."

I moved my hands to his face, the soft hair of his beard silky beneath my fingers. My thumbs brushed gently over his eyelids, urging them to close. I kissed each one softly, feeling the flutter of his lashes against my lips. "Keep them closed."

He complied, a willing participant in this quiet exchange of care. Then I pressed another kiss to his mouth. It was slower, deeper, a mingling of breath and warmth that said everything I couldn't voice aloud. Hunter's arms wrapped around me, pulling me against him with a strength that belied the fragility I had sensed only moments before. As if he were drawing courage from our connection and finding solace in our shared silence.

I relaxed in his embrace. My head found its place on his shoulder, and I stared up at the stars. They were our own private display of light against the darkness, a mirror of the intricate patterns on his skin. And in the quiet of Hunter's rooftop sanctuary, under the watchful eyes of the constellations, I let the unspoken words hang between us.

Sometimes love was loudest when it was silent.

Chapter Twenty-Seven

Hunter

A SENSE of surreal happiness filled me as I swept my gaze around the table, where my siblings and I were celebrating in a corner booth of Conch Republic. All five of us. The air was electric with pride and excitement after our semifinal win against the Marathon Manatees.

"To the Stingrays!" Maia's face was lit with victory as she raised her glass. "One more win and we're taking home that championship trophy."

Evan tried not to laugh as he elbowed Stella. "And here's to our dear sister's sliding catch in the seventh. Thought for sure you were going to face-plant and cost us the game."

"Hey now," Stella protested good-naturedly. "It's called style."

As laughter erupted among us, Luke, the bartender, ambled over with his sandy hair falling into friendly hazel eyes. He set down a frosty pitcher of beer and four glasses. "Heard the good news, so this round's on the house. And some victory chips and salsa to keep you going." With a practiced flourish, he added a large bowl of tortilla chips.

"Thanks, Luke!" Stella called as he headed back to the bar. The tangy scent of salsa mixed with hoppy beer as she poured everyone a glass.

My gaze flicked from face to face around the table— Maia's eyes sparkling with mirth, Evan's easy smile, Gabe enjoying a rare laugh, Stella's wide grin. Something unspoken passed between us, an acknowledgment of the significance of this reunion.

The last time only us siblings were gathered around a table, I was a gangly teenager and more focused on immersing myself inside a book or under the water than appreciating family. And then I became a ghost, haunting overseas locations for years at a time. Now I understood just how precious this was. Maia caught my eye and tilted her head slightly, a silent question in the quirk of her brow. I shook my head almost imperceptibly.

Don't say it out loud. Don't break the spell.

It felt like we were all holding our breaths, afraid that by pointing out the extraordinary nature of this gathering, we'd somehow shatter the fragile magic that had brought us here. Like naming a fear could make it real.

So we sipped our beers and munched on chips, the conversation flowing around safer topics—the game we'd just won, the best dive spots, Stella's latest culinary adventures. But an undercurrent of something deeper hummed beneath the easy banter. Our shared history.

A bond bent and twisted, yet now being repaired.

I leaned back in my chair, and warmth bloomed inside me. I wanted to bottle this feeling, to tuck it away somewhere safe and pull it out when needed. Because despite the laughter and camaraderie, I knew it was tenuous. And so did everyone else around this table.

Gabe's face sobered as he raised his glass. "To family and baseball."

As five frosty glasses clinked in the middle of the table, we all echoed his sentiment, a ripple of tentative acknowledgment going around. And in true oldest brother fashion, Gabe deflected the heavy moment by bringing the conversation back to baseball. "So, championship game coming up. And against those damn Barracudas."

Maia's brow furrowed as she snagged a tortilla chip. "We'll need to get a handle on their ace pitcher and that big slugger of theirs next time."

Stella grinned, her eyes dancing. "Oh, I think we match up rather well with them now," she drawled, her gaze flickering between Evan and me. Pride flared in my chest. Stella had always been our biggest cheerleader, even when we stumbled.

Evan ducked his head, a sheepish smile playing on his lips. "I don't know. I feel like I chickened out by only pitching the first few innings. Manuel really stepped up and secured the win for us."

"Hey, none of that," I said firmly, but I wasn't ready to give his shoulder a supportive squeeze. One step at a time.

Maia's smile faded as she stared at him. "Ev, what you did out there was a massive step, and you were your usual lethal self. You were the one who dug their grave. Manuel just hammered in the nails."

"The Enforcer in action," I added quietly, bringing up Evan's nickname when he'd been a holy terror on the mound. The pitches he'd thrown today might not have been in the same league, but he'd gotten the job done.

Gabe's eyes met mine, a moment of perfect understanding passing between us. We knew the enormity of what Evan had achieved today, the inner battles he'd fought to get here. I'd had my own share of problems, but I wasn't the one who ended up in a wheelchair.

As Evan's posture straightened, tentative confidence settled over him. I leaned back against the worn booth, and the peeling vinyl crackled under my shoulder blades. I inhaled the camaraderie and support swirling around our little corner of Conch Republic, hardly able to believe it.

This.

Right here. Sitting in a dimly lit bar and celebrating with my siblings filled a void that had gaped inside me for too long. Well, partially filled.

I took a long swig, savoring the cool amber liquid sliding down my throat. As much as I relished this reunion, my mind drifted to Brenna. I'd asked if she wanted to attend the semifinal game, but she demurred, citing a family get-together. I was a little surprised at her hesitancy over informing her family about us, given that she was the one who wanted to end the Markham-Coleridge feud.

Then again, I understood better than anyone how complicated family interactions could be. But dammit, I wanted to share this win with her, to have her right next to me amidst the celebratory atmosphere. Was now to time to tell my siblings about us?

The chatter around the table faded into the background as her image consumed my mind. The softness of her skin, the warmth of her smile when she talked about a book. I couldn't shake the feeling that I was getting in too deep. And I still wasn't quite sure how it had happened—I'd tried to make it obvious that I wasn't the man she needed. But every time I saw her, those doubts crumbled, only to double once I was alone and had time to reflect.

"Hey, Hunter, you with us?" Stella's voice brought me back to the present, a teasing smile dancing on her lips.

I blinked, forcing myself to focus on her words. "Yeah. Uh, just lost in thought for a moment there."

"Something wrong?" Gabe asked.

Evan also turned his attention to me, the eyes of all four of them searching mine for answers. The weight of their gazes pressed against my chest, making it hard to breathe. How could I explain the whirlwind of emotions churning inside me, especially when they involved Brenna Coleridge?

"What's wrong, Hunter?" Maia asked, no trace of teasing now.

I hesitated, my fingers tightening around my beer glass. Condensation dampened my palm. But looking at their faces, I knew it was time to come clean. "Nothing's really wrong. Well, maybe." I rubbed my forehead, wondering why the temperature had suddenly shot up.

Gabe gave me a long, evaluating stare. It had been a while since he and I sat in this very bar discussing Brenna, but he could put two and two together. "Let me guess. Is this about a woman?"

My shoulders dropped as I nodded. "Gabe already knows something about this, but I'm involved with someone. Brenna Coleridge."

Silence descended over the table, broken only by the clink of glasses and the low hum of conversation from around us. As I braced myself for their reactions, my heart thudded against my ribs.

To my surprise, a slow, knowing smile spread across Stella's face. "Ha! I suspected as much when I visited your apartment. The way you two looked at each other... it was pretty obvious there was more going on than just the damsel in distress dynamic."

Relief washed through me, followed quickly by a flicker of brotherly irritation. "There wasn't anything going on when you barged in. That all happened later. Is this the part where you tell me we're making a huge mistake?"

Stella's expression turned thoughtful. "Not exactly. I just want you to be careful, Hunter. I know how deeply you feel things, even if you try to hide it behind that tough exterior. And with Brenna's family... well, it could get complicated."

I nodded, unable to refute that. Brenna and I were in uncharted territory, and I knew it wouldn't be an easy path. But as I thought of how we could talk books for hours or the way her smile made me feel, I didn't give a shit about any of it. She was worth it.

"I know it won't be easy," I said, meeting Stella's gaze. "But I'm in this. Brenna... makes me want to be a better man." Heat washed over my face. I felt like a goddamn teenager confessing to his first crush.

Of course, she pretty much was.

Stella reached across the table and patted my hand. "Then I'm happy for you. And I'm here for you, no matter what. We all are."

Gabe leaned back in his seat, a thoughtful look on his face. "Who knows? Maybe this is what our families need. A Coleridge and a Markham together... it could be the catalyst to finally put this stupid feud to rest."

I raised an eyebrow, Gabe's optimistic perspective surprising me. "You really think so?"

Gabe shrugged, a smile tugging at the corners of his mouth. "Why not? It's about time we all moved on from the past. Including me and Ben. We actually managed to have a civil conversation recently. If you and Brenna can find happiness together, then I say more power to you."

Evan nodded in agreement. "Look at me and Liv. Our relationship was anything but easy at first. But in the end, we fought for each other." A grin spread across his face. "And now we're getting married."

Maia rolled her eyes. "Ah yes, the mythical grand event. Have you managed to pin down a date yet? Or maybe the wedding is just fake."

Evan burst into laughter, raising his hands in playful defense. "Easy there, sis. We're ironing out the details as we speak. As soon as Liv and I settle on a date, I promise you'll be the first one on earth to know."

Maia huffed and grabbed a chip from the bowl, then tossed it at Evan. He laughed as it bounced off his chest, catching it with lightning-fast reflexes before it hit the table.

I couldn't help but smile at them. But even as I did, a familiar pang of loneliness struck me. Evan and Maia bantering back and forth reminded me of just how close they were. How much history they all shared. And me? I was the outsider. A youngest son who had finally returned home but still didn't quite fit in.

Would I ever truly belong anywhere?

Stella turned to me, her expression growing serious. "Speaking of relationships, how does Brenna's family feel about you two being together?"

I shifted uncomfortably in my seat, avoiding her gaze. "She hasn't told them yet."

Gabe and Evan exchanged a look, and Maia cocked her head. "Really? Why not?"

I shrugged, feeling defensive. "I don't know. She just hasn't gotten around to it."

Gabe leaned forward, his eyes narrowing. "Or maybe she's worried about how you'll be received."

I bristled at his words, even though I knew he was right. "Look, I'm only telling you guys about it now, so I can't get pissed at her for not telling her family."

Stella sighed, her expression softening. "Hunter, I know this is new for you. But if you and Brenna are serious about each other, you're going to have to face this eventually."

Gabe sprawled back in his chair. A slow smile rose on his face, instantly alerting me. "Maybe it's time to invite Brenna over for a friendly family dinner."

I groaned, imagining the awkwardness, verging on horror, of that scenario. "That's the *last* thing she needs right now."

Laughter rang around the table. I joined in, trying to shake off the unease that had settled over me. But deep down, I knew Gabe was right. If I wanted this relationship with Brenna to work, we needed to test the waters of this supposed feud and see what was really there.

As the laughter died down, our conversation returned to next week's championship game. I pictured myself in the batter's box, staring down the Barracudas' ace. I glanced around the table at my brothers and sisters, and a swell of gratitude rolled through me at their support. Including Evan.

As the night wore on and the beer flowed, I let myself get swept up in the excitement of the moment. But in the back of my mind, I knew there were bigger battles ahead. Battles that had nothing to do with baseball and everything to do with the wounds of the past.

And I couldn't help but wonder if I was ready to face them.

Chapter Twenty-Eight

Brenna

SIESTA SUNSET RESORT resembled a painted postcard as I pulled into the sandy parking lot, the seafoam green buildings gleaming under the midday sun. Plumeria trees swayed in the breeze, and the salty tang of the ocean filled my lungs as I stepped into the humid air.

After climbing a few stairs leading to a light-blue building, I walked through the open-air lobby, my flip-flops echoing on the tile. Comfy furniture with bright floral cushions was clustered in cozy seating areas. At the front desk, Harper grinned and waved me over, her golden-brown curls bouncing.

"Hey, baby sis!" she chirped, leaning over the polished teak counter to wrap me in a tight hug. Her usual cloud of coconut-scented sunscreen enveloped me too. "What brings you around today?"

"Just wanted to say hi." I shrugged, tracing the mosaic of sea glass embedded in the countertop. The truth was I wanted to know if the Dove Key rumor mill had kicked in yet. I trusted that Ben had kept quiet about Hunter and me, but after our PDAs on Main Street, I was curious to see how the old homestead received our new relationship.

"Uh-huh. Hi yourself." Harper arched one shaped brow. "You sure there isn't anything else you want to tell me? Like maybe about your love life?"

And there it is.

My stomach lurched. "What about my love life?"

"Missy's cousin swore she spotted you locking lips with Hunter Markham the other night. At Rousseau's, of all places."

I groaned inwardly. Missy's cousin had a bigger mouth than a grouper, but it had to come out sometime, right? I met Harper's guarded gaze. "It's true. Hunter and I are seeing each other."

She deflated before me, and alarm flitted over her face. "Come on, Bren. Hunter Markham? That man is trouble with a capital T. I saw him running the other morning and could hardly believe my eyes. Sure, he's hot as a habanero, but he's been a complete mystery for years. And what we have heard isn't good."

"Maybe you shouldn't believe everything you hear," I shot back. "People change."

"Sometimes. But he's still a Markham."

Frustration welled that I couldn't deny that, even if I thought the point was stupid. "So what? He's also one of the sweetest, kindest people I've ever known. And I've known him a long time."

Harper folded her arms on the counter and leaned forward. "I don't want to see you get hurt again, not after Knox—"

"I know," I cut her off tersely. The last thing I needed was a reminder. "But Hunter isn't Knox."

Harper pressed her lips together, looking me over with concern softening her eyes. "I just don't want you getting in over your head. Look, I understand that the heart wants what it wants. But some risks aren't worth taking."

I suddenly felt like the walls of the lobby were closing in on me, the cheerful colors too bright, the shell-shaped lamps too glaring. Maybe Harper meant well, but I was a grown woman. I could sleep with whoever I damn well pleased. Even if that someone had a complicated past. Even if our families couldn't stand each other.

I ran an agitated hand through my tresses, blowing out a heavy sigh. "Harper, I love you, but my love life is not up for public debate. The rumor mill in this town is utterly ridiculous."

Harper's brow lowered, and she reached out to touch my arm. "Hey, I'm not trying to meddle. I'm your sister, and I care about you. I just don't want to see you make a mistake by getting involved with the wrong kind of guy. Again."

I rolled my eyes toward the slowly rotating ceiling fan. "Hunter isn't a mistake. He's... different than what people think." I wanted to tell her about the tenderness I'd seen beneath his rough exterior, the way his eyes saw deep inside me, but I bit my tongue. Those were private moments.

"I'm sure he has his good qualities," Harper allowed. "But there are plenty of men in this town! Do you have to be with a Markham? You know the history."

"Our history is just that. History." An edge crept into my voice. "It doesn't have to define the future. Or the present."

"How can it not? The day a Markham met a Coleridge marked the very moment our fortunes changed. Theirs for the better, and ours for the worse."

Sympathy made my heart clench tight. "I know. And I

know you're the one holding it all together and trying to keep the one part of Dove Key we've still got."

"Siesta Sunset isn't in danger of going under, but I won't deny it's a struggle." She gave me a tired smile, then fiddled with the stack of welcome brochures on the desk. "I just don't want to see you get caught in the middle of some generations-old feud. It's not fair to you. And honestly, I'm not sure we can all just let bygones be bygones."

Her cornflower blue eyes shined with love and worry, but that only increased my frustration. "I know you mean well. But you've got to trust that I can handle my own affairs, okay? Let me make my own choices."

Harper stared at me for a long beat. "This might be a situation where we have to agree to disagree. But I'm your big sister, and I'll always be here for you." She came around the desk to wrap me in a fierce hug. "I love you. Even if your taste in men is highly questionable."

"Love you too." I pulled back and grasped her shoulders. "All I'm asking is for you to give him a chance."

She eased out a long sigh. "I can't promise that. Maybe I'm just being an overprotective big sister, but I'm worried you're making a big mistake here. I'm even more worried that Hunter Markham is dangerous. Be careful, okay?"

"He's not Knox. I already said that."

Harper just stared at me. "I know he's not. And that's what scares me." Then she glanced back at the counter. "I'd better get back to work. Keep me in the loop, okay?"

I promised I would and headed for the door, hardly seeing the familiar red-and-yellow Florida Keys mural as I passed. As much as Harper's probing questions had set my teeth on edge, I knew they came from a place of love. But what now? I'd always suspected dating Hunter would cause waves with my family, but confronting the rollers was more daunting than I'd expected.

I skirted the edge of the resort pool, the overhead sun sending shimmering patterns on the surface. Laughter and conversation drifted from Braden's bar, mingling with the splashing in the pool.

I had a sinking feeling this situation with Hunter would get messy before it got better. And as much as I wanted us all to get along, I couldn't force anything. When I rounded the corner of the main building, I spotted Ben hunched over a flowerbed. His blue Siesta Sunset polo was dark with sweat between his shoulder blades. He glanced up as I approached, rising to his feet and swiping an arm across his brow.

"Hey, you." He set aside his spade and pulled off his gardening gloves, giving me his full attention. The furrow between his brows deepened as he took in my expression. "Everything okay? You look a little... rattled."

I blew out a breath, tucking a wayward strand of hair behind my ear. Leave it to my perceptive big brother to zero in on my unease. "Yeah, Harper just grilled me."

Ben's lips pressed into a thin line, and he nodded. "I didn't tell her, by the way."

That made my smile reappear, though it was tentative. "I know. It was the patented Dove Key rumor brigade."

He leaned against his shovel like something out of an old painting. "I'd really hoped this thing between you and this guy would have run its course by now."

And just like that, the smile fell off my face. "Well, it hasn't. This isn't some casual fling, Ben."

"Great." He scrubbed a hand over his face, then his blue eyes flashed. "I thought you had more sense than this." I opened my mouth to respond, but he barreled on, his words tumbling out in an agitated rush. "Have you forgotten what happened with Gabe? The fight that landed me in jail? And Hunter's got an even worse reputation than his brother." His nostrils flared, the vein in his temple pulsing.

"That fight was several years ago, Ben. And look at how you've changed since then." I lifted my chin, meeting his gaze head-on. "Who's to say Hunter can't do the same?"

Ben let out a humorless laugh and shook his head. "Leopards don't change their spots. You're playing with fire."

I bristled at his dismissive tone, my nails biting into my palms. "That's not fair. You don't even know him."

"I know his type." Ben's voice was hard, unyielding. "Reckless, volatile, secretive."

My temper flared, and I drew myself up to my full height as I squared my shoulders. "Like you were, you mean? Before you got your shit together?"

Ben recoiled as if I'd slapped him, hurt flickering in his eyes. Regret twinged inside me, but I pushed on, determined to make him understand. "If you can turn over a new leaf, why is it so hard to believe Hunter might be trying to do the same? That he might be more than his reputation or his family name?"

Ben's stony expression wavered—a crack in his armor. He looked away, and his throat worked as he swallowed. "I just... I don't want to see you get hurt again. You're my little sister, you know?"

My heart clenched at the raw concern in his tone even as frustration simmered under my skin. Why did our families' feud have to taint every aspect of our lives? I took a deep breath and let the salty air fill my lungs. "I know you're trying to protect me, and I love you for that. But I need you to hear me out."

He crossed his arms, his biceps straining against his sweat-dampened T-shirt. "I'm listening, Bren. But I can't promise I'll like what you have to say."

"I know our history with the Markhams is... complicated," I spoke slowly, choosing my words carefully. "But we can't let the mistakes of the past define our future."

Ben's jaw clenched, a muscle ticking beneath his tanned skin. "It's not that simple. There's too much bad blood between us."

"But what if it could be that simple?" I challenged, desperation edging into my tone. "What if we chose to see people for who they are, not just their last name?"

I reached out, grasping Ben's work-roughened hand. "Hunter isn't responsible for the choices his family made. And neither are we. We have a chance to break the cycle, to be better than the generations before us."

Ben's gaze dropped to our intertwined fingers. "I'd like to believe that. But..."

"No buts," I cut in fiercely. "Forgiveness isn't weakness. It's strength. And holding onto this animosity is only hurting us in the end. I'm not asking you to forget the past. I'm asking you to help me build a better future. Can you do that?"

Ben's broad shoulders slumped as he blew out a heavy sigh. When he met my gaze again, I saw a flicker of acceptance in his eyes. It looked like the first ray of sun after a hurricane. "I'll try. For you."

"That's all I'm asking." Hope unfurled in my chest like a sail catching wind. After squeezing his hand, I let my arm drop to my side. "We've got to start somewhere."

"Just keep Gabe and me out of jail, okay?"

I laughed as we embraced, and I soaked in his familiar feel. Even during his bad times, Ben always stood up for me.

Always watched out for me. As he returned to his landscaping, I marveled at the unexpected ally I'd found in my brother. I'd come here expecting to win over Harper and to attempt to reason with Ben. Yet the opposite had happened. He'd come so far from the lost, angry boy he'd once been, and pride swelled within me.

But Hunter and I weren't on an easy path, and my family wasn't exactly rolling out the welcome mat for him. And that made me damn worried. I hadn't talked to my other brothers yet. What if my siblings couldn't accept Hunter? What if my mother hated him when she came back home?

What then?

Closing my eyes, I conjured up memories of stolen moments with Hunter—dancing on the moonlit rooftop, his strong arms around me as we swayed to the music of the night. Lounging on my couch, my legs draped over his lap as we lost ourselves in the pages of our favorite books. The way his eyes crinkled at the corners when he laughed. In those intimate moments, there were no family feuds, no painful pasts, no uncertain futures. Only the two of us.

And just like that, I needed to see him.

Driving away from Siesta Sunset, I headed toward Main Street. And Hunter. The drive passed in a blur as my mind reeled from the tense conversations I'd just had. When I pulled into the parking area behind KeyMark Security, I pushed the encounter with my family away.

I stepped into the building, where Hunter sat alone at his desk, his handsome face creased in concentration as he pored over paperwork. The sight of him, so diligent and focused, filled my heart with affection. And more.

At the sound of my footsteps, he glanced up and his

face instantly brightened. "Hello, beautiful. This is a nice surprise."

I didn't speak as I crossed to him, needing his arms around me, to breathe in his familiar, comforting, and very male scent. With that unconscious grace, he stood and pulled me close, and his strong arms enveloped me. I melted into his embrace, tension draining from my shoulders.

His lips found mine in a sweet, soft kiss hello. Pressing my hand to his face, I drew it out, soaking in his nearness.

"Everything okay?" he murmured as he searched my face.

I nodded, not trusting my voice. How could I burden him with my family's disapproval when we were still finding our footing as a couple? I needed to protect this precious, fragile thing blossoming between us.

Hunter brushed a thumb across my cheek. "I've been thinking... I told my siblings about us, and I want to introduce you. What do you say we take a trip to Calypso Key this weekend? I'll work out something low-key and fun. No pressure."

My heart stuttered. Meet his family? After the reception I'd gotten from Harper and Ben, the prospect filled me with equal parts longing and dread. Could I handle more skepticism about our relationship? Judgment over our families' bitter history? Judgment about me?

But the hopeful gleam in Hunter's big brown eyes melted my defenses. I couldn't deny him, not when he was trying so hard to show how much I meant to him. So I pushed down the doubts churning in my stomach and plastered on a bright smile.

"I would love that," I said brightly, praying my voice didn't waver. "It's gotta happen sometime, right?"

"Exactly. And don't worry about meeting my family. I'll

be right there by your side." Hunter sealed his declaration with a kiss, and I lost myself in the delicious slide of his mouth on mine, the soft rasp of his beard against my skin.

Even as desire coursed through my veins, unease lingered in the back of my mind. Given how my family had reacted—especially Harper, normally the reasonable, supportive one—how would Hunter's siblings feel about seeing us as a couple? Could the Markham-Coleridge feud truly be laid to rest, or were we fooling ourselves by thinking we could overcome generations of resentment?

One bridge at a time.

For now, I'd focus on making a good impression, on proving that Hunter and I belonged together no matter what. If only I could silence the small, insistent voice in my head warning me that we were sailing into dangerous waters. And that maybe neither of us would make it back to shore unscathed.

Chapter Twenty-Nine

Brenna

THE BLACK RANGE ROVER'S tires crunched against sun-bleached sand as we pulled into the Calypso Key parking lot. After exiting the SUV, Hunter's fingers laced through mine. His thumb traced soothing circles on my skin as if he sensed my nervousness about facing a boat full of Markhams. I squeezed his hand, trying to absorb his steadiness as we stepped onto a cement path that wound through manicured foliage.

Glancing around the quiet, serene resort, I tried to deny the sensation of being in enemy territory. I was thirty-one years old, and this was the first time I had set foot on the fabled resort grounds. In school, Hunter and I had always met on neutral ground. But no booby traps snapped on my Coleridge ankles or bound my Coleridge wrists. Calypso Key Resort was decidedly upscale and beautifully modern, and I could hardly keep from staring at the line of beautiful white cottages lining the white-sand beach, swaying palm trees watching over them. The setting was magnificent.

As we approached the canal where several boats were tied up, a tall figure Hunter had already told me about waved to us from the dock. Aiden was Stella's boyfriend and our captain for the afternoon. The sun glinted off his golden hair and his easy smile helped me relax a notch.

"Welcome aboard *Catch of the Day*," Aiden called out as he ushered us toward a beautiful sailboat, well over thirty feet long, with a grand sweep of his arm. Teak decking contrasted a white hull, all of it polished and shipshape.

"Thank you," I said with a smile. Then I shaded my eyes with my hand to scan the vessel. "She's absolutely stunning."

"Thanks!" Aiden grinned like a proud father. "I lived on her before moving into the cottage with Stella. Still love taking her out any chance I get. So thanks for giving me the excuse. We've got perfect weather for a sunset cruise."

He helped me step aboard while Hunter hopped lithely aboard behind me. Hunter's hand found my elbow, guiding me toward a loose circle of canvas camp chairs that had been arranged on the deck. The chairs were painted in bright hues, standing out vividly against the varnished teak flooring. They were positioned to provide an unobstructed view of what I knew would be a breathtaking sunset. And people whose faces I knew well occupied nearly all of them, though I'd hardly exchanged a friendly word with many of them. The butterflies in my stomach doubled their activity.

Stella was already settled into one of these vibrant seats, her toned physique relaxing with her long legs crossed. I hadn't seen her since that embarrassing meeting when she'd found me staying with Hunter, and her dark brown eyes were calculating as I approached. But she greeted me with a smile that eased the tight knot in my stomach slightly. Evan stood alone near the stern, his face slightly guarded and neutral.

As I sat next to Stella, with Hunter on my other side, she leaned forward. "Dad and Nona are staying ashore today. But on behalf of the younger generation, welcome aboard."

"Thanks for having me," I said and was glad my voice was steady.

"I apologize if Aiden talked your ear off about the boat already. I never thought I'd be competing with a sailboat." Stella's words were dry, but her fond glance at Aiden, who was untying us, let me know she was joking.

A wave of relief washed over me as my gaze landed on two familiar faces among this sea of Markhams. April and Liv, though April was a Markham now, and Liv was close to becoming one. April sat next to Gabe, who gave me a nod but kept his face completely unreadable. His expression quickly softened when he turned to his wife and brushed her hair back from her face. Liv perched next to April, and her bright smile was like coming home after a long journey. Seeing her and April here reminded me that I wasn't alone amidst this crowd. I had allies here too.

As the shore retreated, I let out a breath, savoring the salty tang in the air and the soft lap of waves against the hull. Aiden and Stella made quick work of unfurling the sails. So far so good, and no blood had been spilled yet. Rising from his chair, Hunter lifted the lid of a large cooler and extracted two bottles, then popped the caps off with practiced ease.

"Beer o'clock," he said with a wink, passing me one.

I took a long pull, the crisp, cold liquid sliding down my throat. It tasted like summer and fresh starts. Hunter clinked his bottle to mine before settling beside me once again, our knees brushing. Tension unwound from between my shoulder blades as I leaned back, unable to resist the wind in my hair and the man at my side as we chased the sinking sun.

Stella returned to her seat and leaned closer to me, her long, dark ponytail whipping in the breeze. Her brown eyes held a tentative warmth as she scooted to the edge of the chair. "I wanted to apologize for being such a bitch when I saw you at Hunter's place. It caught me off guard, and I lashed out."

"No worries," I replied, giving her a small smile. "I get it. It's a lot to process for all of us." Stella's apology meant more to me than she probably realized. It signified yet another small bridge being built between our families. And a friendlier start to the cruise than I'd dared hope for.

Stella tucked a flyaway strand of hair behind her ear. "So you've had no word from your ex? You're confident he's out of the picture?"

I blinked, the concern in her voice surprising me, but warming to her. "Oh, yeah. I haven't heard from him in a long time now."

Stella's gaze turned sympathetic. "Breakups are tough."

"Yeah. I'm lucky to have Hunter to lean on. He made sure I stayed safe until he was convinced Knox had left town. I'm just focusing on myself and the bookshop now."

"You two will have to come to Orchid sometime. I'll make sure your meals are on the house."

I laughed and said I'd love to. As she moved off to stand beside Aiden at the console, I released a shaky breath. Stella fitted herself against Aiden's side as he guided the boat through the calm water, one hand on the wheel. He planted a kiss against her head, which brought my smile back.

As the boat glided over the gentle waves, Hunter's

warmth seeped into my side. His protective presence grounded me in this sea of Markhams. The tension I had carried like an anchor began to loosen its grip, and a sense of acceptance and maybe even a hint of hope replaced it.

"Doing all right?" The low rumble of Hunter's voice cut through the chatter and whirr of my thoughts. His hand found mine, his calloused fingers interlacing with my own.

I gave his hand a quick squeeze. "Yeah. I am."

But even as the words left my lips, a niggle of worry wormed its way back in. How would my family fit into this equation? The Coleridges were far more accustomed to brandishing harpoons than olive branches where the Markhams were concerned. And though Ben had surprised me, I had a feeling my three other brothers would treat Hunter with more than a little skepticism. But that was a problem for future Brenna. Now I was determined to enjoy the warm breeze against my face.

Half an hour later, April emerged from the steps leading up from the cabin. She moved slowly over the deck toward us, rubbing a hand over her wide belly. She dropped into the canvas chair with a sigh. "I never thought I could pee so much."

Gabe hovered protectively from the seat next to her, his brows drawn together in a frown. "Come here. Put your feet up."

"I'm pregnant, not an invalid." April huffed, but a smile played at the corners of her mouth. Gabe leaned over to remove her sandals, then set her swollen feet in his lap to massage them. April sighed contentedly, her eyes fluttering closed.

Hunter laughed softly beside me, then leaned close. "I can't believe that's my big brother. You might be right about this whole *people changing* thing."

"It's sweet. They're such a cute couple together." The wind whipped strands of my hair across my face. I brushed them away, my attention drawn to movement at the rear of the boat. Evan leaned against the rail near the stern, his posture stiff as he observed our little group. Liv came up beside him, slipped an arm around his waist, and stretched up to press a kiss to his clean-shaven cheek. Some of the tension bled from Evan's shoulders as he sent a smile her way. After a murmured exchange, Liv floated toward me, her gauzy sundress billowing around her knees, and Hunter took the opportunity to talk to Maia.

"I'm so glad you could make it," Liv said, engulfing me in a lavender-scented hug. Wisps of her curly hair tickled my cheek.

"Me too. Thanks for having me." I returned her embrace a bit uncertainly, conscious of Evan's appraising gaze. She might be a friend, but he was all Markham.

Liv pulled back, her green eyes sparkling. "You'll have to stop by Sweet Dreams soon! I'm working on some new cupcake flavors I need a guinea pig for."

"I'm always happy to lend my taste buds to the cause."

"It's set, then. I'll hold you to that." With a last friendly squeeze of my arm, Liv sauntered off to where Maia and her family stood at the bow.

In her wake, Evan approached, hands shoved in the pockets of his shorts. "Brenna." He inclined his head, the greeting polite.

"Hi, Evan. It's been a while."

Discomfort rolled off him in waves, but I caught a flicker of curiosity in his eyes as they flicked between Hunter and me. "I have to admit, I admire that you're taking on the mammoth task of burying the hatchet between our families."

"It's about time someone did, don't you think?" Smiling softly, I tilted my head and studied him for a moment. Despite his reserved demeanor, there was sincerity in his gaze.

Evan's jaw tensed briefly before he nodded. "Yeah, there's been a lot of ill will between us."

A surge of gratitude warmed my chest for the people surrounding me. "Right. It's time to break the cycle and choose a different path."

I could sense Evan's internal struggle, the weight of his family history pressing down on him. But he was here, making an effort to support Hunter and me. "We learned firsthand recently that people can change. Ben did a standout job while he worked here."

"And that's how change begins. Maybe I'm just picking up the torch my big brother set down."

I shot a quick glance at Hunter, who was now talking to Gabe and April. As if sensing my attention, he looked at me, stiffening when he saw who I was talking to. For a moment, heat blazed in his eyes until I gave him a nod to let him know I was fine. And as quick as it appeared, the angry expression fled and he turned back to Gabe. His reaction was curious, but I accepted his unpredictability—another facet of this complicated man.

I turned back to Evan. "Your brother means a lot to me."

Evan gave me a long, evaluating stare. It was intimidating, but I stood tall and met his gaze. He must have approved because the skin around his eyes softened to give him a more relaxed look. "Having Hunter around again has taken some getting used to. But I have a feeling you've helped with the transition. So for that, you've got my thanks." After a nod, he turned and strode back to Liv's side.

I blinked in his wake. Evan wasn't exactly friendly, but of all of them, he had the most complicated relationship with Hunter. I decided to call our exchange a win. In fact, the whole experience made me wonder why no one had tried to end the family hostilities before now.

Maybe because Hunter and I are something special together?

As the boat gently rocked on the waves, Hunter appeared next to me. He took my hand and drew me away from the others to the railing. The sun was just kissing the horizon, painting the undulating waves in strokes of brilliant gold and deep pink. Leaning into his solid strength, a profound sense of rightness stole through me.

Hunter pressed a kiss to my temple, his beard tickling my skin. "Penny for your thoughts?"

"Just... savoring the moment."

"You seem more relaxed now." His fingers idly stroked between my shoulder blades in a comforting rhythm.

"I am," I said quietly. "This cruise... it's been unexpected. And welcome."

I nestled closer, breathing in his mix of clean linen and the underlying musk that was pure Hunter. The slanting rays of the setting sun burnished his angular features, bringing out the rich brown tones in his neat beard. He'd never looked more handsome. Though quiet and watchful during our sail, he hadn't wandered far from me as he balanced being supportive with letting me find my own way.

I tilted my head. "What about you? This little sunset sail had to give you a few nerves too. You feeling okay?"

He nodded. "I've enjoyed myself. Evan's been a bit standoffish—we're still finding our footing around each other. By the way, Gabe told me a few minutes ago that introducing you like this was a good idea. I think he's convinced you don't have invisible horns and a tail." Amusement glinted in his eyes.

I laughed softly, a tentative warmth filling me. Relief. After giving him a slow wink, I turned back to the spectacle on the western sky. Hunter pulled me tight, and we watched another day end.

Eventually, *Catch of the Day* returned to the tranquil waters of the Calypso Key canal. Aiden expertly maneuvered the sailboat into its spot, the gentle bump against the dock signaling the end of our evening. One by one, we disembarked.

April padded over and clasped my hands. "Don't be a stranger, okay? You're practically part of us now. We'll catch up soon."

I squeezed her fingers back, my heart full. "Book club coming up, right?"

She grinned. "Yep, I'm almost done with the book. And don't worry—so's Liv."

Maia and Wyatt waved from the dock, Skye drowsing against her father's shoulder. Even Gabe, known to be the grouchiest of Markhams, smiled and waved before helping his wife off the boat.

As Evan disembarked, he gave me a measured, polite nod. "See you around."

I smiled, but it was tight. He was the only one who hadn't appeared to warm up to me, but maybe I should count my blessings. As he turned away, his eyes lingered on Hunter for a long moment.

I blinked in surprise as a thought struck me. Evan's aloofness might not be entirely about the feud or even my presence. Perhaps it had more to do with the reemerging bond between him and his younger brother. Evan's guarded politeness, the tension that seemed to coil around him... maybe it was a protective instinct, a desire to shield Hunter from harm. I liked that idea.

Hunter steered me toward where his Range Rover waited in the twilight. He opened the passenger door, but before I could climb in, he tugged me back against his chest and captured my lips in a kiss that stole the breath from my lungs. The heat of it zinged through my veins.

"I've been waiting to do that all afternoon," he rumbled against my mouth, his voice low and throaty.

Dazed, my lips tingled as he sauntered around the front of the car and slid behind the wheel with a satisfied smirk playing about his lips. I folded myself into the passenger seat and buckled in. As the engine growled to life, Hunter reached over and laced his fingers with mine, the calluses rough against my palm. "That went well, don't you think?" Pride colored his tone, and I couldn't help but smile.

"It did. Your family welcomed me more than I expected. I actually had a good time, and I wasn't antici-pating that. I just hope..." I trailed off, the unspoken fear curdling in my gut. The palms whizzed past the window, their silhouettes stark against the deepening dusk.

Hunter's hand tightened on mine. "Just hope what?"

Swallowing hard, I forced myself to voice the words threatening to choke me. "I just hope my family can be as accepting of you. Of us."

The winding coastal road soared over the narrow cut between Calypso and Dove Keys, and the water below had turned to rippling onyx under the night sky. A heavy beat of silence stretched between us as we both thought about the afternoon and the next step.

When we arrived at my apartment, the cozy space felt

different somehow. Charged by the fact that we'd surmounted one hurdle, but another one lay just ahead.

Hunter followed me inside, his presence filling up the room. "So when should I meet your family?"

Anxiety clawed at my throat as visions of Hunter facing off against Ben and Eli played out in my mind like a movie I couldn't pause. And a couple of quick calls over the past few days to Braden and my brother Austin had confirmed my fears. They were concerned about me being involved with Hunter too. The Markham bad boy and my Coleridge siblings, mortal enemies standing on opposite sides of a battle line drawn in the sand long before any of us were born.

"Hunter, I..." My mouth went dry, and I swallowed hard. "Today went so well with your family. Better than I could have imagined. Can't we just... focus on that? Figure out my family later?"

He drew his brows together, a flicker of unease darkening his chiseled features. "Brenna, if we're going to make this work, I'll have to meet them sometime."

I knew that. Logically. But my heart kept searching for an escape hatch. Because even though I wanted this to work out more than anything I'd ever known, the tentative acceptance his family had shown me made me afraid. It was chickenshit, but I wanted a way to hold onto this happiness without putting it to the test.

Because I had a sinking feeling I knew how that test would end.

"I know," I continued. "And we will. But I still think one potentially explosive family meeting is enough for one day."

Seeing the turmoil etched on Hunter's striking features, distress shot through me. He was an irresistible force pulling me into his orbit, and all I wanted to do was make him feel good. Closing the gap between us, I placed my hands against his broad chest, the thrum of his heartbeat steady beneath my fingertips. I rose onto my tiptoes, leaning in closer until our breaths mingled in the air. All that mattered was this moment and the man standing before me.

"I don't want to think about our families anymore," I said in a low, throaty voice. "I want to think about you. Only you."

I pressed my lips against his in a kiss that was meant to reassure as much as ignite passion. It was a plea for him to let go of his worries and focus on us—on what we could be together.

Hunter's arms snaked around my waist, pulling me hard against his body. Softening his lips against mine, he deepened the kiss. I gasped as his hand found its way into my hair, his fingers tangling in the locks as he held me close. His tongue teased the seam of my lips, seeking entrance. A low growl rumbled from him as I opened my mouth to let him in. The deeply male sound vibrated through me and sent a jolt of desire straight to my core. My hands slid up his muscled back, tracing the contours of his broad shoulders before coming to rest on the nape of his neck.

"Come upstairs," I murmured against his lips.

He groaned, hauling me tight against the hard plane of his chest. "That's the best idea you've had all day."

Then he was leading me by the hand up the stairs to my apartment. And as the night wrapped around us like a cloak, I lost myself in his touch, his taste, the heady slide of his body against mine.

Tomorrow and all its thorny complications would come. But tonight... Tonight was for us.

Chapter Thirty

Hunter

THE JINGLE of Brenna's keys mingled with the soft sounds of Bookshop in Paradise waking up. As I stood near the back door, I pocketed my phone after scrolling through the day's itinerary. The biggest item was a new security system for a beachfront mansion. Around me, the bookshop unfurled its charm, shelves stocked with tales waiting to whisper secrets to whoever would listen. The air was rich with the scent of freshly brewed coffee and that unique perfume of new pages—a comforting aroma that somehow always managed to settle the restless parts of me.

"Leaving so soon?" Brenna's voice was playful, dancing across the room to where I lingered.

"Got to pay the bills," I replied. "Not all of us are lucky enough to be surrounded by stories all day."

She moved closer with a sly grin. "Ah, but you forget... Where would stories come from without a little real-world excitement?"

In one fluid motion, I drew her into my arms and buried

my nose in her soft hair. The scent of her tropical shampoo filled my senses but couldn't distract me for long. I pulled away just enough to catch her gaze, hoping she didn't notice the uneasiness that fluttered beneath my steady exterior.

"Excitement in my line of work is overrated. I'll take a cup of your coffee to go, though." I smirked, though it wasn't the quality of the brew that weighed on my mind. I'd lain awake for much of last night while the cruise with my family ran through my head. Including my roaring desire, almost compulsion, to defend Brenna when I'd seen her talking to Evan and hadn't known how he'd react. Fortunately, she'd given me that definitive nod, so I'd relaxed and let them be.

And what did that say about me?

All I'd wanted for years was to be close to Evan again. And a rush of protective energy had almost ruined everything. Evan hadn't caused any problems, and Brenna hadn't needed my protection. Which had led to hours of restlessness as I tried to figure out why she wanted to be with me.

Brenna's laugh pulled me back to the present as she left my embrace to cross the floor. Her eyes sparkling with mischief, she unlocked the shop door and propped it open, beckoning the salty breeze. "Of course you want a cup. I make great coffee. One of these days, I'll teach you my secret."

"And will I get it before or after you introduce me to the rest of the Coleridge clan?" My question slipped out couched in jest, but it poked at the other tender spot I kept trying to ignore—the nagging fear that maybe I'd never fit into her world.

Her face became still as she paused across the room, her hands deftly straightening a display of local authors. "Soon.

You know how important it is to me to move beyond all this strife. Which is why we need to be deliberate."

"Sure."

I poured myself a mug of coffee before leaning against the cool back wall. My phone chimed with a text, and I pulled it out to read the message from Garrett. But the words faded as my eyes became unfocused, the weight of my unvoiced worries pressing close. Brenna's words were steel wrapped in velvet, and I wanted to believe them. But as the morning sun streamed through the open door, the tension inside me tightened. She and I wove a beautiful story together—her with her unwavering support, and me with my silent battles. If only I could shake the shadows of doubt long enough to fully step into the warmth.

Because that was something else that had kept me awake. What if this delay in meeting her family was a stalling tactic? What if Brenna agreed that I wasn't what she needed, but she was working up to telling me? I shook my head slightly as I recalled our passionate night. If she was acting, she deserved an Academy Award.

Seeking distraction, I concentrated on my phone as Brenna opened a cardboard box of books and began stacking them on a shelf. Lost in a sea of texts from Myles and Garrett, I barely registered the familiar hum of the shop around me. It all blended into white noise as I leaned casually against the back wall. Until an unwelcome voice cut through my focus like a serrated knife.

"Hey, Brenna."

I hadn't heard that voice in a while, but I recognized it instantly. Every other sound around me disappeared as an icy shiver of déjà vu rocketed up my spine.

The voice was Knox's.

I slid my phone into my pocket, and my spine stiffened.

Easing off my heel, I moved closer, silent as a predator, though I stayed hidden behind a shelf lined with the latest romance bestsellers. My pulse hammered against my ribs, and each beat was a war drum as I weighed my options—whether to step out and confront him or hang back and observe. Marine training had never left me. It had seeped into my bones to become part of my DNA. I assessed angles, exits, and threats with clinical precision while a storm raged inside me.

Peering around the bookcase, I caught sight of him. Knox looked different—the kind of different that wasn't just surface level. His hair was now cut short and neat, and he wore a crisp button-down shirt tucked into khakis. It was as if he'd shed his former self and stepped into someone new. I remembered my reaction last time. The raw, pulsing need to defend Brenna that had overtaken me, and I'd damn near turned the guy into a soprano. I was still fully capable of a repeat performance. Hell, part of me yearned for that.

Except things were different now. In many ways, I'd grown since that previous meeting. The shadows had retreated somewhat. Except for the biggest ones of all. Evan's specter of forgiveness and the logical consequence of that—that Brenna deserved better than me.

"Knox!" Brenna bolted to her feet, her face slack as she stared at him.

"I wanted you to know that I've been staying with my cousin in Fort Myers. Getting clean, and I'm attending AA meetings." Knox's voice was clear and soft, almost unrecognizable from the slurred mumbles I remembered.

But if he made himself a threat, he was in serious trouble. I studied her carefully, noting her shock and alertness, but not seeing any fear. I'd observe for now.

Knox stepped forward, then halted next to a bookcase as

if he didn't want to alarm her. "I know I messed up, Brenna. But I've changed. I'm not asking for forgiveness—I need to earn that. But I am asking for a chance to prove I'm ready to be the guy you deserve."

His voice threaded through the air with a vulnerability that sounded damn sincere. Desperation shined in his eyes, a hunger for redemption that I understood all too well. But this was Brenna he was speaking to. *My* Brenna, goddammit, and my protective instincts flared as hot as the surface of the sun. Every muscle in my body tensed, ready to spring into action at the slightest sign of trouble.

"Knox," she said, her tone steady but not unkind, "it's good to hear you're doing better."

The tension in the room was like a physical presence. Though the man before Brenna bore little resemblance to the drunken mess I remembered, it wasn't his transformation that reverberated through me.

It was the echo of his plea that gnawed at my insides.

"I'm ready to be the guy you deserve."

Those words should have been mine. Instead, they ricocheted around my skull, stirring up the storm of self-doubt that raged beneath my sternum. My fists clenched reflexively, releasing only to clench again tighter, the skin over my knuckles stretched white. Was I any better than him?

He stared at her arm, the arm he'd damaged. "I need to apologize for grabbing you. And... hurting you. I had no right to do that."

"No, you didn't."

"I was really messed up, okay? But I've come such a long way. I've been working in a boatyard, and I'm sure I could get my job back here. We could make a fresh start."

"Knox." Brenna's calm and assertive voice cut through my inner turmoil. "I appreciate your honesty, really. But you need to understand something." She moved behind the counter, her movements deliberate and controlled.

"Forgiveness isn't an issue," she continued. "I forgave you a long time ago. But that doesn't mean we go back to the way things were. I've moved on." Her hands came to rest casually on the counter, just above where I had installed that panic button—a silent signal that belied her outward composure. She clasped her trembling hands.

And that was it.

I was moving before I made the conscious decision to do so. After closing the space between us, I stood behind Brenna and placed my hands on her shoulders in a wordless vow of solidarity. There was power in that touch, a promise that whatever happened, I'd be there to protect her.

"Don't take another step closer," I said softly but with a steel edge, a skill I'd perfected over the years.

Brenna leaned ever so slightly into my support, her spine straightening as if drawing strength from my presence. "Knox, we're not getting back together. I'm with Hunter now."

Knox's face was a picture of disbelief, his eyes darting between Brenna and me as if we were some sort of apparition. The veins in his neck stood out, taut with the effort of keeping his emotions in check.

"Brenna, think this through." Knox's voice held a note of anguish, but it also carried an undercurrent of hurt. Hurt that turned to hard anger when he met my gaze. "I know who you are." Then he shifted his eyes back to Brenna. "You can't seriously want to be with him. Hunter Markham? And you've been afraid *I'm* dangerous?"

Heat rose in my cheeks, the old accusation hitting too close to home, but I held my ground. Silence could be louder than any rebuttal, and my stillness was a wall, an impenetrable warning.

Brenna's head snapped up, her shoulders squaring under my hands as she faced him squarely. "Hunter has been there for me in ways you never were."

Knox's face reddened. He looked like he wanted to say more, but the sight of me standing there, silently daring him, gave him pause.

"I want to make this crystal clear," Brenna said in a distinct, strong voice. "I forgive you for hurting me, but we're through. Forever. So go back to Fort Myers and start fresh. Build a new life for yourself there. Without me."

"I'd be happy to make sure you stay there," I said, the threat implicit in the steady, low quietness of my tone.

Knox looked at me then, really looked, and whatever defiance he had mustered faltered. It was in the slump of his shoulders and the way his eyes lost their fire, replaced by a dawning resignation.

He opened his mouth, but Brenna cut in before he could speak. "Just leave, Knox. For good this time. Believe me, Hunter can keep me safe from any threat."

Behind her, I squared myself to enhance my full height, staring him down and not giving an inch. I'd faced down more adversaries than I could count—I was sure the battle was over. Now it was just the formalities.

"Fine," he murmured. The man before us seemed to shrink, his presence diminishing as he turned away. He slid a hand into his pants pocket before raising his eyes to stare at Brenna. "I've tried to call you, but I'm guessing you blocked my number."

"That was me," I added.

As Knox withdrew his hand from his pocket, a surge of adrenaline coursed through my veins. I tensed, ready to push Brenna to the ground and spring into action. But as Knox opened his hand, I realized it was just a thin slip of paper. I let my muscles relax again, exhaling a silent breath. Knox turned to place the folded slip on the nearby bookshelf. The light caught it to reveal digits scribbled in hasty lines.

"If you change your mind, there's my number." His eyes searched Brenna's face for something—forgiveness, a flicker of doubt, a sign. I couldn't see her reaction, but I felt her tense shoulders under my hands and could picture her eyes holding steady.

"If your ass isn't out that door in five seconds, you're going to regret it," I said through gritted teeth.

Knox turned on his heel, the store silent as he stepped out into the bright morning light.

The muscles in my jaw flexed involuntarily. It was over, but the echo of his words hung in the air between Brenna and me, stirring the whirlpool of emotions inside me even further.

Maybe it was the way Brenna's head followed him, or how the simple act of him leaving his number felt like a challenge to my own place in her life. Knox's walking away didn't just close a chapter of her life. It opened a floodgate of questions for both of us. Knox was a man trying to start over, to be worthy of her. How was I any different? He was right about one thing—my list of sins was a mile long. So was I just Knox in a different package?

But first I had to know how she was after seeing him pop up like a ghost. "Hey. Are you okay?"

Chapter Thirty-One

Brenna

HUNTER'S QUESTION echoed in my head as I gaped at the empty doorway Knox had just exited through. A maelstrom of emotions churned within me. I felt the echo of his words—his earnest plea to start anew—but they crumbled against the tide of realization that swept through me. Knox's return didn't rekindle old flames. Instead, it had cast a stark light on the depth of my feelings for the man behind me.

Hunter's hands rested on my shoulders. His touch was solid and reassuring, yet I needed to find my feet alone. I stepped away and turned to face him, inhaling deeply as I tried to quell the storm inside.

"I'm all right," I lied. And even to my ears, it sounded unconvincing.

Hunter stood before me, a figure sculpted in black tension. Massive and muscular, his presence filled the room. Yet it wasn't just his physicality that commanded attention —it was the taut line of his jaw, his dark hair falling just so and framing a face that held its secrets close. His eyes, usually so warm and inviting to me, were guarded and wary as they flicked back to the shred of paper that lay on the bookshelf. His mouth tightened even more, catching my attention. The sight of Knox's scribbled number seemed to gnaw at him.

Hunter's fingers curled into fists, then released as if he were grappling with an invisible adversary, one that threatened the fragile peace we'd built together. The air between us crackled, and each glance toward the scrawled digits on the paper amplified the volume of the silence.

"Thank you for being here," I said with only a slight tremor in my voice. "When Knox showed up, I wasn't sure... You were so quiet."

"If I'm around, you're never alone, Brenna. I was assessing the situation." Something unreadable laced Hunter's deep baritone. His dark gaze darted again to the torn piece of paper, and the grind of his teeth made his jaw bulge. "He wasn't acting threatening, so I waited. But when I saw you walk over to stand near the panic button, I moved. I can't believe the son of a bitch just waltzed in here like nothing had happened. How did you feel, seeing him again?"

I met his gaze head-on, determined to convey the truth swirling inside me. "It only confirmed what I already knew. I've moved on."

But as the words left my lips, Hunter's reaction wasn't what I had anticipated. Instead of relief or reassurance, his demeanor shifted subtly. He straightened, growing even taller and more imposing. His eyes held a glint of something male and primal—a mixture of protectiveness and possessiveness that made my gut clench.

Whether it was clenching with warning or desire, I wasn't sure.

Turning, he fixated on the hand-scrawled note. As if Knox's mere presence had rekindled insecurities within Hunter—doubts that now showed clearly beneath the heat of his gaze.

"Wait a minute." Boldness surged within me, driven by the need to understand this enigmatic soul who had unexpectedly become the center of my world. "Are you *jealous*?"

The question hung between us, its four syllables heavier than the air pressing against our skin. Hunter's hooded eyes met mine. For a moment, we were suspended in time—the sound of passing cars, the distant laughter of people strolling by on the street all fading into insignificance.

"Maybe," he admitted, though the word came out grudgingly. And in the slight drop of his guard, I glimpsed the vulnerability he fought so hard to conceal—the raw, unvarnished truth of Hunter Markham laid bare.

His admission hit me, and it took everything in me not to reach out and smooth the lines of concern etched into his brow. Yet I held back. Whatever was building between us needed the freedom to crash upon the shore unrestrained. I turned away from him, my gaze falling on the torn piece of paper perched on the edge of the bookshelf.

With a sudden burst of motion, I crossed the floor, snatched the paper, and tore it into pieces. The sound of it ripping between my fingers was cathartic. Pieces of paper fluttered to the floor like broken wings, each fragment a symbol of my determination to move past the threats to what Hunter and I shared now. "Knox doesn't matter. And neither does his number."

Hunter studied me, his body still as a statue, but his eyes... they were alive with an intensity that scorched the air around us. "Knox is a piece of shit," he said slowly, the words laced with tight bitterness, "but he might be right about one thing. Am I any better than him?"

The self-doubt gnawing at him was written in the hard set of his shoulders and the way one hand tapped against his thigh. He was the embodiment of strength. Yet in his eyes, all I saw was a man who believed he was unworthy.

"Stop that," I said firmly. "You're nothing like him."

He let out a tight, humorless laugh. "No, I'm not. Knox is a small-time loser. He pales compared to the mistakes I've made... the things I've done. You shouldn't be with me. I tried to tell you that."

I stormed back to him, the fury inside me igniting. The fragments of Knox's number crunched under my heel in a satisfying punctuation to my mounting anger. I squared my shoulders, facing Hunter with an intensity that matched what I saw on his face.

"Listen to me," I said, my voice rising. "It's not for you to decide what I deserve. Don't you think I should get to determine who I date? Who I'm involved with? I thought we were past this, dammit."

Hunter faltered, his usually stoic presence wavering under my fervor. He looked away and skated a hand over his beard.

But I wasn't finished—not by a long shot. My hands gestured wildly. "Everyone has a past! What matters is what we do with it. And you, Hunter Markham, are doing everything you can to start again. That's the man I'm standing here with. Not the boy who made one mistake that affected the trajectory of his entire life."

As his eyes met mine again, his voice was a low rumble. "Right. You're so proud of me that you won't even introduce me. Even though your family knows about us."

The question sent ripples through the carefully

constructed walls around my heart. How could I explain? That I was the woman who wanted to end this feud between our families, but now I was afraid I was only going to cement it further.

"That's not true," I said through gritted teeth, but the words tasted bitter on my tongue. "And yeah, maybe I need to work some stuff out too. You Markhams have your storied reputation and your success. And we Coleridges have our difficult, scrappy existence."

"So I'm just a fling to hide away, then?" Hunter's voice, sharper than a blade, cut through the pretense. "Because meeting my family—that went fine, didn't it? But when it comes to yours—"

"Look at me, Hunter. I want peace. Peace between your family and mine. But I can't ignore the reality that as we get closer, it gets even more complicated. I can't tell you my siblings won't throw your past in your face. And I don't want to expose you to that since it is very clear right now that you're still confronting a shitload of baggage. And *that* is what you need to deal with."

His jaw clenched, his burning eyes locked on mine. "What are you saying? That we're just... what? Star-crossed lovers, doomed from the start?"

"No." The word came out more forceful than I intended. I reached for his hand, finding it unyielding, but I held on, needing the connection. "I'm scared, okay? I'm terrified that by bringing you into my world, I might lose you. Or I might lose my family. And I can't—I won't let that happen."

"And what about me?" Hunter's words sliced through the air. "When we stepped on Aiden's boat, I didn't know how my family was going to react to you. If they'd treated you with anything less than respect, do you think I would've stood for it? I watched closely the entire time we were out on the water. Ready to act if necessary. Because I won't let anyone mistreat you, Brenna. Not even my own blood."

Anguish tinged his voice, and his fierce loyalty made my heart ache. "Hunter, it's not that I don't trust you or your intentions. It's just... You know about my family, our struggles. Introducing you now, it could—"

"Make them see you're happy?" He cut me off, pulling his hand away to rake it through his hair. "Or do you think I'm not good enough? That I'll always be the black sheep Markham?"

"Stop it! It's not about being good enough. You understand me better than any man I've ever known. This is all about timing, about making sure when we do this, we do it right. Letting my family get used to the idea of you and me. Us."

"Timing!" He scowled, parking his hands on his hips. He looked as if he wanted to say more, but instead, he just stared at me, his entire being tense and tight.

And something snapped in me. Heat swept through me, a wildfire of indignation sparking in my belly. "Look at what you grew up with, Hunter!" I flung my arm toward Calypso Key and its storied resort. "Your family built that place. That huge house, all those bungalows, the history of it all. The Markhams are practically royalty around here."

His eyes flickered with confusion. But I pressed on as centuries-old resentment rose inside me. "But what about the Coleridges? We lost everything to your ancestors. Calypso Key was ours. We've had to sit back and watch as your family experienced success after success with it. And meanwhile, our legacy on Dove Key has been chipped away over the decades."

I paused for a moment. He knew the story as well as I

did of that high-stakes poker game over a century ago. When his risk-taking ancestor beat mine and gained an empire.

Hunter was still as a statue, but his eyes flashed dangerously. "You have no idea the sacrifices my family has made. Present generation included, Brenna."

"I'm sure that's true. But do you have any idea how hard it is for us? To be constantly reminded of all that's not ours anymore?" My hands flailed helplessly in front of me as I struggled to articulate generations' worth of bitterness and regret. "I'm not trying to make excuses, but can't you see? Our side of this divide is different than yours—we're the ones who lost."

I stared at him pleadingly, willing him to understand. That we were trying to navigate through centuries-old grudges and unhealed wounds. And that wasn't even taking into account the problems Hunter himself faced.

"I understand your family hasn't had it easy," I continued. "I understand you haven't. Or Evan. But dammit, Hunter, this isn't just about you! I'm trying to walk a tightrope here between a century of anger and resentment."

"So am I. Between the light and the shadows."

I wanted to be supportive. I wanted to be encouraging. But dammit, I was frustrated. "So what are you saying? Are you just giving up on us? Is this what happened with her? With your great love you lost?"

His face went completely blank. "What are you talking about?"

The words had tumbled out of my mouth before I could stop them. But now that they had, I was determined to have my say. "You told me you were in love once. But obviously it didn't work out, because now there's no sign of her. Well, Hunter, I've got some news for you. No woman can be in a relationship with a ghost! Is she another part of your tragic past? Or just someone who got fed up?"

A completely unreadable expression covered his shock. "Why do you want to know?"

Because I love you.

But that was the last thing I should say out loud. "Because I want to know what happened. I'm curious, okay? Maybe I'm doing something wrong. Maybe I remind you of her, and that's making you back away."

His face was completely inscrutable as he stared at me. I swallowed, thinking I might have just made a big mistake. Maybe this woman was something he couldn't talk about. "Hunter, if you can't talk about her, tell me. There is such depth to you, and I have a strong feeling she's part of it. But I don't want to push too hard."

Hunter scrubbed both hands over his beard, the gesture one of defeat. "I'm not ready to talk about her. Not yet. Look, I need to go. I can't do this right now." He turned on his heel with military precision and headed toward the back door, each step carrying him farther from me. From us.

"Where are you going?" The question was weak and feeble, even to my own ears.

"Somewhere I can breathe," he said, the door closing behind him with an ominous click.

Left alone, I wrapped my arms around myself as if they could hold together the pieces of my heart, which had just splintered. My shop seemed emptier and smaller without Hunter in it. The silence echoed around me, yet our words still hung in the air, their sharp edges cutting through my thoughts.

I picked up a discarded book from the table near the front door, its pages worn and dog-eared. It was an old copy of Romeo and Juliet. My fingers traced over the faded cover as I thought about our own star-crossed predicament.

As I flipped open the book randomly, a bitter laugh escaped my lips. My eyes had landed on Juliet's famous line: *"What's in a name? That which we call a rose by any other name would smell as sweet."*

Would it? Would Hunter be any less a Markham if he bore another name? And would I be any less a Coleridge? I resisted the urge to hurl the book across the room. Was there even room for us amidst all this chaos?

Hunter said he needed space to breathe. Maybe I needed that too—to step back and look at everything from afar. Maybe we both needed time to figure things out separately before trying to piece them together.

Tears welled up in my eyes as I stared blankly at the deserted area around me—the place where our story had begun again. Now, it was a stark reminder of the gaping chasm between us. I stared at the two lovers on the cover of the book. Were Hunter and I destined to stay divided like some modern-day Romeo and Juliet? Unlike them, we still had a chance to change our ending—to write our own story.

But would we let history dictate our fate instead?

Chapter Thirty-Two

Hunter

CROUCHED LOW, the hem of my pants brushed against the grass as I punched the catcher's mitt on my left hand. The Big House stood sentinel in the background, its windows reflecting the light as the sun looked down upon us. And sixty feet, six inches away from me, Evan wound up for another pitch.

The argument with Brenna hung over me like a thunderhead. After I'd stomped out of the bookshop, I called Myles and had him take over the security system installation I'd scheduled. Instead, I sat in my car and watched the bookshop to make sure Knox didn't return. I was pretty confident the guy was gone for good—Knox was impulsive, not a planner. And he'd been clear-headed and utterly defeated when he'd left.

But I had to be sure.

No matter where things stood between Brenna and myself, I wasn't going to let her come to harm. I was done failing. And being too late to make a difference. In the past few days, neither of us had reached out as we let our tumultuous relationship simmer. Which was why I was here throwing a baseball instead of trying to figure out if she and I were off for good. Because even if I'd screwed things up with her, there was still hope of fixing things with my brother.

I caught the ball with a satisfying smack, and the sting vibrated through my hand. But it couldn't distract me. She'd completely floored me with that talk about my lost love. Where had that come from?

And how could I tell her that *she* was my lost love?

Especially now?

Because shit had gotten very complicated during that argument. And Brenna wasn't the only one who was upset. So was I.

I'd woken up determined to hash it out with her one way or the other. After a brutal weight-lifting session, I'd been lying on my couch and stewing as I stroked Pedro, but coming to zero conclusions. When Evan had texted and asked if I could work with him, I couldn't say no.

We had wrapped up hitting practice, where his coaching had sharpened my line drives substantially. Now he was working on his throwing. His next pitch was well off the plate, and I shifted and snatched my glove out to catch it before tossing it back to him.

"Sorry," he called out. "That one got away from me. Good catch."

"Thanks," I mumbled.

Again, I focused on Evan, but I couldn't shake Brenna's angry, frustrated words echoing in my ears. The unresolved tension between us was an invisible barrier I wanted and needed to tear down. But Evan needed me too.

As he took a brief pause, tossing the ball up and down in

his hand, my eyes darted to my gear bag nestled against the vibrant bougainvillea hedge. The contents hidden inside, and the risk I was taking at last, made nerves knot in my stomach. Brenna's words had rung of truth when she'd told me I had to deal with the whole Evan thing. He and I had come a long way, but he didn't know the whole story about that dive.

Would it make a difference? I had no idea, but what was in my bag might tell me.

I'd become the bad boy who couldn't escape his past, but with Brenna, I wanted to be something more. She was the bridge I needed to get there. But she was right—I couldn't even get to that bridge without Evan.

"Another round?" I called out.

"Let's do it," Evan replied, nodding with the brim of his cap dipping low across his forehead.

The next pitch came hurtling toward me. I hardly needed to move my mitt to catch it, and the sting in my palm was a sharp reminder to stay present despite where my thoughts kept drifting. After removing my glove, I shook out my hand.

"You might need to ice that," Evan said, his voice tinged with amusement.

"Or maybe you could just ease up on those fastballs." I forced a smile as I settled back into position. His laughter was a brief, welcome distraction from the turmoil broiling inside me.

"You getting soft on me?" He wound up for another pitch.

"You're the one who likes to point out that we're playing in a rec league." I almost missed an easy catch and sprawled onto the ground.

"Focus, man!"

"Sorry. Maybe the pressure's getting to me." I straightened and crouched again.

Evan barked a laugh. "Yeah. I could see how catching would be way more stressful than combat."

I smiled behind my mask, but there was little humor in it as he threw a massive twelve-to-six curve toward me. I managed to catch that one.

He peaked a brow. "Or maybe something else is eating you?"

"I've got some shit going on."

"Take five?" Evan suggested, pulling off his cap and running a hand through his sweat-dampened hair.

"Sounds good."

We settled onto the cool grass near our equipment, and I took a long drink of water. My bag called to me once again.

Evan stretched out his right leg and rubbed his knee absently. "You keep looking at your gear. Are you having an equipment problem?"

And there it was.

The opening I'd been waiting for. Now I had to seize it.

Taking a deep breath of courage, I shook my head. "It's not that. I've got something else in my bag. Something I've been holding onto for a long time." I picked at the blades of grass, trying to put the words together. I felt unsteady, like a boat rocked by waves, but it was time to face the storm head-on. "There's something I've never told you about that day we dove the *Benson* wreck."

Evan's gaze snapped to mine, his brow creasing with concern. "What?"

"The reason we were there. Why I wanted to dive that deep room on that particular day. It was supposed to be a celebration." Now my words tumbled out, leaden with the weight of years of guilt. "You were headed to the Major

Leagues, and I... I wanted to do something special for you. Something memorable."

His eyes widened at my admission, and for a moment, I couldn't speak. The silence hung between us like the dense air before a storm. My heart racing, I reached for my gear bag and plunged my hand inside. I grasped the MVP trophy, that tragic symbol of what should have been Evan's greatest triumph.

As soon as he'd texted me this morning, I dug it out of that old box and stuffed it into my bag before I could second-guess myself. Now, it felt cold and accusatory in my grasp when I removed it and held it out to him. His face was perplexed as he took the trophy and turned it around in his hands to study it.

And slowly, haltingly, I told him the story of what I'd hoped would happen that day. And how it had gone horribly, irreparably wrong.

When I was done, I met his eyes, tapping my finger on the grass to emphasize my words. "Not a single day has gone by since. Not. A single. One. That I don't think about what happened." My voice was deep and thick, raw honesty scraping at my insides.

Dropping his eyes, he brushed his thumb over the inscription at the base of the trophy. Words that had gone unspoken for over a decade.

MVP Evan Markham. To the first of many awards. I'm proud to call you brother. Love, Hunter.

"Fourteen years," he murmured.

"I'm sorry, Evan. I wish it had been me. It *should* have been me." At last, my voice cracked with the admission—the truth—I'd believed for so long. I had to swallow hard. The apology hung in the air, a lifeline thrown into the churning sea of our past.

He glanced up at me, and the storm of emotion was clear in his eyes—the pain, the confusion. Then he breathed a sigh that sounded like it weighed a thousand pounds. "That's not true. It shouldn't have been either of us."

His words were soothing, but I shook my head. I wasn't ready to be soothed. "I don't expect you to forgive me. Not when I can't forgive myself."

Without thinking, I did something I hadn't done in years. Until Brenna. I straightened and lifted my shirt up, exposing all the scars. The bullet holes. Evan's eyes flew open even wider.

"I spent years chasing... I don't know what. Oblivion? I didn't care whether I lived or died. Every time I completed a mission, I hoped it would be enough. Enough to somehow make up for what I'd done. But it didn't. Most of the time, it just brought more failure."

Evan opened and closed his mouth a few times, then cleared his throat as he wrenched his eyes to meet mine. "I lived at the bottom of a deep, black pit of self-pity for a long time, Hunter. Seeing you again at the wedding provided the catalyst to see how lost I was. Liv was the one who extended a hand to help me out of that hole. None of us really knew what you did while you were in the Marines. But I'm finally able to see I'm not the only one who's... suffered. This past year has made it clear that I need to come to terms with that day on the *Benson*. And with you."

He turned the trophy around in his hands, then stared into the distance. "And I need to take responsibility for my own part in this. I let myself drown in fury, hatred, and despair for way too long. But after the first few years, I settled into this weird kind of stasis. I made a new life and as long as no one mentioned you, I did okay. All those years, and you never tried to come home. For Christmas, birthdays..."

"I wasn't around for most holidays," I said as he returned his attention to me, and our gazes held. "I spent most of my time overseas on deployments. But I understand what you meant about getting along fine as long as you weren't reminded of... what we'd lost. I pretty much did the same thing. Until Gabe called and asked me to come to his wedding."

Evan barked a laugh. "Yeah. There was no more hiding after that, huh? God, I almost blew it with Liv that night. But in retrospect, it made me understand that it was high time to face the demons and finally try to vanquish them."

The breeze toyed with the edges of my hair as Evan struggled with the weight of the moment. His fingers traced the gleaming surface of the trophy, studying it carefully— the symbol of triumph that had been obliterated by our shared tragedy.

"I forgive you," he said finally. His voice was low, but it carried the strength of a tempest. "We both need for me to do that. Being around you again has made me realize how close we used to be, and I miss that. Forgiveness is the first step, right? And now I hope you can forgive yourself."

Something inside me shifted at those words, like a lock clicking into place after years of being jammed. Relief flooded my veins to mingle with an ache that had burrowed deep in my bones. "Evan..." My voice was rough, emotion thickening each syllable. "That's more than I ever thought I'd get."

"Life's too short to hold onto anger, Hunter." He studied the trophy again before raising his eyes to mine. "Thanks for the trophy and for what you were trying to say with it. We've both been living in the shadow of that day for too long."

"Thank you." My words were simple, but they held the weight of years of guilt and regret, now finally starting to lose their grip. I wanted to reach out, to bridge the physical space between us. But I stayed put, respecting the process that forgiveness required. Evan was the older brother and the one who had suffered most of the consequences of that day. I would wait for him to cross that final divide.

"You're welcome. Forgive and forget. Isn't that the old saying? Yeah, I'm ready to forgive you. But I don't know how to forget about it."

"I don't know that either of us can," I said with a shrug. "But we've made a start, haven't we?"

"We have, and I feel better having gotten all that shit out. Let's just take it one step at a time, okay?" Evan offered a tentative smile, and I mirrored it back at him.

"Of course."

As we sat there on the cool grass, the past no longer felt like an anchor dragging us down to dark depths. For the first time in fourteen years, I glimpsed the surface and saw the possibility of breaking through to breathe freely once again. I plucked a blade of grass, twirling it between my fingers as I tried to shake off the weight of our conversation.

Evan stared at me, evaluating, and pointed the trophy at me. "Is this why you were so preoccupied while we practiced?"

"Partly." The fact was, I needed to talk to someone. And Evan had just reached out in a way I never thought I'd live to see. "Brenna and I got into it a few days ago. It might be time to add something else to the list of my screwups."

Evan's brow smoothed as a faint smile came over his face. He set the trophy down in the grass. "Screwing up with women is something I can definitely relate to. What happened?"

As I recounted Knox showing up, then our strained, tense words afterward, I realized something that had been gnawing at me. Something I hadn't acknowledged yet. "I was upset that she felt the same way as her siblings—the resentment toward us. She doesn't resent me personally, but us as a family? That came through loud and clear."

Evan sat up, brushing off his hands. His expression was serious, but his eyes held a glimmer of empathy. "You two don't have an easy road ahead."

"Understatement of the century," I muttered, my gaze drifting toward the Big House.

"Look." Evan's tone was earnest as he leaned closer. "Our families have been butting heads since before the Titanic sank. One high-stakes poker game spiraled into well over a century of bitterness. And their own holdings have been steadily chipped away until only Siesta Sunset is left." He paused, searching my face. "If I were in their shoes, I'd probably feel the same."

"I don't know what to do. What to say. Am I supposed to apologize for being a Markham or something?"

Evan grinned. "Never apologize for that. I watched Brenna carefully when we went for that sail. I liked her, and she might be right. Maybe it's finally time to move beyond this ill will." He cocked his head. "You've got the guts to challenge the status quo. And I think she does too. Relationships have been built on less than that." He grinned like he'd just said a private joke.

"I'll call her and see if I can string together a coherent thought," I said glumly.

Evan burst out laughing. "You're the poet of the family, so that shouldn't be too hard, right?"

I shot him a rueful look. "Turns out words aren't as easy to find when they're not written on the page in front of you. But I'll give it a shot."

As I flicked a speck of dirt from my catcher's mitt, the leather felt well-worn and familiar against my palm. I took a deep breath, clearly seeing the parallels between the man sitting beside me and the woman who now lived in every corner of my heart.

Mending the ripped canvases, the one with Evan and the one with Brenna, were intertwined. Inexorably. Until I sorted both out, I couldn't move forward. My gaze drifted to the small gold object lying in the grass. Today had been a big step toward that, though Evan and I were both still unsure around each other. But I finally believed more steps would come.

He picked up the trophy and saluted me with it. "Thanks again for giving me this. And for telling me the story behind it. People have been trying to tell me for years that there were two victims that day." He shook his head. "I could never see that—I was too consumed by anger. But now I get it. I'm glad to have you back home, Hunter."

A deep, hard lump formed in my throat. The urge rose in me again—to embrace him. And again, I held back, instead giving him a nod. "I'm glad to be back too. What do you say we get back to it?"

Evan stood, stretching his legs and offering me a helping hand up. His grin was infectious, and despite the weight of the world, it urged me to smile too.

"Guess we'd better start focusing on that championship," he said. "It's this Saturday."

"Right."

The championship. Another battle to win. And if we

claimed victory there, then maybe I could face Brenna with the same determination.

Chapter Thirty-Three

Brenna

A SENSE of déjà vu filled me as I stepped inside Island Breeze Bistro. Months had passed since I was last here, and so much had changed since that day Knox hurt my arm at the farmer's market. Yet the retro diner hadn't changed at all, same black-and-white tile floor, same red booths with cracked upholstery. As I slid into a booth, the comforting scent of hot French fries wafted over to me. Harper arrived moments later and scooted in across from me. We each ordered chocolate milkshakes and handed our menus back to the server.

I was at a loss as to how to mend things with Hunter. He was right about needing to meet my family, yet I couldn't be confident the meeting wouldn't turn into World War III. And after the meeting Harper and I had shared with our brothers, I wasn't sure about that at all. She still had plenty of doubts too but was true to her word to be my shoulder to lean on, and she agreed to meet me here to discuss things further.

"I expected resistance from Eli, but I kind of thought Austin and Braden would be a little more positive about Hunter," I said with a frown.

Harper traced a condensation ring on the table with her finger, her gaze distant. "They're like me, Brenna. We all just want you to be happy. And... they have their doubts about Hunter."

A pang struck me at her words, the same doubt echoing in my own heart. But it was still a jolt to hear it voiced so plainly. "Same old story." When our milkshakes arrived, I took a long pull of the icy sweetness.

"Look"—Harper reached across the table to give my hand a reassuring squeeze—"we've got the most protective brothers on earth. And Hunter is setting off big-time alarm bells for them."

"And for you."

She shrugged but didn't reply, just drank her milkshake. That was all the answer I needed. "I get that this situation is complicated and that Hunter is too." I understood that both of us had a part in building the fence that now stood between us. Me in feeling like I was choosing him or my family, and Hunter needing to overthrow the demons that had tormented him for over a decade. I'd thought he was well on the way to that until our argument, and his phone call to me early this morning hadn't settled anything either.

Harper's eyes locked onto mine with such intensity it felt like she was trying to decipher my soul. "How serious has this relationship gotten, Brenna?"

I took another drink of my shake. The liquid courage did little to untangle the knot in my throat. "I love him."

"Oh dear." Harper leaned back, a frown creasing her forehead. "Even with all the... baggage?"

"So what?" My fingers traced the beads of water on the

cold metal shake container. "He gets me, Harper. In a way no one else has."

"I'm guessing Knox didn't get you."

"Definitely not." I let out a half-snort, half-sigh. "Knox never did understand why I love books so much. It was always 'Why do you need to have a book all the time? Let's go out.' But Hunter"—a smile tugged at my lips despite the turmoil inside me—"he'd ask what story had captured me today, then sit down and read with me."

"Really?" She looked intrigued now, leaning forward, elbows on the table.

"Yes." I thought back to the nights Hunter and I spent curled up on the couch, lost in separate novels, yet together in silent camaraderie. How he would listen, really listen, when I raved about a character or plot twist. And how we exploded together in the bedroom—another area where he understood me like no one else ever had.

"Knox wanted me to be someone I'm not. But Hunter dives into my world with me. He doesn't just tolerate my passions, he shares them. That's rare, Harper. It's special."

I drummed my fingers on the table, the worn white Formica tabletop beneath them representing a familiar comfort. My mind was adrift, trying to think of ways to help Hunter heal his wounds. And knowing that I couldn't—he and Evan had to do that themselves. And until that happened, the twisting knot in my stomach told me Hunter would never emerge from the shadows.

"Are you saying the rumors about Hunter are wrong? That he didn't leave town after almost killing Evan only to move on to... worse things?" Harper's words were soft, searching.

"Hunter's been through hell and back. The accident... he'd just graduated from high school! And Evan wasn't much older. Everyone that age thinks they're invincible. And his time with the Marines? God, Harper, he saw things you and I can't even imagine. He had to make decisions that had life-and-death consequences. So yeah. All of that left a mark on him."

"But is he stuck there?"

"I don't know." Fear gnawed at my insides. "He called me this morning." After days of nothing—from both our sides—I'd been happy to hear his deep voice. But our conversation had quickly deteriorated to a rehash of the other day. "It didn't go well. And I told him we can't be together until he works through his problems. But he's got a point too—with my hesitancy about him meeting you guys. So the upshot is we're talking a little but not getting anywhere."

Harper shot me a small smile, as if she couldn't help it. "But he reached out to you, right? That says something."

I nodded. "He cares, but I don't know if he'll ever stop fighting his feelings. Sometimes I think he's here with me, really here. But other times, there's this distance, a barrier I'm not sure either of us knows how to dismantle. His past."

"And where does that leave you?"

I met her gaze, finding an echo of my own turmoil reflected there. "I'm afraid of being trapped there with him. And it's all tied up with his accident with Evan. This morning, he told me he and Evan were actually talking through things, and that has to be a good sign. But they've been estranged for so long, and I don't want to wait in limbo while they work out their problems." I didn't mention his lost love. That felt too private, but I suspected she was part of this awful mixture of dread too.

"Have you told him this?" Harper pressed, her probing eyes searching mine.

"I don't know how."

"You realize you can't change him, right?"

I slumped in my seat. "I know that. I really do. And what makes this so hard is that it isn't just about Hunter and me. Entire families are involved!" Frustrated, I dragged a hand through my hair. "I wanted us—Hunter and me—to be a bridge between our families. To show all of you that old grudges don't have to dictate our lives."

"I know you did, honey."

"And I can't believe that Ben—" I laughed without humor. "Ben!—is the one who has been sympathetic." I huffed and rolled my tight shoulders. At our little family meeting, Ben had been the only one openly willing to give Hunter a chance. "If Ben's the only ally we have, maybe that's a sign. Maybe Hunter and I are just... tempting fate."

My sister winced. "I don't want you to get hurt, Bren! I don't think any of us feel hatred toward the Markhams anymore. Too much time has gone by. It's more the particular Markham you're involved with..."

My face flushed with heat, a mixture of anger and defense swelling within me. "See, that's what's pissing me off about all this! You're making a rash judgment about Hunter without having truly met him. And that's exactly what people have done to us Coleridges for as long as I can remember."

"Maybe there's some truth to that," she conceded, taking a drink of milkshake.

Pursing my lips together, my frustration boiled over. "And yet, I'm afraid if I bring him to the resort, a brawl will break out! You want to know what else he said? Hunter told me he'd never let his family treat me poorly. That if my meeting with them had gotten ugly, he would have put a stop to it. Can you understand how shitty that makes me feel? That I can't automatically say the same thing back to him?"

Harper stared at me evenly, then arched a brow. "But it's easier for him to say that, isn't it? He's been estranged from them for over a decade."

She had a point, but defensive heat seared through me. I was about to give her a sharp retort when my phone buzzed against the wooden table. Hunter's name lit up the screen, and my heart stuttered.

My consternation must have shown because Harper's forehead grew lined. "Everything okay?"

"Uh, yeah," I mumbled, thumbing the message open. Hunter's words scrolled across the screen, simple yet weighted with emotion. "Hunter just texted me."

> Hunter: I miss you, and I'm sorry about this morning. Hope to see you at the championship game tomorrow.

My fingers hovered above the keypad. What was I supposed to say to that? I couldn't tell him how much I missed him, how much just seeing a simple text gave me hope. Not when so much was in the air. I read his words out loud.

"Are you going to reply?" Harper's question nudged me back to reality, though I wasn't sure where that was anymore.

"I don't know what to say. We have so much to settle, and it's too much to put into a text. I need more time." I stared at the phone in my hand, my heart thumping away.

Harper's gaze was patient but insistent. "How do you feel about going to the game?"

The image of Hunter standing on that baseball diamond, eyes searching the crowd for a face he hoped to see—mine—flashed before me. My stomach churned. "It's the championship, so I'd love to be there for him. But..."

Harper cocked her head to one side, considering me. "You've seen changes in him, haven't you?"

I nodded. "He's not the same guy who left all those years ago. He's really trying to move forward."

Harper smiled. "If there's one thing about you, Brenna, it's your knack for seeing the best in people. Even when they can't see it themselves."

Her words should have comforted me, but instead, they added weight to the decision I needed to make. Was I seeing the best in Hunter, or was I clinging to a hopeful illusion? Groaning, I rubbed my eyes with my palms. "This is a huge mess."

"Look at me, Brenna." I lowered my hands to stare at her. "Are you miserable because you're not with Hunter? Or because of all those complications he brings?"

I sighed, letting the sounds of the diner fill the brief silence. "I don't know. That's the problem."

"Then listen to your heart. It hasn't steered you wrong yet."

When we left the restaurant, the humidity seeped into my bones. We walked to the parking lot, and I leaned against the door of my car. "Thanks for listening."

"Of course. Trust your gut on this, Bren." Harper gave me a half-hug, her presence always steady when I felt adrift. She stepped back, and I watched her retreat to her own car before slipping into the driver's seat of mine. My phone's screen cast a pale glow as I held it. For a long moment, I stared at Hunter's message, reading his words over and over.

I missed him horribly. There was no use pretending otherwise. But could I stand beside him, come what may?

My thumbs hovered over the keyboard before they began to move with a will of their own.

> Brenna: I miss you too. Good luck at the game.

Sending it felt like casting a bottle into the ocean, uncertain if the message would reach the shore or be swallowed by the waves. But I couldn't promise I'd be there, not when my heart was still so uncertain. I needed to think this through, and I only had a day to do it.

Chapter Thirty-Four

Hunter

"COME ON, HUNTER!" Maia shouted from the dugout. "Knock the cover off the ball."

Without reacting to her encouragement, I tightened my grip on the aluminum bat and stepped up to the plate. The early afternoon sun blazed down on us, making the Big Pine Key baseball field shimmer like an emerald. Palms swayed lazily beyond the outfield fence, and the air was thick with the scent of freshly cut grass—a balmy tropical day that seemed at odds with the tension of a championship game.

We were running out of time. The Sugarloaf Key Barracudas were ahead, thanks to their ace pitcher, Tom, who'd been shutting us down all game. Except for Evan. In the sixth inning, he'd launched a solo home run that gave our Stingrays a flicker of hope as he narrowed our deficit to two runs to one.

Evan had pitched a solid game—more than solid, really. But his fastball didn't have the usual sting of our sessions behind the Big House. Last inning, I'd jogged out to the mound, peering at him for any sign of injury. "What's up? Is something wrong with your arm?"

Evan just frowned, the lines around his mouth deepening. "It's a rec league, Hunter." He shook his head. "I'm not gonna throw my best stuff to a bunch of neighbors. That wouldn't be sportsmanlike."

"Sportsmanlike?" I snorted, glancing over at the Barracudas' dugout where Tom was practically breathing fire, no qualms about showing us his best. Not to mention their goddamn slugger, Brent Hannigan. Since our catharsis the other day behind the Big House, Evan and I had become easier around each other. Finally relaxed enough that I could tell him what was on my mind. "Their guys don't seem too concerned with being gentlemanly. And maybe you've been a little too easy on Brent. We're behind, you know."

"There's still time. I'll tighten up if I need to. Don't worry." Evan shrugged, the muscles in his jaw working as he suppressed whatever emotions were brewing beneath the surface. "We play our game, our way."

Our way was apparently him pitching just enough to keep us in the game without making the Barracudas look like fools. It was typical Evan, trying to find balance.

"Fine. Let's get this win, then." I clapped him on the shoulder.

"That's the plan." The determined glint in his eye told me he wasn't going to let this game slip through our fingers.

Now, as I settled into the batter's box in the top of the ninth inning, digging my cleats into the earth, it was my turn to do what I could. For the team, for Evan, and for the second chance we were both scrabbling after. Maybe it made no sense, but I couldn't shake the feeling that my future hung in the balance right now. I took a deep breath and expelled it in a rush.

My gaze involuntarily flicked to the bleachers for the hundredth time. To where Brenna sat, her willowy figure unmistakable even at this distance, sitting beside April, who looked about ready to pop. I couldn't believe Brenna had shown up. After her text, I'd been positive she wouldn't come.

I was wrong.

"Come on, Hunter!" Aiden called from first base, snapping me back to reality. He'd just hit a single and was itching to advance. I nodded, gripping the bat tighter as he took a healthy lead.

Tom wound up, his arm a blur as he released a fastball that cut through the air like a knife. Time slowed as I tracked its path, every muscle coiled and ready. I was laser-focused on the ball, not even thinking as I began my swing. Pure instinct.

And then, contact.

The crack of the bat meeting the ball resounded like a thunderclap and sent the crowd into a frenzy. I watched, almost in disbelief, as the ball arced high.

Higher.

Then it sailed over the outfield fence.

"Yeah, Hunter!" The shouts from the dugout reached me, distant and muffled as if underwater. But I was already in motion, legs almost numb as adrenaline surged through me. Rounding the bases, I didn't dare look into the stands, afraid to break the spell of the moment.

I crossed home plate and fell into a back-slapping hug with Aiden as reality hit me—we'd just taken the lead. Three to two, just like that. A raw and exultant cheer ripped from my throat as I scanned the crowd for Brenna's face. She cheered wildly for me, on her feet. Her eyes held a note of pride and suspense I tried not to read too much into. Her presence here was a curveball I hadn't seen coming, and yet it felt so right. Our gazes held for a long moment, and my body felt light and free as Aiden and I strolled off the field.

As I entered the dugout, Evan was waiting. He raised both hands, and I met them with mine in a solid high ten, the slap echoing our exhilaration. His eyes blazed with that old fire. "Way to bring it home!"

Stella stepped up to bat next, her stance confident, her eyes fierce. She swung, connecting a sharp crack, but the ball skimmed low—a grounder speeding toward the short-stop. The throw was quick and precise, and she was out, ending our turn at bat.

"Nice try!" I called, applauding for Stella as she trotted back to the dugout.

As I strapped on my catcher's gear, the weight of the pads felt like armor, the mask a visor for the final battle. This was it—the last half inning to defend what we had fought for all season.

Maia clapped her hands. "Okay, guys! All we have to do is hold them. Holy shit, am I nervous now. Let's keep our same positions. It's worked all game—"

"Maia." Evan stepped forward and cut her off. "I think we should change it up."

Her face went blank. "You do? What do you mean?"

Evan stared straight at her. "I want to take over as manager."

Silence blanketed us for a heartbeat, then under-standing rippled through the team. At what it meant for Evan to step up at long last and take center stage. Everyone straightened a little as those sharp blue eyes raked over us.

Then they stopped on Maia. "But it's your call. What do you say?"

She bit her lip, then nodded. "I'd love it if you led us, Evan."

He gave her a brief smile before his expression hardened, his eyes becoming fierce. "Hunter just scored the go-ahead run. All we have to do is hold them for a half inning and this game is ours, guys."

Liv's hands twisted together, her face pale beneath the brim of her cap. "Maybe I should sit this one out, honey. I missed my last catch in the sixth inning, and that gave them the lead. Someone else could definitely do better than me."

Evan's expression softened as he brushed his knuckles over her cheek. "None of that. We all got here together, remember?" His gaze swept over each of us before settling back on her. "Everyone plays, including you."

Then he straightened, and all of us followed suit. I damn near stood at attention from the authority he was radiating. "Aiden," Evan said, pointing to the doctor. "I'm moving you to shortstop. Your speed is what we need right now."

"Got it," Aiden replied, his face setting into determined lines.

"Gabe, you're on first. Maia, take third base. I want you on the hot corner. Wyatt, be on high alert out there at center." Evan's commands were met with immediate nods from everyone. "We play as one, and we win as one. Let's show these assholes how it's done."

While everyone else trotted to the diamond, I strapped on the rest of my catcher's gear. Evan and I were alone, and I caught his eye. "You've got your game face on, but what about Brent? He's up third." In addition to scoring all the Barracudas' runs, Brent Harrigan had hit the ball Liv was worrying about, which only made me more pissed at the guy. Plus, he'd been a jerk the whole season.

Evan's lips curled into a grin that was anything but friendly. "Brent? I went toe-to-toe with that prick in the minors. Trust me, I've got his number."

Laughter rose from my chest. "What about keeping it clean enough for the rec league?"

"I'm not a dirty player, but I'll do what it takes to win," Evan snapped. This was the Evan I remembered. The Enforcer, his nickname when he'd been notorious for not giving an inch. "Don't worry. He'll get what he deserves."

As Evan settled on the mound, I crouched behind home plate. I risked a quick glance at Brenna, who chewed on her lips as she sat with her hands pressed between her knees. Next to her, April was frowning and shifting on the bleachers. Everyone was feeling the tension.

As Evan struck out the first two batters with ease, pride filled me. He was pitching at full capacity now, and the two Barracudas hadn't even made contact with his fastball. Redemption suited him well. Our Stingrays were more than just a team—we were a family making ourselves whole again.

The Barracudas' slugger approached. His bat tapped an impatient rhythm against his cleats, then he settled in with his toes hugging the line.

"Careful, Brent," I said casually. "You're a bit close there."

He shot me a dirty look, the corner of his mouth twisting. "I'll stand wherever I damn well please."

God this guy is an asshole.

Enough. Focusing on the pitcher's mound, I signaled for an inside fastball. My brother's response was measured —a slow nod I remembered very well. Evan wound up and let it fly. The pitch hurtled toward home, a streak of white fury that nearly kissed Brent's nose. He whirled into a crouch, cursing, while I launched upward to catch it.

"Whoops!" I smirked behind my mask. "Shit. That one could have gotten away from him. Told you."

Ignoring me, Brent stood up again. He glared at Evan, who stood tall and unyielding on the mound, the Enforcer personified. The moment stretched taut as Brent settled into his batting stance once again. I debated about what pitch to ask for and settled on a curve. Evan shook me off.

Yeah. I guess he's not messing around.

I knew what he wanted and gave him the signal. His next pitch was a fastball that Brent took a mighty swing at and completely missed. This time I kept my mouth shut, not wanting to rile him too much. Evan wound up again and delivered a fastball that screamed toward home plate.

Brent swung hard, and I flinched as he sent a high fly ball arcing toward right field. My heart lodged in my throat as Liv shuffled her feet, eyes skyward, tracking the motion.

"Oh, no! Oh my God," she squeaked, a note of panic lacing her voice and audible even from where I stood.

"Come on, Liv," I muttered under my breath, willing her confidence. "You got this."

She took a few steps to her right, never taking her eye off the ball. The rest of us froze, only able to watch as the drama played out. The white streak finally reached the top of its arc and began to fall. When her glove opened, the ball dropped neatly into it.

"Out! Game's over!" I roared, tearing off my mask and throwing it to the ground. The Stingrays erupted around me, a resounding chorus of cheers and laughter. All of us rushed the mound, clustering around Evan. Still in the outfield, Liv stared at the ball in her glove as if she couldn't understand how it had gotten there.

The uproarious cheers echoed in my ears, punctuated by Evan's infectious laughter. In the midst of this euphoria, Stella and Maia weaved their way through the throng of players. With a warmth that only family could muster, they enveloped Evan in a flurry of congratulatory hugs. Their faces were radiant with pride for their team and especially for their brother.

Then they turned to me. Stella was first. Her dark eyes were full of emotion as she wrapped her arms around me in a tight hug that spoke more than words ever could. Maia followed suit, her embrace equally as warm and comforting.

Finally, Liv made it to us from right field, her expression still bewildered.

"There she is!" Maia shouted. "The game-winning catch. Good thing we've got such a great manager, huh?"

Evan's grin could have lit up the entire Key, his pride obvious as he boosted Liv into the air. Her bewilderment gave way to a beaming smile after he planted a kiss on her lips.

"Way to go, Liv!" I yelled. Several hearty slaps landed on my back—an age-old gesture of camaraderie among family. Among Markhams.

And I was a Markham, goddammit.

The noise around us seemed to fade into a distant hum as I absorbed the moment. How an echo from our past had been brought to life again in this triumphant present. And that it had taken all of us to get here.

I turned to find Evan in front of me, wearing a gigantic grin. "That last inning felt like old times. I knew you were going to call for me to back that son of a bitch off the plate."

I nodded, the weight of this moment filling my chest.

"And you did it perfectly. Great job, Evan. You're a force of nature."

"Hey, you're the one who hit the game-winning home run, remember?" Then his face went serious, and I felt the shift in the air. He glanced at the ground, then met my gaze again. "I've missed this, Hunter. You and me."

My throat tightened. "I have too," I managed to say, every word laced with years of regret and longing. "More than you could ever know."

"Then let's put it all behind us. Once and for all. Why don't we start again, right from this moment?"

I couldn't speak, so I just gave him a big nod. Numbness swept over me in a wave.

Evan stepped in close and wrapped me in a hug that held the promise of new beginnings. I returned it fiercely, my eyes stinging as I fought the tide of emotions threatening to spill over. He might have been shorter than me, but he would always be my big brother. His arms were strong, his body solid as I held him, still barely able to believe it. I didn't want to let go, as fourteen years of pain and harrowing, soul-crushing guilt trickled away. My eyes were damp, and I didn't care.

When we broke apart, our entire family had gathered around us, and I wasn't the only one with misty eyes. Evan's were glassy too. Stella's cheeks were wet with tears, and Maia was wiping her face. Dad and Nona had approached from where they'd watched the game in the stands, and their resemblance was clear in their similar expressions.

"I've waited fourteen years for this moment," Dad said, his voice thick as his gaze bounced between us.

The weight of history, of feuds and failures, evaporated in the tropical heat.

"So have I," I rasped, my voice rough with emotion.

We all came together in a huddle, a tangle of arms and shared memories, family by blood and found family from the resort. It was perfect, the reunion I'd kept locked up in the most secret places of my heart but never thought I'd experience.

Then April's voice cut through the celebration from where she stood at the edge of the circle. Her eyes were wet too, but the expression on her face was strange, a mix of embarrassment, fulfillment, and... pain? Her arm cradled her swollen belly. "Evan and Hunter, I can't tell you how happy I am for this moment. But I'm afraid I need to grab Gabe away from the celebration. Pretty sure I'm in labor."

Gabe spun on his heels. His face was a picture of comical panic, eyes wide and mouth agape. "Your bag," he muttered, swiping a hand over his brow. "It's back at the Barn. Oh my God."

April, cool as an ocean breeze, just patted his arm with a smile. "Honey, breathe. You're the one who's been through this before, remember? We've got time to swing by Calypso Key. It's not like this little one's in a hurry."

Her gaze swept over the rest of us. "We'll keep you guys updated, okay?"

"You better!" someone hollered from the back. It sounded like Stella and sparked a round of cheers and laughter. As excitement rippled through us, Evan's arm found its way around my shoulders, pulling me close in a brotherly embrace. I leaned into him, the weight of years lifting with each shared breath.

"Feels like we're finally getting things right, huh?" I asked quietly.

Evan nodded, his grip tightening for a moment. "Yeah, we are."

It was a moment I had never truly allowed myself to

imagine—Evan's arm around my shoulders, a connection deeper than happiness coursing between us. As he held me close, a sense of belonging enveloped me, forgiveness that transcended mere words. And looking around at our family gathered around us, tears in their eyes, I realized this celebration was not complete yet.

One person was missing.

If Evan and I could finally be fully reconciled, brothers again, then the Markhams and the Coleridges could bury the hatchet too. I'd do whatever Brenna needed me to. I'd loved her since I was in high school, and my own demons had nearly drowned us both. All she'd asked for was patience, but I'd been too locked in my head to give it to her. Too damn scared to admit to her that she was the great love of my life. It was time to step up to the plate one last time, and I couldn't wait. My heart filled with determination as I turned to the bleachers.

Brenna was gone.

Chapter Thirty-Five

Brenna

I FORCED myself to walk away from the stands, and my heart squeezed tight as the cheers for the Stingrays' victory faded behind me. The sun kissed the horizon, casting long shadows across the baseball diamond where Hunter and his brother shared a moment that might have healed years of damage.

After the thrilling game ended, I'd watched them embrace from the stands as I sat next to April. I felt like an intruder. Theirs was a private celebration, one that made my chest ache. Because even though Hunter and Evan appeared to have completely reconciled, the Markhams and Coleridges were still estranged.

And that was my fault.

Hunter had done everything possible to make up with Evan, and mended bridges in a way that brought tears to my eyes. And yet here I stood, too scared to even start that journey between him and my own family.

So when April went to join them, I left too. As I slipped

into my car, I couldn't shake the image of Hunter's face. The vulnerability in his eyes when he looked at Evan made me long to comfort him, to tell him how incredibly proud I was.

But what about us?

How did he feel about me?

Even though I loved him, I'd never said the words out loud. And neither had he. My mind turned once again to his lost love. The one he never wanted to talk about. Was she part of why he had such a hard time moving out of the past? My hands tightened on the steering wheel, my knuckles turning white as uncertainty filled me. Maybe he still mourned her. Maybe I was just a stand-in for what he once had.

Sighing, I rolled down the window to clear my head. The sea breeze whipping through was bracing as I drove away from Big Pine Key. And I knew where I had to go.

I headed west on Main Street, which led directly to Siesta Sunset.

When I got there, Harper was ready to close up shop. The two of us headed toward the beach and Tidal Hops. The comforting hum of lively conversation and the soft clinking of glasses greeted me as I nudged open the door. The brewpub's beachy charm, a blend of laid-back comfort and pale turquoise walls, somewhat soothed my restless spirit. A smattering of tables spilled out from the indoor space to an inviting canopy-covered outdoor area with the sand as a floor. My brother Braden's great passion was a casual, welcoming place. Harper and I sat outside, enjoying the warm air now that the sunset was just a faint line on the horizon.

"Well?" She laid both hands on the wooden tabletop,

pressing them into the surface. "Don't keep me in suspense. Who won the championship?"

I forced a cheerfulness I didn't quite feel. "The Stingrays. Yay!"

"Good for them!" Harper's eyes lit up as she leaned forward. "How did Hunter play?"

"Good. Well, more than good. He hit the game-winning home run."

Harper cocked her head, her forehead growing lined. "So why are you here instead of celebrating with him? Haven't the two of you made up? You went to the game, after all."

But before I could elaborate, Braden appeared at our table, wiping his hands with a cloth. Two years younger, my brother was the epitome of beachy charm, with tousled Coleridge-colored light hair that caught the overhead light like spun gold. His casual attire accentuated a toned physique earned from years of rolling kegs and tending bar. But it wasn't just his good looks that drew people in. His infectious energy and genuine warmth made everyone feel at ease in his presence. "Hey there, ladies. What can I get you tonight?"

"How about shrimp baskets and some beer?" I asked.

He nodded. "You got it. Is this private girl talk, or can I join you?"

Harper remained quiet, so I smiled at my brother. "Nothing private at all. Please do." Since I was here to talk about mending feuds, I needed him here. After placing our order, he returned to the table with three frosted pint glasses and a pitcher of his signature IPA.

Harper gave him a quick rundown of the Stingrays game. "And she was just about to inform me why she's here instead of celebrating with the victors. So spill, sis."

I had a hard time finding the words. "Because... I felt like an outsider. I wanted him to have this time with his family. And I got a little insecure about how much Hunter cares about me."

Braden's blue eyes clouded, and his face grew tight. "What do you mean? Did he blow you off?"

I lifted my palm out before my little brother could fully rev up that protective streak. "Not at all. The moment wasn't about us. I didn't want to butt in."

Their expectant gazes encouraged me to continue.

"Hunter and Evan reconciled, right there on the field after the game." The words tumbled out, laden with the significance of the moment I had observed.

Braden's eyebrows shot up, and Harper's mouth formed a perfect O.

"Wow," Harper breathed out and took a quick sip. "You mentioned they were trying to mend things. But they were estranged for a long time. Now all's well between them?"

"What I saw was very different," I confirmed, nodding solemnly. "The entire family was on the field."

"Huh," Braden murmured, leaning back in his chair. "Never thought I'd see the day. Guess we'll have to find a new source of gossip now."

I swatted his arm, ignoring his grin. A weird mix of pride and sadness enveloped me. Pride for Hunter's courage and sadness that confronting my own fears seemed an insurmountable task. Sadness that I couldn't share this momentous occasion with him.

"Good for them," Harper said finally, a note of admiration threading through her voice. "It takes a lot to bury the hatchet after so long."

"Isn't that the truth." I sighed, staring down at the

polished wood of the table, tracing the grains with my finger.

"Are you okay, Brenna?" Braden asked. He cleared a space in the middle of the table as a big basket of fried shrimp and French fries arrived.

"Me? Yeah, I'm fine," I lied, offering a smile that didn't feel very genuine.

Harper studied me, her intuition always attuned to my moods. Then again, she knew there was more to my story with Hunter than Braden did. "No, you're not," she said, her eyes locking onto mine. "You've got that look."

"What look?" I reached for a handful of crispy fries but dropped them on my plate, my appetite suddenly waning.

"The *Hunter's invaded my thoughts and now I'm spiraling* look. You can't fool me, Bren."

I exhaled slowly. "It's just... watching him make peace with Evan today. I felt like I was seeing the old Hunter again. No, that's not quite right. Maybe a brand-new Hunter—the good man who's always been beneath all the trauma, you know? And I just couldn't handle what was happening. So I got up and left without saying anything to him."

"Why?" Braden's question was gentle, but it sliced through the haze of my uncertainty.

"Because I felt so apart from everything, and I don't know where things stand." I glanced away, watching the ebb and flow of the patrons around us. "We got into a fight and haven't really talked since. Which is my fault—he reached out to ask me to attend the game."

"Have you thought about talking to him? Like, actually sitting down and laying it all out on the table?" Harper asked.

"Every day," I admitted. "But fear's a powerful thing. It keeps telling me I might not like what I hear."

"Or," Harper countered, pointing a French fry at me, "you might find out he cares about you more deeply than you realize. Especially now that he's got his family problems settled. Is that worth the risk?"

"Probably," I murmured.

"Look, I'm no expert on love, but if there's one thing I understand, it's taking risks." Her gaze turned pointed, unwavering. "You keep talking about how Hunter is willing to fight to turn his life around. Maybe it's your turn to fight for what you want. For who you want."

"And that brings us back to square one," I said as I pushed some shrimp around on my plate. "It's not just about me and Hunter, is it? It's about all of us. Coleridges and Markhams."

"So you keep telling us," Braden said, and Harper elbowed him. I shot her a smile at the support, much more obvious today, as if hearing that Hunter and Evan had made up reassured her about him.

Trying to gather my thoughts, I ate a crispy fried shrimp. "Seeing Evan forgive him today... it helped me find my own courage. This feud has served nothing but to keep people apart. If Evan can put aside years of resentment, of a shattered life, surely my own family can sit down with Hunter—without casting judgment or bringing up the past."

"I've had my doubts about you being involved with him," Harper said as she swirled a finger over the rim of her pint glass. "And I've had plenty of resentment toward the Markhams. The hostility between Evan and Hunter only solidified it for me. So the two of them reconciling today... I didn't think it would ever happen. I'm big enough to admit when I'm wrong about someone."

"Does that mean…" I trailed off, hesitant to get my hopes up.

Harper's smile rose. "Yes, Brenna. I'll meet Hunter, provided he's willing to fight for what you two have. Everyone deserves a chance. So I'll stand by your side to help convince the rest of our family."

"Thank you." I reached across to give her a quick hug. "That means the world to me."

I turned to Braden. "Okay, Mr. Protective. Ben has already agreed to give Hunter a chance. What do you say? You willing to bury the Coleridge-Markham hatchet?"

He shrugged as he stared at me steadily. "All I want is for you to be happy, okay? So yeah, I'll give the guy a shot. But fair warning—I don't care that he's the size of a gorilla. If he mistreats you, I'm gonna have some choice words for him."

I laughed out loud, my mood lightening by the moment. "You don't need to worry about that. He might be ferocious on the outside, but Hunter is a gentle giant."

Harper raised her beer glass. "Then let's drink to ending feuds."

I CLIMBED the stairs to my second-story apartment, its familiar creaks greeting me like an old friend. Inside, the silence was complete, and in its stillness, my determination solidified. As I paced across the worn wooden floorboards, the weight of what I was about to do settled on my shoulders—not heavy but undeniably present. I rehearsed lines in my head, scenarios playing out like dog-eared pages of one of the romance novels our club read each month. But

Hunter was not a character I could rewrite to suit the narrative.

I stopped at my bookshelf to run my fingers along the spines of countless stories that had seen me through sleepless nights. Each one held a piece of me, echoes of dreams and desires etched between the lines. My eye fell on a worn paperback of *The Old Man and the Sea* that I'd borrowed from Hunter. No one else had ever understood what books meant to me. How they were more than pages between thick paper or leather. They were doorways to different worlds.

Spinning on my heel, I marched to my purse and withdrew my phone. My thumb hovered over the call button on Hunter's contact, a prayer whispered under my breath for courage. I exhaled a breath of nerves. "Okay, here we go..."

Chapter Thirty-Six

Hunter

NIGHT HAD SETTLED in like a thick blanket over Dove Key, smothering the day's excitement with a serene quiet. Main Street was nearly deserted, save for me and my restless thoughts. I walked with no particular destination in mind. Above me, hanging flower baskets swayed gently in the ocean breeze, their vibrant colors dimmed to softer hues in the lights from the streetlamps.

After the baseball game, I had been riding high on adrenaline and deep, deep fulfillment. Evan and I had embraced like the brothers we truly were. It was a moment I'd visualized in my head countless times, never quite believing it could happen. But the cheers faded into a distant hum when I scanned the stands, searching for the face that would make this scene truly complete.

The face that wasn't there.

Evan clapped me on the back, his grin wide and infectious as my family discussed where to go for our victory party. But my heart tugged elsewhere.

"I'm not going out with you guys," I told him quietly, pulling him aside as the team celebrated around us. "I need to find Brenna."

Evan's eyes softened as they darted to the empty stands and back. He nodded. "I understand. Go get her back."

As the elation of having things finally right with Evan ebbed away, it left behind a stark realization that my world was incomplete without Brenna by my side. With determined steps, I left my teammates behind.

I went home, but a quick shower to rinse off the sweat did nothing to wash away the unease. I changed into jeans and a T-shirt, only to find the walls of my apartment pressing in on me, suffocating me.

And that was how I found myself walking down Main Street, trying to figure out how to approach Brenna. The air around me appeared to have a new clarity like I'd put on a pair of glasses. Except it felt like the opposite. Since embracing Evan on that field, I felt like everything holding me back had been stripped away. If he was willing to put the past behind us, then so was I, dammit. I thought of Ayesha and her small family. Part of me would always feel the ache of my failure to protect them, but now I realized that guilt didn't have to be a life sentence. The Afghani family was a part of the past, and it was time to move on. Brenna was also a part of my past, but she was my future as well.

She was everything.

A flicker of light from the old antique shop caught my eye, and surprise at seeing it still lit up brought me up short. Without any help from me, my feet carried me forward until I pushed open the door. The bell overhead announced my entrance with a jingle.

"Oh my!" came the surprised voice of the owner, his

eyes lifting from the innards of an antique mantle clock. "I didn't realize I'd left the door unlocked! I lost track of time repairing this clock." His weathered face cracked into a smile after studying me more closely. "Well, come in, Hunter."

"Sorry for barging in, Mr. Jacobs," I said, smiling that Dad's old friend had remembered me.

Of course he was older now, his hair a steel-gray with a liberal amount of scalp showing. But his blue eyes were still kind as he waved off my apology. He straightened, wiping his hands on a cloth as he looked me up and down. "Nothing to apologize for. The rumor mill is true for once. You have grown into quite the strapping fellow. But you still have the same eyes—I recognized them. Though I think by this time they've seen a thing or two. But what brings you here so late?" He peered at me through his round spectacles, curiosity etching his features.

"I was walking to clear my head, and your lights pulled me in here." My gaze traveled over the various items that filled the shelves and tables.

"Ah, the restlessness of youth," Mr. Jacobs mused, leaning against the counter. "Reminds me of those times with your father. Out on his boat before dawn and trying to outsmart the fish."

"Dad used to tell me how you guys would compete on who'd get the biggest catch."

"Compete? Ha! More like I was always trying to keep up with him." The twinkle in his eye faded slightly. "We had good times, your dad and I."

"Hey, how's your wife doing? I still remember her apple pie."

Mr. Jacobs's gaze softened, a shadow flickering across his eyes. "She passed away three years back."

My shoulders slumped. "Really sorry to hear that. She was a wonderful lady."

"Thank you. She sure was. But life has its seasons, and we learn to cherish the memories." Mr. Jacobs's voice was gruff with emotion, then he cleared his throat busily. He gestured around the shop. "Every piece here holds a story, much like life. I opened the shop shortly after she passed, and it keeps me company, you could say."

I smiled. "Guess that makes you the keeper of stories, then."

"Something like that," he agreed, his smile returning. "Now what can I help you find tonight? Or are you just browsing?"

"Maybe just looking."

"Take your time. There's lots to explore." The shop-keeper returned to his workbench.

I meandered aimlessly through the aisles, hands clasped behind my back. I wandered past the large picture window display that Brenna and I had admired before dancing under the stars. Instead of classic books, now it held a selection of handcrafted furniture. Continuing, my eyes roved over brass compasses and vintage cameras, each with their silent tales, but nothing snagged my attention.

Until I reached the glass case at the counter.

The book shined like a beacon, lying innocently between a pocket watch and an ornate cigar box—a first edition of *The Sun Also Rises* by Ernest Hemingway.

And the memory sprang up. Brenna's nose almost pressed against the window, eyes wide with yearning as she recalled the book and her longing for it. And the owner's refusal to sell. But he wasn't a faceless mirage anymore. Mr. Jacobs and I shared history.

And what better way to bridge the chasm between our

families than for a Markham to give a Coleridge a piece of Hemingway?

"Mr. Jacobs," I called, nodding toward the case. "How much for the Hemingway?"

He looked up, following my gaze to the book. A pained expression briefly crossed his face. "Oh, that one? It's not for sale, Hunter. That book belonged to my late wife. She loved Hemingway, and I keep it here for sentimental reasons."

My fingers tapped a nervous rhythm on the glass, the cool surface sending a shiver up my arm. "Mr. Jacobs." My voice was reassuringly steady despite the storm of emotions brewing within me. "I understand the value this book holds for you and why it's precious. But it's more than just a rare find to me. It represents... hope."

"Hope?" Mr. Jacobs echoed. His eyebrows knitted together as he approached me at the case, the tools from his clock repair forgotten.

"Well, there's a woman I'm seeing," I confessed. A small, knowing smile hinted at the corners of his mouth, as if he'd already pieced part of the story together. "We had a fight, and I said some things I shouldn't have. She's everything to me, and she's longed for this book for years. So this book is a symbol—of new beginnings, of bridging divides. Giving it to her would be my way of showing her that she's my future."

Mr. Jacobs studied me for a moment before one gray brow lifted. "That woman wouldn't happen to be Brenna Coleridge, would it?"

A surprised bark of laughter escaped me at his astuteness, and I met his gaze with a shy smile playing on my lips. "Yes."

"Now I understand. She's wanted that book for years."

"It's symbolic. We Markhams are the ones with the Hemingway link. So it would only be fitting for me to give her the copy of *The Sun Also Rises* that she's always coveted."

The shop owner's gaze flickered to the book, then back to me, and I could see the wheels turning behind those aged eyes. "Symbolic gestures are powerful things, Hunter. But so is the memory of a loved one." His voice was thick with emotion, an echo of loss resonating in the quiet of the shop.

"Mr. Jacobs, if there were any other way..." My words trailed off. How could I explain that this wasn't just about me winning Brenna back? This was about healing wounds that went deeper. "I need it. Please."

"I can't sell you this book, Hunter." Mr. Jacobs's voice was firm, and my stomach twisted before crashing to the floor. Which was why his next words caught me so off guard. "But I'll give it to you."

"Give it to me?" My heart slammed against my ribcage.

He nodded slowly as a bittersweet smile graced his lips. "Maybe it's time for that book to be part of a new story. One of hope, forgiveness, and a different future."

"Thank you." The two words sounded paltry compared to the gratitude swelling inside me. "I can't tell you what this means."

"Take care of her, Hunter. The book and the girl." Mr. Jacobs unlocked the case and handed me the Hemingway. As we shook hands on the exchange, the transfer was one of trust as much as it was a book.

I tucked the Hemingway against my chest, and it felt like a talisman as I stepped out into the night air. Knowing exactly what I had to do, I took off at a trot. It wasn't far to go.

I reached Brenna's apartment, and my palm was sweaty

as I stared at the alarm pad. The one I'd installed what seemed like a lifetime ago. After a brief hesitation, I entered my code and opened the exterior door instead of ringing the bell. I didn't want to give her the chance to say no without seeing me face to face. I padded softly up the stairs and held the book behind my back. I knocked on her apartment door before I could second-guess myself.

"Harper?" I could hear her faint voice, then she opened the door with her phone in one hand. "Did I forget some—" Her green eyes flew open wide. She went completely still, shock making her mouth slack. "Hunter!"

"Hi."

"I was just going to call you..." She gestured vaguely at me with her phone.

"Can we talk?" My voice came out gruffer than I intended, betraying the turmoil inside.

"Okay. Fine. Yes." Blushing, she stepped aside to let me in. She set the phone on the table near the door, and that small sound was unusually loud.

We settled onto her couch, an ocean between us despite the close proximity. Beside me, I hid the book underneath a throw pillow. The weight of it pressed against my thigh as my heart raced wildly.

"I was really happy you came to the game tonight," I said, unable to meet her gaze just yet. "But when you left... it felt like all the air got sucked out of the field."

She shifted, her fingers twining together in her lap. "Hunter, I'm sorry—"

"Wait," I cut in, needing to get this out before I lost my nerve. "I've been thinking a lot about what you said the other day. You brought up the woman I loved. I've been too afraid to talk about her."

"I know that's a painful subject for you to talk about."

"It's not that. I just needed to find the courage. And now I have."

Brenna stilled, her mouth tightening as if bracing for impact.

That involuntary reaction pulled an unexpected smile from me. "You don't realize, do you?" Gathering my nerve, I turned to face her fully. "I've only loved one woman my whole life. I fell in love with her in high school, then had to leave her behind. One woman who was the memory that got me through some of my roughest times. One woman who has always been the light for me, even during my darkest hours... You, Brenna. It's always been you. I've just been too screwed up to tell you how much I love you."

The air hung between us, charged with words that had taken too long to say, and emotions I'd bottled up for what felt like an eternity. But saying them now felt like coming home. At last.

Brenna became absolutely still, and her mouth hinged slightly open. Tears welled in her eyes. "I love you too."

The depth of emotion in those words pulled at every thread of my being. And once again, she gave me the courage to continue. "Today. Fixing things with Evan, and with my family... it made things so clear to me. We all stood on the pitcher's mound, celebrating. But the most important part was missing. You. You're the piece that's always been gone."

A hesitant smile touched her lips, and it was like a sunrise after the longest night. I reached beside me, slipping the book from its hiding spot. The cover gleamed dully in the dim light as I held it out to her.

Her hand flew to her mouth as she recognized the book, her eyes wide with astonishment. "How did you get him to part with this?" She reverently took it in her hands, tracing the title with a trembling finger.

I couldn't help but grin, the corners of my mouth pulling wide. "It was the only way to win the heart of the woman I love. I told him that."

Laughter spilled from Brenna like a melody, the sound that only comes when joy and relief collide. She clutched the book to her breasts. Its spine was creased with history, much like our own tangled past.

"I can't believe this is happening right now. I never needed grand gestures, Hunter," she said, her voice wavering slightly. "But this—this is beyond beautiful. It's like... a peace offering between the Markhams and the Coleridges."

Her words filled the small space of her apartment, heavy with the weight of generations of rivalry and the hope of reconciliation. I nodded. "That's exactly what it is. That old book is more than just paper and ink. It's a symbol of new beginnings."

And before I could stop myself, I leaned forward and touched my lips to hers. Brenna cupped the back of my neck and slanted her head, kissing me back fully. It was the best kiss I'd ever experienced.

Brenna broke our kiss with a teary laugh. She brushed a hand over her wet cheek and set the book gently on the coffee table. "Actually, I have a bit of a gesture myself. I went straight to Siesta Sunset after the game and talked to my family. They're ready to meet you. Seeing you and Evan embrace like that gave me the courage to face my family and explain what you mean to me. And that I'm willing to fight for you. I'm proud to show you off to anyone, but especially them. We can go over there right now if you want."

I shook my head slowly. Not because I dreaded the

introduction, but because the very core of my soul screamed that I couldn't bear to be anywhere but here with her. Desire stirred within me, drawing me closer to her on the couch until the distance felt like nothing. "Thank you. And don't worry, I'll be on my best behavior when we meet." I brushed a finger down the length of her arm, smiling at the goose bumps that rose on her soft skin. "But you know what? Introductions can wait until tomorrow. Right now, I want you all to myself."

With a boldness that took me by surprise, Brenna grabbed me by the shoulders and yanked me forward. She pulled me into a searing kiss that shattered the careful distance we'd danced around the past few days.

"God, I love you," I breathed against her lips, the words spilling out raw and unguarded.

The admission seemed to ignite something within her, and she pressed back with equal fervor. "There's no one else for me. Ever. I love you, Hunter."

Our passion erupted like wildfire, consuming any last traces of restraint. I felt exalted, my soul free at last. Desperate hands tugged at zippers and buttons until nothing separated us. Her gorgeous, curvy figure was a siren call I couldn't resist, and every touch felt like a homecoming.

As we fell back onto the couch, our bodies pressed together. My fingers trailed over her breasts, delighting in the feel of her hot yet silky skin. A gasp escaped her lips when I lowered my head and took one of her peaks into my mouth, gently sucking and drawing circles around it with my tongue.

Then I groaned, a deep wrenching sound of frustration. "Shit. I don't have a condom."

"It doesn't matter," Brenna said as she traced her fingers

over the lines of my tattoo, lighting me on fire. She lay back on the couch, pulling me with her. "I'm on the pill. Safe."

"Me too," I managed to say, already anticipating the feel of her without any barrier between us. I couldn't resist the overwhelming urge to claim her as I nudged her legs apart with my knee. "You're mine. Now and always."

"Yes. And you're mine."

With a deep, rough growl, I rammed into her warmth. Her heat enveloped me completely. And in an utterly new way. Brenna's moans grew louder, matching my own as our bodies moved in perfect synchronization. My desire built with each deepening thrust, my movements becoming more urgent and desperate. The sensations were so raw, so intense, I could hardly stand it. Brenna's nails dug into my back as she cried out. The sweet pain only fueled my desire, sending shock after shock through my entire being.

This wasn't just sex—it was catharsis.

It was two souls cementing their bond, using a language older than words to express what they felt. We continued to move together, our bodies speaking a rhythm of desire and need. And so much more. As her hands gripped my hips, pulling me deeper, I could feel every beat of her heart echoing inside me.

She latched onto my shoulder with her teeth as she moaned my name, her voice hoarse. When her muscles tensed, her body convulsing around me, I was close too. I thrust harder, deeper, and at last, she shuddered beneath me. Arching into me, her mouth opened in a wordless cry.

The sight of her climax was enough to send me over. Every muscle in my body tensed and then released in a euphoric rush. I clenched my eyes shut and drowned in the intensity of the moment, feeling her body respond to mine like we were meant to be together.

Because we were.

As I was overcome completely, a guttural roar escaped my lungs. Brenna's name fell from my tongue like a prayer.

Afterward, with her head on my chest, I traced lazy patterns on her back as we lay on her couch. The heat of the moment had cooled to a warm ember, but the fire she ignited in me was far from extinguished. It never would be.

I stared at the book with its worn cover. "I need you to know something. No matter what happens with our families... I'll be here. I'm not going anywhere."

"I promise you the same." Brenna lifted her head, her green eyes catching the moonlight. Then a stunning smile rose on her face that made my breath catch. "But, Hunter, I don't think we'll need to worry about that."

"Oh?"

"Both of our families are tired of holding onto old grudges. They're ready to move forward, just like us."

With a grin that held no dark shades, only light, I pulled her closer. "So you know what this means, right? Romeo and Juliet got their happy ending after all."

We laughed together, the sound harmonizing with the distant, gentle breeze outside. In this room, in this moment, and for all those to come, the world was ours.

Chapter Thirty-Seven

Brenna

PEDRO WAS SPRAWLED across the windowsill, his once tiny frame now spilling over the edges in a display of adolescent feline grace. I grinned at the sight, then my eyes were diverted to the framed photo hanging prominently on the wall. Evan and Hunter as kids, grinning with their arms casually looped around each other's shoulders. He'd hung it the other night, mentioning that after keeping it for years, it was finally where it belonged. Hearing footsteps, I turned to see Hunter emerging from his bedroom in black jeans, which wasn't unusual. But his royal-blue shirt most definitely was.

"Look at you, stepping out in something other than your signature black," I teased, my gaze traveling appreciatively over the clean lines of his jeans and the way his shirt contrasted the ink on his upper arms and chest.

Hunter shot me that crooked smile that always made my stomach do somersaults. "Figured it was about time I stopped dressing like I was attending a perpetual funeral."

Closing the distance between us with a few easy strides, his arms circled my waist, pulling me close enough that I could count the different shades of brown weaving through his irises.

"You look..." His words trailed off as his warm lips found mine. The sensation was familiar now, yet every kiss felt like rediscovering a favorite book after a long time. "Delicious."

"Thank you," I murmured against his mouth, and a blush warmed my cheeks. The light green sundress I had chosen this morning fluttered around my legs as I stepped back reluctantly. Pedro hopped off the windowsill and sauntered over to meow at Hunter.

He frowned at the cat. "You better not be complaining about the new treats I bought you. I got three different kinds just to make sure you liked one of them."

I couldn't resist giggling. "So are you finally ready to admit Pedro has earned a permanent place in your heart?"

A rueful look crossed Hunter's face as he met my eyes. "Guess it's pointless to deny anymore, huh?"

"Very. Good thing you've got a big heart. Plenty of room in there." I patted his chest with a solid thump, enjoying the hard muscle, then exhaled a sigh. "We should get going. I promise this will be nice and casual."

"I keep telling myself if I can handle a cave full of Taliban, a gaggle of Coleridges shouldn't be too much trouble." Hunter released me but kept one hand entwined with mine as I burst into laughter.

"May I suggest that you not compare my family to the Taliban in their presence?"

He winked. "I was only kidding."

In the end, we'd had to wait more than a day to arrange this get-together. A week had passed since he gave me that wonderful book, now in a place of honor in the bookcase in my apartment. Together, we descended the stairs and exited into the brightness of day. Hunter's Range Rover sat like a sleek, mechanical beast, ready to carry us off to new territory—a casual lunch with my family. There was tightness in my stomach, but it was smaller than it had been half an hour ago. Lighter somehow, as if Hunter's choice of attire signaled a shift in the universe.

Once inside the vehicle, I settled into the plush leather seat as Hunter took his place behind the wheel. The engine roared to life under his command. The drive to Siesta Sunset was a blur of anticipation and the occasional stolen glance. When we pulled into the parking lot, Hunter's hand found mine, giving it an encouraging squeeze.

We made our way toward Tidal Hops, nestled among palm trees rustling in the gentle sea breeze. Hunter's gaze swept over the pastel-colored buildings, the pool where several guests were enjoying a game of water polo, and the laughter of kids chasing each other on the beach.

"The place has a great vibe," he commented, turning to me with a smile that crinkled the corners of his eyes.

I laughed, a little self-conscious as we continued next to the pool. Tall palms swayed above us. "Thanks, but we're no Calypso Key. Our budget is... well, you know."

"So what? The whole place is charming. It feels real, cozy, and approachable. You guys are doing an amazing job."

Warmth spread through me at his words. We stepped inside Tidal Hops, and here I didn't feel any misgivings about the Coleridge budget. Braden had done a fantastic job with his surfboards hung on the light turquoise walls and glass buoys hanging in nets from the ceiling.

Though I also couldn't deny the soft tension hanging in

the air. The kind that precedes any family gathering where everyone is trying just a bit too hard to get along.

"And here's the man of the hour!" Harper, true to her word to welcome my love, approached with her usual vibrant energy. Her eyes glinted mischievously as she craned her head at Hunter. "You sure you're not doubling as a lighthouse? Because you could guide ships to shore with that height!"

Hunter smiled, a faint blush creeping onto his cheeks. "Guess I'm just built for better views."

Standing next to him, I studied this man who'd once been the town's bad-boy mystery, now slightly shy in the face of a compliment. My heart felt too big to contain. Hunter had come so far from the shadows that once defined him. He stood tall in a world of color.

And it was completely, utterly adorable.

My brothers sat around a worn wooden table, and I was relieved to see alertness but no hard stares on any faces. We took our chairs with Ben sitting next to me, leaving Austin across from us. Our fishing guide, Austin's gray eyes were watchful as he gave Hunter a nod. Catching my imploring eye, he smiled and smoothed his brown hair. "Welcome to Siesta Sunset."

"Thanks," Hunter said, shaking his hand. "This is a great bar."

Braden, with his easy smile, placed a couple of large, steaming pizzas on the table, along with a pitcher of frothy beer. "Thanks! Sorry for the simple spread. Pizza's just quick and easy when we've got to feed a crowd."

"Hey, don't apologize." Hunter flashed an easy smile and showed no signs of nerves. "I've never been one to turn down pizza or beer." He raised his slice in a salute as Braden took the seat next to Austin.

"Speaking of which," Hunter commented after taking a long, evaluating taste of the golden liquid in his glass. "This beer is something else. Perfect amount of hops."

Harper groaned. "Oh God. Please don't compliment him! Braden never shuts up about beer."

I laughed, relaxing at last as Braden merely gave Hunter a regal nod.

Eli, who'd been quiet until now, cleared his throat. "We're all pretty protective of our sisters, and I'd be lying if I said I was happy when I heard you and Brenna were involved. All of us were. But a lot of time has passed since that poker game, and maybe Brenna's right. Maybe it is time for a new beginning." He lifted his glass high and smiled, lighting up the room. "To the official end of the Coleridge-Markham feud. And maybe the start of new friendships." His sun-streaked, tousled hair matched his carefree disposition. Sometimes I envied Eli's ability to get along with people.

"I will absolutely drink to that!" I said, winking at Hunter.

"Cheers," the rest echoed as our glasses clinked in the middle of the table. The final tendril of residual tension I'd been carrying melted away like foam on the beach.

As we dug into our meal, I turned to Ben. "How's work going?"

Ben sighed and set his pizza down on his plate. "I got laid off from the landscaping gig. Hank had to cut back and kept me on as long as he could. So now I'm turning over every stone for part-time work."

I felt a pang of sympathy for him. Ben was trying so hard to find his footing, and life kept yanking the rug out from under him.

But before I could say anything, Hunter chimed in,

"I've been thinking about hiring someone to do on-call work at KeyMark Security. You interested?"

Ben's eyebrows shot up, and he leaned in front of me to level a long stare at Hunter. "You'd give me a job?"

"It wouldn't be full-time, but I could use someone reliable now and again. I think you'd be a good fit. You can handle yourself in a pinch, and you know the town better than most."

Ben blinked, clearly working it out in his head. "That could work. I'd love a job without set hours so I could get caught up on projects around the resort."

Hunter's nod was measured, a quiet acknowledgment of the gravity of the moment. "I saw firsthand the good work you did at Calypso Key with that landscaping project. I'd be glad to have you on the team. Besides, I know what it's like to start over."

"Yeah, I guess you do." Ben's acceptance came with a hint of disbelief, as if he couldn't quite grasp the truce forming before our eyes. Finally, Ben gave him a firm nod. "Okay. Thanks. Maybe it's time a Coleridge and a Markham started working together."

"More than time." I smiled and caught Hunter's eye, mouthing a silent *thank you*.

Rising to his feet, Hunter smoothed my hair with one large hand as he topped off my glass. Then he filled everyone else's, emptying the pitcher. "If we're celebrating, we can't do it with empty glasses. To the Coleridges!"

Laughing, we all clinked mugs once more. He asked Austin about fishing, and they discussed the merits of wahoo versus dorado. Eli got into the conversation, chiding them for catching fish instead of enjoying them underwater. It was an old argument between Eli and Austin, and the exchange made me smile.

I caught Harper staring at me, pride all over her face. She leaned around Ben to murmur, "I'm proud of you. Look at what you've accomplished here. And I admit I was wrong. Hunter's got a pretty good personality. I like him."

Hunter burst into laughter at something Braden said, and I studied his handsome face. This was yet another side of him, another shade. My brothers had been reserved to start, but he'd managed to put them at ease and find common topics of conversation. And that shouldn't be surprising, should it? Hunter had spent the better part of a decade as part of a tightly knit team. He was highly experienced at meshing with others and reading the room. I hadn't given him enough credit.

I stared around the table at the people I loved best in the world, wondering why on earth I'd been so nervous about this.

After lunch, Hunter and I strolled along the salt-and-pepper beach, the grains soft and warm under our bare feet.

"What a cool beach," he said, kicking the sand with one foot. "Even the dark grains are soft."

I nodded as I swung our joined hands. "The dark sand is from worn-down rocks. They're old enough that they're the same consistency as the white grains. I've always thought the beach was one of the prettiest parts of the resort."

He winked at me. "Not even close. That honor belongs to you."

I nudged his shoulder and we continued until we reached a secluded spot at the beach's end. The sound of waves gently lapping against the shore filled the space around us.

"Thank you for reaching out to my brother," I said, turning to him. The warm breeze played with strands of my hair.

Hunter shrugged before stuffing his hands in his pockets. "Ben deserves a shot. Besides, someone taught me all about second chances."

I smiled. "And you've done so much with yours. I'm proud of you, Hunter."

He glanced away, focusing on the horizon where sea met sky in a perfect line. "You gave me courage all those years—made me hope that one day I'd be able to see beyond the shadows."

"Well, maybe I played a part, even if I didn't know it," I teased, my fingers tracing the lines of tension that had eased from his face over time. His admission that *I* was his lost love still floored me, and I vowed to make sure he knew how special he was. "But you did the work, and don't forget that. You're the one who fought through the darkness."

"Maybe. But you gave me the light to look for."

As our lips met, the depth of our kiss mirrored the vibrant colors of the ocean before us. It was a kiss of unity, of shared promises and intertwined destinies.

A kiss that whispered forever without a single word.

He reached out to smooth my hair, his expression growing thoughtful. "Who would've thought? Brenna Coleridge and Hunter Markham, the stars of our very own love story."

"More like the bad boy redeemed and the bookshop owner with a penchant for happy endings," I quipped as the warm water washed over our feet.

"Sounds like a romance novel. Think your Sips and Books club would approve?"

"Only if it's steamy enough," I shot back and we both laughed, the sound mingling with the gentle rush of palm fronds above.

Our laughter faded to contented silence, and I marveled at how natural it felt to be here with him—love and the steady determination to better himself had softened the bad boy's hard edges.

"Thank you," Hunter said suddenly, his voice low and full of emotion. "For believing in me when I couldn't. And for giving me the prod to act when I needed to."

"You've always been worth believing in," I said softly and lifted my gaze to meet his.

He smiled, the kind that came from deep within, and it made my heart soar. I rested against his broad chest as he wrapped both arms around me. Tall and solid, Hunter was a presence to lean on. And I gave him something too. A sort of mirror, a way to see other sides of himself. We were each a half, and together we were whole. After over a decade apart, each chasing our own dreams and facing our own trials, we found exactly what we'd been looking for in each other.

And it was perfect.

Epilogue

Hunter

THE FOLLOWING JUNE

CALYPSO KEY's annual Sea and Sand Festival was in full swing, a panorama of sounds, scents, and colors across the broad meadow between the Barn and the Big House. The scent of salty ocean air mixed with the savory aroma of grilled seafood, while flame trees dotted the landscape, their fiery blossoms vibrant against the clear blue sky. I hadn't attended since I was a teenager, so today would be extra special.

For multiple reasons.

The day was picture-perfect for festivities, but the main attraction for us was the sandy area where an age-old rivalry was turning into a friendly match of beach volleyball. The Markhams were on one side of the net and the Coleridges the other. This marked the first time the Coleridges had ever set foot at the festival, let alone played in a game, and the positive energy buzzing between our two families was something I never thought I'd witness.

Brenna stood beside me, her ponytail swishing as she got ready to serve the ball. We were playing the first half of the game with her family, and despite our history, the camaraderie felt as natural as the sand beneath our feet.

"Hey, Hunter, who are you two rooting for?" Evan's voice rang out across the net, his grin sly.

"Whichever side we're on!" I shot back, unable to suppress my own smile. In addition to Brenna and me, Ben, Harper, and Eli made up the Coleridge contingent. Ben moved with a sense of newfound purpose, his past troubles shedding with each leap and dive. And his return to Calypso Key was much more encouraging this time. As the ball sailed toward us over the net, Brenna dove, sending it spinning to me. I set it up, and Eli launched into the air to spike it home.

Brenna and I switched sides halfway through the match. Gabe and Aiden stepped out for a breather, and Austin and Braden took our places on the Coleridge side. Evan and I played like two sides of the same coin. He had a knack for setting up the ball just right, and with my height, I loved to spike it into the sand.

Many of the guys around us were shirtless, including Evan. I doubted I'd ever be comfortable exposing my scarred torso in public. But I'd continued to add color to my wardrobe, and today I wore a dark orange T-shirt to go with my black board shorts. With Brenna by my side, every spike and every serve felt like a small victory.

Stella was taking a break from manning the barbecue both, and her competitive edge was evident in every move she made. Wyatt's laughter was a constant backdrop to our plays as he rushed to tap the ball over the net. The Coleridges won the next point, then Eli performed a high, arching serve. The volleyball soared against the brilliant June sky toward us. I could almost feel the collective breath of the crowd held tight as Evan watched its movement, then set it up perfectly. With a resounding smack, I sent the ball hurtling over the net, securing another point for the Markhams.

"Game point!" Stella called out. We rallied, sweat-slick and sun-glazed, our eyes locked on the Coleridges.

"Come on, Danny, cheer for Uncle Evan and Uncle Hunter!" April's laughing voice lilted from the sidelines, where she cradled her son close to her chest. She held his arm up in a mock cheer as he stared at the crowd, eyes round with fascination. Gabe stood beside her with his hand resting over her shoulder. Young Daniel was the spitting image of his father, pure Markham all the way. Though he was blessed to have inherited his mother's happy personality, thank God. Despite me being several inches taller, Gabe would always be my big brother. The pair had blossomed in their new role, and Hailey positively doted on her little brother.

My eyes were pulled back to the match as Harper served, and the game climaxed in a long volley that tested the limits of reflex and resolve. We were all gasping for air, muscles burning, when Wyatt made a daring save, setting me up for the final shot. Leaping into the air, I spiked the ball into the sand on the far side.

"And that's the win!" Evan proclaimed with raised arms, but there was no sting in his triumph, only the warm embrace of shared exultation.

"Next year, we'll take you down," Ben said, smiling as he offered his hand to Evan.

"Looking forward to it," Evan replied, clasping Ben's hand firmly.

I watched my brother shake hands, but the vision filling my mind was of a sunrise morning several months ago. A ceremony where he pledged his life to Liv on the bluff behind the Big House. When Evan had asked me to be his best man, it was one of the best moments of my life. And I'd stood there just behind him that morning, feeling pride and love so fierce it threatened to crack me open.

My heart was still full as I caught the sun glinting off his wedding ring when he walked off the court. It struck me how much everything had changed, and my gaze panned back to Gabe, April, and their little family. Their wedding was the catalyst that had started all this.

And we weren't done yet.

Brenna's hand found mine as we walked away, her fingers weaving through mine like they'd always belonged there. Around us, the festival buzzed with life. Parts of our families peeled off toward the Conch Republic beer garden, while others fell in behind us to take in the rest of the activities.

"Feels like we've rewritten history, doesn't it?" Brenna mused, taking in the people around us.

"Rewritten, or maybe just... continued it in a better direction."

The blending of our families today was a testament to Brenna's vision, her unyielding belief that the past didn't have to dictate the future. It wasn't always smooth sailing, of course. Careless words occasionally slipped out of a mouth. But now they were forgiven. Then forgotten.

"Either way, I'm glad you're part of my story," she said, leaning into me slightly as we navigated through the crowd.

"I plan to stay that way."

We passed Garrett and Myles, exchanging good-natured hellos with them. They were with a group of guys they'd become good friends with. I was glad to see them settle into Dove Key and make it their home, and I occasionally hung out with the gang too. But more than anyone, my two friends understood that today was about family for me.

We still made rounds at Calypso Key as members of KeyMark, which now included Ben on a part-time basis. And we provided a physical presence to reassure guests and dissuade anyone else who might not be thinking happy thoughts. But no further security incidents had happened, and I was confident we were providing my family's business with the perfect amount of security.

Brenna and I entered the long stretch of booths facing each other with a wide, grassy aisle between. Face painters, artisans, carnival games made for a fun, raucous atmosphere.

"Looks like there's a shooting game up there," I said, pointing to a booth just ahead. "It's been a while. Wonder if I can still hit anything?" Of course, that was a white lie and Brenna laughed at me. I went to the range regularly.

We stopped at the tent—a row of toy rifles and a series of targets that beckoned challengers. A small crowd cheered, and the competitive spirit was infectious as our two families gathered behind us.

"Come on, let's see what you've got." Brenna grinned, and her eyes glinted with challenge.

"All right. You asked for it," I said with mock seriousness. As I stepped up, the familiar itch resurfaced—an old friend from days when my targets had been much more serious. Nerves swirled in my stomach.

Don't screw this up, Markham.

But when I lifted the play rifle to my shoulder, my body

settled into the stance that still felt second nature. Relaxing, I aimed down the sights and let out a breath. I squeezed the trigger. The rifle made a sharp crack, and for a moment, everything else faded—the cheers, the music, the smell of the ocean—all of it secondary to the bull's-eye winking back at me from afar. The bull's-eye that suddenly had a big black hole in the center.

Behind me, the combined family crowd cheered.

I moved on to the next shot, and the rifle felt like an extension of my arm, a muscle memory from years of experience guiding each movement. I took aim, and the trigger gave way beneath my finger, resulting in another hole in another target's center. Three more followed in quick succession as I adjusted to the toy rifle. Each bullet met its mark, and our assembled family erupted in applause that rippled through the warm June air.

"I'd say you've still got it." Brenna laughed, her eyes alight with an admiration that made my chest puff up.

"What, you doubted me?"

"Never for a second."

"Choose your prize," the game attendant announced, gesturing to the array of stuffed animals and trinkets that adorned the booth's shelves.

I gestured grandly to Brenna, and her gaze swept over the prizes. I tried not to exhale in relief when her attention snagged on one particular item—a whimsical bookworm with oversized glasses perched on its plush face and a tiny book clutched in its soft limbs. The plush figure I'd given to the booth attendant hours ago.

Her eyes sparkled as she jabbed a finger at it. "That one! That little bookworm is just too cute."

"I'd say that one's perfect for you," I agreed, reaching out and claiming the prize from the attendant.

"Here you go," I said, handing the stuffed animal to her with another flourish. "A worthy addition to your bookshop, milady."

"Thank you," Brenna said, her eyes dancing as she hugged the bookworm close. "I love it!"

Holding it out again, Brenna's fingers danced around the edges of the tiny book clutched in the bookworm's limbs.

"It looks like the book opens," I said, nudging her softly.

With a curious tilt of her head, Brenna obliged and unfolded the small cover. The moment froze, a soft breeze playing with her light brown hair as her eyes widened in unguarded astonishment at what lay inside.

"Is this what I think it is?" Her voice trembled, and her eyes glistened as they met mine.

"Only if you think it's a ring."

My attempt at nonchalance failed spectacularly. Every muscle in my body wanted to twitch, and I resisted the urge to wipe my hands on my shorts. A collective gasp rose from our families behind us when realization dawned.

Taking a breath that seemed to draw in the whole of the earth's atmosphere, I plucked out the ring. The sun caught on the diamond and scattered prisms of light across her perfect, gorgeous face. I dropped to one knee on the soft meadow grass, my gaze locked with hers.

"Brenna Coleridge," I said, my voice steady and sure, "you've done something no one else could. You brought together two families who were more used to feuding than friendship. You've shown them—shown me—what it means to feel whole again."

Her hands flew to her mouth, stifling a sob, and I continued, pouring every ounce of my truth into the words. "You are the peace after the storm. You're the reason I believe in second chances." The crowd hushed, and a blanket of expectancy draped over us as I reached for her hand and slid the ring on. "I love you more than the depths of the ocean that surrounds us. Will you marry me?"

Tears shimmered in Brenna's eyes as she stared at the ring, then lifted her gaze to mine. "Of course," she called out, her voice clear and resolute as a bell's chime. "Yes, Hunter. One hundred times, yes!"

As cheers erupted around us, the applause cascaded from one end of the meadow to the other. Two families, once divided by old grudges, now stood united, their clapping hands and joyful shouts echoing around us.

"Who would've thought?" Brenna said, her voice tinged with amazement as she glanced at our families. "The Coleridges and Markhams cheering for the same cause!"

"History is overrated," I teased, pulling her close. "We're writing our own story now. One page at a time."

And then, as if the moment couldn't get any more perfect, her arms wound around my neck, pulling me down into a kiss. It spoke of long nights and sunny days, of quiet moments and roaring passions. My heart filled to the brim, like it couldn't contain the euphoria I was experiencing.

When we finally broke apart, breathless and grinning like fools, the world faded into a blur of colors and cheers.

"Ready for forever?" I asked with a thick, hoarse voice.

"I always have been," she murmured back with her fingers tracing the line of my jaw.

As the sun watched over the festival, we sealed our vow with another kiss. It was a beginning, a declaration, and a promise made under the watchful eyes of flame trees and the approving roar of our families. The end of the old and the start of something brand new.

It was a shared excitement for the next chapter of our

love story, for a Shakespearean tragedy we'd spun to have a happy ending.

———

THANK you for reading SHADES OF YOU! I absolutely adored writing this book, and I hope it resonated with you too. Hunter is one of my favorite characters ever, and seeing him get his redemption had me drumming my feet with happiness. I loved how this couple was so perfect for each other. They fit together like a lock and key.

I don't think we're through with Dove Key and Calypso Key yet... Stay tuned for more to come!

And if you're not quite ready to say goodbye to Hunter and Brenna, or to the other Markhams we've come to know and love, I have a bonus scene for this book!

This and all the other bonuses for the Calypso Key series are exclusively available to my mailing list subscribers. Sign up here to claim your bonus scene for SHADES OF YOU:

Beach Read Update
(www.erinbrockus.com/shades)

My Beach Read Update subscribers hear about all my free content, plus exclusive offers and sales. I'd love to have you along! Plus, you'll stay up to date with cover reveals, sneak peeks, and exclusive content about my upcoming series and my other beachy universes.

If you're already on my list, I've got you covered! At the bottom of each newsletter is a link to all my free content for subscribers. Just find your last email from me to read this bonus, as well as any others you might have missed. Or you can simply sign up again—you'll have your bonus in a flash.

Also by Erin Brockus

CALYPSO KEY SERIES:

Main Novels:

Visions of You: A Small Town Single Dad Romance

Because of You: A Small Town Fake Relationship Romance

Memories of You: A Small Town Second Chance Romance

Shades of You: A Small Town Forbidden Romance (Coming Oct, 2024)

Associated Short Stories and Novellas:

Traces of You: A Small Town Rivals to Lovers Romance*

* Subscriber exclusive

HALF MOON BAY SERIES:

Main Novels:

Finding Hope: Half Moon Bay Book 1

Defending Hope: Half Moon Bay Book 2

Rising Hope: Half Moon Bay Book 3

Forever Hope: Half Moon Bay Book 4

Half Moon Whim: Half Moon Bay Book 5 (Standalone)

Half Moon Ember: Half Moon Bay Book 6 (Standalone)

Half Moon Aqua: Half Moon Bay Book 7

Crowning Hope: Half Moon Bay Book 8

Associated Short Stories and Novellas:

Tropical Dawn: A Half Moon Bay Prequel Novella

Tropical Chance*: A Second Chance Half Moon Bay Novella

Tropical Hope*: A Half Moon Bay Prequel Short Story

* Subscriber exclusives

Standalone Books:

In Too Deep: A Second Chance Romance

Beached in Bali: A Friends to Lovers Romance

About the Author

Dive into steamy small-town romance, where passion meets paradise!

Erin Brockus writes steamy small town romances that transport readers to exotic, tropical destinations, and provide a perfect beachy getaway from everyday life. Her mature, relatable characters are impossible not to root for, and she weaves breezy romantic adventure into her stories, emphasizing scuba diving and the ocean.

Drawing on her twin passions for diving and travel, Erin infuses her characters and narratives with a sense of excitement and passion. Her idea of the perfect day involves sipping a cocktail on the beach after exploring the ocean depths.

Erin lives in Washington wine country with her husband, who is also a scuba instructor. She is currently hard at work on her next island adventure. When she's not writing, you might find her out for a run or cycling through the countryside on the next quest for adventure.

Printed in the USA
CPSIA information can be obtained
at www.ICGtesting.com
JSHW081337140924
69664JS00001B/2

9 781957 003399